W9-CBX-044

"Former Marine Coughlin and bestseller Davis combine a well-paced, credible plot with a realistic portrayal of modern combat . . . The climax . . . will leave readers cheering." —*Publishers Weekly*

DEAD SHOT

"Compelling." —*Publishers Weekly*

"The [plot] propels the pages forward, but this one isn't all about action: Swanson proves a surprisingly complex character . . . *Dead Shot* suggest[s] a hardware-heavy story that only an armed-services veteran could love. Surprisingly, it's completely the opposite. Readers will be compelled . . . and will look forward to another Swanson adventure." —*Booklist*

KILL ZONE

"Stunning action, excellent tradecraft, insider politics, and the ring of truth. Just about perfect." —Lee Child

"Tight, suspenseful . . . Here's hoping this is the first of many Swanson novels." —*Booklist*

"The action reaches a furious pitch." —*Publishers Weekly*

SHOOTER

The Autobiography of the Top-Ranked Marine Sniper

"One of the best snipers in the Marine Corps, perhaps the very best. When I asked one of his commanders about his skills, the commander smiled and said, 'I'm just glad he's on our side.'"

> —Peter Maass, war correspondent and bestselling author of *Love Thy Neighbor*

"The combat narratives here recount battlefield action with considerable energy . . . A renowned sniper, Coughlin is less concerned with his tally than with the human values of comradeship and love."

> —*The Washington Post*

"Coughlin is a sniper, perhaps one of the most respected and feared in the Corps, and his memoir, *Shooter*, offers a uniquely intimate look into the life of one trained to live in the shadows . . . some of the most poignant action ever recorded in a modern Marine memoir."

> —*Seapower* magazine

TIME
TO KILL

A SNIPER NOVEL

GUNNERY SGT. **JACK COUGHLIN**, USMC (RET.),

WITH **DONALD A. DAVIS**

PAPL
DISCARDED

St. Martin's Paperbacks

TIME TO KILL

Copyright © 2013 by Jack Coughlin with Donald A. Davis. Excerpt from *On Scope* copyright © 2013 by Jack Coughlin with Donald A. Davis.

All rights reserved.

For information address St. Martin's Press, 175 Fifth Avenue, New York, NY 10010.

Library of Congress Catalog Card Number: 2012041269

ISBN: 978-1-250-04375-7

Printed in the United States of America

St. Martin's Press hardcover edition / May 2013
St. Martin's Paperbacks edition / February 2014

St. Martin's Paperbacks are published by St. Martin's Press, 175 Fifth Avenue, New York, NY 10010.

10 9 8 7 6 5 4 3 2 1

CHAPTER 1

NEWPORT BEACH,
CALIFORNIA

Kyle Swanson leaned on the white railing of the deck on the second floor of his house as the sun edged down toward the horizon and wondered if he had time to get out in the surf one last time, paddle down to the Wedge, ride a few sets, and get back before it got too dark. Madeline, his girlfriend of the past two weeks, was coming over after her shift in a beachfront restaurant and was expecting him to grill some tuna while she whipped up a salad. They would drink cold *cerveza* and eat on the open patio with the glass doors all the way open, with a fresh ocean breeze coming in while music spilled into the night. They might take a midnight dip, and he would be dazzled by her body in that red bikini with her blond hair reflecting the moonlight. After that, a strategic retreat to the big bedroom to make love while boarders, bladers, dog walkers, tourists, and other lovers strolled the boardwalk out front, unable to see them.

No, he decided as he rubbed the freshly painted railing. He didn't have time for that one last swim, and he and Maddy would have to part in the morning, but it had been a hell of a leave. The United States Marine Corps wanted its top sniper back on duty.

His telephone rang, as if it had been waiting for just the right moment to ruin the idyllic mood. A glance at the screen showed Lieutenant Colonel Sybelle Summers was calling from Washington. "Hey," he said.

"Are you out of the lazy vacation mode yet?"

"Did I ever tell you that you have a sultry voice?"

"I am your superior officer, Gunnery Sergeant Swanson."

"But we slept together once, Sybelle," he said. "Remember? A rainy night in France?"

"I've never been to France. You must be thinking of your current chippie, what's her name? Michelin, like the tires?"

"Her name is Madeline, and your memory is slipping. I thought you and I had a deep and special relationship."

There was a slight, pleasant change in her tone. "Some people just are not that memorable." They both laughed.

"Sybelle, why are you bothering me on my final evening of leave? Gimme a break, girl. The sun is just about down, I'm drinking beer, watching the beach, getting ready to grill a dead fish, Maddy is coming over, and the California weather is perfect. Washington, where you are sitting, is clogged with snow, according to the Weather Channel. I don't want to come back."

"Quit whining, Kyle. You built that big house and now you start acting all rich instead of like the raggedy-ass jarhead you are. Maddy, is it? Maddy? Is she out of high school yet?"

"Here's a suggestion; why don't you come out here instead? No snow."

"Miss Maddy Michelin would be upset if I did that. Let's get to business. You are wanted back here right away."

"I'll be there tomorrow afternoon anyway, Sybelle, and I can't get back any faster than that." He tilted back the longneck bottle of Corona beer, which was getting warm. The sky had deepened into a band of solid orange that was being chased by the heavy purple night coming from the east, and the sun was moving so fast that it seemed to be falling.

"Change of plans. A plane will be waiting by the time you get out to John Wayne. I'll meet the flight here, then we go directly to a meeting. Take this thing off speakerphone."

He closed the speaker and picked up the receiver. "OK. I'm listening. This line is not secure."

"Really? I had no idea. Does Maddy know that?"

"Can you get to the point?"

"Some of your father's friends have contacted the boss, and they want us to talk to a guy lives out on the Maryland shore. We'll drive out from Andrews."

That was a jolt. It was her way of advising him that Sir Geoffrey Cornwell in Great Britain apparently had pulled the original string to start this ball rolling, and that was Kyle's real other life. The man had been a colonel in the British Special Air Service Regiment before a broken leg forced him into retirement. Refusing to be shelved, he had set out to design technical applications and new weaponry for the military, and was on the cutting edge when the War on Terror dollars started to flow like cheap wine. Eventually, he persuaded the Pentagon to lend him a sniper for technical assistance on a unique project to develop a new kind of long-range rifle, the Excalibur. They had sent Kyle Swanson over to England, and before long, the project was successful, and Jeff and his extraordinary wife, Lady Patricia, who were childless, had found a new friend in Kyle Swanson, an American orphan.

Over the years, through some very good times and some very bad and dangerous times, they unconsciously knitted together as a family. Sir Jeff branched into other fields and had a golden touch for business, and although Kyle remained a Marine, he was brought into the business, too, for the Pentagon liked having its own liaison man in the thriving Cornwell pipeline. It had been a special day for Kyle when the Cornwells adopted him as their son.

So if Sir Jeff, who was always helping out clandestine operations for the United States and Great Britain, was behind this thing—Kyle still didn't know what it was—then Swanson would consider it important and worthwhile. The problem had probably gone from Jeff to his friends within the British intelligence service and perhaps even into the prime minister's office before leaping over the pond to the White House. That was enough for Swanson, but a last night with Maddy would have been nice.

Kyle paused. "So General Middleton himself is ordering me back?"

"Not that boss, Swanson. The *big* boss. Anyway, Task Force Trident is now involved."

That more than aroused his curiosity, but he couldn't swallow it whole. "You want me to give up my final night, fly coast-to-coast, get off the plane a few hours before I would get there anyway, and go straight to work in Maryland? That urgent?"

"Damned straight, Gunny. Consider yourself back on the government dime." She ended the call.

"Aw, man." Kyle folded his phone and returned it to his pocket. The rim of the sun was almost totally gone, sinking into the Pacific Ocean. It was the moment he always watched for but usually missed, because it happened so quickly. Then there it was, for only a heartbeat, a brilliant sparkle of emerald as the final rim of the sun disappeared. Maybe it was an omen, he thought, an official ending to his two weeks of peace and quiet. Now it was back to being the triggerman for Trident.

Reluctantly, he hit the speed dial number to give Madeline the bad news of the broken date. He had to leave right away, he tried to explain, and no, he couldn't say where, and no again, sorry, but he didn't know when he would be back. She was totally unsympathetic and went from angry to cold as fast as the green flash had blinked out. "Look, Maddy, I've built this damned house right on the beach. You think I'm going to let it stand empty? Of course I'll be back. And I'll call you the minute I arrive; even before I arrive, I promise." She said something extraordinarily vulgar and hung up on him.

Two hours later, he was the only passenger aboard a small executive jet that was hauling him from John Wayne Airport outside of Newport Beach, heading to Andrews Air Force Base, just over the Maryland line outside of Washington, D.C. Swanson was in the wide, soft seat and had already finished reading the *Time* and *Newsweek* magazines that were in the seatback. It was a government plane, so there was no flight attendant, but he could fix a drink on his own in the galley, and somewhere over Missouri he would probably test the shrink-wrapped turkey and cheese sandwich.

Both magazines had covers showing the mobs demonstrating in the cities of Egypt, and their lead articles were about the latest treacherous political storm that was roiling that ancient country. The situation was deteriorating, just as it had been when he began his leave thirteen days earlier, just as it had been doing for years, if not centuries.

He tossed the magazines onto the empty seat across the aisle, settled back, and tried to puzzle together why he was being called back so suddenly. Sybelle's guarded conversation had given him only some very broad parameters for consideration, but they were startling. First of all, she had mentioned Sir Jeff, and also had said it was the big boss calling him home, and emphasized "big." His actual commander in Task Force Trident was two-star Marine Major General Bradley Middleton, and the general's only boss was whoever happened to be the president of the United States.

More than a decade had passed since terrorists had flown fuel-packed civilian airlines into the Twin Towers in New York, the Pentagon in Washington, and the Pennsylvania dirt. In response, the entire U.S. government had reshaped itself both at home and abroad to make sure such attacks never happened again, and that gave birth to the behemoth Homeland Security Department. Even that wasn't enough, because the inevitable bureaucratic friction soon appeared along the seams of the various departments. Numerous plots had been foiled since 9/11, involving crude devices like explosive shoes and underwear, which proved the system worked as long as people remained alert and paranoid enough to maintain their vigilance.

There were always going to be maniacs out there who would try to kill Americans, but airplane hijackers had lost their advantage. The nature of air travel had changed dramatically: Now there were tedious searches by TSA workers before boarding, flight attendants would willingly die rather than open the cockpit door, and every passenger on the plane, from a semipro athlete to a college girl, was ready to jump on a hijacker like a pack of crazed dogs. The willingness of a terrorist to give up his life to achieve his goal was of no use when his targets were equally as willing to die to stop him.

The military had also finally changed to accept the talents of Special Forces; elite operations like the Army's Delta Force and the Navy SEALs, and the futuristic

technology of remote-controlled drones, had changed
the landscape of the battlefield. The Pentagon had met
the challenge of terrorism head-on, as had the CIA, the
FBI, the NSA, and the rest of the alphabet agencies.

Nevertheless, there were still holes in the protection
net, for publicity, budgets, congressional oversight,
and the huge numbers of people supporting and carrying out any operation always tended to multiply over
time. The heroes had become *known*. It had been a
short step from that inevitability to the creation of Task
Force Trident by people who still cared fervently about
secrecy.

Trident was invisible by military standards, with a
total roster of only five people, including General Middleton, who ran the show. The offices were in a hard-
to-find area of the Pentagon, and the budget came out
of Homeland Security via the Department of Agricul-
ture. The team was far outside any chain of command
other than Middleton's reach to the president.

Sybelle Summers was the ops officer, and Master
Gunnery Sergeant O. O. Dawkins handled the adminis-
trative end, working the inner paths of Pentagon power.
Double-Oh could borrow anything in the arsenal, from
individual troops to stealth bombers for a Trident mission. The team's only non-Marine was a squid, Commander Benton Freedman of the Navy, a quirky geek
whose proprietary electronic net could kick the combined computer butts of Google and Facebook without
breaking a sweat. They called him "the Lizard," a cor-
ruption of his college nickname of "Wizard." Swanson
handled the wet work. Few people even knew about

Trident, but the president always knew where they were, in case they were needed. Like now.

He left his seat, went to the head with his Dopp kit, and studied his reflection as he shaved. Swanson was not a big man, standing five feet nine inches, and weighed exactly 176 pounds, with sandy brown hair. Only yesterday, he had been a beach bum wearing baggy board shorts, and now he was back in his Trident uniform of jeans and a dark blue sweatshirt. His Marine dress blues, on a hanger in Washington, carried the three gold stripes and two rockers on the sleeves to denote his USMC rank of gunnery sergeant, with rows of ribbons and awards, including the Congressional Medal of Honor. He loved the uniform and the Corps, which had been his home during long years of training, fieldwork, and assignments around the world and had taught him the trade of the sniper. In doing so, it had honed him into a fierce weapon.

He seldom wore the blues these days; he worked in places where he dressed the part he was playing. Jeans and sweatshirts today, maybe a business suit tomorrow, with authentic credentials to match the character.

Swanson cleaned his face of leftover lather, replaced the razor, then picked up the alleged sandwich and a can of tomato juice on his way back to his seat. The sandwich was tasteless. He took a few deep breaths, and his mind continued the shift back into the counter-intelligence mode. It was like time travel, bridging the freedom he had enjoyed during the past few weeks back into the complex and deadly world of Trident, where only the mission existed.

He went to sleep to the hum of the dual engines, leapfrogging in time as the plane moved eastward. The four-hour flight would arrive in Maryland seven hours after he left California. Three hours he wouldn't get to live.

The descent to land at Andrews was swift. The plane circled quickly and dropped into the approach path of the most exclusive airport in America, the one that *Air Force One,* the president's official plane, called home. It was too dark for Kyle to see the trees when the little jet's tires squealed as they caught the runway. The front tilted down until the forward wheels made contact, the reverse thrusters screamed, and the brakes clamped hard to slow the bird.

"We're here, Gunny," said the copilot as he stepped out of the cabin. "The flight OK for you?"

"Anytime the landings come out even with the take-offs is good by me," Kyle replied with a grin.

"Ain't it the truth." The pilot popped open the small hatch and dropped the stairs. "Snowing out there. Watch your step going down, it'll be slickery."

Sybelle Summers was waiting on the tarmac nearby beside an old Ford Crown Vic with a single blue light blinking brightly atop its roof. She was as tall as Kyle, with a classic face that never carried much makeup, and snowflakes were catching on the black hair cut to collar length. She wore leg-hugging stretch twill black pants and soft boots, a white sweater of Irish wool, a gray scarf hung loosely around her neck, a rock of a Rolex, and a lot of attitude. The only woman ever to pass the

Marine Recon course, she had become a special ops and counterterrorism expert and was on a fast track to someday become a general, if she lived that long. There was nobody Kyle would rather have at his side if the going got rough.

Tonight, she had her game face on. A worn black leather gun belt was buckled around her waist, and a big gold badge flashed on her right hip, just in front of the holstered Glock 19.

"Working undercover, Lieutenant Colonel Summers?" he asked.

She thrust a padded nylon briefcase at him. It was zipped closed. "Homeland Security creds for you tonight and your .45 Colt ACP, loaded and racked with one in the chamber. Grab your gear and get in the car."

"What's going on?" he asked.

"This guy we were meeting tonight? He's dead."

CHAPTER 2

The big car had a winter coat of scuffed black paint and dirty curtains of slush caked around the tires. Sybelle was at the wheel, and the big V-8 was thrumming at idle. After two weeks on the beach in California, the icy cold of the wet Washington winter slapped Kyle before he had even thrown his bags in the rear seat. When he climbed in front, the heater was blasting to fight the chill. Sybelle turned on the full rack of lights behind the grille and in the rear window, and a cop who had been waiting for her signal stepped into traffic and held up a hand to stop all oncoming vehicles. Bundled in a black jacket with a fur-lined hood and thick gloves, he looked like a grizzly bear. With a double yelp of siren to warn those in front, Sybelle took off.

The wipers brushed away an easy snow, and the big tires gripped the pavement as they thundered away from Dulles on the long access highway, using the emergency lane to pass other cars that could not get out of the way fast enough.

"Dead, huh?"

"Yep. We're going over to check it out. Police are saying he caught a bullet in the throat."

"Want me to program the address on the navigation system?"

"Don't bother. I went to the Naval Academy, remember? This little town is just south of Annapolis, and I used to sail down in that area. We'll be there in thirty minutes." Sybelle was a lead-footed speeder, more reckless pilot than safe driver, and with plenty of horsepower at her command and not caring about the dismal miles-per-gallon rate of the large car, they soon were out of the airport and headed east.

Swanson settled in for the ride. The seat was lumpy. "So bring me into the loop. What's up?"

She flicked her dark eyes at him for a microsecond, then back to the highway. The snow had been cleared, but patches of muck and ice hugged low places in frozen puddles. "Don't know too much more than I told you on the phone. Sir Jeff said this guy, his name is . . . was . . . Norman Haynes, was an experienced auditor for one of the big accounting companies, with a lot of contracts abroad, including Sir Jeff and Excalibur Industries. Did you know him?"

"No. I'm not involved in the day-to-day business stuff."

"So just what do you do as a senior vice president there, besides make a lot of money to spoil your surfer chicks?"

"Sybelle, get back to this story. Please." She was jabbing his ego. Kyle Swanson was already wealthy, and someday he would inherit the company, but he would not discuss that with anyone, even with himself. Talking about money embarrassed him, which was why Sybelle enjoyed doing it.

"So this number cruncher Haynes dropped by London on his way back from Egypt and met privately with Sir Jeff. Said he had been spooked by his trip to Cairo," she continued.

"I imagine all of Egypt is a pretty spooky place right now. Revolutions are messy. People take their families and assets and run away to safe havens."

"Not necessarily." Summers blew past a snowplow that was kicking up a thick storm of road gunk behind it. "Instead of being on the ropes financially, the company where he was running an audit, the Palm Group, had money pouring in."

"So what? Investors looking for an edge is nothing new. Make a bet on a developing nation that is in the shitter, and when the economy turns around, you make a fortune."

"This apparently went beyond risk-reward. Haynes found discrepancies and refused to approve the books. That's a pretty big deal. Other companies and banks won't do business with a firm blacklisted by its auditors. Bonds won't sell, banks won't lend, and customers won't buy. One of the Palm Group vice presidents actually threatened him."

That got Kyle's attention. "Threatened him? Most

companies try to keep auditors happy. What the hell did he find?"

"Iran. Big money coming in from Iran."

Swanson thought about that for a while as the snow danced before the headlights. "I don't know much about the auditing game, except that accountants can face prison time for divulging the private results of their work or making money from their inside knowledge." He shifted in his seat, but comfort was impossible. "So our boy Haynes went against the ethical code of his profession and confided that Iran is in the playpen. It would have taken a lot for him to put his career at risk. Meaning he may have stumbled upon a national security issue for the United States."

She nodded. "The bad news is that he would not say exactly what he knew. The Palm Group security people had taken his computer, his briefcase, and all of his notes and papers, claiming his access was voided by his refusal to sign off. Haynes, like most accountants, had a better than average memory, and he convinced Jeff that he recalled most of the important material and would divulge everything in a private meeting with an appropriate American authority. That was to be us."

"And now he's dead."

"Yes. We had the Lizard start a file on Haynes and tag him in the system, so the 911 call from his wife pinged the Web, and cop radio chatter confirmed it was a homicide. They'll already be at work by the time we get there. The background file is in your door pocket."

Swanson picked up the folder and punched on the

visor light. As usual, the Lizard had put together a thick dossier on short notice. Norman Haynes grew up in a middle-class neighborhood in Ohio, and was a good athlete and student who enlisted to be an Army grunt and earn money for college. He drove a 3rd Armored Division tank in Desert Storm. After that, he traded Army green for Yale blue and picked up a degree in economics. The man was totally clean, made good money over the years, and was a registered Republican, married with three children in college, and cleared to audit military contractors. A high security clearance.

"How much longer?" Kyle asked.

"Twenty minutes," Sybelle replied.

"I'm going to sleep. Wake me when we get there." With that simple statement, he eased the lumpy seat back and closed his eyes. Hard years in the field had taught him how to sleep anytime, anywhere, whenever he could. The growling roar of the big V-8 engine was like a lullaby for him as it ripped along Highway 50 toward Annapolis, and he set his mental alarm clock for twenty mikes.

"Know what I'm thinking?" Sybelle asked.

"Nukes." He did not even open his eyes.

"Yeah."

"We're here," Sybelle said as she steered onto Dietrich Way. Swanson opened his eyes and smelled saltwater. It was easy to identify the correct address, for every light was burning in a two-story white Cape Cod–style house and around the snow-covered grounds. Emergency vehicles of every sort were parked haphazardly, and Sybelle shut down her own flashers as she coasted to a stop at a checkpoint at the end of the long driveway.

A young patrol cop with a plastic cover over his hat approached, his eyes sweeping the car, driver, and passenger.

Sybelle had the window down and both of their creds extended as he arrived. "Lousy weather for standing post," she said with a smile of sympathy.

"Yes, ma'am. It truly is. Can I help you?"

"We need to talk to whoever is heading the investigation. I see local and county cars, so who's on top?"

The policeman studied the badges. "You from Homeland Security? What's your business here?"

"Do you have Beyond Top Secret clearance?" It was a quick turf battle that she won by answering his question with one of her own. She retrieved the credential wallets and tossed them to Kyle, then laughed to break the tension. "Don't worry, Officer, we come in peace, not to bigfoot your investigation. In fact, we just want to provide some off-the-record information to your detectives."

"Yes, ma'am. Follow the drive up to the house, park on the left, and I'll radio Detective Payton that you're on the way."

"We can find him," she said. "Keep us off the radio. Thanks. In fact, you never even saw us tonight." There was no "please," the smile had vanished, and the window buzzed up again. The automobile ground on, following the ruts made by the earlier arrivals. She parked beside the band of yellow crime scene tape.

Kyle hated to give up the warmth of the car but zipped up the unmarked blue aviator's jacket he had brought from California, flipping up the fur collar around his ears. "Damn," he muttered as he stepped out. "Colder than a witch's tit." So much time in the sun had made him soft.

"Man up, Marine," Summers said, leading the way to another patrolman who stood at an opening in the tape. Again she showed the creds, this time asking for Detective Payton. The cop pointed to a boathouse about fifty feet from the back door.

"Quite a spread," Kyle said as they crossed the broad lawn that sloped down to a long dock. "About an acre of prime waterfront property. Price must be more than a million bucks if it's worth a dime."

"This channel feeds directly into the southwest side of the Chesapeake Bay. With the calmer water, there's a lot of sailboat racing here in the summer."

Colorful small boats and kayaks were racked neatly in the boathouse, covered and safe from the weather, while the ropes, paddles, and other gear had been dumped outside to provide room for a police command center. Radios were popping, and video feeds were online, dumping information directly into computers in Annapolis. She asked, "Detective Payton?"

A solid man in his midforties zipped up tight in stained khaki canvas overalls and work boots turned from a computer screen. He had narrow, busy eyes and a badge on a chain around his neck. "That would be me. Who are you?"

They handed over the fake credentials once again,

and he studied them, then gave them back. "What's up? We're kind of busy here with a homicide, you know." The tone was not hostile but suspicious. Locals never liked federal officers showing up unexpectedly.

"Can we find somewhere private to talk?" Kyle nodded at all of the people jammed into the boathouse, which had grown warm with their combined body heat and the electronics.

"Sure. Come on. Let's go up to the porch, and I'll introduce my partner. There's hot coffee up there, and I'm going to tell him whatever you tell me anyway."

Kyle nodded, and soon they were under the roof of an enclosed deck jutting out from the house itself. Detective Allen Jones was sipping warm coffee. "Bitch of a night for murder," said Payton. "The snow has fouled up any hope of tracks."

Sybelle accepted a coffee cup from Jones. "We know some basic information on the victim."

Jones, a thin man with light brown skin, frowned at that news. "How?"

Swanson stirred some creamer into his own coffee. "The reason we're here is that we had an appointment to meet Mr. Haynes tonight."

"Why would Homeland Security be meeting an accountant?" Payton asked.

"Let's trade a little more information first. All will become clear," Swanson promised.

Payton chewed his lip for a moment. "OK. A single large-caliber gunshot apparently was fired from the end of the dock, blew out a window, and nailed the vic right in the throat. Hell of a shot from a football field away."

"Anybody else hurt?" Kyle did not mention that a hundred yards was almost rock-throwing distance for any trained shooter.

"No. The wife was right there in the room with him, and the kids were upstairs. The scumbag killer was apparently only interested in Mr. Haynes."

"Neighbors and witnesses have anything?"

Payton finished his coffee and threw the paper cup in a trash can. "We're not finished with the questioning, but some say they heard a loud gunshot, and then an outboard motor heading down the channel at high speed. Sometime between seven and nine o'clock for a preliminary time of death." Payton paused. "Now it's your turn. Until you tell us why we should be telling you anything at all, that's as much as you're going to get."

"Fair enough," Sybelle said, removing a sanitized version of the Lizard's background file on Haynes from her jacket. "This will save you trouble on putting together his background, and I can bring you up to speed while Detective Jones walks my guy through a quick look-see around the site. Then we'll be out of your hair. This is a homicide; your case, not ours. All we know is that he wanted to report some sort of international financial scam."

"Hunh," said Jones. It was not like Feds to give in so easily.

"We're not detectives," Swanson said.

"Exactly what are you, then?" Jones asked.

"Little fish in a big net, Detective Jones, just like you. We have other specialties."

Jones examined Kyle. The smaller man had the build

of one of those monsters who could run forever, then fight a dragon and not break a sweat. The gray-green eyes were colder than the weather, maybe colder than Antarctica. "I'll just bet you do. Come on."

Jones led him outside until they stood side by side with their backs toward the house, where four broad windows faced the water. The lot had been graded at a gentle slope and was anchored at the water's edge by a big oak tree that was bare of leaves. A picnic table was layered with snow like thick frosting on a cake. "The killer probably coasted in down there with his engine off, tied up, got out and lay down prone on the dock, and waited to take his shot. Blowing snow has erased the pressure images."

"But if it walks like a duck," Kyle said.

"It's probably a fucking duck," Jones responded, his face hunched inside his collar. "Back during the drug wars in Miami, rival mobs would send hit men in boats on home invasion missions to reach their targets. That stopped with more police water patrols. Somebody may be trying to revive the idea. Once away from here, he could have escaped in a car, or met a bigger boat out in the bay. Or have chartered a plane."

They turned around, and Jones said, "Here's what's left of the window."

Kyle looked inside the house, where forensic people were still at work, bagging and tagging. Morgue attendants had the lifeless body in a bag, lashed to a gurney, waiting for permission to move it.

"Do you need to see the stiff?"

"No. Do you have a caliber on the bullet?"

"Not final. It looks military grade, probably a 7.62 millimeter round. The ghouls dug it out of the wall directly behind where it passed through Haynes. No brass has been found."

Inside, the walls were painted a teal green, and a ceiling fan rotated slowly beneath the off-white ceiling. The room was well decorated, with a long dark green sofa and a matching chair at right angles around a dark coffee table that seemed to be made from old wood. A wet bar with bottles of liquor and empty glasses dominated one corner; a huge potted plant with broad leaves owned the other. Everything was laid out for enjoying the water view.

Jones pointed through the empty frame. "The kids were upstairs. Mrs. Haynes was in the chair, reading a magazine. The victim had poured a Scotch and was standing in front of the window, looking toward the water, when he was shot."

"There was no light at the end of the little pier? You know, to warn off boaters?"

"Maybe that was what Haynes was looking at. He would have known there should be one shining out there but probably thought the bad weather may have knocked it out. We found that the wires had been cut, leaving the killer shielded by the dark."

Kyle snapped on a pair of latex gloves and knelt in the snow to take a closer look at the windowsill. He touched a couple of points of jagged glass that still protruded along the edge like the teeth of a saw blade. A carpet of shards had spread inside. "OK. Thanks, Detective."

By the time they were back on the porch, Summers had finished briefing Payton, telling him almost everything about the planned meeting. She was saying, "I'm not an accountant, so I don't have any idea what Haynes wanted to tell us. We can't rule out that this guy maybe had enemies on Wall Street, was about to drop the dime on a Ponzi scheme, or had pissed off a drug lord, discovered an international money-laundering racket, or whatever. I don't even know enough to guess. We see no obvious evidence of a security threat, and that's what I'll pass back up my chain of command. The homicide part is all yours." She looked at Swanson. "We done?"

"Afraid not," Kyle said. "This thing may just have jumped way above the pay grades of everybody here, including us."

"Whoa up. You found something!" Payton exclaimed. "I know when somebody gets a hunch about a murder."

Swanson looked at the cop. "This is a personal guess, with nothing to back it up, Detective Payton. Totally speculative, but based on my experience."

"Talk to me, son."

"You've got to make it plural now. There were two killers here tonight, not just one."

"How's that? The neighbors heard only one shot."

"Glass does specific things to a bullet on impact," Swanson said, falling unconsciously into his sniper-lecture mode. "It changes the trajectory, depending on the thickness of the glass, and causes the round to lose its point of aim. The first shot did nothing but blow out the window. Then a second shot was fired only a half second later. It would easily have blended into one noise for someone not paying attention. Witnesses really would believe they heard a single sound."

Detective Jones interrupted. "Only one bullet was found."

Kyle changed his angle to face the dock so he could use his hands to frame what happened. "A single bullet like a 7.62 would have just punched a hole in the glass before hitting the target, leaving the window intact. So Shooter One used a smaller round, like a 5.56 millimeter, to totally shatter the glass, which is why there are so many shards inside. That allowed a clear path for Shooter Two's 7.62 round to impact the victim. Your forensic people saw only a single wound, therefore expected to find one bullet, and they found it."

"Our crime scene people would not have missed something like that." Jones put an edge on the comment.

"No criticism intended, Detective," said Kyle. "But did they really conduct a detailed study of the entire room? Most likely, they will find the second bullet in there somewhere, probably imbedded in the wall behind that fiddle-leaf and the other big plants in the corner. Shooter One would have aimed at a place where the bullet would do its job of taking out the window but would neither cause the target to shift nor be easily found."

"You know about this sort of thing?"

"Seen it once or twice."

"So you think we're dealing with some trained snipers?"

"Not really, but they were obviously good enough as marksmen with military training. Shooter Two actually missed his target. No sniper aims for the throat, because the target zone is too narrow. That's movie stuff. And the bad weather would have affected the bullet's path." Kyle pounded his fist into his palm for emphasis. "A big round right into center mass, the chest, is much easier, and death is just as certain."

"Jesus H. Christ," said Jones, putting the picture together in his mind. "Suddenly, I'm wishing this was just a drug hit."

Payton gave a long look to Sybelle and Kyle, and seemed to deflate. "Shit. Now I gotta call the FBI. You two might as well stick around. It's gonna be a while." He stomped through the snow back out to the comm center that was set up in the boathouse, muttering to himself.

CHAPTER 3

CAIRO, EGYPT

Yahya Naqdi was running for his life. He was ten years old and scared. The sand and rock of the desert pulled at his sandals like a hungry thing holding him rooted to the spot, immobile on a plain of sudden, ugly death. Explosions and screams, shrapnel and fire, and dirt, dirt, dirt everywhere; it filled his nostrils and his eyes and his mouth. The voices of soldiers behind him were bellowing for him to run straight and hard at the enemy, for he was in the lead element of the Army of Twenty Million, and they were surging forward in a human wave attack against the entrenched Iraqis. Despite the religious cries of the mullahs, the threats of his own Iranian sergeants and the thrill of becoming a martyr and going to paradise, he had come to a halt in the middle of the screaming charge when his best friend, only twenty feet beyond, stepped on a land mind and was blown to pieces. The bloody head bounced back toward Naqdi like a soccer ball with white eyes. There was a thundering drum roll of explosions as dozens more mines were triggered. The concussion of another blast smacked the boy hard, knocking him to his knees. He bent forward and vomited, then fell into the bile when a piece of flying shrapnel knocked him on the back of the head and tore away a slice of scalp. More boys ran over him, calling at the top of their lungs that God was good. That was the plan: Thousands of boys would dash through the minefields to clear the way for the real attack. The last thing he had heard was the Iraqi artillery starting to fire to rain even more destruction on the charge of the children. While he lay unconscious on the battlefield, more sharp metal tore at his body.

He came out of the dream sweating and clutching the sheets in fear. He coughed once, twice, hacking to spit the dirt from his mouth, to breathe through clogged nostrils. For more than thirty years since the Iran-Iraq War, he had been haunted by the terrible dream of his friend's head skidding along, bloody and sightless, and staring back at him from paradise.

He lay in bed as his breathing slowed and the terror faded. He had never married, for he would never let anyone detect this weakness. Better to be alone than pitied and ridiculed behind his back. He threw off the covers and began the daily ritual of again becoming Colonel Yahya Naqdi, the feared and mysterious intelligence officer who ran foreign clandestine operations for Iran's Army of the Guardians of the Islamic Revolution.

He slid his feet into comfortable slippers and walked naked across the carpet of the comfortable hotel suite in downtown Cairo, avoiding looking in the mirror. A tiny refrigerator yielded a chilled carton of orange juice, which he drank while the shower warmed to the proper temperature. Within the glassed cubicle, clean water, foamy shampoo, and a good scrubbing sluiced away the filth that accumulated with the dream. He turned off the shower and dried with a soft towel, and only then allowed the mirror to throw his image back at him. It was a disturbing sight.

Two puckered scars were on his right shoulder from where bullets had struck him in an alley in Istanbul during a mission gone bad early in his career. A healed knife slash curled up from his left hip, another memory, this one from Beirut. The long, ragged one across his stomach dated back to when he had almost been gutted by shrapnel during the children's charge. He did not bother to turn and see the others on his back. Fingertips traced the old scar in his scalp, and he turned away from the reflection.

He applied body powder and deodorant, then took his time shaving close to the skin. Other Muslims were sometimes offended by his not having a beard, but Naqdi ignored them, for he walked among the barbarians, and a long, unruly, dirty beard would be as good as a beaming light to identify him as a terrorist. Anyway, in his heart, he had no time for Allah, or God, or Buddha, or any other superstitious nonsense. Prayers were a waste of time. You are who you are, and when you die, you are dead, and that is truly the end. There is no paradise, no heaven, no afterlife. He still performed the ritual prayers to Allah if among Muslims, because not doing so would draw attention; he did not listen to the words he recited.

He carefully brushed his hair and energetically scrubbed his teeth, attacking his gums hard with the bristles. Personal hygiene was important, for details were important. He cleaned his manicured nails, then washed his hands again, and imaginary dirt still clung to him.

Naqdi was fifty-one years old, of medium build and had sprinkles of white dusting thick black hair and eyebrows. One of his trademarks was to always dress as well as, or better than, whomever he might be meeting. With a generous budget from his masters in Tehran, he had become a clotheshound, to fit in better with the infidels. His spacious closet was stocked with laundered clothing, and this morning he chose a fresh cream-colored shirt that buttoned at the neck, gray trousers with sharp creases, a soft tweed sport coat, and a pair of shoes that had been made in London. These gave him the cultivated look of an intelligent and successful businessman. Finally, the colonel was ready to face the new day.

A BMW limousine was waiting downstairs, and a bodyguard opened the door to the spacious and cool backseat. The armed guard got in the front, and the driver moved smoothly into traffic. Naqdi took note that the streets of Cairo seemed calm and cheery this morning, for soccer mania had temporarily calmed the ongoing street protests staged by the rival political parties that comprised an uneasy coalition beneath the banner of the Muslim Brotherhood. The mobs were only a mask, for the intelligence colonel from Iran was the guiding hand, and the man with the money.

He had sent word to the various parties to stop squabbling for the day because the all-star Iranian soccer team, one of the best in the world, was coming to Cairo for a friendship match with the Egyptian squad. The mood of the people was important, and he wanted a rather neat revolution.

In the not-too-distant past, running such an Iranian special mission in the heart of Egypt was unthinkable, but with the fall of the dictator Mubarak, and the political takeover by the Muslim Brotherhood, things had changed. Now it was easy. Colonel Naqdi had designed a masterpiece that would deliver an intact and functioning Egypt into the political grip of Tehran.

Less than ten minutes later, the BMW ducked into the basement garage of a large office building that headquartered the Palm Group, and Naqdi was escorted up to his office near the top floor. Breakfast and hot coffee were waiting for him.

Major Mansoor Shakuri, the colonel's aide, had been alerted by the BMW driver that their boss was on the way, which gave him just enough time to rush to the bathroom and shove two fingers down his throat to force a violent spell of vomiting. Colonel Naqdi terrified him. The man oozed intrigue and misdirection, and he did not care how many lives and careers he smashed to achieve goals known only to himself and his powerful masters back home. The aide had come to learn that for his boss, a simple double-cross was never good enough when something more complex could be developed.

The major splashed cold water on his face, gargled some mouthwash, adjusted his suit and tie, combed his hair, and was ready by the time he heard the colonel enter the office. The man's phobia about neatness had trained the aide to also be immaculate. If Shakuri had so much as a smudge on his shirt, the colonel would frown, and that was never a good thing. Taking a deep breath, the major knocked twice and went into the private office, immediately feeling the head-to-toe visual scan by his boss.

"Good day, Major Shakuri," the colonel called to his chief of staff as he settled in to eat, check the news on the Web, glance at his private messages, and receive the morning briefing.

"Good morning, Colonel," answered Mansoor Shakuri as he placed a folder of information beside the food tray. Shakuri, forty-five years old and six feet tall, had been at work for two hours to prepare the colonel's day. His reports were concise. The men had worked together for more than a year, and the strain and tension had given Shakuri painful stomach ulcers.

"The mission in the United States was successful," he said, standing with his hands folded before him. "The bothersome accountant, Haynes, has been eliminated."

The confirmation did not come as a surprise. The colonel expected such results in his clandestine operations; in fact, demanded them.

"Our team made a clean escape. One has already flown to Los Angeles, where an Iranian community thrives in an enclave around Beverly Hills. The other is driving to a similarly safe area in Houston, Texas. Once settled, both can be used again."

Naqdi sipped some of the strong coffee and savored a bite of sweet pastry. He had been forced to expend a sniper team that had been inserted into the Washington area three years earlier, and the colonel despised exposing skilled talent.

"Good," he said. It was not a moral thing. Killing people did not bother him if it meant accomplishing the mission. He would leave such worrying to those unlucky men who had a conscience.

Sometimes, people simply had to be removed, and this was one such case. This man had completed the required auditing duty for the Palm Group and then stupidly had dug deeper into the business's extended financial network. He had not been required to do so, had personally been warned by the colonel not to do it, and became a walking dead man when he persisted. The continued economic health of the Palm Group, where the colonel had the cover of being a vice president, was much more important than the life of any certified public accountant.

"What of the audit?" asked the colonel.

"A more compliant company based in Hong Kong has already assumed that task, with a guarantee from Beijing that it will receive the needed approval."

"Fine work, Major Shakuri. We're not quite finished with it, however. I want an investigation to re-create

Mr. Haynes's movements and meetings from the time he left our offices to the moment he was killed. Did he confide in anyone, or did he just run home to report about how he was mistreated?"

"Yes, sir. I already have someone assembling that."

Satisfied, the colonel changed the subject. "Who am I meeting this morning?" He dabbed a napkin at his lips and brushed crumbs from his coat.

"A Muslim Brotherhood representative wants more financial assistance for his faction, one of the centrist groups. Fifteen minutes at the most, although he would probably like to spend the day here."

Naqdi shook his head. These political gangs never ceased their little intrigues, no matter who was in power. "Anything else?"

"You are then clear until after lunch. At one o'clock, the navy people are finally ready to brief you about the Suez Canal."

"Excellent." The major was relieved to see a smile. "And what about our soccer team?"

"Everything is in order, sir," replied the aide. "They should arrive on schedule."

"Excellent. Excellent." The colonel turned to the written reports and his maps. The major left the room with a heavy heart.

EVERGREEN, ALABAMA

Trooper Horace Milbank of the Alabama Highway Patrol had backed his Dodge Charger SRT8 into a cutout at the edge of a pine forest along I-65, about halfway between Montgomery and Mobile, and sat there a while wondering why his wife could not understand that cops only really felt comfortable in the presence of other cops. Their dinner at home two nights ago with her co-workers from the real estate agency had been a disaster, because he had gotten drunk and angry when none of the pansies wanted to see his gun collection. Another cop would have jumped at the opportunity. Hell, nobody in the dinner group had sold a house for three months, and they were all drinking his liquor. Mrs. Milbank had withheld sexual favors since then. The trooper relaxed in the broad front seat, keeping an ear cocked to the radio chatter as he watched the broad corridor that had been carved through the pines.

This was a quiet section of interstate, one of those long stretches where drivers lose track of what they are doing and gradually increase their speeds to well beyond the 70 miles per hour limit. From his hideaway, Milbank could see traffic coming from both directions. Nothing had come up from the south for five minutes, the last being a truck loaded with a mountain of cut timber. Way out at the edge of his vision, he saw the single bright light of a motorcycle pop into view, a bike that was moving fast, which made the trooper more alert. He decided to clock the guy with radar and kicked his big V-8 engine to life, anticipating a short, happy chase. Alabama had long ago inserted some luxury sport sedans into its motor fleet in order to keep up with the new hot wheels of the bad guys. His Charger's 470 horsepower would get him up to 60 miles per hour in only five seconds, and he had a top end of 175 mph. If this turned into a flat-out road race, Milbank would be all over the guy.

As the light loomed closer, Milbank changed his attitude. It was not a motorcycle after all but a one-eyed jack, a car with a burned-out headlight. When it passed, he saw that it was hauling a small covered rented trailer. The trailer had no lights at all on the back. *Idiot.* Still going too fast and overrunning his only headlight. With the extra weight pushing from behind, the driver would not possibly be able to stop in time if something happened. Milbanks flipped on his light bar and laid tracks of hot rubber on the pavement as he accelerated out of his hiding spot and swung in behind the car, catching it in ten seconds flat. He tapped the siren, and the car slowed and pulled to a stop in the safety lane.

The trooper had a feeling about this, one of those cop-gut forebodings that warned him to take things slow and easy. After halting, he had notified Troop Headquarters of his position and told the dispatcher to stand by. He had parked at an angle in order to bathe the target car with a high-intensity spotlight as well as with the headlights, effectively blinding the driver.

"Keep your hands on the steering wheel," he ordered, with his voice magnified by a loudspeaker system. Then he unlocked his Winchester pump 12-gauge shotgun and laid it on the front seat as he slid out, leaving the door open. Keeping his heavy flashlight in his left hand and unsnapping the holster of his Glock 23 pistol, Milbank walked to the left rear of the car, watching the hands of the driver as he cautiously approached the side window.

A dark face, but not African American, more of an olive skin. The first thought was that he had stopped an illegal immigrant. "*Habla usted inglés?*" asked Milbank.

The driver blinked. "What?"

"Use one hand only, and give me your driver's license, then the registration and insurance."

"Why? I have done nothing wrong." The driver dug out the necessary identification and handed it to the trooper.

The funny accent, a thick beard, and now some attitude. A drunk? "Sir, would you please slowly open your door and step out of the vehicle?"

The driver stayed where he was, turning a grim face toward the trooper. "I refuse. I want a lawyer!"

Milbank decided against the Taser in this developing situation. He drew his handgun and pointed it. "Get out of the damned car. Right now. Keep those hands where I can see them!" Using his shoulder radio microphone, the trooper summoned backup help.

The driver opened the door slowly and swung his legs out, then unfolded from the seat. Overweight, dirty sneakers, rumpled jeans, and a shirt hanging unbuttoned over a T-shirt.

"Put your hands on the car and spread your legs."

The driver began to turn but planted his right foot hard on the pavement and in a quick movement broke into a run, cutting around the front of the car, passing through the headlights, and reaching the darkness beyond. The trooper hesitated to fire his weapon at someone he had just stopped for having a busted headlight.

Milbank did not chase him but walked to the runoff

ditch alongside the road and shined his flashlight along the perimeter. "Go ahead and run, Bubba," he called out. "Nothin' out there but pine trees, poison ivy, skeeters, and snakes for twenty miles in any direction. Try not to hurt yourself before daylight when we bring in the hound dogs." He stayed alert, with his pistol ready, and walked the roadside for another five minutes until a county police unit rolled up, then two more Highway Patrol cars, one bringing his sergeant.

The license and tags and registration all matched to the name of Pejman Mobili of Tuckahoe, Virginia, and Trooper Milbank identified the license photograph as that of the driver. Now having probable cause for a search, police went through the vehicle and trailer, found a stash of weapons, ammo, and a Kevlar vest, and impounded everything. The limping suspect was arrested by eight o'clock the following morning, dehydrated and hungry, with a sprained right ankle and a face so puffy with mosquito bites that both eyes were swollen shut.

CHAPTER 4

WASHINGTON, D.C.

Lieutenant Colonel Sybelle Summers and Gunnery Sergeant Kyle Swanson were the only uniformed personnel in a late-morning conference room deep within the Washington Field Office of the Federal Bureau of Investigation. Unless you counted dark blue suits as uniforms, thought Swanson; then it would include everyone else. Representatives of all of the alphabet agencies were around the polished table, a show of teamwork for the Anti-Terrorism Task Force—the ATTF. Everybody in the room was supposedly equal, but of course that was not true. The ATTF flow chart had mushroomed over the years after being founded on the dreadful rubble of the 9/11 attacks. Back then, the American intelligence agencies hardly spoke to each other as territorial wars and budget battles were legendary. Now at least they all talked, but the ATTF itself had become as Byzantine as anything that could be found two blocks away in the International Spy Museum.

The only one to whom Kyle and Sybelle paid attention was the obvious big dog, their old friend David Hunt, one of the FBI's five special agents in charge of the powerful Washington Field Office, also known by its own acronym as the WFO.

The lights were dim in the conference room as one of the ATTF agents flipped through a PowerPoint presentation concerning the arrest of Pejman Mobili by the Alabama Highway Patrol. A legal resident of Tuckahoe, Virginia, the Iranian national had been elevated from the cause of a mere state traffic beef to the subject of intense federal interest when law enforcement computers spat out a ballistics match on a 7.62 mm Dragunov rifle found in his trailer to the bullet that had killed accountant Norman Haynes in Maryland the night before.

"To sum it up, we've taken a highly trained Iranian sniper off the board. Good work by the troopers, and a bit of good luck for the home team," the agent said, wrapping up his slide show. He seemed pleased. The ATTF was hungry for success, particularly for one that might even be made public in a sanitized version.

Swanson and Summers glanced at each other, and Hunt caught the look. After the initial round of greetings, the two Marines had remained silent as ATTF specialists had spoken in turn, covering the case from a counterterrorism standpoint. Hunt addressed them. "Colonel Summers, Gunny Swanson, I asked both of you to this briefing because your unexpected presence at the original crime scene helped break this case. What are your opinions at this point?"

Sybelle placed her hands flat on the polished table, and every eye was on her. "You are giving this guy way too much credit. He was never any superman. Just look at his picture. He's a slovenly mess."

"Excuse me, Colonel Summers, but his mission in Maryland demonstrated a high degree of competence. Becoming such a good sniper required serious military training, obviously in Iran." The speaker, a serious young woman from the CIA, lowered her half-glasses to the tip of her nose.

"Bullshit," Kyle exclaimed abruptly and leaned forward on his elbows. "Since I'm the only scout-sniper here today, let me tell you that this guy is not a real sniper. His so-called training is just a bunch of jackassery. The Iranian military found a guy who could shoot straight, gave him some basic principles of marksmanship, and told him he's a sniper. Their physical training is just an obstacle course where they swing on monkey bars and jump into holes. It's nothing. A Girl Scout could do it."

"Easy, Kyle," said Hunt. "You were the one who figured out what happened in Maryland. Now it sounds like you're changing your tune."

Swanson pointed to the big flat-screen television hanging on the wall. A list of objects found in the car and trailer was still shown on it. "No, Dave, we're just readjusting our thinking, based upon what came from the arrest. I agree with Colonel Summers."

The woman CIA agent glared. "He had the murder weapon—a sniper rifle—in his possession, Gunnery

Sergeant. A Russian-made Dragunov rifle like that is accurate to about nine hundred fifty meters. He was a dangerous guy."

"What he had, ma'am, was a broke-ass old Russky hand-me-down. No matter what you may have read in *Jane's Infantry Weapons,* the Dragunov may work up to six hundred and fifty meters, max, on its best day."

Hunt took over as the CIA woman settled back in her chair, seething. "Kyle, I don't understand why you are belittling this guy. We consider this a direct attack on American soil. It might even be considered an act of war."

Sybelle answered. "Ladies and gentlemen, the gunny and I are just trying to bring a military viewpoint for your consideration. If Iran was staging a direct attack on the United States, don't you think they would use the best people available, and do something more than grease an accountant? This guy Mobili looks like he has never passed up a Happy Meal and is a stranger to soap and shampoo. He may have been planted here as a mole, but he went native once he got a taste of the U.S. Your PowerPoint says that the trailer contained not only the weapons but also a PlayStation, an iPod, an upscale computer rig, and a bunch of porn videos. Once Mobili tasted what it was like to live free, he decided to enjoy the opportunity, and he wasn't going to leave his toys behind when he ran."

The CIA woman came back, a bit quieter now after parsing the logic. "What is your read on the second shooter?"

"My guess is that he will be much the same. Snipers

need to train hard all the time, burn a lot of ammo, and keep sharp. That takes open space, dedication, time, and money. I don't see Mobili and his partner being able to do that. A couple of Middle Eastern men with beards and big guns would certainly draw the attention of any hunters or gun enthusiasts who might stumble across them while they practiced in some North Carolina forest or the Utah canyons."

Kyle nodded. "What has Mobili told you so far? Has he identified his buddy, admitted the shooting?"

Dave Hunt shook his head. "He lawyered up right away and hasn't said a word other than he wanted a Koran for company. Apparently he has decided the time has come for him to forsake the pleasures of the infidels and resume being a faithful jihadi."

"He'll talk. Sooner or later," the CIA woman said with solemn confidence.

Swanson agreed. "Look. For us, this began with a tip about the accountant who uncovered some financial crap in an Egyptian business that is an Iranian front. We're going back to our original source and see if we can find out more, which we will turn over to everybody here. But before we do that, Colonel Summers and I would like to have some time alone with the prisoner. Let me talk to him, sniper to sniper, unofficially. Maybe I can pick up something. I promise not to hurt him."

Dave Hunt stifled a chuckle that was heard as no more than a cough. There were definite limits to interrogation techniques, but he knew that Swanson and Summers seldom paid much attention to limits. He glanced around the table and saw no objections. "Let's work something out after the meeting," he said. "We can lay on a plane to Alabama after lunch."

A pair of United States Marshals arrived a few hours later at the FBI field office in Birmingham, Alabama, for prisoner transport. Pejman Mobili had been taken from his holding cell and was ready to go, shackled, hand-cuffed, and wearing an orange prison jumpsuit with a dirty white jacket thrown around his shoulders. He held tightly to his religious book. The transfer of custody was a brief formality of paperwork and signatures.

"Y'all have a nice ride, now," drawled the special agent holding the clipboard.

"Piece of cake," said one of the marshals as they hustled the prisoner to a waiting dark SUV with a metal cage enclosing the backseat. "We drive straight through and deliver him in Washington like he was a pizza. Should we expect any problems?"

"No," replied the FBI man. "Only thing is he may drive you nuts spouting verses from the Koran."

The marshal shrugged. "We've had worse. The man's entitled to his beliefs, right? We'll just turn up the radio."

Mobili was put into the backseat and strapped into a seat belt, and the hand and leg cuffs were locked to a chain attached to a steel ring welded on the floor. There was nothing he could do. The doors closed, locks clicked, and the SUV blended into the morning traffic and was gone.

The prisoner settled against the seat and studied his two new guards. Both wore dark blue windbreakers with US MARSHAL stamped on their backs in bright yellow. One was a man no bigger than himself, and a woman was driving. Just a couple of stupid American cops moving him to a new jail where somebody else would try to ask questions. His lawyer had emphasized that he should not answer anything; the less he said, the harder it would be for law enforcement to compile evidence.

The man in the front turned to face him with a startling mirthless smile and eyes that seemed to glitter with anticipation. "Make yourself at home back there, Mr. Mobili. Read your prayers. We won't be long." Kyle Swanson looked at his big wristwatch. "Let us know if you need anything."

The prisoner ignored the guard's clumsy attempt to establish some relationship. He said nothing and opened his Koran. His lips moved silently with the familiar beloved words, and he began rocking back and forth as their power gripped him. He shut his eyes and recited a sura, letting his thoughts wander. How had he ever drifted so far from the teachings? He had been a faithful servant until a year after coming to America, when the temptations of the flesh and the senses had gradually eaten away at the truth of his life, and he gave in. It was all the plan of Allah, wasn't it? He had been instructed to adopt the dreadful ways of the West and live as one of them until he was needed. Once called, he had carried out the assignment, then was caught by a traffic cop. Surely that had been his fate? Would it end there? No, Allah had kept him alive for a bigger purpose, something as yet unknown. Being killed by the American police had never worried him, for to die as a martyr was a fitting, noble end. Mobili had finally turned away from the infidels. Between now and whatever his destiny might be, he would immerse himself in the teachings of the Book. He hoped Major Shakuri would pay the lawyers.

ALABAMA

They had been moving steadily on Interstate 59 to the northeast from Birmingham for about an hour when the woman driver slowed, went up a ramp, and turned left at the overpass where a combination gas station and restaurant was the only structure. Big trucks were parked side by side, some with their engines running and exhaust fumes blooming white from their pipes. She stayed on the smaller state road that ran as straight as an engineer could draw it for about five miles, and the intersection and the passing vehicles on the busy highway gave way to a rural setting of flat fields and files of hardy trees along the meandering creeks. "There's the truck, Kyle," she said, "and the Lincolns are right beside it." She coasted the SUV to a stop.

When Kyle Swanson opened the door, the overwhelming stench of pigs swept into the vehicle.

The smell jarred the prisoner. "What is this place? Why are we here?" The pig was a filthy animal, and the blood and flesh of the swine were an abomination in Islam.

"Shut up," Sybelle said, and she also left the SUV to join the small group.

Mobili stared. The two black men wearing filthy blue denim bib overalls were solemn. *Not police.* One slapped his palm hard against the ventilated trailer of the eighteen-wheel rig and laughed when the cargo of pigs squealed in fright.

Swanson turned away from the group and returned to the SUV, threw open the door, and unlocked the chains. He hauled Mobili out.

The odor almost made the prisoner gag. "What are you doing?" Mobili shouted. "Police cannot inflict cruel and unusual punishment in this country."

Kyle grabbed him by the shirtfront and threw him hard onto the ground. The surprised prisoner rolled over but came back with a sneer. "I know my rights!"

"Things have changed, and the sooner you understand that, the better. You are nothing but a terrorist asshole from Iran who infiltrated into my country and murdered an American citizen in his own home. That means you have fallen into a black hole, because you have now been declared an enemy combatant. You no longer have a lawyer, no constitutional protections of any sort, and you will never see the inside of a public civilian court." Swanson jerked him to his feet and forced him toward the trailer. "Also, I'm not a cop, and I can do to you whatever the fuck I want. From now on, you belong to me."

Mobili struggled to keep his balance. "I refuse to answer any of your questions."

"I haven't asked you anything." He ripped the Koran from the prisoner's grip and shoved him toward the pair of men, who caught him with steel-strong arms. "These gentlemen are Buster and Jim Lincoln, who work a pig farm near here. Buster used to play football for Alabama and Jim for Auburn."

"Roll Tide," said Buster.

"War Eagle," snapped Jim.

Kyle resumed. "Buster was a Marine."

"Semper fi!"

"Jim was an Army Ranger."

"Hoo-ah."

"They had a sister, Beatrice, who was an attorney working in the North Tower of the World Trade Center in New York on 9/11. Not a shred of her body was ever recovered after your jihadi buddies smashed a big plane into her office. So, Mr. Mobili, you're going for a ride with the brothers Lincoln and their pigs. There are some things they would like to discuss with you. Maybe you will live through the next few hours or maybe you will become a smelly pile of digested pig shit, and I really don't give a damn one way or another."

CHAPTER 5

CAIRO, EGYPT

Were the admirals satisfactory, sir?" Major Shakuri asked Colonel Naqdi when he came into the office for the evening briefing, dreading it, for he brought some bad news.

"Moving slowly, as usual," the colonel replied. "They are afraid of putting their expensive toys in harm's way, and I have to remind them firmly that those ships were built or bought to do exactly that. What do you have for me?"

Mansoor handed over a single sheet of paper containing a summary of the Egyptian Tourism Authority's dismal monthly report. The industry that was the nation's primary source of jobs and revenue was drifting toward total collapse. Almost fifteen million tourists had visited Egypt in 2010, more than ever before;

then, immediately after the fall of the dictator Mubarak, that number went off the cliff. Tourism was now down 80 percent.

The illusion of personal security had been crushed, and foreigners were taking their MasterCards to safer destinations instead of coming to Egypt to drift down the Nile and visit the Pyramids and the Sphinx. Millions of dollars were being lost every month, thousands of Egyptians were cast out of work, and the coalition governments that came and went with regularity were blamed.

"This is excellent," said the colonel. "Keep the pressure on. Come up with some incidents where other tourists with camera phones capture the action for television. Maybe a German riding a camel, or a Canadian woman shopping for a rug, or some American hikers who believe they are exempt from the world's woes."

"Yes, sir." Major Mansoor sucked in a sharp breath. Better to get this next part over with. "There has been an unwelcome development concerning the death of the American accountant. The sniper who was supposed to fly to Texas decided to drive instead and has been arrested on a traffic violation in the state of Alabama."

The colonel closed his eyes tightly, fighting his temper. There was no need to argue about this, because Allah had willed it so. He remained quiet for a moment, letting his thoughts churn through the problem. "We must assume that the U.S. government has assumed custody of this fool by now. Can he hurt us?"

Mansoor felt almost giddy with relief that he was not being blamed. "No, sir. He knows nothing. If he remembers any of his training, and is faithful, he will not say a word to them, even under torture, particularly if we maintain his legal representation."

"Why did he drive instead of fly?" That made no sense. The man should have been safe in Texas instead of in a jail cell.

"I have no idea, sir. His instructions were explicit, to get on the first plane available."

The colonel pushed away from the desk a bit and crossed his legs, straightening the creases in his pants as he did so. The black shoes still gleamed in the overhead light. "You gave those instructions to him personally?"

"Yes, sir, in the usual way, sir, through encoded e-mails on a pornography site. The links were taken down after each use. He knew only enough to carry out the assigned task."

The colonel cocked his head to one side. "So there's really nothing we can do." It was a statement, not a question. "The man made a serious error and it came back to bite him."

"He cannot hurt us, sir. I'm certain of that, but it is unforgivable that he disobeyed orders."

"Instruct our people in Tehran to kill the fool's mother, and have that news passed along when Washington allows him to communicate with a lawyer. That will encourage him to remain quiet."

Major Mansoor smoothly moved to the next subject. "We have had a positive result, sir, on your idea to follow the accountant's route home to determine if he met with anyone. Aside from the travel and hotel people, his only private meeting was in London, with an industrialist named Sir Geoffrey Cornwell." He slid a typed biography and a photograph across the desk.

The colonel studied it. "I know of this man. Retired colonel in the British SAS, a wealthy industrialist and an expert in weapons development." He shut his eyes once again in thought, wondering what Cornwell might have done with the information from the accountant. "Major, I want you to dig deeper on Cornwell. Examine his schedule for the next few weeks to see if there is an opening through which we can get to him."

Mansoor made a note on his pad. "Yes, sir."

The colonel was studying the biography again. "And one other thing. Take a look at his wife, this Lady Patricia Cornwell, too. Perhaps we might reach her with less trouble. If we take her, Sir Geoffrey will be much more willing to have a conversation with us."

ALABAMA

Jim Lincoln held their unwilling guest in a steel-tight grip as Buster Lincoln opened a rear door of the enclosed truck trailer. When Pejman Mobili struggled, Jim said, "Be still, boy. I'm looking for a reason to hurt you."

"Where are the police?" shouted Mobili.

"Don't know."

"What about that man and woman? Give me back to them."

"You really don't want that," Jim answered. "Pair of

badasses, the both of them. Kill you without a thought. You better off ridin' along with us for a while."

"Hey, Jim?" Buster's deep voice came from inside the ventilated trailer. "We already got a dead piggy back here. Damn."

"Can't sell a dead pig," Jim explained to the prisoner. "We do our best to get them all to market alive, but they are fragile little things. Even these two-hundred-pounders."

"I demand that you give me back to the police! My lawyer!"

"We don't use electric prods or slap 'em around. Grow up on our farm and they get treated pretty good. We even work close around them so they get used to being near humans. They're afraid of their own shadows, and getting them to market is a chore in itself, ain't it, Buster?"

Mobili heard the other man rattling things around inside the truck. Pigs were squealing and snorting. "Sure is. Can't be too hot, not too cold, not too wet, not too dry. Just the right kind of bedding. Partitions to keep the groups separate so they don't fight and bite tails or kill each other. OK, hand him up here, brother. We can put him in with the dead one."

Mobili squirmed, but Jim Lincoln easily lifted him up, and Buster caught him under the arms and hauled him in the rest of the way. "No! Please!"

The brothers securely tied him in strips of silver duct tape. When he continued to shout, Buster hit him hard in the stomach.

"Kyle said we shouldn't kill him."

"I know, brother. I just had to do something . . . for Beatrice."

"I understand. Slap some tape on his mouth and let's get going."

While Buster applied the gag, Jim lifted the partitions in the surrounding pens. Then they jumped out and closed the door. The Iranian had been thrown onto the cold dead pig, and now other swine began to snort and stumble around him. When one snot-covered snout licked his face, Mobili began to cry.

CAIRO, EGYPT

Colonel Yahya Ali Naqdi dismissed the major for the day, then took a minute to encrypt a message and download it into the micro SDHC memory card of his cell phone before leaving for dinner with the two visiting admirals at the Pool Grill on the fifth floor of the Four Seasons Hotel. Following the main course of stuffed sea bass, but before dessert of cinnamon rice pudding, he excused himself to use the bathroom. After washing his hands, he received a warm towel from a wizened old man who was there to attend the customers, and in doing so, exchanged his cell phone memory card for an identical one.

It was good to have a lot of different friends and contacts in this new world in which everything he had ever known had changed; up became down, backward was forward, and there was no right or wrong anymore in politics and power, only survival. The very sands of the desert seemed unsteady after the coups of the Arab Spring, and nothing was ever certain.

Several months earlier, during the initial planning stages for his ultimate actions, Colonel Naqdi had opened a secret line of communication with British intelligence in London. He fed them just enough background information concerning the turmoil in Egypt to keep them interested, although it was usually delivered after an event had happened. It was still worthwhile, because it was always detailed and had proven to be accurate, so the British considered their new agent to be intelligence gold. They knew the material came out of Egypt, but they didn't know who he was, so they gave him the code name of Pharaoh.

A few hours after the dinner, as Naqdi prepared for bed and the tremendous events that would happen tomorrow, his latest message reached MI6 in London. The Pharaoh had confirmed that the sniper arrested in America was an operative of Iran's Army of the Guardians, and the assassination of the accountant had been carried out on orders of an intelligence officer named Major Mansoor Shakuri.

ALABAMA

Kyle Swanson was at a large rectangular table in the kitchen of Janetta Lincoln, drinking strong coffee with a taste of chicory and slicing bright red tomatoes the size of softballs. Warm aromas of a home-cooked meal clouded the air. Sybelle Summers was washing huge leaves of lettuce that had come straight from the family's hydroponic greenhouse and joking with the Lincoln girls, Mara, fourteen, and Becky, sixteen, who swirled around her in a friendly storm of energy.

He and Sybelle had driven straight from the rendezvous to the Lincoln home, where a long three-rail white plastic fence lined the road for about two hundred yards. A spacious open gate was anchored by decorative rock columns. The SUV bumped across the cattle guard when they turned beneath a large sign that read LINCOLN PRODUCTS. The grounds were winter bare but neatly laid out, with a number of barns and metal warehouse outbuildings flanking a spacious brick and wood home set back on several hundred acres of prime dirt. A greenhouse was attached at the rear of the house, and two more were in the distance. The girls had come charging across the broad porch to bring them in when Sybelle parked beside the wide stairs. They had not seen each other for about two years and had a lot of girl-talk catching up to do. Both had lost their baby fat and had the long-legged, coltish figures of two beautifully developing young women.

The kitchen was a madhouse for a while, then settled down as routine kicked in and a big lunch was prepared, and conversation became less excited. Another thirty minutes, and Kyle heard the downshifting grumble of a big truck and saw the ventilated pig-hauling trailer maneuvering into the driveway, then branching off on another path to one of the more distant barns. It disappeared inside, and the door was closed. Buster Lincoln emerged from the barn and stopped in an outbuilding near the house that served as a giant mudroom, where the dirt and grime and stench were washed away before setting foot in the house. He wore jeans, a faded wool pullover, and clean boots when he came through the door and pecked his daughters on their foreheads before sweeping Janetta into a hug and spinning her around the kitchen. The table was almost filled to its length with dishes and pans and plates when they were all seated, and Janetta closed her eyes and said grace.

"Isn't Uncle Jim coming in for lunch?" asked Mara. "Did you know Sybelle carries a gun? She's like some kind of cop!"

"We have a visitor who is interested in the Hogzilla Project. Maybe an investor. Jim is giving him the tour. He'll be in later."

"Eewh. I hate those big hogs. They stink."

"I told you, little girl. They smell like money."

Kyle took his cue to change the subject. "How's the Hogzilla thing going? I mean, making a commercial product out of wild boars has got to be pretty challenging."

"It's a start-up enterprise, so we go one step forward and two steps back and throw a lot of money into the pigpen. Actually, some upscale restaurants are showing interest, and zoos and nature parks have bought some. Big rascals, though. Some more than five feet long, up to four hundred pounds." He laughed. "Janetta raises giant vegetables, and I raise giant hogs."

Sybelle finished a bite of salad and asked, "Why bother?"

"Why not?" Buster replied. "I studied business, and Jim did animal husbandry, and we've got ten years of experience now building on what our family left us. We think it might be an opportunity. Nothing is ever a guaranteed success. Maybe we'll find a slot somewhere for them."

"Meanwhile, they still stink." Becky crossed her arms and rolled her eyes.

Jim Lincoln was standing on a concrete floor, with a rack of sharp knives within reach and blood pooling around a drain as he butchered the pig that had died on the truck. He worked methodically beside a set of four pens, each containing a wild boar excited by the feeding. Lincoln stripped out the guts and hurled them into a pen, and a huge hog would attack the food in a frantic rush. The big shoulders would hunch over as the tusks on the bottom jaw helped scoop the meat into the chewing mouth. Their bodies were smeared with the bloody offal, and they banged against the gates, wanting more.

Pejman Mobili was lashed naked to a post overlooking the boars, and his eyes rolled in fear. The ride in the back of the truck had seemed like a vision of hell, but the pigs had not actually hurt him, although one had fallen heavily on Mobili's right foot, almost crushing it. At present, he would willingly go back among the tame swine. These four bristly, ugly hogs were terrifying, and they seemed to be eyeing him as they cried out for more food.

"Wow," said Sybelle. "They are huge."

"We call them Hogzillas. Each weighs over four

hundred, and capturing them is a fight." Buster Lincoln nodded grimly toward the captive sniper and told him, "They can make you disappear, totally and forever." Mobili was shaking.

Kyle Swanson stepped close to the Iranian. "OK. Here's the deal. We gave you a safe ride with the little pigs just to get your feet wet. Now you have to make the biggest decision of your entire life—look at me, not the pigs. I am your only hope of reaching paradise." His voice was quiet and unhurried. Jim dangled a fat strip of gooey intestine over a pen, and a boar lunged for it, his weight crashing against the fence.

"You tell me everything I want to know within the next hour, without wasting my time or making me ask the same questions over and over, and I'll take you out of here safely. You will go to Guantánamo Bay or maybe a maximum security prison for the rest of your miserable life, but you will be alive. Fuck around with me and you go headfirst into the Hogzilla pens. That's the only deal you will be offered today, you son of a bitch."

"They would start by eating the soft and easy parts," said Jim, a specter in boots and bloody rubber apron and holding a dripping cleaver. "Ears, eyes . . . your little dick and balls."

Mobili wept again, tears coursing wet paths through the filth on his cheeks. He had never felt so lost. "Yes. Yes. Ask me anything."

Kyle stood with his feet spread, arms crossed, and cocked his head. "Don't think I won't do it."

"I know. I understand."

Swanson nodded to the others, and they walked

out as Kyle started asking questions. Jim went to the mudroom to wash off while Buster and Sybelle headed back inside. "Would the Hogzillas really eat him?" she asked.

"Probably not. Mess him up a bit, though, just by rooting on him. We maintain them on top-quality forage and grain. Those ugly beasts are almost vegetarians."

LONDON

"A fresh pint for you, Billy-boy, from the bloke in the back corner booth. Asks a minute of your time." The bartender whisked away the empty glass, made a quick swipe at the remaining circle of dampness with a cloth, and plopped down the fresh and foaming mug of beer. Bill Gorn did not touch it for a moment, nor acknowledge the benefactor waiting at the table, for he was usually a cautious man. He was built like a fireplug, with a mop of unkempt dark hair, a thick neck, and sloping shoulders that led to arms corded with muscle from a lifetime of heavy physical work around the docks along the Thames. The scarred hands were large. When not earning an honest wage, he worked part-time as a leg breaker for a bookie, and he had spent a few years in the lockup on his only assault conviction. Turning slowly from the bar, he stared into the gloom at the back of the smoke-filled pub and saw a gent in a black suit sitting alone. The man looked directly at him, held up an envelope, and laid it on his table. Billy Gorn smelled money.

There were no other strangers in the pub, just the usual congregation of dock workers and watermen clustered in rowdy conversations at the other tables and along the bar. Gorn picked up the beer in his left hand and went to the back booth, using a moment sidestepping through the crowd to dip into his right trouser pocket, pull out the switchblade knife, and palm it up his sleeve. "Thanks for the pint, sir," he said as he came to a stop at the table.

The stranger was a medium-sized man with gray hair and gray eyes. Ordinary to the point of being invisible in London. "There is a ten-pound note sealed in this envelope," he said. "It is yours, for your time. I have a proposition through which you could earn nine thousand, nine hundred and ninety more."

Billy Gorn visibly struggled with the arithmetic, and the tall man rescued him. "Ten thousand pounds, sir. Would you like to make ten thousand pounds?"

"Wot's your name and how is it that you walk into my pub and ask exactly for me, who's never laid eyes on you before?" Gorn took a bite of the beer and wiped foam from his lip.

"My name is unimportant, but I am a solicitor by trade, and I was asked by a client to find someone like you, someone reliable for a special task. A former client suggested your name." He took a small sip from his own pint.

"Well, your client knows that I'm no killer, if that's what you are after. I can break them, but they can always be mended."

"Indeed. You will not be asked to kill anyone. Just

the opposite, in fact. You are to keep her alive and safe. Another of my clients wishes to speak with her husband and believes this may be the best avenue to have such a conversation. Now are you interested?"

"Ten thousand quid for snatching some woman?"

"Just so." The solicitor laid a twenty-pound note on the envelope. "No bodyguards involved, so there probably should be a minimum of rough trade. Would you be interested, then?"

"For a kidnapping, I'll be asking twenty thousand pounds, then. Ten for a friend to help me." Billy Gorn was confident in his negotiation style. The thick eyebrows came together, the ledge of his forehead wrinkled, and his little eyes hardened.

The solicitor was familiar with dealing with criminals, however, so he reached out and picked up the fresh twenty-pounder and put it back in his pocket. "You may ask, but the offer remains ten thousand."

Gorn was taken aback at seeing money removed from the table. He thought quickly. Clyde would help him for a thousand, and be happy to do so. "Twelve, then."

"Ten."

"Ten it is. Half up front."

"No." The lawyer had not broken a sweat but pulled a larger envelope from his briefcase. "You are not to be totally trusted, Mr. Gorn. So I shall give you a thousand pounds now to pay for your expenses, and the rest when the job is done and I see the woman is alive and safe. Everything you need to know, including the place she is to be held, is in this packet."

Billy tipped up his pint and finished it. "What is the time on this job?"

The solicitor slid out of the booth and took a moment to straighten his suit. Bland as wallpaper, Billy Gorn thought. "As soon as possible. And if it all goes well, I shall include a bonus."

"How much of a bonus?"

"Please, Mr. Gorn. Stop being foolish and just take care of the job." With that, the gray man drifted toward the door, cigarette smoke swirling around him, and disappeared.

Billy remained at the table and watched him go. Then he caught the eye of his mate, Clyde, still at the bar and gave a slight nod. Clyde peeled away and followed.

CHAPTER 6

CAIRO

A TV set in the colonel's office was tuned to the live coverage of the airport arrival of the Iranian national soccer team. Shouting fans surged along the police security cordons, cheering wildly.

"We have a good team," observed Colonel Naqdi. A newspaper lay folded on his desk, with a front-page photograph showing strong young men in Iranian soccer uniforms, those in the front row kneeling, and all smiling for the camera. "A very good team," he repeated.

"We are favored to win the Asian Cup," his chief of staff agreed. "They are rising in the world standings."

"Which is exactly why this exhibition goodwill match with Egypt is so special. I am pleased that the Cultural Ministry pushed through a popular sports competition so quickly." He looked across at Major Mansoor Shakuri.

"I will not forget that this was originally your idea. Well done."

"Thank you, Colonel." He had several months ago suggested a friendship match, not something like what was unfolding before him at the moment; never something like this.

On the screen, the aircraft came to a halt far short of the terminal. Stairs were pushed into place when the door opened at the front, and a welcoming group of Egyptian sports officials boarded, along with the customs authorities to clear the visitors.

Major Shakuri went to a sideboard and poured them both tea. The colonel gave him a hard look and said, "Let us hope it all goes smoothly. You could use a win about now yourself, Major, after that failure in America."

"No excuse, sir." Shakuri stiffened in the chair. Any thought that the arrest of the sniper would be treated as a minor mishap was crushed. This man never forgot failure.

"I like you, Chief of Staff, and you have great potential, but you must consider more variables in your planning. I detect a sense of urgency in your work, when you should be more patient. Get it done, but do it properly. Time is our ally," the colonel cautioned. "The historic events that will break the stranglehold of the Egyptian army on the current government's leadership are well under way. We will get there eventually."

"I understand clearly, sir," said the major. *Change the subject!* "We hired some hooligans in London through several cutouts to kidnap the Cornwell woman.

It was better to send local infidels to do the job rather than use brothers of the faith who might be under police surveillance."

The colonel rubbed his hands together. The soccer team was deplaning and waving to the cheering admirers. "Keep me informed on that one. The old man who is her husband is a dangerous enemy."

A large blue-and-white bus was waiting for the team, parked between a lead army truck that would push a path through the crowd and an armored car in back for extra security. Uniformed Egyptian army troops were seated in the open-back truck, and another helmeted soldier manned the .50 caliber machine gun atop the armored vehicle. A phalanx of civilian police on motorcycles would stop traffic at the intersections all the way to the hotel where the team would stay overnight. Security was ironclad.

The athletes boarded the bus, took seats, and pushed open the sliding windows to continue waving. They were goodwill ambassadors, and it was easy for sports heroes to be friendly. The door hissed closed, and motorcycle engines roared to life.

"Watch now. Now we start," the colonel said, picking up his teacup.

The helmeted gunner in the rearmost armored car opened up with a long rip of fire that destroyed the engine in the back of the team bus in front of it; then more bullets crashed the length of the bus toward the front. The heavy armored car accelerated out of line, bent into a sharp turn, and headed straight for the immobilized bus as the heavy machine gun pumped short, sharp bursts into the trapped soccer team. The army troops piled out of their truck and began shooting into the shocked crowd of onlookers.

Inside the bus, the athletes and trainers scrambled over the bodies of their teammates to try to escape through the windows on the far side away from the incoming fusillade of bullets that ripped and tore without mercy. Before they could get out, the armored car slammed into the thin skin of the bus with such power that the two vehicles were meshed into a single tangle of metal. Then a bomb exploded, lifting both vehicles off the ground for a moment before they crashed back down to burn furiously.

In his office at the Palm Group, the colonel and his chief of staff watched and drank their tea. Idiot television announcers were horrified, and that weakness was passed along to their tens of thousands of viewers. The screen showed the welcoming crowd breaking apart and stampeding like a herd of goats. Many had been killed or wounded, and others were trampled. The station switched to a replay of the armored car shooting, then ramming the bus and exploding, and then the Egyptian government ordered the station to shut down. The screen faded into a fuzzy, buzzing blackness that only fed the fears of those watching.

"It appears you have your win today, Major Shakuri. My congratulations," said the colonel. "The team was martyred for the greater cause."

The major was trying hard to keep himself together. "It is sad that such fine young men had to be sacrificed."

"Nonsense, Major. Your plan caught the attention of the world," the colonel said. "Any investigation will show this to have been an outrageous attack by the renegades within the Egyptian army. People will lose trust in all of their security forces."

"How will our country respond?"

The colonel smiled. "Demonstrations in Tehran and a very strong diplomatic protest."

WASHINGTON, D.C.

Kyle and Sybelle dumped Pejman Mobili back with the U.S. Marshals in Atlanta and flew back to Washington. Major General Bradley Middleton, the two-star commander of Task Force Trident, was waiting behind the big desk, rocking slowly with a foot braced on a lower drawer. Master Gunny O. O. Dawkins was immersed in his favorite pastime, reading online newspapers and blogs and Web sites on his iPad tablet, with his big fingers scrolling on the little flat screen as smoothly as those of a texting teenager. Commander Benton Freedman was picking at the information from the prisoner.

"He didn't know much, did he?" Freedman, the Lizard, asked.

"Wouldn't expect him to, Liz. He was a shooter. Nothing more."

"This name of his partner might be good, and I'll get that over to the FBI right away. He's probably changed it by now, but who knows?"

Sybelle Summers spoke. "And give priority to that other name he dropped, that Major Mansoor Shakuri who gave him the order."

"On it," the Lizard confirmed. "He may have been lying."

Summers shook her head. "No. He wasn't lying."

"What did you do to him?" asked O. O. Dawkins, glancing up from the business page of the online *International Herald Tribune*.

"Nothing, really. Not a mark on him. He just felt like talking, I guess. Guilt, maybe."

Dawkins snorted, grinned, and started clicking through some broadcast network sites. A celebrity mother and her two daughters, all strikingly beautiful, were having a public quarrel over a sheer dress the mom had worn to a premiere, and every network was running pictures as if it all meant something. "I don't even know why these women are famous," he said, nevertheless deciding to check out the dress that was causing the furor. It wasn't all that sheer. Couldn't really see anything.

Kyle Swanson moved to the window and looked out at the bright, chilly day. "Liz, that major is stashed somewhere in Iranian intelligence, but I think you can narrow the search to the counterintelligence units. He's got some power."

General Middleton pushed back his chair and suddenly stood up, leaning on the big desk. "Goddamn it. I cannot believe the Iranians were so stupid as to actually attack the United States in the open."

Dawkins shifted back to Binging hard news sites. "But they did. Hey, guys, terrorists just blew up the whole Iranian soccer team during a goodwill trip to Egypt. The Iranians are blaming the Egyptian army."

"Fuck. Still something else that does not fit," the general snapped back. "Tehran traditionally keeps a low profile beyond their borders because nobody trusts them. Eventually, we will probably have to go after them because they are developing a nuclear weapon. To pick a fight with us over something like an accounting scam makes no sense because it gives us a valid excuse to bomb their nuke facilities. That's just the way it works."

Swanson turned toward him. "I talked to the prisoner about nukes. He knew nothing. Is the White House considering a strike?"

"They consider everything. Now that we can prove the sniper was Iranian and his orders came through the Iranian command structure, political pressure will build to do something."

Summers, wearing battle dress fatigues, crossed her legs and picked at her boot laces. "We will be extra cautious, sir. Nobody wants to be wrong about this one."

General Middleton absently waved a hand. "What has gone on before is ancient history, Summers. I want you to continue working the sniper angle. See where it leads."

Swanson's eyes moved from face to face. "Then my next move should be to get to the U.K. and see if Jeff can help us unravel it. He gave MI6 everything he remembered about the accounting deal, but if the two of us go through it a couple of times together, maybe something else will pop up."

The general nodded in agreement. "OK. Get your

butt over there. Remember you're a Marine and you're working for me, not him. Do that Excalibur shit on your own time."

"Aye, aye, sir."

"And give my regards to Sir Geoffrey and Lady Patricia."

LONDON

Lady Pat loved the theaters of London, having never totally extinguished the actress spark. She had abandoned a stage career when she met and married a rugged, handsome young captain in the Special Air Service, Geoffrey Cornwell. That had been years ago, and many things had changed. They had become wealthy, received awards, and seen the world, but she still dearly loved the boards. Instead of begging for a minor role in a play, perhaps being rejected because the director didn't like the shape of her nose, she was now courted as a potential investor. Being a financial angel opened all doors. Although she was now sixty years old, she yearned for the burn of a spotlight.

She and her private secretary, the beautiful, dark-haired, and efficient Delara Tabrizi, had been making the rounds all day. A new musical was being cast, and they lunched with the producer before moving on to a fringe venue that was struggling to put together a small production by a dynamic new writer. She was unimpressed but gave compliments to the creator and his four-member cast. Lady Pat always had kind things to say to actors, whose fragile egos could be crushed with a glance. She gathered this group in a hand-holding circle, smiled, and started reciting "An Austrian army, awfully arrayed," the first line of the alliterative poem by Alaric Alexander Watts. The verse was about a battle fought so long ago that it had been forgotten, except for the poem about it that became a voice exercise practiced by almost all actors.

"Boldly by battery besieged Belgrade," continued the ingenue, and the leading man boomed out, "Cossack commanders cannonading come," then the breaking voice of a boy, youngest of the troupe, followed with "Dealing destruction's devastating doom." They continued, line by line, through the entire alphabet. She led them in applause and hugs, for she was one of them.

Then it was out to the West End for some street shopping at the Chapel Market before a rehearsal at the historic King's Head Theatre, of which she was a patron. She and Delara preferred to leave the car behind on such days and do their London prowls by taxi, foot, and subway, for they could see so much more. The chauffeur, alerted by Delara's cell phone, would be waiting to take them home when they got off the train. If need be, they could always spend the night in the city. They were in no rush, and now that the workday was over, they decided to take the Tube back to do some more shopping.

They joined the steady, jostling crowd entering the Islington High Street station and stepped carefully onto the first of two long, steep escalators heading down. Staying to the right side to allow others to pass on the left, Delara found herself wedged between a large man immobile on the step in front of her and Lady Pat behind her shoulders. They rode down with the crowd in silence and made the right-angle turn for the second escalator, facing another sharp decline. Delara was jammed against the same man, and when she glanced back, there was another large man right behind Lady Pat. Turning to face forward, she tapped her left hand against Pat's leg hard to alert her to the possibility of trouble.

Almost immediately, Lady Pat felt a sharp point against her back, and the man behind her, with a knife covered by a folded jacket, leaned in close and said with a soft but threatening voice, "You and your friend will be coming with us now, ma'am. Any trouble, and I will be havin' to put this blade between your ribs." The man in front of Delara turned and glared at her.

Lady Pat took a deep breath and unleashed a tremendous scream from deep in lungs that had been trained to reach people in the last rows of a theater, and it almost stopped time. The eyes of the man in front of Delara Tabrizi widened in surprise, and Delara hit him on the bridge of the nose as hard as she could with a downward strike of her fist. The nose cracked, blood flew out, he saw stars, and his knees went wobbly on the moving escalator. Everyone was turning to stare.

The man with the knife momentarily froze, which was enough time for Lady Pat to turn and jam a wedge of stiff fingers into his testicles. The sudden pain made him drop the knife, and she grabbed the front of his shirt and jerked him forward and to the side, letting gravity and momentum roll him over her left hip. She had not lived with an SAS officer for so many years without learning some self-defense tricks. The attacker went tumbling past her, then past Delara, who kicked him in the face as he went by. Both of the men were down and entangled in a clump as others in the crowd piled on them in a noisy rugby-style scrum.

By the time the escalator emptied onto the long station platform, a pair of constables of the British Transport Police were waiting with handcuffs to take charge of the bewildered assailants. Delara gave them her business card and said that charges would be pressed against the hooligans who tried to steal her purse.

Lady Pat had stepped into the background and refused to be fussed over. She was fine, she said, but had a constable escort them back to the surface and into a taxi. When they were finally alone, she told Delara to immediately call for the Bentley to come into the city and pick them up at Brown's Hotel in Mayfair as soon as possible. The chauffeur should bring along a few of Jeff's security lads, for there had been a spot of trouble.

CHAPTER 7

WASHINGTON, D.C.

Swanson was looking forward to a good night's sleep. He had been on the go almost constantly since the telephone call from Sybelle had jerked him away from his California vacation. Catnaps in cars and planes could not replenish the energy his body craved, and the fatigue of sleep deprivation was setting in. He locked the door of the Georgetown apartment, and the safe familiarity of the place eased him down so that he was asleep as soon as his head hit the pillow an hour later.

The transatlantic telephone call came from England at one o'clock in the morning and changed him instantly from sound asleep to wide awake. It was Sir Jeff, sounding weary and worried as he described the attack on Lady Pat and Delara in the Tube station. They were fine, he said, although he could not say the same about the two thugs who botched the attack. Jeff said he already had everyone under tight security, so there would be no repeat of such a thing, but Pat had wanted Kyle to be personally told before he heard about it from some other source. The older man's voice choked up when he said the company jet had already been dispatched to fetch him to London. It would meet him at Reagan International.

Kyle felt a moment of déjà vu, because he was already booked on a flight tomorrow. He would take the Excalibur plane instead, just as he had canceled a commercial flight to get to Washington in a hurry. There was no question this time; he needed to see them. He could sleep on the plane. He could sleep when he was dead.

Swanson hung up, went to the bathroom, then stood by the bedroom window to look out at darkened Washington and entertain murderous thoughts. Why would anyone go after Pat and Delara, and in such a public place? Obviously, it was no random mugging attempt, although Jeff had said the police had not yet gotten any answers from the goons that did it. He lifted up on his toes and stretched, then dropped down to do some push-ups and sit-ups before climbing back into bed, knowing he would be unable to really sleep. He closed his eyes, breathed deeply, relaxed, and slowly lowered into the hazy zone somewhere just north of oblivion, quiet but with his senses alert to everything, the still place he always went to before going into a big fight.

Again he was the only passenger on the aircraft, but this one had a pretty hostess who welcomed him aboard and did everything but tuck him in as the Lear settled into its long flight home. She dimmed the lights, set the volume low on a CD of soft jazz, and gave him a pillow and a blanket after converting the seat to a bed. Kyle was flying five hours forward in time on this jump.

He did not know how long he had been asleep when he heard a paddle stroke in water, then a forlorn voice tinged with humor. *"So it begins."*

"Maybe," Swanson said. *"Maybe not."*

"Oh, yes. You will soon cause me to be very busy. There are many things you do not yet know."

It was a familiar haunting, a playing out of defined roles. Kyle was being visited once again by a character he knew as the Boatman, a tall and ghastly creature who piloted a little boat to ferry souls from earth to eternity, souls that Kyle Swanson had killed. Over the years, the nocturnal visits had become less and less surprising as Kyle had learned to let his subconscious roam and be open to all hints and suggestions.

"Why are you here? I am not near any battle. Therefore, no fresh bodies for your little boat."

A ghoulish giggle rose to challenge. *"There will be many of those, and we will have our usual deal: You will kill them, and I will haul them away. Or maybe I will take you this time. Or someone close to you."*

"I'm not going to kill anybody." In Swanson's dream, he could detect the flicker of a holocaust burning on a distant horizon and smell the ashes of cremated beings. It caused him to grind his teeth. *"This time, you are wrong."*

The Boatman grinned, and there was a glimpse of

his toothy skull. *"Not wrong. I am just early. Even by your standards, this time many people have to die."*

"Not by my hand."

"Oh, yes. You are wrong. Very wrong." The long paddle dug hard into the water at the stern, and the boat slid away on unseen water.

"Go to hell," Swanson said.

"Yes," replied the Boatman. *"I always do."*

Swanson felt his body loosen, the muscles fully relaxed, and his mind went into an even lower gear. He had lied to the Boatman, of course; not that it mattered, because those meetings were always just a reverie to remind him who he was and to let his subconscious mind assess the facts. He was certainly planning to kill whoever had attacked Pat, and that reckoning would come even if he had to overturn God's green earth to do it.

He puzzled for a moment about how the Boatman could have come for a visit while Kyle was flying at twenty thousand feet. Soon he was snoring, and the flight attendant snipped off the light and adjusted the blanket.

CAIRO

Curtains of black smoke spiraled and swirled above the Egyptian capital as civil order broke down following the destruction of the visiting Iranian team. The people were blaming the elected government and the generals for the airport massacre, and the major cities had endured a night of looting and murder, beatings, rape, and robbery. Mobs were in the streets, those supporting the fragile government clashing with equally fervent antigovernment factions, although they were all mostly members of the Muslim Brotherhood. The powerful army generals dithered, not knowing what had really happened and wanting to test the political winds before cracking down on one side or the other. From his office window on this bright new morning, Colonel Naqdi watched the smoke and crowds with deep pleasure and almost smelled fear and opportunity.

"We are not quite there yet," said Colonel Naqdi.

His chief of staff, Major Shakuri, thought carefully before speaking. "The government seems at the edge of collapse, sir. I've never seen such open mayhem. The Egyptians may soon be at war with themselves."

"They are just confused, Major, because they sense that events far beyond their control are at work. The elected men cling to power through a coalition of different parties, and the Brotherhood is not satisfied with its current political status—they want it all. The generals who have the real power seem lost. Everybody is yelling at everybody else."

"Confusion that we manufactured," said the major.

"It was not difficult to do, was it?" the colonel asked. "Two Brotherhood martyrs with military experience were in the armored car, one to shoot and one to drive. The bomb was just a few artillery rounds wired together. It was an army vehicle, the driver knew the proper codes, so no one questioned its last-minute addition to what was supposed to be a totally routine escort duty.

This was a wise investment in every way, and you see the result of careful planning."

It was still another implied threat against Major Shakuri. He had vomited again in private that morning before reporting to his colonel that the London attack on Lady Patricia Cornwell had been unsuccessful.

"Another failure?" the colonel had sneered.

"Sorry, sir. The lawyer I used as an intermediary to hire the attack team has been silenced. Should I try to pursue the woman again?"

The colonel had given him a cold stare, as a man would regard a beetle, a creature of no consequence. "No. The old man will have her covered with bodyguards by now. Neither will be reachable for a long time." Naqdi moved on to other things, but the major knew there was another black mark against his name.

Now the colonel returned to his desk and used the remote control to turn up the volume on the large television screen hanging on the wall of his office. Al Jazeera news was reporting on demonstrations in the streets throughout Iran, too, protests demanding revenge for the deaths of the beloved soccer stars. Speeches were being made in parliamentary bodies around the world, including at the United Nations. To anyone who followed the news on television, the entire Middle East seemed to be on fire again, although it was all being orchestrated for the purpose of whipping up anger and enthusiasm in both countries for what lay ahead.

He looked up suddenly at his chief of staff and asked, "Is the ship on schedule?"

Mansoor Shakuri was glad he had checked the sailing

plan before the briefing. Something positive that he could report. "Yes, sir. She will be on station at the proper coordinates at the correct time." In his heart, he thought: *More martyrs*. The colonel dealt in high body counts.

"I don't trust the navy," the colonel said. "Stay on top of that movement and do not let them become tentative. Make sure that ship is where it is supposed to be, Major. If the admirals argue, tell them to talk to Tehran—after they follow my orders."

"Yes, Colonel. Is there anything else?"

Colonel Naqdi grew quiet as he mentally ran through his timetable. It was too early to bring the missile crew to full alert status, for that could arouse unwanted interest at a time when suspicion was already high in Egypt. "No," he said and dismissed the major.

Then he walked back to his window to watch the demonstration below as he weighed the situation. There was a lot yet to do. The Muslim Brotherhood and its leading clerics were trying to take over the legislative branch of the elected government, the People's Assembly. The Brotherhood was still a minority after last year's vote. The prime minister sided with the Supreme Council of the Armed Forces, and he was still in control because the generals were reluctant to surrender power, despite the outward appearance of supporting civilian rule.

Colonel Naqdi recognized that the fires of revolution burn brightly for a only brief time; then demonstrators go back to their day-to-day and leave only the predators to fight for the ultimate power. He knew this to be true because he was one of those predators. The risks were great, but the potential payoff was enormous.

The costly American experiment to establish democracy in Iraq had failed, but it had deposed the Sunni dictator Saddam Hussein. Baghdad and its firebrand preachers and figurehead politicians now rested easily in the pocket of the religious rival Shia government in Tehran.

So now it was again Egypt's turn at the altar, and Colonel Naqdi was to deliver the strategically important country as still another puppet state. At the end, he would have the Egyptian armed forces also under the control of Iran, and it would become a Muslim Brotherhood dagger pointed straight at the Israelis. In addition, the standing armies in both Egypt and Iraq would sandwich Sunni-led Saudi Arabia, and Iran also would have military control of the vital sea routes that fed the world's unending appetite for oil.

What could be better? That kind of geopolitical shift was worth the sacrifice of the soccer team. A few more hammer blows, a handful of soldiers, a little time and a little luck, and he would have it.

CHAPTER 8

A private car was waiting at Heathrow. Swanson was a bit surprised that it was not a white luxury vehicle of the Excalibur Enterprises fleet but rather a dark police sedan with a pair of plainclothes types as an escort. Other than a preliminary greeting, neither man in front spoke as they cruised along the direct route between the giant airport and a modest and totally secure safe house where the Cornwells had been hidden in the university city of Oxford.

Kyle fidgeted in the backseat. One of his core principles as a sniper was to consider that going slow was almost always better than too fast. This was not one of those cases. He felt as if he had been poking along like a man on horseback, exactly one horsepower, when he wanted to travel at the speed of light. Even the hottest military jet would not have been fast enough. He chewed on his anger as the big car ate up the miles.

The stone house was normally used by visiting academics at Oxford and had the exterior look of an old English home, with base stones that reflected the weak winter sun in shades of soft orange. It was unremarkable in every way and blended perfectly with similar cottages nearby. Another policeman was at the door and required Kyle to show identification before being allowed to pass. Just inside was an immaculate, small reception room with a uniformed cop at a little desk, his hand casually resting on a submachine gun. He logged Kyle in as an approved visitor, then touched a buzzer.

The door at the far end of the room was opened by an attractive woman in dark slacks, a pink cowl-neck sweater, and low heels. "Gunnery Sergeant Swanson," she said, offering a hand; the grip was firm. "I am Tianha Bialy," she added, with no further explanation. Her voice had a low pitch, long black hair fell over her shoulders, and the distinctive bump of a holstered pistol showed beneath the sweater at her waist. "Please come in. Lady Pat and Sir Jeff are in the living room."

A few paintings of someone's ancestors hung on the walls, shelves were jammed with old books and files, and Lady Patricia Cornwell stood drinking a glass of beer before a fire that burned in a wide hearth of gray stone.

Kyle walked straight to her, his eyes searching for any damage, and she laughed and embraced him. "Relax, Kyle. I'm fine."

He turned to Jeff, who remained seated in a cushioned chair, a knobbed wooden walking stick tilted against one arm. Kyle went over and gave him a hug. "I'm sorry I wasn't here sooner," he said.

"It's all good now, boy," Jeff said with a deep laugh. "Have no worries about us. The security jockos have us locked up like the queen's jewels, and our Pat even broke a leg of one of the toffs."

There was a gleam of excitement in the older man's eyes. Kyle noticed a framed map of Egypt propped on the mantel above the fireplace. Something had been under discussion when he arrived, and he could guess what it was.

Jeff turned toward the other person in the room, a middle-aged man with thin brown hair, who was in a common bureaucrat's vested suit and black shoes that were scuffed in places. "Kyle, let me present Sir Gordon Fitzgerald, the chief of MI6."

"Delighted," said Fitzgerald, lifting his whisky and taking a sip. Known more commonly by the letter *C*, the head of the British Secret Intelligence Service that handled foreign threats looked more like a tradesman than a spy. Kyle supposed that was the point.

Swanson got right to it. "I want them. I want both of the bastards who attacked her." His eyes reflected the frustration that he had been holding in for hours.

The small and portly MI6 chief was unperturbed by Kyle Swanson's outburst. He had been prepared for it and was used to handling high-strung field agents. His voice was steady and quiet. "That is quite out of the question. They are in the custody of the queen's government. It will remain that way."

"Do a rendition, then," Swanson said. "Put them on

a plane to a country that specializes in making prisoners more cooperative. Your hands remain clean, I will get what I want there, and whatever happens is not your fault."

"Now you are just being insulting. My friends Jeff and Patricia assured me that you could put aside your personal feelings so that we might work together. If you cannot, then I have no further use for you. You can fly right back to America, as far as I am concerned."

Swanson put his hands on his hips and stared at the seated security chief. "What?"

"You see, I know quite a lot about you, Gunnery Sergeant Swanson. In fact, I had a word with your General Middleton at Task Force Trident in Washington about an hour ago. He has issued new orders for you to lend all assistance possible to us. Paperwork to follow, if need be. Are you prepared to do that?"

Swanson turned to face Cornwell. "What's going on here, Jeff?"

"Things are looking rather nasty, Kyle. Forget the attackers; they are little fish."

Lady Pat came over. "Sit down, Kyle, and put on your thinking cap. It seems the attack on me was just part of some big plot. I am a bit put out that I was not the big prize. I thought I was the star."

Swanson sat, breathed deeply, and relaxed his tight muscles. He really had no choice. "All right. I'm in, Sir Gordon."

"Grand. There is a lot of ground for us to cover. First, let me set your mind at ease—the unsavory chaps who attacked Lady Pat have already assisted police with our inquiries to the maximum of their limited abilities. They were just common waterfront riffraff hired by an anonymous solicitor to do the kidnapping. One of them followed their unsuspecting benefactor all the way home and thus obtained his name and address. By the time the police ran round to that apartment, it had been destroyed by fire, and the bodies of the solicitor and his wife were discovered in the debris. It was murder and arson." C lifted his glass again.

"Murder."

"Someone was tidying up after the attack to break the connection," said Sir Jeff.

"Even then, MI6 was not involved. The assault on Lady Pat had been under investigation as an ordinary criminal matter." The director placed his glass on a side table beneath a lamp and leaned toward Kyle. "What I am about to disclose is very highly classified, which General Middleton says you possess appropriate clearances to hear."

"I understand."

The voice of the MI6 chief remained neutral. "We have a valuable source in Egypt who goes by the name of Pharaoh. We do not know his true identity, but his material is flawless and without fault. A message from the Pharaoh arrived overnight that contained information on the dead solicitor, the kidnap plan, the two men who were hired, and the person who gave the orders."

Swanson put his teacup aside because he was tempted to throw it into the fireplace. "An Egyptian ordered this attack?"

Jeff coughed to clear his throat. "No, Kyle. Not an Egyptian. An Iranian officer by the name of Mansoor Shakuri."

"Shakuri?" Swanson felt the chill of recognition. "That's the same guy who was behind the hit on your accountant friend," he told Jeff.

"Apparently. Your people shared that with us," said C. "Then earlier today, the Pharaoh informed us that it was Shakuri who had planned and carried out yesterday's awful slaughter of the Iranian national soccer team in Cairo. It's a bit much to believe it to be a coincidence. Iranian intelligence is stirring up trouble in Egypt to get an excuse to strike back hard. Working through the Muslim Brotherhood, they could take over that country."

"Complicated," Kyle observed.

"Yes. Quite," agreed the MI6 director. "That is where you come in."

"You want me to take out this bad guy?"

"No. Not at this point, at least. We need more information. It seems a bit too easy to have found the name of this Major Shakuri popping up from multiple sources. He may be nothing but a diversion. I want to know what is really happening, Gunnery Sergeant. Egypt is critical, it is in trouble, and we must be certain before we act."

Sir Jeff stirred in his armchair. "Kyle, I have been in contact with an old business acquaintance in Cairo who swears to me that Egypt's more popular politicians, plus the commercial leaders and government experts, have had nothing to do with these outrageous attacks. Just the opposite. They want stability, so things can calm down and they can bring the country back to being a prosperous business partner in the international arena. So I am going down to Egypt to meet personally with him, and I want you to come along."

Kyle shook his head abruptly. "The hell you are. You and Pat will stay in this safe house until this all settles down. Send me instead."

"Precisely what we intend to do," said C. "I was arguing with this stubborn old man about that very thing when you arrived. Since you are a vice president of Excalibur Enterprises, you can go in with Dr. Bialy and do some advance surveillance under the cover of routinely setting up a meeting for Sir Jeff at some unspecified time. Instead, the people we need will meet with you."

"Dr. Bialy? Who's that?"

The MI6 woman whom he had believed to be an assistant to C smiled from her watchful position along the wall. "That would be me."

"I don't want a civilian woman along on a mission that could become dangerous. I won't have time to wet-nurse her."

"Doctor Bialy is a native of Egypt, sir, and is a recognized expert in Egyptology. She speaks the language and has personal contacts, which you do not. Tianha is also a fully trained MI6 operative, and she is going with you, or she will be going in alone, and you remain here."

"You threaten people a lot, don't you, Sir Gordon?"

Jeff deflected the subject. "My so-called meeting is

set for next week in Sharm el-Sheikh. You two will arrive there the day after tomorrow."

"Sharm? Why Sharm? Wouldn't this be better up in Cairo?"

C heaved himself from the chair and walked laboriously over to the map. "Normally, that would be correct. But Cairo, despite the mobs and the unrest, is not what has us worried. This map shows it clearly."

"Shows what?"

"You do this one, Tianha," said C, wandering away to read some book titles on a shelf, his chin jutting forward as he became lost in thought.

"Yes, sir." She stood before the map, with her arms crossed, not needing to look at it because she knew it from memory. "That attack in America and the attack on the soccer team are, in our opinion, diversions. Iran really gained nothing through such actions other than inflaming passions. So they must have some ulterior motive, a higher purpose. We were thinking more about water and oil."

Kyle stared at the map. Egypt was a vast, squarish country that shared the desert in the west with Libya, and another desert border with Sudan in the south. The broad Mediterranean Sea occupied the entire north, while the Red Sea provided most of the eastern edge. Saudi Arabia was on the other side. A smaller finger of water, the Gulf of Aqaba, branched off to the right and ran up to a point where Egypt, Israel, and Jordan all met. The second fork from the Red Sea branched left and became the Suez Canal. The place where the split took place was the coastal resort city of Sharm el-Sheikh.

"It is our opinion," Dr. Bialy said, "that those horrible acts are setting up some kind of strike to take control of Sharm." She tapped the map with a bright red fingernail. "It would be an enormous strategic coup and allow them to control shipping in the Red Sea, wreck European trade, and give the Iranian Navy easy entry into the Mediterranean."

Swanson remembered that warships of the Iranian Navy had been making bold ventures into the Red Sea in recent months, showing the flag and letting the navies of other nations know that there was a new player on the block. "The U.S. would never allow that to happen. It's too much of a choke point."

"The politics of the region changed with the Arab Spring revolutions, Kyle," said Jeff. "A strident Muslim government in Egypt allied with the Iranian theocracy could tilt the entire region as we know it today. Once the Iranians are lodged in tight, it will be difficult to evict them."

Kyle was incredulous. Iran had to know this would mean war, and that would provide the final answer to whether or not Tehran possessed a nuclear weapon. The mullahs would paint the situation as a holy conflict and throw everything into the battle, with millions of Muslims in other countries being sympathetic to their calls. Israel could be obliterated, and the Western nations attacked. "Has your Pharaoh reported anything about this?" he asked C.

"No. Another reason that Tianha is going along is to

try to establish a personal contact with him. You are to sniff around Sharm and see what's what down there of strategic value. We need every shred of information that we can get, Gunnery Sergeant Swanson."

Lady Pat came up behind Kyle and wrapped her arms around him, peering over his shoulder. "And you must stay out of trouble."

"Right," he said.

CHAPTER 9

OXFORD, ENGLAND

Kyle Swanson put on a jacket that evening and went for a walk, alone, to clear his thoughts. The historic town was quiet and brought up automatic thoughts of all things English—benign tales of Robin Hood and King Arthur and Lady Diana, and the rough histories of warriors such as the Desert Rats and Lord Nelson and the Special Air Service. A chilly mist was settling over the area as he passed through Gloucester Green near Worcester College, headed east on Beaumont Street, and then up St. Giles until he found the Eagle and Child Pub. He went in for a pint. The place was packed with students, and they all seemed like kids. By comparison, at thirty-six, he was probably the oldest man in the room, aside from the barkeep.

He found an empty corner in which to nurse his beer.

A pretty young brunette at a nearby table checked him out and whispered to her girlfriend, and they giggled. He ignored them. Not tonight. Even amid the crush and chatter of the young people, Swanson had the uncomfortable, creeping feeling that he was old and alone.

Normally, even when deep in enemy territory, that seldom bothered him, for there were times that he preferred to operate totally on his own. He knew that he was a U.S. Marine, and therefore a member of an elite force of more than two hundred thousand brothers and sisters whose fighting prowess was known around the world. From the newest recruit to the four-star commandant, they all had his back. Then there was Task Force Trident itself, a little five-person unit with clout far beyond its size, for it answered only to the president of the United States. If he was in trouble, usually all he had to do was call, and help would be on the way, sometimes through methods that lay far outside of normal channels.

That was what was really troubling him; in Egypt, Swanson would be beyond the reach of his security blanket. He would not be going into a potentially hostile situation as a Marine, much less in his specialty of the Trident sniper. His position would be that of a civilian, a prosperous business executive. He would move in open luxury, not evading surveillance. His only backup was a woman MI6 agent who knew more about King Tut, the kid monarch who died a thousand years before Christ was born, than she did about twenty-first-century terrorism. Things had changed a lot since the time of chariots. If he didn't really know her, how could he trust her? It would be up to her to win that trust, not his responsibility to make it happen.

The pint was empty, and he went to the bar, ordered another, then returned to his corner. It was such an automatic move, back to the wall, view of the door, that he did not give it a thought. His camouflage on this trip would be the dark suit of a corporate vice president, and his hide would be a hotel suite, not a hole in the dirt. As long as nobody questioned him closely about business affairs, he could fake the corporate role because he had watched Sir Jeff lead meetings of the Excalibur board of directors. Swanson wondered how any serious business could be conducted at all in Egypt, which was wrapped in convulsions of change, but money did not rest, no matter who was in power.

At a table against one wall, two serious-looking young men with backpacks hanging on their chairs were immersed in a game of chess. That steered Kyle into thinking about pawns and strategy and MI6. The Brits were firm allies, of that he had no doubt, but government intelligence services were always playing games within games. Could C, Sir Gordon Fitzgerald, be using Jeff and Pat and Kyle as bait for some unknown purpose, or multiple purposes? Jeff was not an easy man to fool, but C knew more than all of them put together about what was really going on in Egypt, where the double-cross was an art form. C had used vague terms about his unidentified source without really saying anything about the contact. Did the director of British intelligence even know who it was? Was he being used, too?

Over at the chessboard, one of the players sacrificed his white knight to the black queen. Kyle's brain was beginning to hurt from stirring around all of the ingredients in the assignment, and he puffed out his cheeks in exasperation. He was nobody's white knight, and he had no intention of being sacrificed.

Once they arrived in Sharm el-Sheikh, Swanson would fall within the operational control of MI6 and be beyond the normal reach-back to Trident for support. Their local contact and guide was to supply him with a handgun. Instead of being overprepared, he thought that would leave him almost naked for firepower. He drained the beer, left the pub, and pulled his personal encrypted phone from his jacket pocket, speed-dialing Washington. Within a few minutes, the Trident team was working to sharply upgrade Swanson's capabilities during his venture into the land of the Pyramids.

"One final thing, guys," he said. "Do a workup on my mysterious new partner from MI6, this Dr. Tianha Bialy." He spelled the name, and the Lizard confirmed it.

"I have already done that. MI6 sent me her particulars. Highly educated and a recognized Egyptologist. She's clean, Kyle."

"That's what worries me. With all of her years studying her academic specialty, she cannot possibly be an expert operative. I doubt that she has had any field training beyond the minimum needed to qualify, although they are passing her off as an experienced hand."

"Want me to dig deeper?" The Lizard laughed. "That's a joke, Kyle. Archaeology. Digging up tombs. Lara Croft?"

The voice of Lieutenant Colonel Sybelle Summers cut in. "Stay on topic, Liz," she ordered, then changed her tone. "Kyle, if you don't want her, we can just abort the mission. It's dangerous enough without saddling you with more difficulty."

"No. They insist that she knows the turf, and they will send her on alone if I cancel out. I'll just keep a close watch, and if we can't rely on the Brits, we're in trouble."

"When do you and this mystery woman leave for Sharm?"

"Tomorrow."

"Stay in touch."

"Roger that."

LONDON

Tianha Bialy sat cross-legged on the soft carpet of a tidy four-room apartment, snug in a thick blue bathrobe and with a towel wound around her wet black hair. A cup of hot tea was within reach, Arabic music swam softly from hidden speakers. Her packing for the trip was done. All she had to do was snap the latches and she would be ready. Passport, documents, cash were in her purse. Makeup would be kept at a minimum. A smart gray skirt and jacket with a modest white blouse were waiting on hangers in the closet. She was ready. She was prepared. She was nervous and welcomed the feel of her fiancé's strong hands on her shoulders.

"Why are you doing this, Tianha?" Jonathan Blake

was an archaeologist and geologist who had spent most of his working days digging in faraway places in search of clues about the world of old. Somewhere along the line, his interests changed to the more lucrative occupation of hunting for oil.

"It's an assignment, Jon. The orders came straight from the top. I can't refuse it." She leaned back against him.

He gently kissed her shoulder. "You are a brilliant academic, my dear. Your phenomenal talents are best suited for archaeological sites and computer searches. Just look at your work in the last five years. Your reputation is already made, and you can lecture at any university you wish."

"But I am also an MI6 agent."

"You were conscripted by them because of your expertise in the Arab world, my dear, to be an analyst, not some spy adventurer."

"That's why they are sending me down there. I know the people and the culture and the politics. We want to find out who is likely to inherit the levers of power in Egypt before the whole place explodes." She closed her eyes, and he peeled back the robe from her shoulders, sliding his hands over the soft skin that had the scent of lavender.

"Anyway, if there is trouble, my American partner will protect me." She gave a slight shiver.

"Do you trust him?"

"I don't know. He is an absolutely frightening person, Jon. He is not very big, certainly not as tall as you, but there is an absolute sense of confidence about him.

He moves like a ghost. He's smart and obviously lethal, with narrow gray-green eyes that see everything."

Jon eased Tianha to the carpet and lay beside her, sliding a hand beneath the robe to cup her breast. "What did MI6 say about him? Surely they gave you his file."

She sighed in comfort. "There is not much of a file, believe it or not, because most of it has been blacked out. He is thirty-six years old, a career Marine gunnery sergeant, one of the best snipers in the world, and holds the U.S. Congressional Medal of Honor. Almost everything else has been erased because of security matters. Kyle Swanson officially fell off the map about six years ago."

"Can you control him?"

"I don't know, but that may not matter. He has his job and I have mine."

Jon kissed her, more roughly. "And what is your job down there, Tianha?"

"Remember the Official Secrets Act, Jon. I can't tell you. We could both end up in prison." She grimaced a bit because he was hurting, but also exciting her.

He pinched her nipple and twisted, and she closed her eyes against the bolt of pain. "To the devil with the Official Secrets Act. What you find could be worth a fortune if we use it properly. Tell me." He smiled down at her, leaning on his elbows. "I can make you tell me."

Tianha leaned up and bit him lightly. "No you can't." She laughed.

Blake curled his hand in her hair and pulled it hard. "You are being a naughty girl, Tianha. You know you will tell me eventually, so make it easy on yourself."

She began to struggle, and Blake moved atop her naked body, pinning her to the floor. The belt from her robe was in his hand, and he wrapped it around her wrists when she extended her arms to him. "Not this time, my love," she whispered, staring into his dark eyes and handsome face. "I go to serve queen and country."

"Everything," he said and lowered his face to her belly, nibbling at the soft flesh. "Tell me everything."

"Never." She slipped her bound wrists over the back of his neck and pulled him down as he spread her legs. "I will never tell you about the Pharaoh. Never."

CHAPTER 10

One hundred and forty-six people boarded EgyptAir flight MS780 at Heathrow Airport in England for the long southeastern flight to Hurghada International Airport in Egypt. Kyle Swanson was the last passenger to cross the threshold, delaying in order to study the others. After boarding, he told a flight attendant that he needed a moment to go through the coach section and say hello to an old friend at the rear of the aircraft before taking his own seat in the first-class cabin. The attendant asked him to please hurry, for the crew would soon be closing the door and preparing for takeoff.

The stretch wide-body Airbus was carrying only about half of its capacity, and the cavernous coach area loomed like an empty frame on a wall, a testament to the reluctance of people to travel to the troubled country. Passengers were spreading out, staking claims to vacant seats, as Kyle went down one aisle all the way to the rear, circled through the galley, and came up the other side without seeing anyone suspicious.

An attendant arrived to take his suit jacket and hang it up, and Swanson settled into the comfortable wide seat next to that of Dr. Tianha Bialy, who gave him a strange look. "Why did you wait so long to get on?"

"I had to go to the bathroom." Kyle buckled his seat belt.

"They now have bathrooms aboard the planes."

"Really? I'll try to remember that."

"Are you planning to be rude for this entire trip?" she asked.

Swanson turned a bit, the hardness of his face slightly easing. "No, not at all. In fact, the better we get along, the better we can work together. I just wish we would have had more time to get to know each other before heading out as partners. That's certainly not your fault. Happens all the time on missions."

The twin engines below the wings growled to life. "I agree. Then let us make the best of a strange situation. Shall we shake hands on it?"

"Sure," replied Kyle. "Three days in Sharm, three days in Cairo, maybe a side trip to Alexandria or Port Said, and then back to London. A straight-up business trip for all intents and purposes. We should be able to get through that without gashing each other too much."

She laughed at that. "You must call me Tianha, and I probably should not refer to you as a gunnery sergeant when we are in public."

"Kyle." He noticed she had a charming smile when

she was relaxed. Just like that, the tension had seemed to drain away from her. "Are you worried, Tianha?"

"Of course." The airplane began its long crawl to get in line for the taxiway. "This could be very dangerous. For a woman, even someone like me, it would be impossible to do on my own. How about you, Kyle? Aren't you worried?"

"No. I've had a lot of experience in volatile situations. I try to keep nasty surprises to a minimum." The plane shuddered and stopped on the tarmac before moving slowly forward again, and the engine noise grew a notch. An announcement came from the intercom that they were next for takeoff, and the attendants should take their seats.

"Well, you look very nice in your company's vice presidential suit and tie instead of a camouflaged battle dress uniform."

He laughed as the Airbus began its roll. "Tianha, the suit *is* my camouflage."

By the time the plane was airborne, each knew the other was lying. Nothing had been settled between them.

HURGHADA, EGYPT

The flight coasted uneventfully across France and down the length of Italy, Greece, and then the broad Mediterranean, with Turkey to the east. After entering Egyptian airspace, they followed the deep crack of the Suez Canal all the way to the Red Sea. As the pilots began to shave off altitude, Swanson examined the approaching coast, where the pale desert sand met blue-green waters. "Not much to this place, is there?"

"No," Tianha said. "Hurghada is just another fishing village that has grown up to be a medium-sized city. I've been through here a few times before while doing research projects around Aswan and Luxor. Being on the proper side of the canal, it has always been a jumping-off spot to some of the more historic places down south, but mostly they are promoting the diving and fishing opportunities on the nearby islands. The tourism crisis must be pretty severe down here."

The Airbus circled lower and sped in for a smooth, one-bounce landing on one of the two long runways. As they coasted to a stop, Kyle noticed that only two other commercial planes were parked before the long terminal area, which was topped by spiky tentlike coverings. Far away, though, were plenty of military aircraft: several varieties of helicopters, a squadron of American-made F-16s, and what looked like old Soviet-era MiGs. Hurghada lived on tourism, but it was also the home of a major Egyptian Air Force base beside the Red Sea. Why had she not mentioned that?

When the door opened, there was no gate extending into the building, which meant that even on the hottest days when temperatures soared well above 100 degrees, the passengers would deplane on the scalding tarmac and hurry indoors to the air-conditioning. He was glad it was January.

"Your people have someone meeting us, right?" Kyle asked as they went through customs. "Look at that mob of taxi drivers. The natives seem restless."

"They are hurting for fares. Usually, it's pretty orderly in the taxi ranks."

The first passengers to pick up their bags were besieged by drivers offering deals in various languages. To one side, beside a row of yellow molded plastic chairs, stood a middle-aged man wearing white trousers and a short-sleeved white shirt and a skinny dark tie that was slightly askew. He held a simple sign that bore the name of BIALY, and she beckoned to him rather imperiously. He hurried over, bowed politely, and retrieved their bags, then led them outside to a clean hire car waiting beside a decorative garden.

After securing the suitcases, he removed a package from the trunk, got behind the wheel, and drove away. "Tianha, it's good to see you again." The subservient demeanor fell away, replaced by a calm and confident ease.

"And you, Omar. This is Kyle Swanson. Kyle, meet Omar Eissa, formerly a flight sergeant of the Royal Air Force, and our local contact."

After retiring from the RAF, Omar Eissa had drifted back to Egypt, the homeland of his family until his grandfather had moved to England as a student many years before, and his father had fought against the Nazis in World War II. The reward for the exemplary military service to the crown was British citizenship for the entire Eissa family. In trade, the country had received three generations of strong boys in uniform. Omar had become bored after his retirement from active duty, but he had noticed something in his travels throughout

Egypt, something that might be interesting in his less active years.

Tourists and professionals and businesspeople always preferred spotless private vehicles with air-conditioning and a competent, knowledgeable driver who spoke English and other languages to the clattering taxis with open windows and mulish men who smoked vile cigarettes as they drove. The Flighty reached out to old friends and was guided into MI6, which offered financial help to establish a string of hire car agencies throughout Egypt. As a driver himself, he could poke around for intelligence without drawing the attention of the authorities. The more he did it, the more he became just an ordinary piece of the local scenery.

"Ah. The American. Pleased to meet you, Mr. Swanson." The driver exited the airport and turned toward the city.

"Just call me Kyle. Did you bring a pistol for me?" Kyle saw no point in dancing around the main issue. He wanted to gun up as soon as possible.

Eissa handed the box over his shoulder, and Kyle opened it: a .45 Colt for him and a 9 mm Beretta for Bialy, with spare magazines and a soft shoulder holster for Swanson.

"Terrific," Kyle said, working the slide and checking the weapon. "Where are we staying tonight?"

"You are in adjoining suites at the Marriott down at the beach. It's the best hotel around, and they were glad to get the business. To stay in character, you will go directly there now to freshen up, like a couple of normal, exhausted travelers."

"No argument from me," said Tianha.

"Right. At six o'clock, you tell the concierge to call my car agency because you have made dinner plans. Then we will do a full ride around town after dark."

From the backseat, Kyle looked in the mirror at the driver's dark eyes. "You have something special in mind?"

Eissa grimaced and tightened his grip on the steering wheel. "Things have been pretty calm around here because the people were making decent livings, and jobs are the best reason there is for not overturning the economy. Also, we are far away from the population centers and the rioting. This morning, however, I came across something rather unusual, and I need your opinion before reporting it to London."

"What is it?" Swanson asked.

"You'll have to wait a couple of hours," Omar replied. "I don't want to influence your thinking."

"Come on, pal. Don't fool around if it's important."

"This is my territory, Kyle. I'll know when to go. I have already driven past it twice, and I don't want to attract attention." There was no hesitation in the agent's voice now. "As for importance, well, let's just say it could change the entire cricket match."

Omar pulled beneath the canopy of the Marriott as the sky was purpling just before sundown. A chubby doorman moved forward with a friendly smile, his hands clasped behind his back. He knew Omar, and he knew there would be a five-dollar U.S. tip for him to allow the preferred parking spot.

"Well, what is it tonight, my friend?" The doorman held up his hand. "No, let me guess. You brought that couple in this afternoon, so it's time for an authentic camel steak and some belly dancing, followed by a romantic stroll on the beach."

"If we all don't get murdered in the process," Omar said, pressing the folded bill into the doorman's palm. The instability of the country had sent the foreign exchange rate rocketing for the U.S. dollar.

"The fucking revolutionaries are murdering our entire country, Omar. I have heard of no problems around here tonight. Do you require protection? I could get a trustworthy man to ride along, or follow in another car."

"No, my friend, but thank you. I have an AK-47 on the front floorboard, and my pistol. Anything beyond that, well, we would be dead enough to be no longer concerned. Here come my people now."

Tianha and Swanson appeared at the door. Before the doorman drifted away back to his post by a small platform, he whispered. "They are booked into separate suites, but I think they are probably sleeping together. There is a connecting door. I will let you know."

The English woman and the American man were both in cool, casual attire, ready for a night on the town. She wore long sleeves, a traditional black shawl covered her head, and her skirt was modest. Her matching expensive purse carried, out of sight, a pistol and a camera.

"Hello again, Dr. Bialy. Did you have a good rest?" Omar Eissa asked with a slight, polite bow.

"It was excellent, Omar," she said as she slid into the rear seat of the car. "Just what I needed after that long flight." Kyle walked around and got in the other side, surveying the scene as he moved. No serious watchers.

As soon as Eissa pulled away from the entrance canopy, they put aside the acting. "Hurghada, as you know, is near the choke point for the Red Sea and the Suez Canal," he said. "Ship traffic moves freely through the area all the time, which gives it strategic importance. Not to give you a geography lesson, but just to put what you are about to see into proper perspective. Tianha, get your camera ready. We will be there in just a minute."

They looped south through streets of small, white-walled homes where people lived who could never afford a single night in a luxury hotel. "Omar, Hurghada is just a dot on the map. Sharm would be the defensive bulwark around here because it controls more of the vital waterways," Bialy said. "I'm as curious as Kyle. What are you talking about?"

The quiet sedan turned onto Al-Farouk, the main coastal highway. "You are absolutely correct. Sharm would be the prize for any real battle, so what do you make of this? Over there at the ten o'clock position."

A large olive green truck with the markings of the Egyptian Air Force was parked in a turnaround off the highway, its nose facing the sea. It had a stubby little cab, but the broad rear deck and heavy load required three sets of double wheels on the back. Flat on the deck was a rack of four missiles.

"Jesus!" exclaimed Swanson. "Are those Harpoons?"

"Yes. My sources say that the air force bought that particular mobile missile battery system several years ago from the Royal Danish Navy. It is served by a two-man crew, and both of them are over there with it."

Kyle noticed the truck was not protected by a large guard detail, nor even a stack of sandbags, giving the impression that it had just pulled in there to park temporarily, as if in the middle of a long trip. He heard Tianha's camera clicking images into the memory chip. "Back in the day, Harpoons were the shit," he commented. "Over-the-horizon capability and a range of about seventy miles, with a big boom on some ship at the end. Consider that to be a significant threat, boys and girls, and go ahead and report it."

Tianha put the camera aside. "A threat to what?"

"Four Harpoons could cause some major damage out there, although I can't imagine why Egypt would want to sink an oil tanker." Eissa turned back inland. "I don't want to pass them again so quickly."

"Yeah. The good news is that the tubes were flat on the platform, and they have to be raised for a launch, so nothing immediate is happening. We can give it a final check in the morning before we leave." He briefly considered going after the missile battery tonight and monkeying around with the hydraulic lifting system. That would probably require killing the two crewmen, which would compromise the overall mission. He decided to leave it be and let the allied intel services, which would have Tianha's photos and report, keep an eye on the installation from a satellite. If the launcher went to an offensive posture, someone else could make the decision on whether, and how, to take it out.

"I would love to know if it has a specific purpose, or if it is just there as a precautionary defense measure during the troubles," Tianha wondered.

"Oh, it has a target," said Kyle. "Bet on it. Otherwise it would be parked at the base rather than be out here on its own. Now let's go get some dinner."

CHAPTER 11

CAIRO

Colonel Naqdi of the Army of the Guardians was at his desk in the Palm Group headquarters offices early and watched a majestic dawn break on what was to be an important day. Urgent messages from the commander of the First Naval Zone in Bandar Abbas were waiting on his desk, but the rear admiral's pleas would be ignored. The man had already been told that the mission would not be canceled under any circumstances at this point. Either he cooperated or he would be replaced, just as a broken-down old ship could be replaced. The admiral needed to be reminded that the creaky Iranian Navy was gone forever, a relic of the shah's regime, and that he was now just another cog in the reorganized Navy of the Army of the Guardians of the Islamic Revolution.

The ship in question was the old *Babr,* an antique Pakistani-built utility vessel of the Delvar class with a 1,300-ton displacement and a crew of twenty officers and sailors. More than fifty years old, its only armament was a single ZU-23 23 mm antiaircraft gun. The superstructure sat aft, near the blocky stern, and the midships was broad and flat, suitable for the role it had been playing as a replenishment vessel for the Iranian fleet that had been chasing Somali pirates in the Gulf of Aden. That gave the colonel a pause to chuckle to himself. The United Nations itself had let this little wolf in sheep's clothing go on the prowl by stating that vessels of different countries could enter the area of the Gulf of Aden to combat piracy, and the Iranians had actually done well in that role. From that position, the Iranians had expanded their reach to penetrate north in the shipping lanes into the Red Sea.

The *Babr* was innocent and scruffy enough not to draw much attention as it meandered up the coast. Its only possible hostile military use would be to lay mines, so it would be kept under loose observation. The captain had orders to proceed to a point that was carefully plotted on his map through the use of a military-grade GPS navigational system, then slow down and maintain only enough speed to keep headway when his ship reached the invisible mark on the water. A high-frequency beacon would be activated; then he was just to await further orders. Since he carried no commercial cargo, the skipper deduced his ship was being used just to push the envelope of tolerance of the other nations for having an Iranian presence of any sort in the energy-rich shipping sector. When the secret mission was over, the *Babr* would probably return to the 16th Fleet and help chase some more pirates. He could feel the vibration as the twin diesel engine lazily turned the propeller shafts. The captain realized he probably would never know the real purpose of this little voyage, for that was the domain of those higher in rank than he. His job was to follow orders. The sun had come up to starboard, and he was sitting in his padded chair, sipping a cup of hot tea, and watching the giant vessels plying the shipping corridor.

Colonel Naqdi was finally satisfied that everything was as it should be, and he issued a final flurry of encrypted communications and orders. Last among them was an official letter of commendation for his chief of staff, Major Mansoor Shakuri, citing the excellence of his performance in coordinating today's complicated action.

HURGHADA

Kyle Swanson whipped through an hour's worth of isometrics, crunches, and push-ups before stepping into the steaming shower and pondering Tianha Bialy. Why was she really on this trip? So far she had accomplished absolutely nothing other than setting up a good car service with a decent undercover agent who had happened upon an antiship missile battery. Omar could easily have replaced her as a translator, if needed. Granted, Hurghada was just a stopover on the way to Sharm, so maybe he was expecting too much, and she would perform some MI6 magic over there.

He took his time getting into another rich-guy tailored business suit and knotting a branded silk necktie that Lady Pat had bought for him. The shoulder harness for his pistol ruined the line, so he left the jacket unbuttoned. Showtime. He called the concierge to send someone up to collect the bags, because that was what rich guys did.

Tianha was waiting at a table in the restaurant, reading news from her laptop computer. "Not much to report, Kyle. A lot of unrest after the Iranian soccer team massacre in Cairo the other day." She had a cup of coffee to one side, and a basket of pastry was in the middle of the square table, along with fresh flowers.

A waiter appeared, poured a hot cup of coffee for her, and took Kyle's order for fruit and cereal. "Perhaps nothing much is being reported, Tianha, but this place is strung tight as a violin."

She looked around to be sure no one was listening. "I made contact about that missile battery to London last night. No further orders."

"Another piece of data for a big picture that we can't see."

"I just feel we should do something more about it."

Kyle bit into a fresh croissant and chewed thoughtfully. "Not our job. Well, it might be yours, because I still don't know your assignment. But it's highly doubtful that you are supposed to have a shoot-out over a parked Harpoon battery."

Bialy sniffed and went back to her computer. "We

will discuss this later," she said. "This is not the proper place."

"Well, if we ever get to the proper place, will you let me know? Freezing your partner out of the loop sucks."

Her dark eyes looked steadily at him. "I'm under strict orders, Kyle. You just have to believe me."

"I want to. Just try not to get us killed while you follow those orders, OK?"

Thirty minutes later Omar Eissa arrived at the hotel to pick up Swanson and Tianha, right at nine o'clock, and was assured by the doorman that the maids had told him that the two wealthy visitors had not slept together the previous night. The connecting door remained closed and locked on both sides. The doorman thought it strange, he said, accepting the usual tip while he helped load the luggage. The American businessman must be sick for not pursuing such a beautiful woman and for being so obviously cool toward her. They did, however, tip better than the Russians, who wanted everything for nothing. The Germans were the worst of all, but right now he would welcome any customers at all, even Greeks.

Omar cut the conversation short and got his customers into the car. The fast ferry ran over to Sharm three times a week, as did a slow ferry, although the schedules of both had been disrupted by the revolution. If they missed the ten thirty departure, there was no telling when another would sail. Omar told the doorman he wanted to be early.

He swept the Mercedes out into traffic and retraced the previous night's journey along the coast road, slowing down as they approached the parked military truck. "Oh, no," he said. "That's trouble."

Swanson and Bialy followed his stare. The truck was in the same position, but the rack of missile tubes had been raised to a 45-degree angle, with steel struts planted on the ground around the deck to soak up recoil. The two technicians who had appeared lazy yesterday were now busy on the platform.

"What does it mean?" Tianha asked.

Swanson gave a fatalistic laugh. "Getting those tubes up means the missiles are probably hot, programmed, and ready to fire."

"My God. We have to stop it," she exclaimed, her eyes wide.

"Will you stop that? If we attack with a couple of pistols and an AK-47, we could take out the technicians, but that would also expose us to arrest. All you can do is update London. Other people have to handle this, Tianha."

Omar had been watching and listening as he drove. "Swanson is right, Tianha. My hope is that they are not going to shoot at our ferry. We had best get to the pier."

They remained in the automobile while the aft ferry ramp was cleared and the barrier opened. Omar followed signals into a short line of vehicles that disappeared quickly into the broad covered parking deck. At a signal, he shut down the ignition, and all three got out as the Mercedes was chained into position, bumper to bumper with cars in front and behind. A biting wind channeled through the open space, chilly enough to make passengers hurry up the metal staircase to the shelter of the twin lounges for the hour-and-a-half crossing to Sharm.

About 150 people were aboard the sparkling white Hurghada Turbo *Sea Jet 1,* half of its normal capacity, and it carried only a dozen vehicles. The absence of weight would allow the ferry to lift almost out of the water when it picked up speed and headed across the Red Sea. The frequent travelers had already staked out seats away from the metal bulkheads and near heating vents so they would be warmer than the tourists who clustered at the windows to view the passing scene.

Omar and Tianha grabbed a table while Kyle went to the cafeteria bar and brought back coffee and bottled water for them all. Orange midmorning sunshine poured into the lounge, giving it an almost cheerful glow, an oasis of peace in a country that seemed intent on devouring itself. Kids were already restless and zooming through the aisles, or just standing in place, staring at each other until a new friend was made.

"Things are always like this at the start of a crossing," Omar said. "By the time we disembark, these quiet people will be rude and impatient, ready to commit mayhem to get one place ahead in line."

With the rumble of engines and a loudspeaker announcement, the *Sea Jet 1* dropped its lines and headed away from the long pier. Omar opened an Egyptian magazine, and Tianha spread out a tablet and two textbooks. Neither was inclined to talk, for there was little more to say. "I'm going on deck for a while," Swanson said, pulling on a Burberry trench coat. Ignored by all, he walked away, tying the belt and flipping up the broad collar. The deep right pocket sagged a little and jingled as he walked.

"He is going to freeze out there. Just because the sun is shining does not mean it will not be cold on the water." Omar put aside his magazine.

"Good." She looked at Omar hard. "Safe to talk here?"

"Yeah, as long as Swanson stays gone. What's happening, Tianha?"

She glanced around and lowered her voice a bit. "MI6 has a new source in Egypt who has been furnishing us with extraordinary information that proves the Iranians are orchestrating much of the unrest, in concert with the Muslim Brotherhood."

"So? Everybody knows that already."

"This is not rumor or hearsay, Omar. The source is providing ironclad proof, including names and numbers and exact times and orders stretching all the way back to specific people in Tehran."

"Who is this person? How does he have such access?"

"We don't know. He, assume it is a *he,* goes by the code name of Pharaoh, and I have been sent to find him. Right now, he is operating on his own, and we want to give him protection and guidance."

Omar smiled. "You want to run him as an MI6 agent."

"Just like us, Omar. Just like us. So far it has been a one-way street, with him contacting us when he wishes. We have sent a message back down the chain that someone is being sent to Egypt to establish a point of contact and provide him with protection, or whatever he wants, plus offer a way out if things go bad for him."

"And you are to be that agent contact?"

"Yes. Eventually."

"You gave him your name?" Omar was astonished. An agent never intentionally unmasked his or her identity and walked around in the open. "Not only is that suicide, Tianha, but it will ruin your cover as a respected academic and researcher."

"Of course not. We are sending a quiet alert to him, but I also want you to spread the word through your networks that an influential new friend has arrived and wants a private meeting with the Pharaoh. The contact's name is Kyle Swanson, and he works for the U.S. Central Intelligence Agency. You already have our schedule, so you can put that out there, too."

Omar puffed out his cheeks and blew out a long breath. "Does Swanson know about this?"

She gave a small smile. "No, so let's keep that between ourselves for the moment, shall we? I'll tell him when he needs to know."

"You're playing a hard game, Tianha." Through a lounge window, he saw Swanson staring at the water with his hands shoved in his pockets. "Is he really CIA?"

"No. He's just an American Marine."

Kyle was not uncomfortable on the open deck. With the heavy overcoat, only his feet were cold. Supple leather shoes were made to look good, not to repel frostbite. The harsh January wind bit at the exposed skin of his face, but the brightening sunshine was warming things fast. He fished in his pocket for an Egyptian one-pound coin and plugged it into the slot of a big telescope mounted on the deck so tourists could watch the harbors and the passing ships. No one else was interested in taking a look, so he stayed with it; two minutes for an Egyptian pound, which was worth sixteen U.S. cents and falling.

The shipping lanes seemed filled; giant oil tankers and container ships lumbered forward and stopped in a delicate dance of elephants as they lined up for access through the Suez Canal to the Mediterranean. Smaller vessels easily moved about them with discipline and care: a few yachts, fishing boats, and speedy pleasure craft. Here and there he picked up the silhouettes of naval ships. The Red Sea was busy. Swanson edged the big lens back down the swirling wake of the *Sea Jet 1* to look back at Hurghada.

So far, so good. Maybe the Harpoons were just there for a regular drill, because one of the strengths of a missile platform mounted on a truck was a mobility that could quickly move it to a point of threat. Every branch of every armed force on the globe regularly ran exercises, so would the Egyptian Air Force be any different? He hoped that was so. The Harpoons were not exactly surgical tools, and even the best guidance systems would be challenged to pick one specific ship from among a cluster of targets. Many neutral fishing boats, airplanes, and human beings had been destroyed over the centuries simply for being too near, or mistaken for, legitimate military targets.

Two minutes elapsed, and the telescope shutter snapped closed with the suddenness of a triggered rat trap. He stood upright and wiped away some tears brought by the wind. *Please let me be wrong about this.* Kyle fished in his pocket, retrieved another coin, and was in the process of inserting it into the machine when his eye was drawn back toward Hurghada by a flash of light that was followed by a rising white column of exhaust smoke. *Launch!* He spun from the telescope and pounded on the window of the lounge to get the attention of Tianha and Omar, and was back at the scope, watching a second launch, by the time they ran onto the deck. He didn't even have to point; a pair of shipkillers were in the air, chalking their way high into the sky and accelerating.

The Harpoons seemed to be looking down at all of the sea traffic as the launch codes transferred to inertial guidance and GPS settings. The deadly birds completed the climbing arch and dove toward the water, flattening into an attack mode at almost the speed of sound. The missiles covered the first ten miles before any of the ships reacted; then a steady chorus of bells and alarms grew in a cascade as battle alerts sounded and the Harpoons bored in on the noisiest ship in the target area, an Iranian naval vessel named the *Babr,* which was holding station while giving off more than enough radar and radio signals for the missiles to ride a true track.

The first Harpoon punched in ten feet above the waterline and drilled a burning hole through the crew compartment and the galley before detonating in the engineering spaces, the explosion going upward and outward. A gust of bumpy air lifted the three-foot-wide stabilizing wings of the second missile, and it smashed directly into the bridge, killing everyone there. The ship rose from the water with its top sheared away and its back broken by the dual direct hits. A fireball wreathed in smoke bloomed over the wreckage as the *Babr* rolled to starboard and began to sink by the stern.

For miles around, surprised crews stood momentarily frozen as the surprise attack unfolded and the concussion wave of the mighty explosion spread across the sea. Captains on every ship snapped out of the moment, ordered the highest possible alerts, and activated their missile defenses. Boats were ordered lowered to rescue any survivors from the stricken Iranian naval vessel. Almost all eyes were on the tower of black smoke rising into the sky.

"Here come the other two," Swanson said, leaning into his telescope with more coins in his palm.

The white exhaust trails in the clear sky were especially menacing now, because the original target ship was destroyed and no longer able to broadcast and assist the guidance systems of the incoming missiles. They went up, curved over, and dove to begin the sea-skimming run into the crowded sea lanes at 537 miles per hour.

Flashes of countermeasures erupted from every ship carrying a weapon. Tracers crisscrossed in interlocking fire, and a nearby British frigate pumped off anti-missile missiles that swept toward the incoming Harpoons. The combined speed of the weaponry closed the gap fast, and the lead Harpoon in the second wave ran headlong into the defensive web, was peppered by

bullets and fragments of antiaircraft shells, and tumbled into the sea.

The last one kept coming, nicked just enough to
slightly change its course. It buzzed erratically out of
control for another mile before smashing into the broad
side of a 130,000-ton, double-hulled tanker that was
registered in the Bahamas and filled with unrefined oil.

CHAPTER 12

Thick and ugly black smoke pouring from the hulk of the burning tanker could be easily seen from the *Sea Jet 1* as it pulled into the pier, more than twenty miles away from the site of the Red Sea attack. The ferry passengers had panicked with the sudden appearance of death and destruction on the water and were fearfully scrambling to reach the perceived safety offered by solid earth beneath their feet. It was hard for Kyle to blame them. The blast that had rolled across the water was followed by a tremendous set of waves that shoved the *Sea Jet 1* sideways like a toy boat.

He had remained standing, braced against the pedestal of the big telescope while the disaster unfolded, mentally cataloguing everything that was happening.

Bialy and Omar had grabbed the railing and held on tight. Screams of some passengers had blended with the alarm and horns of distressed ships during the first few minutes, until the ferry captain announced over the loudspeaker that bigger ships were surging forward in rescue efforts, and the ferry would stay out of the way and proceed to Sharm under maximum speed. With that, its engines roared and the *Sea Jet 1* leapt forward, away from the danger zone.

"I told you we should have done something!" Bialy yelled at Swanson, her eyes wide in horror. She pointed toward the burning oil tanker and the sinking Iranian ship, blaming him. "We could have prevented this! It didn't have to happen."

"Why don't you just shut up?" Kyle was tired of listening to her. Dr. Tianha Bialy was no field agent, and she was allowing emotion to impact her judgment. He made a decision on the spot. "We're done as a team. You're on the first plane back to London."

Then he gave a hard glare at Omar Eissa. At least this guy had some dirt under his fingernails, some mileage as an operator. *Can I trust you?*

Eissa looked back unflinchingly. "I suggest we all go to the automobile and prepare to disembark as soon as we can. There's nothing more to see here." He gently took Tianha by the elbow and tugged her away from the confrontation.

She shook him off. "You can't make me leave, Swanson. You're not my superior."

"No, but I can refuse to work with you any longer. Things are turning nasty in a hurry around here, and your presence would be almost a death warrant for both me and Omar. Those missiles changed the rules. It's no academic exercise, no series of quiet meetings, but a shooting war. That is no place for a rookie. You just witnessed what could be the start of a war between Egypt and Iran, with God knows who else being drawn in before it's over."

She shrugged away from Omar and crossed her arms, anger rising in her eyes. "I'll be staying, Swanson. You don't even speak the language here. If one of us leaves, it will be you."

His lips barely moved. "You know, come to think of it, that would be fine, too. Next time I come to Egypt, I had just as soon be part of a Marine Expeditionary Force armed to the teeth. If you wish, call London when we reach the hotel and let the big dogs make the 'you-or-me' decision, and tell them I volunteer to leave."

"Good," she snapped. "I will."

"Good."

They fell silent and went below to the automobile parking deck. Deckhands had been briefed by the captain to stay calm themselves in order to help settle the passengers, and they moved about as if this were business as usual, unlocking axle chains and steel hooks and preparing cargo to be off-loaded. Their eyes reflected an inner fear as they worked without the usual shouts and orders and controlled chaos of docking. More than anyone else, the crew was aware that the ferry had been but a minnow out on that broad sea and would have easily been crushed to splinters by any of the big ships rushing to the rescue of the stricken vessels.

The ramp was lowered, and Omar kept his place in the line of cars and trucks, ready to react if another driver panicked to get away faster. On almost every trip he had made, the courtesy and temporary friendships shown during the voyage evaporated as soon as the vehicles cleared the pier, and it became every driver for himself.

Once on the road, Omar looked in the rearview mirror at his two passengers, who sat without speaking against the doors on either side of the backseat. He inhaled a deep breath. "Neither of you has asked my opinion, so I will give it anyway. You are acting like quarreling teenagers. We are a very small team of agents that just happened to be in an advantageous position to see what happened back there. Our report will be invaluable in both London and Washington. If you break us up now because of your petty differences, it will be a long time before another team can be inserted."

"Omar—" Kyle started to respond, but Eissa held up a hand to stop him, waving away any words.

"I've heard quite enough. I expected better from both of you."

The Blue Neptune Hotel loomed like a sultan's castle of some 375 opulent guest rooms that dominated Shark's Bay as the lordly anchor for the luxury hotels that were stacked along the Sharm beachfront. Only the very rich could afford to stay there, and though there might be a tourism crisis in Hurghada, Sharm's hotels were filled, sleek yachts were moored in the busy marina, and a white cruise ship balancing a pyramid of decks was anchored just offshore. It was a mirage of peace, just after noon on a sunny day.

"They don't know what's happened yet. We beat the news ashore," Omar commented as he pulled up to the front entrance, where palm trees and a formal garden softened the look of the thick white walls. A few tourists with binoculars were on a plaza, staring at the dirty horizon, but just below them, sunbathers lounged around one of the hotel's three swimming pools, and farther out, people walked the beach unperturbed, only beginning to wonder what kind of accident had taken place out in the shipping lanes.

He slid from behind the wheel and called a porter with a rolling rack to take the luggage, and they all filed into the exquisite lobby. A domed ceiling soared over three stories of emptiness, with solid balconies surrounding the interior of the room. Thick rugs were on the hardwood floor, and long tapestries depicting the glory days of the Ottomans stretched up the walls. Before they reached the reception desk, Omar motioned them into an alcove. "Obviously, Sharm is still enjoying the good life, so we must take advantage of it. If we are to continue the mission as a team, I will stay and help." He spun his key ring on an index finger, then closed his palm around it. "If not, I'm leaving. Neither one of you can do this alone, and I will not jeopardize my cover. Which will it be?"

Kyle Swanson tugged on his suit, and Tianha Bialy fiddled with her purse. Neither spoke.

Omar scowled at them and shook his head with disgust, turned on his heel, and walked away.

"Well," Bialy asked, "what now?"

"Omar is a good man, but I don't need him anymore," Swanson said. "I'm ready to meet this contact, Sir Jeff's money friend, get the info dump, and then leave tomorrow morning. My job will be done. In fact, I'll have the concierge make my airline reservation right now, before the rush starts. You can take over and go behind the scenes with Omar. That will probably be better without me." He walked toward the reception desk.

"You're a right bastard, Swanson." She hurried toward the door to catch Omar.

A well-dressed woman with high cheekbones, dark hair, and brown eyes was at the reception desk. "Welcome to the Blue Neptune, sir. How may I help you?"

"I have a reservation," he said and handed over his passport.

She called up the account, had him sign in, and exchanged the passport for a key card. "You have two messages, Mr. Swanson," she said. "Your friend Mr. Youssef Gaber asks that you join him in his suite, the penthouse, for lunch at one o'clock. The second message actually is just a note that your other luggage arrived safely. Since it was under diplomatic seal, we have stored it in our vault. This came with it." A small padded envelope had his name on it.

"Thank you," Swanson said. "Could you please send everything up to my room? I need to speak with the concierge about a change in my travel plans before I go up. I will probably be staying only one night."

"Oh? I have you booked down for three, sir, and this is a very busy season."

"I understand, and the hotel can charge my company for those other two nights and rent them out again. Business plans change."

She briefly studied the man, who had just thrown away hundreds of dollars in charges without a thought. Being the vice president of an international corporation must be nice, the clerk thought. "Very well, sir. We will hold those dates open until you check out, then refund the cost if we let them out again."

"Perfect," he said. "Now would you please have the concierge meet me in the bar, and tell him to bring the airline schedules for tomorrow."

"Mr. Swanson," she said, and he stopped. "Did you just come across on the ferry from Hurghada? My computer showed your travel plans."

"Yes."

"May I ask? Did something bad happen on the way? Rumors are floating around about a big ship being on fire, and we heard a distant explosion some time ago."

"Apparently, some oil tanker had an accident. We were miles away and didn't see anything more than what you saw and heard. The ferryboat took us away as fast as possible."

She gave a nervous smile. *Accident!* The word she was hoping to hear. *Just an accident.* She had been around in 2005 when terrorists had set off three bombs in Sharm, wrecked a luxury hotel, killed eighty-three people, and sent tourism into a downward spiral. It took several seasons to recover, and she did not want to live through such a thing again. "Well, I am glad that you all made it safely, sir. You probably need a drink, so the concierge will meet you in the bar immediately and give you a complimentary beverage of your choice."

CAIRO

The coded signal of the successful attack was flashed to the desk of Major Mansoor Shakuri, who immediately delivered it to his chief, Colonel Yahya Ali Naqdi, who was pleased with the additional damage. The job had been only to sink the old Iranian naval supply ship, but the firing of the two extra missiles had bought a bonus with a lucky hit on the huge Bahamanian-registered tanker *Llewellyn,* filled with crude oil. The huge explosion and ensuing fire had brought shipping to a halt at the mouth of the Suez Canal. He smoothed the piece of paper with his hand and read it again. Sometimes things work out better than expected. Amid such confusion, he decided to advance the timetable for Phase Two.

"Major, this opportunity must be seized." Naqdi opened a notebook bound in black leather and flipped to a green tab. "Contact our foreign ministry in Tehran so they can issue an official protest about the unprovoked sinking of the *Babr* and the terrible attack on this *Llewellyn* tanker by Egyptian military forces. They must also call upon the United Nations to condemn those unprovoked attacks as a danger to regional stability and express a lack of confidence in the Egyptian military forces to protect these vital waters."

Naqdi was up and moving about his office in the Palm Group as his mind spun off the needed chain of events. "Then the Muslim Brotherhood will begin the planned demonstrations, claiming that the Egyptian army is launching a coup of the democratically elected government and that the generals are responsible for open hostility and multiple attacks against both Egypt and Iran." He paused to let Shakuri catch up with his notes. "It all must take place as soon as possible, Major. Time is important now; minutes are important. Within two hours, I want the Egyptian Parliament demanding that the UN dispatch a peacekeeping force to Egypt."

Major Shakuri was writing the instructions as fast as he could. He asked, "And when do we begin the operation at Sharm, sir? Within forty-eight hours?"

The colonel consulted his notebook, then used his pen to change the designated times. "Do it immediately. This confusion is our friend, Major. I want the boats in the water by four thirty tomorrow morning, and the attack on the hotels to follow exactly ten minutes later. Our transport planes will already be in the air. By daybreak, we will have secured the airport, and units of Iran's Army of the Guardians will be on the ground in Sharm el-Sheikh."

"Once there, we won't leave." The major gave a tentative smile.

The colonel laughed out loud. "No, we won't. But remember: In this action, we do not want to appear to be a force of invading imperialists. Instead, we are invited guests of elements of the elected host government. We are merely an advance guard for a multinational United Nations peacekeeping force that will derail a military coup by radical Egyptian generals. We plan to help reestablish order in this wicked country, protect our own people and foreign visitors, and stand guard over the most important oil transportation routes on the globe."

"That will present an interesting diplomatic situation for the rest of the world, sir."

"There is one more thing, Chief of Staff." The colonel actually broke into a big smile that left Shakuri sweating. "You will turn over my briefings to someone else in the office and fly down to Sharm immediately. I am giving you overall command down there, Major. I need someone trustworthy and smart in charge on the ground, and no one is better suited for the task than you. You have shown your capabilities many times, and now you are ready for a step up. When this is over, you will get a promotion in rank and a new assignment. Meanwhile, you will run the Sharm operation and let no one get in your way. There will be a lot of soldiers of higher ranks to perform the military tasks, but they will all report to you, Major Shakuri. If they have a problem, tell them to call our superiors in Tehran."

SHARM EL-SHEIKH

The concierge was a polite and sincere young man who had been trained well for the position by growing up in the thriving belt of big hotels along the scenic waterfront. Nothing surprised him any longer about the lifestyles of the wealthiest people in the world. He had seen suicides, assaults, drunks, rapes, drug overdoses, bribery, the bloody aftermath of beatings and murders. He always made sure the ambulances came to the unseen side entrance of the Blue Neptune and handled everything with courtesy, sympathy, and total confidentiality. From what the desk clerk said, this particular meeting with a newly arrived American guest should not take long. He found the man in the bar, staring out one of the big windows toward the sea. "My name is Karam, and I am the concierge, sir. You asked to see me?"

Swanson motioned for Karam to sit down, and almost immediately, a waitress arrived with a bottle of champagne wrapped in a towel and placed in a bucket of ice. "A small welcome from the Blue Neptune, Mr. Swanson. I heard about your ferry crossing. It is a tragic thing."

Kyle put his hand on the bucket. "Thank you, but there is no use ruining this perfectly good bottle of champagne by opening it. Save it for someone else. I won't be here that long."

At a silent signal, the waitress removed the bucket and bottle back to the bar. "Very well. Then down to business. What can I do for you?"

"Did you bring the airline schedules?"

A broad smile revealed gleaming teeth. "No need for that, sir. After so many years, I know them by heart. Where do you want to go, and when?"

"What is the first flight to London tomorrow morning?"

"There are a number of departures available. The

first one is very early, the British Airways seven o'clock. Are you certain that you would not prefer a later departure, say the ten o'clock Lufthansa?"

Swanson had a pair of U.S. hundred-dollar bills folded in his shirt pocket, and he pushed them over to Karam. "No. I'm an early riser. Seven o'clock is good, and make it a first-class cabin, would you? I'll need a private car and driver, not a taxi."

Karam smoothly palmed the money, put it in his own pocket, and stood. "Consider it done, Mr. Swanson. I will send a note of confirmation to your room this evening."

Kyle also stood up and fished out another hundred. "Apparently, I didn't make myself clear, Karam. I want confirmation not this evening, but within an hour. In fact, do it right now."

As the businessman walked away, Karam looked out the window at the smoke smudging the horizon, and everything came together. This man was the first rat leaving the sinking ship that was Sharm el-Sheikh's. The concierge hurried back to his desk and ordered the airline reservation and the car and driver in a matter of minutes, then left a confirmation message on Swanson's telephone. Karam tapped a pen on his fingers as he thought about what he needed to do next.

It was a short walk across the spacious lobby to the office of the in-hotel travel agent, who happened to be his brother-in-law. His sister was at her own desk, and Karam shut the door, locked it, and spun around the CLOSED sign. His relatives stopped what they were doing, and they all moved to a corner to discuss the situation.

Whatever had happened out there on the Red Sea had been very bad, they surmised, worse than was first thought. It would probably bloom into a crisis, which meant that big money could be made from a sudden exodus of scared tourists. Quietly, the family laid hurried plans to reap a financial windfall.

CHAPTER 13

Seven minutes before the one o'clock appointment, Kyle Swanson was in his suite at the Blue Neptune, finishing a quick change of clothes. The suit he had worn that morning was creased and dirty from the ferry ride and smelled faintly of smoke and oil. He had stripped, jumped into a hot shower for a rinse to shock his body back to normal, dried off, and put on fresh underwear and black socks. The shirt, suit, and tie were on hangers in the bathroom to let the steam generated from the shower work on the wrinkles because there was no time for valet service, or even to iron them.

Two large blue duffel bags were beside the closet, and he lifted them to the bed, where sunlight highlighted the official seal of the United States and long zippers that were sealed with locks. Kyle ripped open the envelope he had been given at the front desk and shook out a key that popped both locks; then he hauled down the zippers and opened the bags. *Bless you, Lizard,* he thought. In his last call to Task Force Trident before leaving London, he had asked Commander Benton Freedman to somehow get him a package of what he called "the necessaries." Liz had come through big-time.

The term "diplomatic pouch" was a misnomer, dating back to the days when confidential messages were exchanged between nations. As embassies grew, so did the need to supply them with more things, ranging from crates of liquor to food and medicine. The privilege often had been abused to transport drugs, illegal cash, and once even a kidnapped Nigerian ambassador locked in a box. Stamped with diplomatic immunity, goods pass through customs offices without being opened or X-rayed. Almost anything could be in them, and the Lizard, working through the resources of the U.S. Drug Enforcement Agency in Egypt, had outdone himself. A local DEA agent had dropped the duffel bags at the hotel.

A disassembled M-16A3 match grade rifle was secured inside a backpack, along with eight hundred rounds of ammunition, enough for more than twenty full magazines. He felt like a kid at Christmastime as he dug out the toys: a satellite radio-telephone, four fragmentation grenades, four smoke grenades of various colors, two Willie Petes—white phosphorus—a pair of claymore mines, four bricks of C-4 plastic explosive, and a supply of det cord, primers, and timers. He felt a surge of adrenaline, for although he was standing there in his underwear, he no longer felt naked in this worsening situation. When he snapped the rifle together and shoved in a clip of ammo with a satisfying click, it felt better in his hands than a lingerie model.

Also folded in the bags were local rags of the sort that an Egyptian workingman would wear, so if needed, Kyle could blend in with a crowd. A pair of jeans, two polo shirts, and a tattered and stained heavy pullover hoodie completed the set. The final items were enough bottles of water and MREs, the infamous Meals, Ready to Eat, to last three days. In all probability, he would never need any of the material, but before he left tomorrow morning, he could give the entire stash to Omar for the MI6 agent's future use.

He pushed the bags in the closet and finished dressing, again looking like a businessman but feeling more like a sniper. At one minute before one, he hung the DO NOT DISTURB sign on his doorknob, made sure the door was locked, boarded the elevator, and punched the button to the penthouse.

The door opened smoothly to reveal an immaculate reception foyer and two men who might have been graduates of World Wrestling Entertainment. Both were in suits, but without ties, and the open collars allowed room for their massive necks. Each weighed at least 240 pounds and had olive skin, curly and thick black hair, a broad forehead, and dark eyes that missed nothing. One of the brutes stood directly in front of the elevator, blocking passage with his bulk, while the second was ten feet away, at an angle to give a clear field of fire, with a stylish flat carryall hanging from his shoulder. Inside the bag, his hand was wrapped around an automatic pistol. They stared at Kyle without saying a word.

Swanson had expected guards so had left his .45 with the other weapons in the room. "Kyle Swanson of Excalibur Enterprises to see Youssef Gaber," he said quietly, stepping forward to hand the big guard an embossed business card and to open his own jacket. Under the watchful eye of the man with the hidden gun, Kyle was thoroughly patted down, including a search for an ankle holster and a pat beneath the balls and his ass to determine if anything was hidden between his legs. The guard moved back, knocked on the door behind him, and opened it. The man with the carryall never looked away.

The surprise lay inside the room, not out with the guards in the hallway. Not only was a man that had to be Gaber waiting, but so was a rather frazzled Egyptian army brigadier general, both standing beside a big window that showcased the manicured gardens, and the golden beach that sloped down to the foamy water that shone like diamonds when gentle waves broke in the bright sun. Tourists were still enjoying their holidays, and colorful catamarans with big sails bellied before the breeze were racing out beyond the marina. Boat traffic seemed normal. Everything seemed normal, except for the cloud of smoke on the horizon that knifed into the cerulean sky.

Youssef Gaber waved Kyle over and shook his hand to make the introductions. "Kyle Swanson. At last we meet. Sir Jeff has constantly entertained me with stories about your work together." Kyle also knew the background of his host, who had just turned fifty. He was a native Egyptian whose father had been a merchant, and the boy had developed a sharp sense of how to trade. By twenty-one he was running his own import-export business, then had branched out into real estate, oil, and finance. Having made enough money to last several lifetimes, Gaber had retired from active business, but he sat on the boards of a number of companies and was a director of the Central Bank of Egypt. His gray hair was freshly cut, and he wore white linen trousers and a blue blazer with buttons made of gold.

"Good to meet you, too, Mr. Gaber. Jeff says you attract money like bread crumbs attract ants."

"Jeff exaggerates."

"He does."

"Kyle, would you please call me Youssef? And allow me to introduce Brigadier Mohammed Suliamin of the general staff." Swanson shook hands with the slender man in the tan uniform, who almost seemed weighed down by the olive shoulder boards with gold stars and the rack of colorful ribbon on his chest. Judging by the tired eyes, the general had not been sleeping well and was under pressure.

"Mr. Swanson. It is a pleasure to meet an executive representative of Excalibur Enterprises." The tone of his voice let Kyle know the general was aware of this identity charade, and as a senior officer, the man was reluctant to be talking directly to a Marine gunnery sergeant.

Youssef defused the moment by pouring drinks, a pale whisky.

"Nothing for me, sir. I never drink on the job." Swanson had stopped drinking entirely at one point, just like he had once experimented with being a vegetarian, but had pleasantly discovered that he was not an alcoholic and did not crave the bottle. Everything in moderation was a better way to go. He accepted a glass of water with ice cubes instead, and they did a *salud*.

Their eyes went back to the scene beyond the window as another flash of fire churned through the dark stripe of smoke. "We were speculating about what may have happened out there," said General Suliamin.

"Well, let's take a wild guess." Swanson put his glass down and crossed his arms. "Maybe four Harpoon missiles bearing the insignia of the Egyptian Air Force were fired from a portable launcher parked near Hurghada, and the first two each hit a single ship, the third one was shot down, and the fourth popped the oil tanker."

"We don't know any of that to be fact," said the general.

"Sure you do. That and more, which is why you are looking so worried. I know it because I saw the platform, the missiles, and watched them fly and hit. Now what do you know that I don't?"

The general stiffened and glanced over at Youssef Gaber, who said, "This must be a full and frank discussion, Brigadier. Tell him."

"Very well. The first vessel, the one that apparently was the primary target and was sunk, was a ship of the Iranian Navy."

"Oh, shit," said Kyle.

There was a knock on the door, and Dr. Tianha Bialy of MI6 entered, neat and modest in a white blouse and a long dark skirt. Kyle wondered if she had been given the same thorough search of welcome by the big guard. Her eyes fired daggers at him as she crossed the room and introduced herself.

Gaber and the general led them to a seating area. "There is food on the buffet, if anyone wants lunch. I am not particularly hungry, but let us not worry about such things. If anyone wants anything, please feel free to make a plate. We need to get to work."

"What can we do that the official diplomatic route cannot?" asked Kyle. "Egypt has been the subject of the day for months now."

"And it will remain that way for some time," Gaber answered. "Even after such a long time has elapsed since the revolution that toppled the dictator Mubarak, our country remains fractured. Kyle, you and Dr. Bialy must convey to London and Washington that Egypt has not yet descended into the wilderness of wild-eyed radicals, despite the political gains and outrageous statements made by the Muslim Brotherhood."

Bialy spoke. "They have the presidency now, sir, and have a significant block of votes in the Parliament. That gives them a lot of power."

"Not quite true, Doctor. Ours is a coalition government and Islamist in composition. But the Brotherhood itself is split into many factions. They are not a unified front, no matter what their rhetoric, due to historic tribal and sectarian infighting for power. Also, while they know how to demonstrate loudly, they are still learning how to run a government."

"How do you think can we help?" Kyle steepled his fingers and settled back in the comfortable chair.

Gaber handed off to General Suliamin. "The military still remains as the power behind the throne. There are rogue elements in the ranks, to be sure, but we are weeding them out as they are uncovered. We can be observant of our religious beliefs, loyal citizens, and good soldiers at the same time."

"Can you hold it together?" Tianha wanted to know.

"Doctor, you know better than most how this ancient land has survived for centuries. It is our intent to remain in the community of civilized nations, and we will not be buried by this latest sandstorm of religious zealotry. Everyone who speaks Spanish is not from Spain, and millions of Chinese have never even seen China. The Irish are not the same as the English. So why do Westerners believe that all Muslims are alike?"

"Nine-eleven." Kyle spoke simply but brought up the vision of airliners plunging into skyscrapers filled with innocent civilians.

"Exactly, Kyle," said the general. "It was a terrible thing, but we had nothing to do with it. Except for a few hotheads, the average Egyptian thought it a despicable act. The best proof is that despite this revolution in our country, we are still here, still working hard with our friends so that we remain friends. I went through training at Fort Bragg and have an advanced degree from Stanford. I considered the attack by those madmen to be an attack on me personally, for they tarred the names of all of us."

Tianha had moved to the buffet and dipped a slice of carrot into a bowl of hummus. Gaber said, "We are going to show the two of you secret documentation that will demonstrate that Egypt needs and deserves the continued support of the United States and Great Britain. You will take it back and report to your governments." He booted up a laptop to start a PowerPoint presentation.

Kyle interrupted. "One moment, Youssef. Say we accept everything that you say. Why the attacks on the Iranians—the ship and the soccer team? Is there an outside force?"

"Absolutely," the general shot back with anger. "The Iranians are at the root of the problem. We can prove this with firsthand intelligence from a highly placed source."

Bialy was still at the buffet. She turned and said, "You're speaking, of course, of the Pharaoh."

It was if the air had been sucked from the room. "How do you know that name?" demanded Suliamin, rising from his chair.

She answered the question with one of her own. "Do you know his real identity?"

"You are discussing secret material, Dr. Bialy. Go no further."

She remained unaffected. "It is not very secret, Brigadier. The Pharaoh also has been a source for MI6, and we do not know who he is, either. That's why I have been sent to Egypt, sir, to find him."

Kyle remained silent, but the veiled hostility between the two agents startled the economist and the general. Swanson's sudden decision to leave tomorrow had forced Tianha to change her plan to dangle him as bait to bring out the Pharaoh, for now she had to be the target herself. Omar had already floated the story about Kyle being a CIA agent, and now he would have to openly expose Tianha as the real contact. The Pharaoh would learn about both of them.

"I thought you were together on this," said Gaber, quietly disturbed.

Swanson looked out at the sea, where the midday sun was reflecting as if hitting a mirror. "We have been traveling together, but I'm on a plane back to London tomorrow to deliver the information you give us. With that, my job is done. Dr. Bialy will stay here and do whatever she has in mind with the Pharaoh."

The general stared at each of them in turn, then let out a long breath. "It is not unusual for rival agencies to have different agendas," he concluded. "Dr. Bialy and I can discuss this intelligence source after we have dealt with the more important matters before all of us. Let's get down to business, shall we?"

Kyle picked up a triangle of bread smeared with cheese and cucumbers. *So Tianha and Omar have decided to stay in the game on their own. I'll give my weapons to Omar tonight and be out of here on that first plane. That works.*

CHAPTER 14

SHARM EL-SHEIKH

Karam, the concierge at the Blue Neptune Hotel, along with his sister and his brother-in-law in the travel agency, were toiling hard. News of what had happened out on the Red Sea had finally been absorbed by visitors and residents of the playground city, and simmering worry replaced the holiday joy. Some of the big yachts were already gone, the huge white cruise ship was gathering its passengers for an emergency departure, and most of the other guests were making plans to leave. At the Blue Neptune, Karam was the one who could make the necessary arrangements. Missiles sinking ships and a pending environmental disaster meant his family had to make as much money as they could before the tourists evaporated, with no way of knowing when they would come back. Secret auctions and lavish tips would secure passage on tomorrow's planes.

Brigadier General Suliamin and Youssef Gaber had flown back to Cairo at seven o'clock that evening after the long conference with Swanson and Bialy. The two officials had given the friendly governments of the West the best overview the allies had had in months concerning the real situation within Egypt. Kyle was to personally deliver a flash drive containing the information to London, and he felt there might be a glimmer of hope for future stability if the political picture painted by the money man and the military leader was accurate. The key was to keep Iran on the sidelines and let Egyptians decide their own future.

In any case, he was confirmed for departure, and he decided to have a final truce with Tianha, for there was nothing to be gained by letting personal animosity upset their superiors, who already had enough problems. Swanson was just glad to be out of it all.

It was eight o'clock, and they were having dinner in the near-empty hotel restaurant. Tension and nervousness had caused many of the other guests to order room service while they packed. The bar was doing a brisk business, and there was no chance the two of them would be overheard.

"You're crazy," he observed with a smile that softened the words. "Did you know that?"

"I must establish contact with this source," she replied as she finished a small bowl of seafood bisque. "He, or she, needs control."

"Seems to me that your source's information is always

a day late and a dollar short, and he's shopping his stuff to too many people," Kyle said. "He warns you of nothing beforehand that would let you plan some action to stop it."

Tianha dabbed away a dollop of stray dressing from her chin. "He still provides a lot of rich background material that proves that Iran is deeply involved."

"Having him say that, and basing your decisions on his word, are two different things, Doctor."

"Which is why we have to control him from London. We can assume he is highly placed but untrained in what to report. An experienced case officer can remedy that, and this agent may be invaluable in years to come. Just imagine if we had reliable eyes inside the Tehran government."

Kyle looked around. Nothing happening, and no one watching. "I don't like your plan to draw him out by putting out the word that you are an MI6 agent. He probably will show up with a gun in his hand."

"Knowing that I am not a threat will make it easier for him to contact me, I'm sure. I expect him to be cautious."

The waiter appeared with their main courses, a steak for Kyle and shellfish for Tianha, refilled their wineglasses, and left them alone. "Do me a favor, then. Keep Omar nearby if this meeting ever actually takes place. It never hurts to have backup."

"Of course," she said and sipped the wine. "I thought when we started this adventure that you were going to be my bodyguard."

"Nope. As the man said, you are a trained agent and

you know Egypt as few others do. Just use good sense, and get out if something dangerous starts to cook."

She actually giggled. "You mean like here in Sharm? I don't think anything is going to happen here. It's holiday heaven in the middle of nowhere."

"Remember the Harpoons? Bad things are coming this way. Sharm's a very strategic piece of territory. Cairo has the government, but Sharm controls the petroleum path for the whole world. It's the cork in the bottle for the oil business. How much longer are you staying?"

"Another day or two. If there's no contact by then, I will go to Cairo. Most likely that is where the Pharaoh will make contact. What about you?"

"I will stick around London visiting Jeff and Pat for a few days, then go back to Washington." He put down his fork and leaned across the table. "I'll keep an eye on you from afar. If there's trouble, send up a flare, and I'll do my damnedest to help."

"Oooh. You'll ride to the rescue like the famous 7th Cavalry?" The wine and food and excitement of the day were brightening her mood.

"Not exactly. That was General Custer, and he was slaughtered. I don't get slaughtered."

IRAN

At military airfields surrounding Tehran, a sky train was being assembled. Hundreds of soldiers of the Iranian Army of the Guardians were nervous in the night.

They had moved to the airfields in trucks from their training sites, and officers had gathered the men assigned to each plane and personally inspected them. As with any army, the infantrymen settled down to wait. They smoked cigarettes and wrote letters to loved ones, aware they were facing the biggest challenge of their lives. Each wondered whether he would survive as a hero, die as a brave martyr, or perish in deserved shame if he proved to be a coward.

Cargo was loaded first, the ammunition, food, and minimum equipment to sustain them until aerial and maritime supply routes could be firmly established. While loading crews lashed down the crates and a few vehicles, mechanics and flight engineers combed the planes to be sure they were ready for the long flight ahead. Finally, the commander of each company stood before his men and announced the mission: Egypt had officially requested assistance to put down counterrevolutionary forces within that country's army. They were reminded of the annihilation of the Iranian national soccer team and of how only yesterday an Iranian naval utility vessel—not even a ship of war—had been sunk in the Red Sea in an unprovoked assault by Egyptian missiles. The Guardsmen were chosen to stop that aggression.

Iran had assigned fifteen jet airliners and cargo planes to the task, including huge Boeing 707s and 747s, and there would be about two hundred soldiers with their equipment on each aircraft. It was to be a long and perilous journey out of the country and through the airspace above Iraq, Syria, and Lebanon, with the permission of those Muslim governments. They would not fly over Israel. Finally, the planes would form up in one long line and fly down the Suez Canal to the target, the airport outside of the coastal resort of Sharm el-Sheikh.

SHARM EL-SHEIKH

It was after midnight, but Kyle Swanson could not fall asleep. Normally, he could order his body to shut down and grab a rest period whenever he wanted. Even in fierce battle situations, sleep discipline was important. He lay on the king-sized bed, between soft 1,200-thread-count Egyptian cotton sheets, and stared up at the ceiling for an hour. He turned on the light to read a paperback murder mystery but found it impossible to concentrate. The television set offered a menu of movies guaranteed not to hold his interest. From his window, he could see the reddish orange glow that marked where the tanker *Llewellyn* still burned fiercely. Within a few days, the pristine coastline would be slick and sticky as oil rode in with every wave. He wished he had not yet given most of his guns to Omar. Throwing those two duffel bags into the trunk of the Mercedes felt like tossing his own child over a cliff. Omar could retrieve the MI6 weapons shipment at the airport on his own.

He thought of knocking on the door of the connecting suites to see if Tianha was awake, too. *No. Don't even go there.* One o'clock. Two o'clock. Every sense he possessed tingled with the ominous feeling that something just wasn't right, although there was absolutely nothing going on. *Hell with it. I can sleep when I get to London.*

He got up, dressed in a comfortable black sweat suit, laced up his gray Nikes, tucked his personal weapon, the Colt .45, in a belt clip holster beneath the shirt, pocketed the cell phone, and headed out for a run along the beaches of Hotel Row. The Blue Neptune was strangely active for so early in the morning, as the hired help was preparing to handle the expected morning rush of departing guests.

Kyle did not stop the elevator at the lobby level but descended to the parking area and walked the aisles until he found Omar's white Mercedes parked nose-out and tight against a wall as an extra precaution to keep its cargo safe. Swanson patted the car affectionately, then set off at an easy lope along the main traffic route, heading into the stillness, hoping to do five miles.

The town of about thirty-five thousand inhabitants was mostly asleep as he trotted along, staying within the sphere of illumination from the hotels on his right to avoid tripping over some obstacle along the unfamiliar road. He soon settled into an eight-minute-mile pace and felt the start of the familiar burn as his body shook off the fatigue and the muscles stretched. No one bothered him. With plenty of time and breathing easily, he decided to increase the distance to three miles out, then three miles back. Twenty-five minutes from the Blue Neptune, he found a traffic circle that could serve nicely as a halfway point, ran around it, and headed back, changing his route to rack in some running on the hard sand of the beach.

Then something clicked in his brain, a familiar sound that should not be there, the distant rumble of multiple outboard motors. He took a few more steps, slowed, and stopped and stared out at the water. Already the sound seemed closer. Why would motorboats be out there in the middle of the night? There were the usual warning lights on ships in the channel, and the distant fire on the *Llewellyn,* but that was all, other than the new, ominous humming. It could mean only one thing, and Swanson was too experienced a Marine not to recognize the opening phase of an amphibious assault. Boats were coming in. He ran to an outcropping of rocks and ducked into the darkest shadow he could find, pulled his pistol, and waited.

Swanson got the telephone out of his pocket and hit the speed dial button for the number of Tianha Bialy. It rang three times before her sleepy voice answered, "Hello? Kyle?" She had checked the voice ID. "What—"

"Tianha, listen up. I'm down on the beach, and big trouble is brewing. It looks like an attack is about to begin."

"Hunh? An attack?"

"You've got to get out of there right now. Call Omar and get him up, and meet me at his car. We need to get out of this area as fast as possible."

"Kyle, are you sure?" A yawn.

"Dammit, Tianha. You don't have any time to waste. There's going to be a lot of shooting soon."

"Kyle, I'm standing at the window of my room now, and I don't see anything unusual."

"Stand there much longer and you might be a dead woman. Get out while you can. I'll meet you both in the underground garage." Kyle folded the phone to cut the connection. Whether she did the right thing was now up to her, because the motors were louder and closer. If they were inflatables, commandos would be clinging to handholds with all of their strength as the boats reared out of the water for the final dash to shore. He leapt from the shadows and ran for his life.

In her room, Tianha turned from the window. She was naked. "Kyle says we should get out, Omar. Something about an assault. I don't see anything, though."

Omar Eissa crawled out of bed and went to stand behind her, wrapping her in his arms and holding her close. He turned her loose, stepped to one side, and slid the big window open to the chill of the night air, instantly hearing the shrill screams of approaching outboard motors. At the same time, they saw the crests of white foam at the bows of speeding boats that were otherwise still invisible in the darkness. "He's right, Tianha," he snapped. "I think the Iranians are here."

Major Mansoor Shakuri stood about ten feet back from the waterline and slowly moved a flashlight-sized infrared green laser signal toward the incoming boats. He had flown in the previous day from Cairo to be the advance spotter for the raiders and to assume overall command once they had all landed. It felt good to be out from under the thumb of his demanding superior and back in the field, doing some of the real work for which he had spent his lifetime in training. This was a command worth having.

Ten boats had been scheduled to be put in the water by a wallowing, nondescript cargo ship that had carried the entire seaborne attack force to within ten miles of the beach. Each boat was to contain ten commandos, so there would be a hundred men coming up in the first wave. They would do nothing more than secure the beach while the boats went back for a second load and then fetched in the third and final wave. Shakuri would have three hundred soldiers across the beach by 0400. Even if detected, they were not to move out until ordered. Defend only, not attack, at this point, Colonel Naqdi said. Be patient and give the plan time to unfold.

The first boat hit the sand and slid forward, with the assault force jumping out and running past him to the shelter of a belt of small sand dunes at the top edge of the beach. One soldier, hard and lean with a grease-blackened face, and dressed entirely in black, peeled away, came close, and saluted. A belt of machine-gun ammunition hung around his neck, and an officer's tab was on his tunic. "First Lieutenant Taghavi reporting, sir. First wave is present and accounted for. One man lost his grip and fell off. Perhaps the boats can pick him up on the return trip, although he probably drowned."

"No matter, Lieutenant. Spread your men in good defensive positions and hold. It won't be long before a force this size is spotted, and we cannot be certain of the

Egyptian response. And have the men dig, Lieutenant; the deeper the hole, the better they are going to like it if a firefight breaks out. Assign someone to take over this signal laser for me."

As Major Shakuri turned, he saw the shadow of someone darting away nearby but ignored it. The first wave was safely on the ground.

CHAPTER 15

Major Shakuri forced himself to remain calm as he walked the broad area where a makeshift convoy of vehicles was gathered. The drivers were all members of the Muslim Brotherhood, but not a one had ever taken part in a real battle, so they were drawn to the spectacle of the black-clad soldiers who had stormed ashore in front of the Blue Neptune Hotel. Shakuri, with his pistol out, snarled as he pushed them to regain their attention and focus on their job for the night. "All drivers to your vehicles immediately. Start the engines and stay in your seats, prepared to receive passengers. We will move out as soon as the men are loaded. Do not be left behind, or you will be severely punished."

There were excited whispers as the drivers retreated to their cars and trucks and buses, for they had not been informed of their exact duties tonight. The cover of deception had been pulled away, and the drivers saw

Iranian soldiers on the sands, moving with precision and purpose. Shakuri still had not disclosed the destination to them all; just that they were to get ready to move. In moments, the motors turned over, and the area hummed with the coughs and pops and whine of a traffic jam.

By the time he had completed a quick walk-around inspection, the major heard the boats at the beach again, coming in protected by the first wave of defenders. Another hundred men splashed out of the surf and ran to the parking lot. Shakuri climbed into an Egyptian army J8 Jeep with a 12.7 mm machine gun mounted in the rear and pointed the lead group into the Toyota pickup truck just behind it. Black-clad shock troops filed like ants into the vehicles, remaining totally silent. Even when equipment snagged, someone tripped, or there was a mix-up about who went where, every problem was sorted out with hand signals, with noncoms pushing the troops into position.

Although he had been watching closely, Shakuri was surprised when a soldier appeared at his side, as if out of the night itself. "Ready, sir. Ninety-eight men counted."

Above the rumble of the idling vehicles, the major could detect the higher-pitched engines on the inflatable boats, which were already speeding away to bring in the final wave of troops. He ran a mental count to be sure he had enough wheels and was certain that he did. "Drop a sergeant here to guide the next convoy, with the driver of that Jeep, who has been briefed."

He did not know if the soldier saluted, for the lieutenant had disappeared just as fast as he had arrived. Shakuri's nervousness melted away as he settled into his seat. He was on his own, out from beneath the thumb of Colonel Naqdi, and his confidence was bubbling. "Head out," he barked at the driver. "Airport." Behind him, the gunner racked in a belt of ammo.

On the beach of the Blue Neptune, a security guard in a crisp white shirt and dark pants let his curiosity get the best of him. He opened the door that led from the main building to the swimming pools, walked down the sidewalk through the lush foliage, and stopped when he looked out at the edge of the water. Little boats filled with men were roaring to the shoreline, and more were gathered on the sand below him, not moving. His job had required him to draw his sidearm before, when particularly bothersome thieves and muggers were molesting guests, and the reflex of facing danger made him reach for the pistol. A pair of silenced submachine guns coughed, and the bullets almost cut him in half, dropping him dead on the spot. "Fool," said Lieutenant Taghavi. No one was supposed to die yet. The third force was almost out of the water and heading for the transport rendezvous point. For now, staying with the plan was all that counted.

Inside the building, Tianha and Omar heard nothing other than their own footsteps and heavy breathing as they fled down the concrete fire stairwells, hands grasping the metal bannisters. Each floor had a red door that opened onto hallways, but they bypassed those exits in a dash to the parking basement. Their survival lay in getting to the car and leaving the area before the soldiers closed it down. Regular hotel guests probably would be safe enough in their rooms, but a pair of agents from British intelligence would definitely not fare well in whatever was about to unfold.

WASHINGTON, D.C.

Satellites and computers throughout the Middle East had painted the big aircraft since they had lifted off the tarmac of various military airfields in Iran and joined in a loose three-plane formation and headed east, with permission, through the skies of its friendly neighbor, Iraq. No American warplanes rose to challenge them, for there had not been any U.S. combat troops in Iraq since December 2011, and most of the billion-dollar airbases had fallen into total disrepair after being thoroughly looted. The Iraqi Air Force had only a handful of F-16s and not enough trained pilots to fly them, so they stayed on the ground because they were not being attacked.

The huge Iranian air fleet lumbered along a carefully predetermined route that skirted the American zone of control that still existed over Afghanistan and dodged Israel entirely. Instead of hiding their presence, the planes flaunted it, broadcasting to anyone who asked that they were on a humanitarian mission at the request of the United Nations and the Egyptian government. In both the Mediterranean Sea and the Red Sea, U.S. Navy fighter jets with air-to-air missiles on hard points sat on carrier decks in position for hot launches. Fighters flying Combat Air Patrols above the American battle groups extended their patrols into wider circles. Fighters from Israel zoomed up to take a look. No one could detect any overt threat, and the Iranian planes sped on.

"What the hell is this?" asked Wilson Patterson, a former four-star general who was now the national security adviser for the president. The results from the computer readings were plainly projected on a wall screen in the Situation Room of the White House. "Iran is running a mercy flight to Egypt? That is horse shit!" Patterson had never lost his Marine vocabulary.

"The United Nations has not authorized any such thing. The only request came from the Muslim Brotherhood in Egypt just a few hours ago. No one has acted on anything yet, and there has been no meeting of the Security Council." Belinda Hawkins was the president's chief of staff, and she had come to the big conference room wanting answers, not more questions.

"We can't afford to let them land in Egypt," said Patterson. "Once they have a footprint there, it will take all hell to dislodge them."

"And we can do nothing to stop them, because to shoot down a bunch of transport planes that are citing a nonexistent UN mandate would be condemned as an act of war. We don't even know what is aboard those aircraft. Could be blankets or could be bombs, and no one has asked us to intervene," Hawkins said.

"What kind of assets do your CIA have in the area?"

"Not much. Some people to keep an eye on the oil situation, but they are paper-clippers and worker bees. I could throw a bunch of statistics, Wilson, but this is Sharm el-Sheikh, for Christ's sake. Nothing ever happens there. What do you have?" She looked over at Admiral Kelly Foster, the chairman of the Joint Chiefs of Staff.

"Everything we need to fight two wars at the same time. I have carriers and subs and cruise missiles and all kinds of airplanes, and they are all cocked and locked." The white-haired admiral looked carefully at the CIA chief. "I believe this is part of some kind of pretty shrewd invasion plan, but I'm not advising the shoot-down of a bunch of unarmed transports and passenger planes until we have much clearer intelligence on what's happening."

Patterson straightened his papers and stared at the wall screen one last time. "Nobody is even suggesting that you do that, Admiral Foster. But let's take this mess upstairs to the Oval Office and let the boss know the Iranians have outfoxed us. He won't be a happy camper."

SHARM EL-SHEIKH

Kyle trotted around to the inner street side of the Blue Neptune to use the bulk of the hotel as a shield, found the turnoff for the underground parking garage, and headed down the ramp into the cavernous space, where his steps echoed back to him. Tianha and Omar burst from the exit door from the stairwell about the same time, and they all met at the Mercedes, with Omar punching his personal code into the doorlock pad.

"Pop the trunk so I can get at the weapons." Kyle waited only a few seconds for the trunk lid to spring open, and he grabbed the duffel bags that he had put in there only a few hours earlier. He hurled them into the backseat and dove inside the car. "Go!"

It had barely begun to move when a man came running down the ramp, eyes glittering in a spade-shaped, bearded face. He was spraying long, wild bursts of automatic fire from an AK-47. Bullets clicked off the concrete wall, burst a few overhead lights, and punched into parked cars.

"Who the hell is that? He's wearing an Egyptian army uniform." Omar had started the engine, and the car was rolling.

"Doesn't matter if he's shooting at us," Kyle said, pulling his .45 Colt.

Omar grunted agreement and floored the accelerator just as the gunman ran out of bullets and the weapon clicked dry. The man was standing in the middle of the lane, fumbling to reload, and his eyes grew in alarm as he realized that he was defenseless against the onrushing car. He tried to jump away, but Omar caught him with the bumper, and the impact flipped the gunman against another car, where he hit with a hard thump, bounced to the concrete, and lay there broken and still.

Tianha had her window down on the right side, with her weapon out, while Kyle was in the left rear, also with the windows down and his pistol ready while he scrabbled with his free hand to unzip the bag and reach the better weapons. The noise around the hotel was growing in volume.

Omar flew out of the top of the ramp and threw the Mercedes into a squealing turn. More Egyptian army soldiers were running across the street and into the hotel, firing as they went. A straggler stopped at the sight of the car that swept past only ten yards from him, turned to shoot, but sprawled flat when Tianha emptied her Glock at him. Then they were gone.

"Clear over here," she called.

"Clear here," Kyle responded. "Omar, get your own pistol out while I assemble some gear. You think those guys were really Egyptian troops?"

Omar wedged his pistol under his hip and gripped the wheel tightly. "They're certainly not the Iranian soldiers who are on the beach side, and they have to be more than a bunch of thugs that just happened to be passing by out here early in the morning with AKs. My guess is they are some sort of raiding party of the Muslim Brotherhood, wearing army uniforms." They heard gunfire popping from the street in front of other hotels.

"My God, they are targeting defenseless tourists." Tianha pushed in a fresh magazine. "This is going to be Mumbai all over again. Hundreds of innocent people were killed and wounded."

Swanson looked out the back window at the men

surging across the thoroughfare as he recalled the 2008 massacre by Muslim extremists in India. Pakistan was behind it, of course, because the Muslim Pakis and the Hindu Indians had hated each other for ages. Mumbai was just another chapter of the deadly story the two countries were always writing, and in that context it made some sense. A similar attack on Sharm's hotel row by jihadists, with a highly trained Iranian force right in the neighborhood, was a lot different. It would be bloody and blamed on the Egyptian army. Puzzle it out later.

"Omar, head for the airport," Kyle said, finishing assembling the M-16A3 and placing a couple of grenades within easy reach. "Let's stay focused right now on those Iranians."

Tianha turned in her seat to look at him. "They arrived by boat, Kyle."

Swanson shook his head. "That's just the initial assault team. You land over the beach but immediately grab the airport to bring in planes and support. Same thing we did in Somalia."

"Impossible," said Omar. "Iran is too far from Sharm." They ducked into a side street to avoid a group of men firing at another hotel, sending a scalding surge of bullets into the glass windows and zinging off the concrete.

"I agree. Fifteen minutes ago, I would have said it was impossible for Iranian troops to be down there on the beach. The point is they cannot remain there without external support. It has to be the airport."

"And then?" Tianha was staring out of her window again. "We can't just keep driving around."

"Then? Well, then we just disappear until we can figure out what the hell is going on. Getting us to a safe place is Omar's department."

There was a loud explosion in one of the nearby hotels, and a flash of fire ripped outward over the street from an upper floor. Gunfire rattled like pebbles in a can.

"A lot of people are going to die tonight," Tiana said in a sad voice that was almost a whisper.

Kyle leaned against the seat, rifle across his knees, surrounded by the tools of his trade, finally feeling ready for whatever was to come. By gathering up Omar and Tianha, he had consolidated his forces and increased the available firepower, for three guns were better than one. He was unprepared for anything of the scope of the battle that was happening around them, so all he could do was keep scrambling while he figured it out. In addition, the Lizard had included a sat phone in his package of goodies, so Kyle would finally be able to put aside the charade of cooperation and contact Task Force Trident as soon as he determined what was happening at the airport. "Yes, many will die. But not us. We can hold our own."

THE AIRPORT

The lights around the airport seemed puny in comparison to the glare of Hotel Row. It had been closed all night and was just coming to life, getting ready to handle another routine day of flights. The workers were still sluggish with sleep, and the security guards were totally off balance when the long line of vehicles led by a big military Jeep that mounted a machine gun rolled up to the terminal building and dozens of black-clad soldiers jumped out and ran in with automatic weapons at the ready.

Major Shakuri walked inside and saw only a small security team that had been taken by surprise, disarmed, and pushed to the floor. There was an unexpected feeling of confidence and power swelling his heart. He moved to an airline counter, and a nervous attendant gave him a microphone that tied into the public address system. Clearing his throat, Shakuri announced, "Do not be alarmed. We are a special force from the Iranian army, and we here at the request of the Egyptian government. You are under our protection. If no one resists, no one will be hurt. Again, please stay calm while we go about our duties."

He handed the microphone back to the young woman at the desk and smiled. "Really, my dear. You have nothing to fear." With an easy stride, he walked to the clump of Egyptian security guards on the floor and told them to get to their feet. "Brothers, I need you to take my men to other sections of the airport. We must put a soldier with a gun in every room. Can you do that for us?"

The guards were in shock. The airport had been taken by a military force without a shot being fired, and even as they watched, soldiers were fanning out to create a defensive perimeter. Finally, one of the older guards spoke. He was on the early shift to handle customs duty and had no intention of getting into a fight with these dangerous-looking men, so he bowed his head. "Welcome, brothers. We will cooperate."

"That is good." Shakuri clapped him on the shoulder. "You will please escort my tactical air party up to the tower right now so we can finish our work." A half-dozen technicians peeled away from the soldiers and followed the man out of the terminal area. Others were assigned to the hangars and outbuildings. The major was moving fast to secure the place, and he had remembered to have one truckload of soldiers at the tail of the advance party stop to establish a roadblock. When the reinforcement column arrived, he would extend the perimeter around the runways. Major Shakuri looked at his watch and was pleased that everything had turned out so well. As Colonel Naqdi had promised, the strong and unexpected show of force would determine the outcome. All he had to do was show up.

His handheld radio beeped, and the tactical air team reported they had taken control of the tower and were in contact with the planes ending the long journey from Iran. "Very well," Shakuri said. The facility was safely in his hands. "Send the message. This airport is now closed to all other traffic, and any flights except those approved by us must divert to other facilities."

With help just minutes away by air and by road, only one thing remained on his list, perhaps the most important. He contacted Lieutenant Taghavi back at the

beach, and as the officer answered, Shakuri heard gunfire and explosions in the background. "We have the
airport, Lieutenant. Are you ready to attack?"

"Yes, sir."

"Do it," the major ordered.

CHAPTER 16

THE AIRPORT

The sky above the airport was cloudless in the predawn darkness, and it seemed to Kyle that every light at the facility must be turned on. Corridors of illumination outlined the runways. Stars and planets were still bright in the heavens, and in sharp contrast to that galactic display, a straight line of blinking lights was moving closer, stacked one above another into the distance: planes descending to land.

Wearing his Egyptian-style clothing, he was hidden in the deep shadow beside an air-conditioning vent on the roof of a gasoline station about a mile from the main gate. From the top of the square cinder-block structure, Kyle had a wide field of view for his binos; he saw the soldiers steadily pushing outward and estimated the perimeter would extend to cover the gas station within thirty minutes. Tianha Bialy was crouched nearby, also with binos, watching for patrols.

Back on Hotel Row, they could still hear chaos, but at the airport, everything seemed in order, another sign that the military was in charge and commands were being obeyed. The terminal building was a simple long rectangle with bay windows beneath metal awnings across the front, and the structure opened in the rear directly onto the parking apron for the planes. Dozens of figures moved purposefully about, most with weapons, but many of them also obviously airport staff doing their normal jobs, although under new management. Soldiers were establishing a strongpoint in the long, bare parking lot out front: a machine gun on a tripod and some RPGs—rocket propelled grenades—behind a concrete barrier. A beefy Jeep with a mounted automatic weapon was parked near the roadway entrance. He could not make out the exact types of the weapons at this distance but assumed they were all standard military issue and nothing exotic. The soldiers were showing good discipline, he thought; they were probably members of the elite Quds Force.

Swanson shifted position only slightly when Tianha quietly said, "Omar's here."

There were soft footsteps, and Omar Eissa squatted beside them. "I'm still alive."

"That will be counted as a plus," Swanson joked. "How'd it go?"

"Easier than anticipated. I followed another hire car right up to the gate, and we both raised hell about everything being closed. The other guy turned away immediately, but I recognized one of the security guys and slipped him some cash. I told him that I had clients who were desperate to get out of town on the morning flights, and he thumbed back over his shoulder toward the Iranian soldiers and told me the airport will be off-limits to all civilian traffic for a couple of days. I obediently turned around and drove off. Here I am."

"What is your assessment?" Kyle swung his binos back to the sky. The first plane was on final approach.

"This group is spread pretty thin over such a very large area, but they are showing no nerves because there is no doubt that they are in control."

Kyle scanned the airfield. The troops were indeed moving slowly. "Adrenaline dump. They were all riding a high sense of alertness for several hours before landing and getting out here, all keyed up and ready to fight, only to discover it was a walkover. They burned a ton of energy and now they are thinking, OK, we've got time to breathe. Combine that with this early morning hour, and their leaders are going to be busy kicking the troops to make sure they stay awake."

Tianha said, "I've seen enough. Let's go report to London."

"Make sure they pass it straight to Washington." He did not move the glasses and could now see the first plane swoop down with its landing gear extended like talons, a Boeing 707. It touched down about a hundred meters from the north end of the runway, the great tires squealing and smoking against the tarmac as the engines roared into reverse as it sailed past a squat yellow fuel truck parked beside a concrete turnout.

"Of course they will, but I will remind them none-theless."

"Your mission, looking for that Pharaoh guy, is in real jeopardy now, Dr. Bialy," he said and swept his arm toward the airport. "They should consider pulling you out right away."

She crossed her arms. "In my opinion, it is now more important than ever for me to find the Pharaoh and get him to supply us with information. I won't give up."

"Look. This has turned into one ugly morning, and the arrival of Iranian combat troops means that all bets are canceled. All three of us will be lucky to survive until sundown."

"I'll wait in the car while you debate some more," Omar scolded and hustled away.

Kyle felt the sting of starting to lose his temper again. "I'm sorry, Doc. Didn't mean to start barking. But it is best that you go with Omar and bring our bosses up to speed," he said in a gentler tone. "I'm going to be busy out here for a little while longer. Get yourself into some regular Egyptian clothes and take the opportunity to stuff some food down your throat, because we don't know when we will have a chance to eat again. I will join you guys at the safe house just as soon as I can. Omar told me where it was."

"What are you going to do?"

When he did not answer, she left without further comment, apology unaccepted.

Kyle returned his binos to the airport in time to watch the newly landed plane run to the far end of the run-way, turn, and roll off to a taxiway that brought it back toward the terminal. It stopped, and the door opened, with wheeled ladders pushed into place at the front and rear hatches. Moments later, a line of uniformed Iranian soldiers with weapons descended out of the plane and shuffled into formation. A little tractor hooked to the nose of the airliner and hauled it off toward the hangar area, just as the second plane nosed out of the gray morning sky. This operation was running like an efficient assembly line, everything happening right on time.

He stuffed the binos back into the case and stood still and alone on the rooftop for a moment as his sub-conscious formulated a plan using both facts and logical supposition. An unknown number of large transport aircraft were ferrying in troops, probably hundreds of soldiers, and he could hear an increased volume of gun-fire and explosions back at the hotels. He did not know what was happening back there. From a deep pocket of his loose, dirty white trousers, Swanson removed his satellite phone and thought of hitting the button that would link him to Task Force Trident in Washington, but he was running short of time. He was not quite sure who was killing whom, but Kyle could report that one thing was certain: Iran had just invaded Egypt. Tianha would be giving the same thing to London, of course, which would immediately share it with Washington. It would take time for him to explain everything that was happening, and right now minutes were in short supply.

He could talk or he could act. The darkness was al-ready giving way to faint early-morning light, the planes were coming in at precise intervals, soldiers were fanning out as more arrived, and if Kyle wanted to some-how screw with their efficient plan, he had to move right now. He dropped the phone back in his pocket, slung the rifle over one shoulder and a backpack over the other, and struck out at a slow trot through the shad-ows, headed for the north end of the runway.

THE BLUE NEPTUNE

At the command of First Lieutenant Taghavi, almost a hundred Iranian commandos rose as one from the slop-ing shelf of sand bordering the large hotel and spread into a long line, with a squad trailing in reserve. They had waited as still as statues, except for the one inci-dent with the overzealous guard, while the sounds of automatic rifle fire, the quieter pops of pistols, and the occasional explosion resulted in the screams of trapped tourists being slaughtered in the rooms, in the hallways, and around the outside. Although the soldiers sup-pressed any feelings of humanity until they were told to move forward, they were eager to surge into the melee. The horde of gunmen had worked themselves into a frenzy of bloodlust, but they were so disorganized that they had posted no sentries and never saw the Iranians coming. The gunmen might have been dressed like Egyptian soldiers, but they were just a mob.

Brilliant streaks of red and white flares darted sky-ward, some going off like giant fireworks while others drifted back to earth beneath small parachutes that painted ghastly white or scarlet red shadows that stretched and danced. Taghavi's Iranians advanced almost in step, easy on their triggers but mowing down any armed opposition. Smoke grenades burst to cover the advancing troops; then stun grenades were bounced into the lobby and other ground-floor entrances to detonate with sudden crashes that immobilized everyone inside.

The flanks circled the hotel, with the opposite ends closing together almost shoulder to shoulder, and when the raiders realized that they were now the ones under attack and tried to escape, there was no hole to be found in the security cordon. They were killed one by one, or in small groups, and those who tried to jump from windows were shot when they hit the ground.

The Iranians took control of the ground floor within four minutes, then went through the hotel room by room, methodically clearing the spaces and taking down any gunmen they found. Their orders had been clear: Once the hotel was recaptured, the soldiers switched into a friendly mode toward the surviving civilians. Medical personnel rendered first aid until emergency services ambulances arrived and were allowed to enter. Even the few police cars that showed up were given protection, and the cops were allowed to take over crowd control. Several photographers were escorted into the hellish scene to document what they found.

During the counterattack on the Blue Neptune, the raiders at the other hotels stopped shooting and fled into the night, so that by the time the rescue parties of Sharm police accompanied by Iranian soldiers arrived, little fighting was encountered, although still more flares zoomed skyward, smoke grenades loosed clouds of color, and weapons were fired to maintain the façade of fierce fighting.

It took about an hour to clear all of the buildings. Then the Iranians stood aside and let the civilians and the medics mop up the carnage among the civilians while the Iranian troops collected the bodies of the impostors dressed like Egyptian troops. The corpses would be hauled back to the ship for disposal far from curious eyes.

Lieutenant Taghavi radioed Major Shakuri. "We're done, sir. Mission accomplished."

THE AIRPORT

Good luck for him, bad for them. Kyle saw the pair of headlights approaching along the service road, then heard the growl of the engine, and he rolled into a ditch until the car drove past. There were two soldiers in it, the passenger laughing at something the driver had said. Swanson got out of the ditch and resumed his journey, breathing easily and watching the taillights grow smaller before they flared bright when the driver hit the brakes.

It came to a halt only fifty yards from the runway, not far from the golden glow of landing lights bordering the right side of the approach path, and that illumination compromised their night vision. Kyle slowed his pace and angled his head down and away so the glare would not affect him as much. The soldiers got out and stretched, looking around but seeing nothing of interest because Kyle had flopped back into the ditch and was crawling forward on his hands and knees while listening to them talk. He lowered to his belly, slithered even closer in a measured stalk, dumped his gear, and pulled a razor-edged knife as he waited for the roar that he knew would come.

In less than two minutes, the next big plane came settling in, angling toward the runway while the pilot kept the nose up like some prehistoric giant bird, and the sudden howl of the engines drowned out all normal sound. It was only natural for the two guards to turn and watch it land. It was just as natural for Swanson to use that moment to break cover and kill them both.

He first took the guy on the right, who was standing a bit behind the other, with his head conveniently tilted far back, looking up at the plane. Kyle snaked his left arm over the exposed shoulder and brought his forearm hard against the nose and mouth. A kick behind the right knee forced the man off balance and arched him against Kyle, who snatched up and back hard to stretch the neck even more. A single, rapid left-to-right deep tear with the blade took out the windpipe and main arteries with a ripping sound, followed by a gush of dark red blood. The sound was lost in the roar of the plane engines, but the sudden blur of motion caught the attention of the other guard.

With his surprise gone, this would have to be a scramble kill, and Kyle launched an unrelenting attack with deadly purpose. The body of his first victim was still against him, so Swanson kicked and threw it directly into the startled second soldier. He followed in immediately and hard, taking the man to the ground while stabbing wildly around the body between them, slashing the stomach and legs of the man on the bottom. Swanson violently pushed aside the first victim and mauled the second, who was already in shock and great pain, with his upper body now exposed to the assault. Swanson clamped his left hand over the man's mouth and pushed the point of the knife deep into the stomach, up behind the ribs and into the heart area, then twisted hard and sawed and cut and watched impassively as life left the man's eyes and the bowels and bladder let go. Kyle pulled the blade free, wiped it, and rolled the corpses into the ditch. They would be discovered easily, but that was unimportant.

By Kyle's count, that airplane had been the eleventh big transport to land, and he had no way of knowing if it was the last or if more were coming. He could still see distant lights in the sky, though, and since Omar had confirmed the airport was closed to civilian traffic, it was logical that at least a couple more Iranian aircraft were on the way in the initial lift of troops. They had been arriving at the rate of one transport every fifteen minutes. He would proceed on that assumption and try to slow things down and let the Iranians know everybody was not playing by their rules.

Swanson understood that he was acting without orders, going on instincts that had been honed in battles of years past. One of his personal mottos was that it was sometimes better to ask forgiveness than to seek permission, and he was doing what he thought was in the best interests of his country. It was not the first time that he had run an unauthorized mission. Covert missions were run all over the world, all the time, and this one just happened to fall into his lap. The paperwork would just have to catch up. Official condemnations might erupt later, but any negative fallout would go elsewhere, while Kyle shuffled out the back door as an unseen force.

Meanwhile, he was right here, right now, with a window of opportunity, a bag full of explosives, and nobody asking questions.

CHAPTER 17

Swanson sprinted across the runway, shifting his gaze from the landing lights of the approaching plane to the faraway terminal that was crowded with assembled troops. He did not really have a plan other than wreak some havoc, and the easiest way to do that was to blow some shit up—set the decrepit fuel tank truck afire, crater the runway, or even attack the tower. The most bang for his buck would come from the fuel truck, for it did not matter whether or not it was full of aviation gasoline. The trapped vapors from the last load would be more than enough to amplify the explosion, which would distract the attention of the pilot, and after that, who knew?

The U.S. armed forces had learned a lot about improvised explosive devices, the lash-up planted charges that the bad guys had popularized to face the mechanized American military during the wars in Iraq and

Afghanistan. Not that hard to make, an IED could pop a Humvee apart like a firecracker under a turtle. He ran to the truck with a brick of C-4 plastic explosive already in his hand. A sharp knock on the round fuel tank resounded with a dull thud, indicating that it still contained a good amount of fuel, which made him smile.

He crawled beneath the truck and secured the C-4 directly below the tank so the explosion would point upward, like an erupting volcano. The ignition sequence would come from a blasting cap triggered by a cheap cell phone, all of which had been part of the Lizard's kit of supplies. With that done, he punched nine digits of the ten-digit telephone number into his satellite phone, then crawled back from beneath the filthy belly of the truck, glancing over his right shoulder. Another cargo plane coming down fast, with its landing gear already extended and the engines growing to a howl that made his insides shudder. Swanson did not look at his watch as he ran, for the exact time was unimportant. Either he made it back to the ditch in the next few seconds, or he would be cooked alive by his own inferno. The hard concrete of the runway gave way beneath his pounding boots to softer dirt as the noise of the approaching plane screamed even louder.

Five more steps at a dead run and he hurled himself forward and rolled into the depression. The plane engines were close and deafening as the big bird rode toward touchdown. He planted his face in the dirt, held the sat phone up high, and pressed the final digit of the cell phone number that would trigger the booby trap beneath the truck. In the millisecond prior to the connection, he hoped that Sir Isaac Newton was right with his First Law of Motion: Every object in a state of uniform motion tends to remain in that state of motion unless an external force is applied to it. That meant that the heavy airplane going better than a hundred miles per hour and pointing away from him would normally maintain that momentum and direction until the brakes were applied and the thrusters reversed. Another external force was going to change that orderly line of movement, and Kyle's bomb sparked just as the aircraft was almost directly beside the tanker truck.

The sudden explosion sheared off part of the left wing, tore away an engine, bounced the plane straight up off the runway again, and started it into an out-of-control forward cartwheel while still moving at about a hundred miles per hour. It slid and skipped in a typhoon of golden sparks and lateral trails of flame; then the entire tail section snapped away under the structural stress. The wreckage finally came to a slow, agonizing stop about halfway down the runway, with the front half plowing into the open field beside the concrete strip. There, it settled for a heartbeat before it went up in a whoosh of flames.

Huddled in the ditch, Swanson had opened his mouth and put his hands over his ears as the concussive wave of the blast shook him, then curled into a protective ball while debris from the dying plane splattered the runway like deadly rain. When things quieted, he looked up and saw the aircraft carcass burning hot. He climbed to his feet and hurried to the patrol car, turned on the engine, and drove away with no lights. Although he heard distant screams, no thought was given to how many people he had just killed. That was the job. *Just a little shock and awe to start the day, fellas. Welcome to Egypt.*

The safe house was a furnished apartment on an upper floor of a high-rise building about two miles from the west gate of the airport. A cluster of similar office and apartment buildings had grown up in the space as Sharm el-Sheikh had flourished on the tip of the Egyptian peninsula, drawing in tourists, businesses, and new residents who smelled money. Parked cars and small trucks lined the curbs, and Swanson dumped the stolen auto among a clutch of older vehicles parked in a line in a small lot of sand and downtrodden weeds. Numbers had been scrawled on some windshields with whitewash; it was a used car lot just like those that can be found anywhere in the world. Leaving the keys in the ignition, he was confident that it would soon be stolen.

A siren was wailing urgently at the airport as he shouldered his bag and, sticking to the walls and shadows, walked to the rear of the high-rise and took the service elevator up to the twelfth floor.

The British intelligence service, MI6, had purchased the condominium during an advance sale even before the building was completed because it provided not only a safe haven but also put eyes on the airport, just as there were similar observation posts near the port and the oil transfer stations. The place was leased to a traveling business executive who did not exist, all bills were automatically paid through a local bank, and the pantry and refrigerator were kept stocked. Kyle rapped three times on the door and heard someone come, then pause to check the TV security camera screen. The heavy steel door swung open easily on oiled hinges. "Come in. Quickly," said Omar. "Something has happened."

Large windows in the apartment faced the airport, and Tianha Bialy was at the tripod of a long telescope that was focused on the inferno burning beside the runway. Plumes of fire-retardant foam and water were being sprayed onto the wreckage. "A plane has crashed," she said.

"I see that," responded Kyle. "What else is happening?" He dropped the bag and went into the kitchen to get a bottle of cold water.

Omar was watching the scene through a pair of binos. "Some of the troops on the ground responded out there along with the usual emergency vehicles. The others are still moving into formations. There is no real sign of panic."

Kyle joined them at the windows. "Have any other troop carriers landed since the crash?"

"No. The next one in the landing pattern climbed back to altitude and I guess will lead the rest of them in an orbit to await orders. It does not look like the runway has been permanently impaired, so they might have enough fuel to stay up there until things are cleared away. Are you hurt?"

Tianha looked up for the first time and saw that Swanson was filthy dirty, with dark streaks of dried blood painting his tunic. "My God, Kyle, you look awful!" She looked back at the fire, then at him again. "Did you have something to do with that?"

"No, of course not. I was just doing some recon and ran into a couple of guys and we had a disagreement. Anyway, I didn't have an antiaircraft gun on me. That looks like an accident. Did you report to London?" Deflect. Answer a question with one of your own.

"Yes. They were to pass everything on to Washington. I'm to stay put and continue to feed information."

"Sounds about right," Swanson said, chugging the last water from the bottle. He took the sat phone from his pack and headed for the bedroom. "So I had better check in, too. Time for E.T. to call home."

CAIRO

Well, now. Someone was not playing by the rules, and Colonel Yahya Ali Naqdi of Iran's Army of the Guardians had an idea who the troublemakers might be.

Major Mansoor Shakuri, his chief of staff, had telephoned from Sharm in a panic to report what appeared to be a deliberate attack that had brought down one of the incoming Iranian transports, with the loss of about two hundred soldiers. Tension and worry laced his voice.

Distance between the action in Sharm and the colonel's desk in Cairo had the merit of allowing him to stay on the big picture of the overall invasion, while the major was swept up by emotion. The attack on the hotels had been carried out without any real difficulty, and the force from the beach was right on schedule. The number of troops at the airport was gradually increasing and the major said the runway would soon be open again to accept the remaining aircraft. Security was being increased to prevent further attacks.

The deaths of some two hundred soldiers was not a true disaster, for the colonel had estimated that even more might have been lost before the foothold was secured. It was the way they died that grabbed his attention. According to the major, a fuel truck parked by the runway detonated just as the plane was landing beside it, and the disaster resulted. That was no accident. Fuel tanks don't just conveniently blow up when a military airliner passes over.

Naqdi spent a while settling down the excited major and encouraging him to continue his good work, promising that he would not be held responsible for what had happened. Their daring attempt to bring down the Egyptian government, close the Suez Canal, control the oil flow, and pose a direct threat to Israel was fraught with risk.

All the while, the colonel's disciplined mind had been thinking about other things, particularly some soft messages that had been vibrating along the Egyptian underground intelligence web; the man known as the Pharaoh should come out of hiding and make his presence known. The contact whom the powers in London and Washington and Cairo wanted the Pharaoh to meet was an agent of the U.S. Central Intelligence Agency, and the accompanying schedule showed that the fellow actually was in Sharm. That was expanded with later information that an MI6 agent wanted the meeting. CIA and MI6 agents on the loose in Sharm, and a killed airplane; too much to be a coincidence.

The colonel instructed Major Shakuri to launch a manhunt for an American named Kyle Swanson and a British woman by the name of Tianha Bialy but did not tell him why.

THE SAFE HOUSE

"Are you staying in trouble, I hope?" The deep voice of Major General Bradley Middleton rumbled firm and decisive over the satellite phone, although he was thousands of miles away in the Pentagon office where he commanded Trident.

"Yes, sir. I think you might say that."

"Good. Well, Gunny Swanson, I have you on the speaker here, and the rest of the team with me. Give us a sitrep."

Kyle had been putting his thoughts in order ever since he saw the first boats hit the beach. "A large force of Iranian troops has invaded Egypt and seized control of Sharm el-Sheikh. They did not bring any heavy weapons that I could see, but some small artillery pieces might be arriving by boat or plane. Another force attacked the tourist hotels hard, with unknown casualties. They were dressed like Egyptian army but neither looked nor acted that way. I think they were plants. We now have eyes on the airport, where one of about fifteen troop-carrying planes crashed on approach. The runway was partially blocked. That's about all I know at this point."

There was a momentary silence on the other end; then the general spoke again. "You are certain that the soldiers are Iranian."

"Without a doubt, sir. I met a couple of them up close and personal. Their ID cards said they were with the Revolutionary Guard."

"How many?"

"I estimate they have about three to four thousand men on the ground right now from both the sea and air. Can you brief me what's going on elsewhere? I only know what I can see."

"Hey, Kyle." A higher-pitched voice—Lieutenant Colonel Sybelle Summers. "Mixed reports are coming in, mostly through the media, and we got an earlier info dump from your partner. The hotel massacre also looks like a stage show to us. The attack was pretty savage, but brief, and Iranian troops chased away the bad guys. The Egyptian military is being blamed, while the Iranians are being hailed as liberators by the Muslim Brotherhood on Al Jazeera. The Brotherhood is cranking up the crowds in Cairo to embrace these actions, so the legitimate government is stumbling for answers, and their denials sound weak. Our allies are extremely nervous, trying to figure out a response. It's just too early in the game for us to know much more than you."

The general's voice resumed. "Gunny, no doubt that an organized plan will be pulled together here soon, but it will take hours to implement anything. The one item that you can consider to be true is that Iran will not be allowed to take a foothold in Egypt, particularly by force. Letting them keep Sharm would be a disaster."

"So what do you want me to do? Just overwatch and report in every once in a while?" Kyle put an edge of sarcasm into the questions.

"We discussed it before you called, Kyle." Sybelle again. "You are the only thing we have on the ground right now, so you have to go with your gut. Try to confuse and bother them, because they are operating very close to the edge of their capabilities. At some point, these Iranian visitor units must link up with the big forces of the Muslim Brotherhood for major support, and those are tied down in Cairo and the big cities right now."

The general said, "That can't happen, Gunny. Do what you can to delay and destroy. Make them chase shadows and shake them off schedule until the big cheeses around here figure out what to do. Buy me some hours, Gunny. Buy me a whole clock full of hours. Someone will be here 24/7 if you need to talk."

"Yes, sir." He terminated the call, already starting to think like a guerrilla.

In Washington, the Trident team members exchanged looks around the table until Commander Benton Freedman spoke. "One man going against thousands? Is it a suicide mission—a Jews at Masada or a King Leonidas at Thermopylae thing?"

"No, Liz. We are just unleashing the mutt."

"Sir, are you referring to Marc Antony's call to 'Cry havoc, and let slip the dogs of war'? Shakespeare?"

"Whatever. Get out of my office. I'm going over to the White House to brief the president. You guys sift everything we have to determine how we can help Kyle and whether we can resupply him down there in the middle of nowhere. We need to feed our war dog. I think he's going to bite some serious Iranian ass."

CHAPTER 18

OXFORD, ENGLAND

Sir Gordon Fitzgerald, the chief of the British Secret Intelligence Service, was welcomed at the door of the cottage by Sir Geoffrey Cornwell and guided into the library, where Lady Patricia sat before a large fire, stroking the silver whiskers of a fat orange cat that had wandered in from outside a week earlier and made itself at home. The head of MI6 rubbed the cat with a pudgy finger. "Does this beast have a name?"

"Cat," replied Lady Patricia. "Her assigned job is to keep away the elephants."

"There are no elephants in Oxford," C said, moving to a chair.

"She is very good." The cat purred so contentedly that she vibrated.

Sir Jeff poured glasses of whisky and handed them

around. "So, Gordon, have you come to release us from this ivy-covered prison?"

They clinked glasses and drank. "That would be one of the reasons. We have found no trace of any more threats against you since the attack in the Tube station. We know now that the person behind the scheme, this Mansoor Shakuri fellow from Iran, held a high position with the Palm Group in Cairo—a cover, of course—but he seems to no longer be there. The major has popped up, of all places, in Sharm el-Sheikh."

"I see." Jeff finished off his drink and put the glass aside. "So he is off to fry bigger fish than us."

C nodded and put down his own drink, then folded his hands over his ample belly. "Unfortunately, things are a bit too confused down there at the moment to conduct a thorough investigation, but the international finance boys in Europe and the United States are cracking the records of the Palm Group with the intention of interrupting the cash laundering from Iran. Doubt the Palm Group will be a bother much longer; it looks like nothing more than a front, anyway. Your own security can take over now, and you both can go home."

"I shall abscond with this cat," Lady Pat said with mock severity.

"Please consider the cat a small gift from a grateful government for your trouble and cooperation," C replied. "Now, let us move to a more important point. Have you been in contact with Gunnery Sergeant Swanson?"

Pat and Jeff glanced at each other. "No," said Jeff. "Has something happened to him?"

C lifted a hand as if to bat away any concern, although

there was a moment of uncomfortable silence. "No, no, no. At least, none of which we are aware. Your lad and our agent did not get out before the Iranians arrived in Sharm, and they seem to be caught in the middle of those shocking developments. A report from Dr. Bialy said they are in an MI6 safe house for the time being. If they just keep their heads down, they should be fine until we can plan an extraction."

There was a sharp laugh from Lady Pat, who unceremoniously dumped the large cat from her lap onto the floor and brushed her hands together to get rid of the sticking fur. "Kyle is not going to keep his head down when all of that, that *mess* is going on."

"Dr. Bialy warned us that Swanson is proving difficult, if not impossible, as a working partner. Please, if he calls you for any reason, tell him to remember his role: He was to have the private conference with the Egyptians and then report back here. That was all. Dr. Bialy has the very different assignment of identifying and contacting a valuable source, and he was to assist her in whatever way he could. He has proven unwilling or unable to do that."

Lady Pat went to the bar, poured herself another shot, then refilled the glasses of the men. She picked a thin cigar from a silver box and lit it. "That partnership was doomed from the start, Gordon," she said. "We can dress Kyle up in a nice suit and tell him to act like a civilian and play second fiddle to the doctor, but Kyle is what he is. He has a very low tolerance for bullshit, pardon my language."

Sir Jeff picked up the thought. "With Sharm going

to the devil for the moment, according to the telly, there is simply no possible way that Kyle will sit still. He has probably contacted his people in Task Force Trident back in Washington by now, although I do not know that for a fact. It would be best to understand that he is now back under their command, and no longer under yours."

"Jeff, this American must not interfere with Dr. Bialy's mission!"

"Let us just wait and see if Swanson and Bialy live through this next twenty-four hours, George. There will be plenty of time later to worry about your unknown source."

SHARM EL-SHEIKH

Kyle Swanson stood beneath a hot shower, washing away the muck and blood of the night and letting the clutter of thoughts settle in his mind. Soap and shampoo did not require much mental power, so his mind was free to roam, and possibilities swept along like scenes in a slide show. "Delay and destroy," the general had said, a process that Kyle had already begun. Next step? What's the next step?

He had been up all night, seen action, created some chaos, but was now running on battery power and needed rest. Sleep discipline was important to any operator who needed to maintain his edge over a long period of time, and he had not had much rest since leaving California. He turned his face to the falling water and let it sluice around his eyes and into his ears, then leaned against the tiled wall so the hot stream could work on the knots in his neck. It was interesting that with an invasion under way, the water and electricity still worked.

Recon. That was the next step, and he did not have to do it all himself. The two MI6 people in the next room were virtually indigenous to the area, spoke the language, knew the strange customs, and could go out and mingle with the populace without arousing suspicion. They would be just two more people on the street in what was bound to be a day of unrest. Done with the shower, he toweled off. Were they sleeping together? The way Omar protectively rubbed Tianha's shoulder as they stood side by side last night back at the hotel indicated their relationship was more than casual. So what? Their business, not his, unless he could use that nugget of information somewhere down the road.

It would be best not to shave this morning, for every man in town wore at least a stubble of beard. In the mirror, he saw that a nick on the side of his neck was only a small, clean cut that was already beginning to heal, not much more than the bite of a razor, although it had been inflicted by a piece of flying shrapnel when the airliner blew up. He dug into the shaving kit for the bottle of meds, shook out a five-milligram tab of Ambien, and swallowed it dry. Marines sleep when they are told, but Kyle also believed in better living through chemistry. The sleeping aid would help put him down and keep him down for a couple of hours without being bothered by the bright sun and the noise outside while Omar and Tianha went out to see what was what. By the time they returned, he would be up.

Wearing loose gym shorts and a T-shirt, he went into the living room to discuss the situation, praying that Bialy would go along with his suggestion for a change. He wanted them to find out what was happening around the city and chart strongpoints, comm centers, headquarters areas, gathering places of the soldiers, vulnerable points, and guard positions, then come back and transfer whatever they found to a city map. From that, Kyle would make a target list.

PELELIU LHA-5
CARRIER STRIKE GROUP ONE
PERSIAN GULF

The Eye MEF was defanged almost before it could gather its gear. The 1st Marine Expeditionary Force was the go-to unit to make a sudden and heavy strike into hostile territory where civilians had been slaughtered and Americans were at risk or being held against their will.

As soon as the headquarters at Camp Pendleton in California was alerted to the situation developing on the Egyptian peninsula, mission-planning wheels began turning. Plans were already on the shelf for almost every conceivable place on the globe where hostilities might erupt, so the experts were basically doing a cut-and-paste job on contingencies that had been studied and updated for years. They did it all the time in practice, so doing it in real time made little difference.

The closest suitable unit to the action was the Marine Expeditionary Unit (Special Operations Capable)—known as MEU (SOC)—which was prowling the Persian Gulf. They had reacted immediately, without waiting to be told by Washington to gear up, and elements of the 5th Fleet Carrier Strike Group, built around the massive USS *Carl Vinson,* were surging forward to get within helicopter range of Sharm el-Sheikh.

From a cold start, the MEU could technically launch into an emergency situation in three hours. Leaders of the various sections were in the thick of assembling an attack scenario that could drop more than two thousand U.S. Marines on top of the Iranians at Sharm and back them up with warplanes, support ships, tanks, artillery, naval gunfire, and an amphibious landing. Drones were already flying and the satellites were looking down to help choose a landing zone. Special ops teams were being tasked to hit specific targets, and a precise fire support plan was coming together. Once ashore, the combat fighter-bombers and land troops would retake the airport, and the Iranians wouldn't have a chance to recover.

One member of the strike team was Captain Aaron Clay, who was out on the broad flat deck of the *Peleliu* LHA-5, chilly in his olive drab flight suit even as the morning sunshine promised forever visibility once over the target. He watched the crew arming up his stumpy AV-8B Harrier jet with the five-barreled 25 mm Gatling cannon, the 70 mm rockets, and the CBU-100 cluster bombs that would seriously put a hurt on somebody. Clay was feeling twitchy, as he did before any mission, prebattle nerves. All of the other Harriers on the deck were getting fueled and ready, too, and the troop-carrying helicopters were being nursed as if made of gold. Below deck, Marines were gearing up for the fight, and the AAV-7 amphibious assault vehicles were being given a final going-over.

"Looks like the package is coming together good, Fearless Leader," said Lieutenant Andrew McCore as he walked up beside Clay. "You ready to fly through the valley of death and fear no evil?"

"Born ready, Andy. Have they finalized our targets yet?"

"Nope. Should be ready pretty soon. I came out here to bother you while the analysts nail things down. I have a question."

"Wait a second until the COD lands." A big twin-engine transport plane that routinely ferried material and passengers to and from the carrier roared in with its engine at full power, caught the three wire, and jerked to a spine-jarring halt, going from about a hundred knots an hour to zero in a heartbeat. As the noise subsided, Clay said, "Go ahead. Shoot."

"We're going to hit the Iranians with everything we've got, right?"

"One could assume that." On the horizon, Clay could make out the bulk of the *Vinson,* and he knew the big carrier was humming with activity, preparing its own squadrons. Destroyers were cutting through the sea, throwing aside foam, and cruisers were preparing missiles. Mine-clearing ships were way out front, and all around were support ships; running deep under the water, two submarines were on the prowl.

"So if we know it, don't you think the Iranians know it, too? They don't want to really mess with us. Little isolated force like that wouldn't last a day of serious fighting."

Clay folded his arms across his thick chest, licked his dry lips, and nodded in agreement. "I am a big believer in using brute force. The more violent, the better."

"Spoken like a true Marine aviator. One more question."

"What?"

"Sir, if you die, can I have your watch?"

"Sorry, Andy, but I've already promised it to somebody else. You're too late, as usual, which is why you are still a mere lieutenant."

"Well, fuck a duck." McCore wandered off. "I'll go try Reese. He's got a Rolex."

Clay sucked in a deep breath of sea air that was heavy with aviation fuel. *Goin' to war soon.* He would shake off the nerves as soon as he climbed into the cockpit of his vertical takeoff machine and started the checklist. *Just another mission; out, boom, and back, rearm and do it again. Can't lose.*

Everything was ready. Nothing could stop them now.

His eyes roamed over to the COD, which sat with its propellers motionless as it discharged a small group of people: five men in camo, lithe and solemn. No one was there to greet them, and they disappeared into the base of the tower as quickly as they had arrived. Captain Clay had never seen them before, but there were hundreds of men around wearing camo.

SHARM EL-SHEIKH

A link had been established from the Blue Neptune Hotel to the CNN bureau in Cairo, and an Iranian Army officer appeared on television screens around the world, calmly preparing to read a short statement. His uniform was neat, and there was a sense of confidence about him. He looked directly into the camera while listening to directions through an invisible bud in his right ear. When the invisible voice said, "Now," he spoke.

"Good afternoon. I am Major Mansoor Shakuri of Iran's Army of the Guardians, and I am broadcasting from the Blue Neptune Hotel in Sharm el-Sheikh. A terrible attack on civilian tourists by radical Egyptian army troops has been defeated. I must report that casualties among the civilians have been substantial, but I now can also report that Iranian peacekeeping troops have stopped the bandits and Sharm el-Sheikh is once again safe."

He paused for effect, then continued. "During this entire turbulent time, we have been aware that other nations have been concerned about the safety of their people. Let me offer this comfort: No foreign nationals are being held prisoner, and steps are being taken to fly out anyone who wishes to leave. Your people are safe, and your wounded are being tended with the best of care. All are free to contact families and friends.

"Although the airport will remain closed to civilian traffic for the time being, airlines will soon be able to resume normal operations. Media representatives have already been allowed in, as evidenced by the broadcast. We urgently appeal for medical help from international organizations and look forward to assistance from the United Nations. Once an appropriate UN force arrives to provide protection for all the people, and are able to secure the Suez Canal and the oil routes from the renegades in the Egyptian military, the troops of Iran will leave." He put aside his papers and looked at the camera. "Thank you."

In Cairo, Colonel Yahya Ali Naqdi had watched Shakuri's performance with a great deal of pleasure, and now he clapped his hands in applause. Perfect. Just as you win some battles with bullets, you can also win some by stringing words together like pearls. Shakuri's statement on worldwide television would blunt military responses from America, Great Britain, and NATO. By delaying the actual departure of the foreign nationals, the Iranians would, in effect, have human shields against airstrikes. Russia and China would veto any swift UN deployment with many speeches over a period of weeks, or even months. Iran was there to stay. The colonel was satisfied with the speech, and with how Major Shakuri had become the face of the invasion, another cutout between the colonel and repercussions—what the Americans called a "fall guy."

In Washington, the lights were bright in the hallways of power and the mood somber in the Oval Office. "Where does this leave us?" asked the president of the United States.

"As I see it, we can mount covert operations and threaten sanctions, but with the safety of our people guaranteed, we no longer have just cause to attack." The secretary of state ran a finger down the transcript of the broadcast. "All lies, but good ones."

"General?" The president raised an eyebrow at the chairman of the Joint Chiefs.

"The *Vinson* Strike Group and the Marine Expeditionary Unit are en route and waiting for our decision. You guys have to make that call."

The national security adviser said, "It's a damned chess game, and we're playing against someone who is pretty good at this, thinking two steps ahead. Giving permission for civilians to use e-mails and Facebook is nothing but free publicity. We cannot attack the Iranians now without looking like the bad guys."

With everyone in the room agreed, the president issued his decision. He knew that Kyle Swanson was already on the ground and hard at work, so things were not totally at a standstill. Perhaps some special ops unit could go in to back him up. There would be another briefing in two hours, but for now, he made the only logical call.

The chairman summoned his aide, who was waiting outside the door. "Get on the horn back to my office. Stand down the MEU (SOC) and all strike packages, and await further orders."

Captain Aaron Clay had peeled out of his flight suit, put on his khakis, and found a bench in the mess deck of the *Peleliu* LHA-5. He was decompressing with a hot cup of coffee while digging into a meal of steak and eggs. No more butterflies in the gut; just a sense of deep disappointment.

CHAPTER 19

Swanson slid awake at noon, his eyes opening as easily as elevator doors parting to show a new world. He felt renewed, ready to take the next step, whatever it might be. His subconscious had mulled the situation thoroughly while he slept, and he recalled the first President Bush's words when Iraq invaded Kuwait, "This will not stand." Obviously, this illegal invasion of Egypt by Iran, no matter how it was spruced up as a diplomatic and humanitarian mission, was a slap to the face of the West; it also would not be allowed to stand.

Things had to be in motion in the world capitals, and although he did not know what actions were being considered, he did know that he had not a moment to waste. *Don't let them get comfortable.* Kyle rolled from the bed and padded to the kitchen, the tiled floor chilly on his feet. He made a quick snack of juice, sliced cheese and melon, and an apple and walked to the big window overlooking the airport. It looked quiet. No planes arriving or departing.

He put his eye to the big telescope and scanned slowly left to right, coming to focus on large piles of boxes and crates stacked in and around a maintenance hangar about four hundred yards from the terminal building. Forklifts were carrying more crates to the pile, and guards were walking lazy patrol around the perimeter. Kyle pulled the telescope back away from the window to avoid being spotted by anyone doing countersurveillance by studying the windows of every building that overlooked the critical airstrip. The safe house wasn't going to be all that safe if the Iranians and their pals in the Muslim Brotherhood got their act together and cleared the area. Omar would have to find something else within the next few days.

Back in the bedroom, he raided the closet and found a fresh pair of white cotton pants; they were a little loose in the waist, but a cloth belt took care of that. He chose a knee-length, loose dark blue *dishdasha* with an open Nehru collar. A checkered blue and white scarf covered his shoulders, and a cream-colored knitted cotton kufi went on his head. With that and the face stubble, he could go out in the daylight for a while, as long as he didn't have to speak.

At the small desk in a corner, Swanson laid out a one-time code sheet and spent thirty minutes composing a report, then checked in again by sat phone with Trident headquarters. The Lizard answered instantly, and they greeted each other with inane-sounding passwords.

"How's the weather down there?" asked Commander Freedman.

"Pretty cool. How about there?"

"Always the same. Shackle."

"Right and ready." Liz was ready to take the secret and guarded transmission. It was known as the Simple Shackle, and they each had preset identical pads that were a series of connected squares that gave them the look of a chessboard. Each square corresponded to a letter in the alphabet, but each number was really the number that followed it; a *four* actually was a *five,* which might correspond to a vowel the first time used and a consonant the next. The code was no match for a computer but was perfect for ease of communication. Afterward, the code sheet would be destroyed. Swanson had four that he could use on this mission.

Slowly, Kyle read the appropriate numbers that briefly reported that he was still good, the resort city of Sharm was quiet, and the airport was standing idle for the time being as far as plane movements. Then it was his turn to receive, and he jotted down the numerical series. When he decoded it, he found a surprise: The Saudis had already reacted and were shifting forces into position along the northwestern border to face Egypt. That would cover from the Jordanian border to the Red Sea, close the side door to the east, and dash any hope the Iranians might have of leaving that way. *This will not stand.*

He read on with a surge of pleasure that made him chew his lower lip. The next part of the message added another item to his list for this afternoon's chores, one that he was happy to do. Then the piece of paper was ripped to pieces and flushed down the toilet.

He took a moment to disassemble the rifle, wiped the parts with gun oil, and wrapped it all in a pillowcase to cushion it and break up the straight lines, then dumped it into a trash bag made of heavy-duty black plastic. The pistol went into the back of his belt and was covered by the loose *dishdasha*. After adding a wire hanger from the closet to his bag of goodies, he left the apartment, locking the door behind him.

He walked casually, with the bag over his shoulder, taking on the appearance of an average businessman just trying to get by during this surprising and dangerous time. The sun was bright and the sky clear, giving everything a confusing veneer of normality, although Sharm el-Sheikh was anything but normal. Still, awnings hung along storefronts to provide shade, and goods were stacked outside for sale, everything from bicycles to fruits and vegetables. Women, who could dress with some style in Egypt, had ducked back into the anonymity of their traditional ankle-length robes and covered their faces. Kyle found he did not have to worry about speaking, for not only were the crowds of civilians unusually silent, no one was meeting the eyes of anyone else. The best way to survive was to not be noticed. He kept moving, back toward the lower-income outskirts where he had left his stolen car, for he needed to steal another one for the day.

It took some shopping because many of the automobiles were either too small for his purpose or too new, with the cutoff SUV look or a hatchback. Within a half hour, he narrowed in on a dirty white Renault parked at the edge of a field. It probably dated back to the mid-1980s, and it had slick black tires, four doors, and the scars of having been in more than one fender-bender during its long life. It was a small box on wheels, but with a spacious trunk. It took only a couple of minutes to bend his wire coat hanger into a hook, slide it down the door beside the window, pop the latch, and get inside. His knife tore the ignition away from the steering column; he twisted the wires and sparked the engine to life. The Renault gave a couple of coughs, then chugged away, and he drove downtown, happy that his new escape-and-evade platform would never draw a suspicious glance.

A few bunkered-up guard posts manned by Iranian soldiers had been erected at key points throughout Sharm, although civilian police still directed traffic and apparently were also handling ordinary law enforcement duties. It was obviously an uneasy alliance, and the cops, none of whom were allowed to carry guns, were also staying low to the ground, fearful of the hard looks cast at them by the soldiers with automatic weapons. The soldiers were at ease, smoking cigarettes, laughing, and watching the women more than they watched the men or the passing vehicles. Perfect, thought Kyle. With nobody opposing them, the occupiers were getting sloppy, and their vigilance was dropping every minute that nothing happened.

He drove by what appeared to be the central government administration building, which stood out from its surroundings just as a county courthouse dominated so many small towns back in the United States. Over here they were almost always simply called "Government House." Four soldiers wearing the deep olive green uniforms of the Iranian Revolutionary Guard were clustered outside the front entrance. Two were simply standing there with weapons over their shoulders, watching civilians approach a young officer seated at a table stacked with papers beside the front door. He was apparently there to give army permission for some errand to be run, or something just as mundane. There was only a short line of five or six men waiting their turns, and they hesitantly approached him one at a time. At an adjacent table was a communications setup that connected the officer to a higher command level if there was a question. There were no questions; whatever its purpose was, the line moved along rapidly. The radioman was bored, leaning back in the chair with his ankles crossed, and flipped his cigarette into the street.

Good enough. Kyle kept going, scanning the opposite side of the street. Since he was near the center of the city, there were a number of multistory buildings that seemed in decent repair, and boxy air-conditioning units hung from some of the windows. That made sense, he thought, and also signaled that windows that were closed were to unoccupied rooms, for without any cooling air, the rooms would be unbelievably hot and stuffy, even in January.

The building was a definite possibility. He did some mental measurements and chose a pair of windows on the fourth floor of a building about two hundred yards down the street with unobstructed sight lines to the soldiers. The old fashioned double-hung windows gawked at him like open eyes. Decision time: inside or outside?

The whitewashed building was some kind of office complex, the natural habitat for a lot of lawyers and businessmen who would want to be near the main government building. It offered Kyle the definite advantages of all-around concealment and height for a sniper's hide, and since most of the lawyers and other workers were probably staying home today, there would be only a small chance that anyone would interrupt him if he could occupy that supposedly empty room with the dirty windows. Get in, shove a desk in front of the door, throw together a hide in the back shadows of the room, then slowly open the window about a foot. That would work.

The downside was that he was alone and could not really watch his ass and the target at the same time. He could not be certain the offices were empty, and getting up and down the stairs, through open hallways, breaking locks, making the shot, then getting out across sidewalks and streets was definitely the more risk-laden move. Somebody could stumble upon him at any moment, for pure chance and the real world could always intervene, and it was wise to keep such dangers to a minimum. As much as he hated to admit it, some things were just beyond his control. Go to Plan B.

Swanson drove on until he found an abandoned shed outside of town, not far from the road, swung in behind it, and killed the motor. Pulling on a pair of gloves, he opened all four doors and wrestled the backseat out of the car, leaving it beside the shed as if were an outside sofa. After that, he burrowed through car junk into the trunk and tripped the lock from the inside; the lid rose smoothly for a few inches, then stopped. He got out and went around to the back to lift it all the way.

Unloading the clutter went quickly as he rolled away two spare tires and tossed the jack, a sealed quart of oil, and a wooden box of tools. In this area of the world, owners worked on their cars rather than drop the vehicles off for a day with an expensive mechanic. Within minutes, the trunk space was empty. He covered the flooring with the pillowcases with which he had wrapped the rifle, so as not to smear old oil and dirt on the clean *dishdasha* and attract unwanted attention.

Newer-model cars all have release triggers inside the trunk to prevent anyone from getting stuck, but his Renault was of a different day. He would have to improvise. A roll of duct tape from his bag performed the needed magic, as he taped over the locked mechanism to disable it, then used some thin 550 parachute cord to create a handle of twined loops on the inside of the lid. Back in the trunk again, he sprawled out to test if he could fire from the prone position. It would be tight, but he was satisfied. He pulled the lid closed with a rope made by twisting a sturdy length of duct tape and lashing it to the cord handle. The trunk was then taped shut on the inside, still unlocked but secure enough to avoid its flying open while he drove.

The final chore was to ready his M-16A3, and he snapped the two pieces of the semiautomatic rifle together, fitted in the pair of cotter pins, and attached the silencer. The scope was dialed in to two hundred yards, virtually point-blank range. A fresh magazine of ammo was clicked home after he polished each of the standard 5.56 mm NATO rounds for a last time. He laid it down and spread the black bag over it, weighting the plastic sheet with his duffel.

A few minutes later, he was back cruising the target zone, a Joe Average Civilian looking insignificant but with a large pistol wedged beneath his thigh. The soldiers were still at the Government House, doing their paperwork thing as he passed without looking directly at them. The street might have been choked and busy on a normal day, but not under this cloak of a menacing military presence. With many people sticking close to home, a lot of parking spaces were created, and Kyle steered smoothly into one about two hundred yards from the officer at the table on the other side of the street. He parked before a two-story facility that apparently also housed a number of small businesses that dealt with the local government. Windows were closed or the air conditioners were on. No one was on the two small balconies overlooking the street, which was virtually empty.

The boxy Renault had become a sniper's mobile hide, and Swanson took it out of gear, pulled on the emergency brake, but left the motor idling as he made one last visual sweep of the street. A few people were around the open Government House, but no one was looking his way. He slithered into the back of the vehicle and took out the weapon, squelching the normal urge to hurry and keeping his breathing normal. *Slow is smooth, smooth is fast.*

Now on his stomach, he peeled the tape away from the lid and held the handle to keep the trunk lid closed while he also stripped off the tape from the lock catch bar. Gun in one hand and the makeshift rope handle in the other, he allowed the trunk lid to rise another few inches. He saw an open lane to the target and let the lid rise even higher. Swanson listened to the sounds of the street. He disdained using the earplugs preferred by some snipers, because they dulled the senses and the shooter could not hear the enemy or what's around him. Kyle would rather be deaf than dead.

Elevation was no problem since they were all almost at street level, and there was no detectable wind, which in any case would have made no left-or-right difference at this range. He eased the lid open the rest of the way, brought the M-61A1 to his shoulder, and acquired his first target, the busy officer. The view in the scope was so close and clear that Swanson could see that the man's cheeks were pitted with acne scars, and the sniper exhaled and turned the job over to his muscle memory; he had practiced this very shot thousands of times. The finger caressed the trigger with a gentle, steady pull and unleashed a round that struck the officer right at the bridge of his nose, the fabled medulla oblongata shot, which impacted the lower brainstem and tore through the area that controlled almost everything in the body. The back half of the officer's head exploded away and the body cartwheeled back over his chair, fanning up a wave of blood.

Before that body hit the ground, Kyle had moved the rifle slightly and shot the radioman through the head, which was totally pulped. The victim had been so totally relaxed that his arms just fell to his sides and the body stayed in the chair.

The semiautomatic rifle and its shooter were acting as a single unit, cycling through the job, and Kyle swung the other direction by a few degrees and popped the two guards with shots to their hearts. *Boom, boom,* pause, *boom, boom,* and it was all over in five-point-seven seconds.

He pulled the rifle back with his right hand while lowering the trunk lid with his left until it locked with a firm snap. The few people in the plaza were on the ground in fear, shocked by the unexpected gunfire and staring at the dead soldiers, as Kyle climbed back behind the steering wheel and released the emergency brake. The battered Renault puttered away at an average speed, turned at the first corner, and disappeared.

CHAPTER 20

CAIRO

Iranian Colonel Yahya Ali Naqdi of the Army of the Guardians took a great deal of pride in viewing things not as he wished they were but as a situation actually was. Artists lay down one careful brushstroke at a time, and time and talent determine whether the painting will be great or just colors scrawled on canvas. His invasion had proceeded nicely up to this point. The first phase was a success. He had gotten Iranian troops on Egyptian soil without opposition.

With the massacre of the soccer team, the attack on the Iranian ship, and the atrocities inflicted on tourists in Sharm el-Sheikh, most Egyptians felt their military forces, their police, and the coalition government had failed in their primary duty of protecting the people. In the public eye, the Iranian troops were regarded as rescuing heroes. In reality, Naqdi had established military control over the vital oil routes and effectively controlled the Suez Canal. Oil and gasoline prices were already spiking around the world, a problem that would continue.

The colonel understood, however, that the few thousand soldiers he had down in Sharm might look powerful, but they could not hold out there indefinitely. It was time for Phase Two: for the Muslim Brotherhood to capitalize on the opportunity. All Naqdi's men had to do was keep up the peaceful facade in the south while the Brotherhood stirred the mobs into a frenzy. The Brotherhood had made substantial political gains, even winning the presidency, but it was not in real control. That lay, as always, in the hands of the generals. Now was the time to reorganize the unruly mobs into an alternate army supported by the people, drive south and link up with his Iranian commandos. Supplies and ammunition were sufficient to last until that main force could reach them.

The colonel unfolded the latest communiqué from his chief of staff, Major Mansoor Shakuri, down in Sharm. Four soldiers had been killed at a government office building, and the evidence indicated that it was the work of a sniper. Another brushstroke. The colonel added in the two murdered soldiers whose knifed bodies had been found in a ditch by the airfield, and the downed plane that had mysteriously exploded while landing, killing all of the troops who were aboard.

He had learned of the separate development in which soldiers of the Kingdom of Saudi Arabia were being moved into the general area. That hardly mattered, because Naqdi had no intention of fighting them. Still, the Saudis' maneuvering was a sign that a great snake was beginning to stir.

This apparent sniper attack indicated that special forces, probably Americans or British, were being inserted and hiding. It was expected. Major Shakuri would just have to brace for more minor attacks, and the general in command at the airport would have to make the men extra vigilant. Just keep the lid on for a couple more days, he thought, and it should all be over.

He also was interested in Shakuri's search for the CIA agent, Kyle Swanson, who had not yet been found. The sweep by intelligence officers had discovered that Swanson had been a guest at the Blue Neptune Hotel at the time of the attack and had a flight reservation on one of the passenger planes that never took off. He probably was still lurking around the area. They had also determined that Swanson had been traveling in the company of the well-known British Egyptologist Tianha Bialy, who the colonel now believed was also a British spy. She, too, had disappeared.

SHARM EL-SHEIKH

After hitting the Iranians at Government House, Kyle Swanson drove the Renault carefully toward the waterfront. Help was on the way.

The intel weenies back in the States had been busy with their maps, overlays, look-down images, drones, and computer models, and the Shackle communication from the Lizard had instructed him to do an eyes-on confirmation of a proposed landing site for a small unit. Four operators and an Air Force Combat Controller would be fast-roping down from a stealth-modified Black Hawk helicopter at 0300 tomorrow morning to link up with Kyle and become the pathfinders for a large assault that almost everyone thought was inevitable, sooner or later. Along with the Combat Control Team communications suite, they would be bringing in a lot more toys, firepower, and talent. Importantly, he would no longer be alone.

The GPS coordinates took him away from the heart of the Red Sea Riviera and up the coast to a quiet point across from the two small islands that comprised the Ras Mohammad National Park a few miles offshore. Normally, it was a tourist playground that featured spectacular diving into underwater caves, but this area also had cleared out for safer surroundings. He kept driving around until he found a small coastal shelf that was rugged and bare around the land edges, impractical for earning a living by farming or fishing but ideal for a surprise special ops landing on the dominant jagged ridge. He parked and sat for thirty minutes, letting the fresh breeze sweep through the open windows, and he did not see another soul. Even the usual ferry service over to the islands had been suspended. It was too far from Sharm for roving Iranian land patrols, and they had nothing at sea. Barring an unforeseen development, this place should do just fine.

He headed back. The next job was to dump the car,

since it had probably been seen at the shootings in the city, so he drove up the road for a few more miles and parked on a side path heading north, with the windows open. Still with a half tank of gas, it would be gone before nightfall. If Iranians found it, they would assume the driver was headed to the mountains to hide. If it were found by an ordinary enterprising Egyptian, which was much more likely, it would be stolen and taken elsewhere. With that bit of misdirection complete, Kyle policed up the brass in the trunk, disassembled the rifle, slung his black bag containing the gun over his shoulder, tucked the pistol in his belt, and began the long, slow trudge back to the safe house. It had been a good day so far.

Sharm glittered in the distance beneath the cool midday sun but was like a tarnished jewel needing a polish. Swanson had walked less than a mile when he heard the sound of an engine approaching from behind, the *chug-chug* of a tractor instead of the smoothness of an automobile, and he immediately pretended to be limping and slouched his shoulders, bending his back forward a bit, his face toward the ground in front of him. Sure enough, a farmer hauling bags of beans into the city pulled to a stop beside Swanson, but when he called out, Kyle retreated off the road and looked at the driver with suspicion, wrapping his package close to his chest, as if in fear. The bearded old man laughed at the thought he might be a thief preying on some unfortunate who was obviously sick in the head, for a good Muslim would not do such a thing. He made hand motions for Swanson to climb in the cart, and Kyle approached with great caution, face down as if humiliated, and climbed aboard to huddle in a corner. The tractor moved out.

Swanson kept his head on a swivel as the driver chugged along, talking loudly and constantly. If the farmer was hauling his beans in to market, then he anticipated customers for his crop. Commerce was returning to the city, which meant things were settling down. The ride lasted a few more slow and dusty miles, and a couple of automobiles passed, going both ways. Traffic was out and about, but the vehicles were not stacked with belongings, and there was no outflow of refugees.

The Iranians were playing this hand well, he thought. Calm the people, show them safety, be friends. He was sure that by now, international media companies had hired boats out of Hurghada and news crews were on the ground in carefully escorted groups to document the disciplined Iranian soldiers, happy Egyptian children, women shopping, men working, and no terrorists blowing up hotels: images from the noninvasion of Sharm el-Sheikh. They would not have been shown the wreckage at the airport, nor the slaughter at Government House.

He slid from the moving cart as they neared the city without a word to the driver, who was still talking and happily singing to himself, as if all were right in his own little world and he didn't realize his passenger had departed. Within forty minutes, Kyle was back at the safe house, where Tianha Bialy and Omar Eissa were waiting.

They were at the small table in the kitchen, studying a city map and preparing notes from their journey through the streets. When Kyle unlocked the door and came in, they both looked up with relief. "We were getting a bit worried about you, mate. Are you all right?"

"I'm good. I went down by the waterfront for a while." Swanson dropped his bag and went to the little fridge, where bottles of cool water and juice stood in ranks. He could smell fresh food, and the counters were stacked with vegetables, fruit, canned goods, and the leftovers of sandwiches made of eggs and cheese. Enough to feed an army, Kyle thought. At least to feed the recon team coming in tonight. He decided not to mention that before hearing what his partners had discovered.

"Did you find anything?"

"Some. Not much. The freighter that landed the beach force is still anchored out there and has started to unload supplies. With all of the men and equipment it carried, they can't have much of a load, and I didn't see any increase in the actual force. Two-man patrols are on the beaches, and some static positions are being built at the level of the berm. Strangest damned thing is that some asshole foreign tourists are actually down on the beach in their bathing suits, saying hello to the soldiers and acting like this is just an extra adventure on their holiday, and the destroyed hotels and casualties meant nothing to them."

Omar spoke, his eyes on Kyle. "That's yesterday's news. Things are generally quiet all around the city, but there was a shooting downtown today. Four Iranians were killed."

Kyle spun the top from a chilled water bottle and let the liquid gurgle down his parched throat, hydrating his insides.

"You didn't know about it?" asked Bialy.

"Un-unh. You guys have any problems being out this morning?" He sat at the table with them.

"No. Like you, we saw that the tourist crowd has calmed down quite a bit since the action. The bodies are gone, the wounded are in the hospital or being tended to, and the hotels are scrubbing away the blood, mending the glass, repairing the bullet holes, and painting everything. It's like a construction bonanza, and every workman in town has a job. Even kids are pushing brooms." Tianha got up. "Let me make you a sandwich. The marketplace was busy, everybody jammed in selling foodstuffs. Every stall open. Just as you saw on the beach, this has gone from a horrible disaster to just another day in paradise, if you can just ignore the bodies and the Iranians carrying weapons."

"Sure. Thanks. I'm tired after my walk." He pulled the long shirt over his head and tossed it over the back of his chair. His T-shirt was soaked with sweat.

She sliced two thick slices of bakery-fresh bread, smeared on butter, and put it in a frying pan to toast while she cooked a quick egg over easy and melted a chunk of cheese on top of it. "A million calories in one serving will do you good," she said during the three-minute cooking drill. "Omar says you are too skinny."

Swanson took the sandwich. "You're in a good mood today. What happened? You find a bottle of happy pills?"

"Not at all. It's just that we've come up with a great idea. You go ahead and eat while we brief you on what we saw during our prowl, and then we'll discuss the plan."

Swanson took a bite. Delicious. He chewed slowly, and except for an occasional question, he let the others do the talking. They had actually done a good job of putting together an overview of the situation within the city, marking Iranian military concentrations and checkpoints to be avoided and reading off a rather wordy report they would transmit to London. The most remarkable comment was the accurate observation that nobody in Sharm was calling for help.

"That's good work," he offered. "What is your new idea, then?" Tianha almost had a gleam in her eye. *She thought of this, whatever it is. Omar's just along for the ride.*

"All of the work going on to get Sharm back to almost normal can be used to our advantage. Because of the lack of transportation out of town, other than the few ferries being allowed to operate, there are a lot of tourists still in the hotels. The Blue Neptune took the brunt of the attack and sustained severe damage, but I have made a reservation to check into a suite at the Four Seasons."

Swanson covered his surprise by taking another drink of water. "Why? You're good right here."

"But Kyle, the Pharaoh will never find us here. At the hotel, with my name in the register, I would be easy to track down."

"Are MI6 and C cool with that?"

"I haven't told them, but I don't need permission. Omar can look out for me, and by being out in the open, I can move more freely and gather even better intel while we wait." She smiled. Omar shrugged his shoulders.

"What's your cover story?"

"That's the best part. I'm a scholar, so I was en route to do some independent research in the fabulous library at St. Catherine's Monastery near Mount Sinai. My academic credentials will support that. But I got scared and ran away when the attack hit the Blue Neptune and hid out overnight. Since calm has been restored, I am back in a big hotel, hoping to get on the list of people allowed to leave. It is best to act like an innocent abroad."

Since Kyle did not give a damn about the Pharaoh and had no control over Bialy, he said, "OK. Sounds like a winner, as long as we keep in close touch. I will stay here for a while longer, and you call me if you need me." The two British agents moving to the hotel had a huge plus side for Swanson, for he would be able to use the safe house as a hide for the incoming recon team. Tianha and Omar didn't need to know about them at all.

"Omar, I'll need a car for my own use. I can't keep stealing them off the street, so can you arrange something before you guys leave? I would prefer some kind of 4x4 in case there is some rugged driving needed when this place goes to hell. Complete with good papers."

"Sure. I have an SUV at my local office. I'll park it

in the underground garage here and leave the keys for you."

"Well, good luck to you both. Tianha, you be careful in dealing with the Iranians and with your Pharaoh, and stay in close contact, OK? You know this isn't over."

"What are you going to do?" Bialy asked.

Swanson yawned and stretched. "I don't know. Right now, I think I'll take a nap."

CHAPTER 21

SHARM EL-SHEIKH

Major Mansoor Shakuri was feeling the pressure of command. Brigadier General Medhi Khasrodad of the Iranian Revolutionary Guard was in charge of the ground troops in the Egyptian peninsula, but Khasrodad was little more than a figurehead whose job was to be certain the men performed their duties. Shakuri held the actual power, and he answered only to Colonel Naqdi in Cairo, and Naqdi was the critical strong link in a chain that stretched all the way back to Tehran, where it was anchored in theology and politics. In this unusual case, the general answered to the major, so the pressure was eased somewhat by the pleasure of being in charge. Finally free of the colonel's fearsome presence, the major could do as he pleased. He had learned much during the months of stern tutelage—much more than the colonel suspected, for Shakuri had used his position as chief of staff well. The colonel would be very surprised to know that the major was such a deep well of inside information.

Naqdi actually had been quite effusive in praising his former chief of staff, allowing Shakuri to become the public face of the successful military action that had disguised the invasion. The major's photograph in a crisp uniform had appeared in many newspapers, his televised appearance had been on screens around the world, and the social media was passing him around like a party favor: the savior who defeated the terrorists' savage attack on the hotels of Sharm el-Sheikh! A promotion and a citation for his record were almost certainties. Nobody was talking about Colonel Naqdi.

General Khasrodad had his headquarters with the troops out at the airport, but Major Shakuri saw no need for austerity. He instead confiscated a cluster of apartments at one of the luxurious seaside hotels, from which he could watch the beach and the blue water from his desk, and where he could have refreshments served on shining silver platters by hotel waiters. The bad part of command was that each decision carried risk, and the commendations and promotion and bright future could vanish in an instant, leaving him in disgrace, if not in prison. Despite the new job and beautiful surroundings, Shakuri had not forgotten that his colonel had a low tolerance for failure.

As a silent acknowledgment of who was senior, Shakuri was at his big desk, listening to the report of

General Khasrodad, in a chair opposite him. The take-over of Sharm was complete, but there was at least one viper in the nest, maybe more. Four soldiers dead at the Government House, two sentries gutted at the airport, and the troop-filled transport plane that crashed, al-though that was officially listed as an accident. The major knew better. To him, it had the look of a growing partisan movement. Khasrodad had argued that such guerrilla actions were to be expected during an occu-pation phase, that the casualties sustained by his force thus far were still well below the predicted parameters, and that security procedures had been tightened to pre-vent further losses. Shakuri considered that to be a pas-sive response and one that would only invite further trouble. He wanted a more aggressive posture. If there was indeed an underground guerrilla movement afoot in the city, he intended to snuff out the danger before it could flame into rebellion. There had to be a show of retribution. What good was command if you did not exercise power?

Following the conference, the general had to slink away and reluctantly prepare to carry out his new or-ders to arrest half a dozen Egyptian men from different strata of society and different parts of the city and hold them in the local jail. Major Shakuri summoned his clerk and dictated an order that was to be broadcast promptly over the local broadcast stations, then repeated every thirty minutes.

ATTENTION ALL CITIZENS: Six peacekeeping soldiers of Iran have been brutally murdered in this city while in the performance of their duties. Such cowardly attacks will not be tolerated. Iran was invited to Egypt by the government and the United Nations to help secure its safety against anti-Islamic terrorists, and we shall do so. The people of Sharm el-Sheikh are required to participate in their own defense, but some outlaw elements have engaged in rebellion and have killed members of the IRG without provocation. Those evil attacks require a response to ensure that rebels will not swim unmolested among the law-abiding citizenry. They must be denied all forms of shelter and assistance.

To underline our determination, a price must be paid for the terrorists who have spread mischief upon the land and are attempting to destabilize the society. The holy word of the all-merciful Prophet, praise be unto him, instructs us that punishment must be in proportion to the crime: "Life for life, eye for eye; nose for nose, ear for ear; tooth for tooth, and wounds equal for equal."

Therefore, it is decreed that for every Iranian soldier killed, one citizen of Sharm el-Sheikh is to be executed. Six soldiers of Iran were slaughtered, so six Egyptians must bear the responsibility for those heinous acts with their own lives. These executions by firing squad will be carried out in the public square at nine o'clock tonight.

By order of Major Mansoor Shakuri,

Commandant of the Iranian Peacekeeping Mission

THE SAFE HOUSE

Kyle Swanson had not showered all day, because the dirtier he looked, the better his disguise as a common man on the street. The accompanying itchiness and filth did not matter. Tianha and Omar had already left for the Four Seasons, so he was alone to putter around the apartment, killing time and restraining the urge to get out there and do something, *anything,* to throw another wrench into the Iranian plans. *You're a sniper; you know how to wait.* Here he was sitting on his ass during a sunny afternoon, with absolutely nothing worthwhile accomplished.

He felt almost like a prisoner in the spacious apartment, but his rendezvous with the Pathfinders in a few hours was too important for him to expose himself unnecessarily. He had to remain hidden for a while longer. Still, he could not help being restless and aware that vital time was slipping through his fingers. The longer the Revolutionary Guards remained unmolested, the more likely it was that they would succeed in securing their foothold in Egypt.

He did not listen to the radio nor turn on the television set, although he checked briefly with Washington and was advised that the Pathfinders were still on schedule. Once they were in place, other options would open up, but meanwhile he still had permission to act independently. The political side was wrestling with the rapid developments, and the Muslim Brotherhood–orchestrated riots in Cairo and other countries seemed to have reached a temporary stalemate, as if the core of the movement were being reorganized into a more military-oriented force. Neither side held the upper hand twenty-four hours into the invasion.

After the messaging, he dropped to the floor to pump out some exercises, made a good meal, and thought about creating some kind of diversion that would keep the Iranians busy looking the other way when he went to fetch the Pathfinders at 0300. He found the keys that Omar had left and made a quick trip down to the garage to check out the new set of wheels, a like-new Toyota 4Runner Trail with automatic transmission, four-wheel drive, and a powerful V-6 engine that ordinarily was used to run tourists out to distant attractions in the desert. The back windows were tinted, which made it perfect for hauling in the Pathfinders tomorrow morning. Satisfied, Swanson went back upstairs.

Knowing he would probably get no more sleep for a while, he planned to take another nap while he could, and the idea came to him while he dozed, forcing him awake with a start. The Iranians had to be tight on ammunition, having only what they carried on their persons and in the aircraft that brought them and whatever was being unloaded among the beans and tents and other gear back on the beach. They could be leaning on the locals for food and some supplies, but each bullet might become worth its weight in gold until this advance force was relieved by some other force. The weakness was their inability to resupply. If he could somehow damage the supply line, they would have trouble.

He went to the telescope and examined the airport again until he found that stack of crates that had to be the ammo dump, then studied the scene and drew a detailed map. Swanson stepped back, drank some water, and thought, *I want that!* Pleased to finally have found another goal, he ransacked the closets. The problem of sneaking up on the airport stash crossed his mind only in terms of the possible tactical approaches. He never doubted success, particularly when he had a cushion of several hours to assemble a homemade ghillie suit that would help him vanish during the approach.

He assembled his camouflage suit out of the darkest cloth he could find, cutting it apart and then using a sewing kit from the bedroom table drawer to stitch it back together in the rough shape of his body. Dirt from some potted plants in the safe house helped ugly it up, as did splotches of black paint and ripped rags. Finally, he tried it on before the full-length mirror and saw something that appeared misshapen from head to foot, more like a couple of mounds than a human form. It was lacerated with tears at frequent intervals, into which he would insert vegetation from the immediate area of the stalk once he was on scene. A pillowcase became a camouflaged bag that he would drag along behind him.

As the sun began going down, Swanson lugged his gear down to the 4Runner and joined the evening traffic through the outskirts of the city. As opposed to the earlier complacent freedom he had seen, there now seemed to be some tension in the town. Groups of people were talking and gesturing on the corners, arguing in public, and the few soldiers that he saw were grim instead of being placid. Perhaps everyone was settling into the idea that Sharm el-Sheikh was no longer a good place to be, that the Iranians were here to stay, but he wondered if something had happened that he did not know about. The problem with being cut off from Omar and Tianha was that he could not keep up on the local gossip. No matter; that could wait.

A good place to stash the Toyota opened up when he found a small market that had closed early. The lights were out, latticed steel bars were padlocked on the windows and doors, and the small parking apron was shielded from view by an adjacent industrial building. He pulled into the most distant parking spot, got his gear, locked the Toyota, and began to walk casually toward the southern end of the airport. He looked back down Hotel Row, where many of the usual lights had not been turned on tonight. Darkness slammed down. Perfect.

By eight o'clock, Swanson was only a mile away from his target, unseen in the night with his face blackened with soot, his ghillie filled with thistles and brush, and his drag bag tied to his ankle. The painfully slow stalk was going surprisingly smoothly, although he did not rush things; the closer he got, the slower he went, until he was moving even slower than the gentle breeze coming across the water. Time did not matter as he progressed an inch at a time in a belly-scraping low crawl, down with the worms and the beetles.

THE PARK

The examples, for Major Shakuri preferred to think of
the six Egyptians who were about to die as *examples*
and not real people, had not been brutalized when they
were arrested. They were neither clubbed nor kicked
but were treated almost as if they were invited guests
of the Iranian military. Shakuri, after all, was not a bar-
barian. The prisoners had been told what was going to
happen, and why; then they were allowed private time
with their families and a period of solitude with the
comfort of reading the Koran. Food and drink were
made available, but most barely touched it.

At exactly eight thirty in the evening, Shakuri's
driver parked the commander's Rolls-Royce alongside
the main entrance to a five-acre circular park in the
middle of the city, a peaceful oasis of green grass and
trees that was tended carefully all year because it was
a favorite place for residents and tourists to stroll, for
lovers to rendezvous, and for children to play. Clean
sidewalks edged the circumference of the park, and
two wide lanes flanked with benches crisscrossed the
circle, meeting in the middle at a large fountain that
splashed geysers of water. Decorative blue tiles lay in
patterns beneath the ripples. Very nice, the major
thought.

When he lifted his eyes, the image was jarred by a
wall of sandbags that sprawled with menace beside the
southern walkway to the fountain, awful tiers that measured seven feet high and twenty feet in length. Lined
directly before the sandbag barricade were six thick

posts that stuck out of the grass at three-foot intervals. This would be the killing ground, and it would be left in place to remind the Egyptians not to assist enemies of the Iranians. The major was puzzled that only a small crowd had gathered. Maybe a hundred people, not much more than the families of the prisoners. He had thought there would be more.

The troops that had erected the wall and the posts had returned to the airport, for the duty that came next could be trusted only to hand-chosen soldiers who would not flinch from an unpleasant task. The firing squad of ten strong young men was at parade rest, wearing green-patterned camouflage uniforms with white scarves tucked around their necks, green berets, and white gloves on their hands. AK-47 assault rifles with curved magazines that were loaded with thirty rounds each hung from their right shoulders. Major Shakuri was saluted by the captain in charge, then did a quick review of the smart-looking troops, their neat garb reflecting both the solemnity of the occasion and respect for the men they were about to kill.

When Shakuri took his place to one side, ten paces behind the soldiers, the captain ordered the captives brought forward, and the six prisoners emerged under guard from a pastel-colored building on the east side of the park. Their hands were cuffed behind their backs, and they wore clean clothes. Five watched the ground, while the sixth held his head erect, staring with anger at the Iranians, and when his gaze swept to Major Shakuri, it locked there in challenge. Shakuri recognized him as the mayor of Sharm el-Sheikh, who had argued with him against the reprisals only to be added to the list. He was a popular local figure, the owner of a marina, and Shakuri knew that putting the mayor before the guns would definitely send the message that the Iranians were not to be attacked.

Each man was placed in front of a post and tied tightly; then black cloth hoods were placed over their heads. Shakuri had held the strange man's stare and had felt the heat of those dark, accusing eyes. He heard low voices muttering prayers. Some women wept.

"Attention!" roared the captain, and the firing squad soldiers assumed their proper stances and brought up the AKs, jamming the wooden stocks into their shoulders. "Prepare to fire!"

Shakuri forced himself to remain immobile, rooting himself to the spot, but felt his entire body tighten as if he were one of those unfortunates tied to the posts. His face betrayed nothing, but his heartbeat increased to an irregular, hard thump in his chest, and the arithmetic of the moment came to mind: Ten automatic rifles with thirty rounds apiece equaled three hundred rounds to expend on six men. Fifty bullets each and please, Allah, let that be enough. *Inshallah.* God's will.

"Fire!" shouted the captain, and the ten triggers were pulled simultaneously, unleashing a storm of bullets at the helpless targets, raking up and down the line and hitting each man again and again. A layer of smoke flattened in the space between the firing squad and the condemned men, and Major Shakuri noted the bright orange flashes that spat from the multiple muzzles. Once the shooting started, it did not stop until the magazines were empty. Most of the defenseless victims surged forward upon the impact of the first strikes, then twisted or slumped toward the ground, still hanging from their posts. The bodies were ravaged by the continuous fire until there were no more bullets, and the captain said, "Cease fire." The soldiers dropped their weapons across their chests and came to attention, their faces blank.

There was no moaning and not a twitch of life from the destroyed bodies, and Shakuri's hearing came back to the sound of wailing from wives and children and other family members of the deceased. The captain saluted, and he returned it, then made the long walk back to his waiting limousine, struggling to hold himself together. During the trip back to his headquarters, he remained haunted by the flood of blood that had spouted from deep, gouging wounds and the fragments of brain and oozing trails of intestines and torn flesh that had been flung against the sandbags and covered the ground around the men. Most of all, he remembered the calm, furious stare of that one brave condemned man, the mayor, who would not be intimidated and cowed and bent to the will of the Iranians just because someone put a gun to his head.

The major took a few minutes to go to up to his suite, and when he looked in the bathroom mirror, he saw that his face was bright red. His stomach twisted, and he made it to the toilet just in time to vomit up his dinner, going to his knees in pain. He thought he might be having a heart attack, and he lay on the cool tiles until his breathing slowed while the visions of the execution continued to flash through his mind. *I had to do it! There was no choice!*

CHAPTER 22

THE AIRPORT

Swanson had frozen in place, nose to the ground, when he heard the long burst of automatic weapons fire in the distance. AK-47s were buzzing in a sustained staccato of fire, but it was far behind him, somewhere back in the city. He glanced at his watch: nine o'clock. Plenty of time.

Slowly, he surveyed the area around him again and saw nothing had changed. A static guard position forty yards away still remained quiet, with one soldier sitting on a lip of sandbags, a rifle across his knees, and talking down to his partner in the hole. The Iranians had not yet even thrown coils of barbed wire around the ammo dump, depending for security on the human eyes of men with guns, who generally saw only what they expected to see.

By ten o'clock, he was within a quarter mile of the small mountains of cases and crates, which were showered with bright lights. To Kyle, that also meant the reverse—those same glaring lights created helpful corridors of darkness between the stacks. He paused and checked his surroundings once again. The static guard post was now behind him, and a single roving soldier was on duty around the dump. Swanson had timed the man passing the same point every ten minutes. That opened a huge window of time.

Their training was working against them. The commandos were honed to be frontline fighters and were not accustomed to the rear-echelon garrison duty that had been thrust upon them; it was demeaning, and they were not good at it. When the rover guard passed the next time, Kyle eased his right leg forward and untied the drag bag, then slowly and softly assembled the M-16A3, putting in a fresh magazine. The faint clicks of the metal against metal sounded like thunderclaps to him but were unheard by anyone else. He waited another ten minutes for the guard to pass again before moving to his final position.

It was a little after eleven when the guard went by on his usual route, watching the ground as if studying his own footsteps, and ducking his eyes from the bright lights that blazed from portable wheeled stands all around. Kyle grinned: *He's blind as a bat!*

Swanson had maneuvered to a spot where the illumination changed sharply into shadow, and slowly rose up beside a row of tall telephone poles, letting them mask his bulk. Five yards away was the deep valley of crates and containers, and he crossed it with three easy strides that would not draw a curious eye. Then, once in the wider cavern of shadow, he ventured deeper into the complex, his path determined by the patches of dark, until he was fully surrounded by the peaks of the containers loaded with explosives, bullets, grenades, and shells. No guards patrolled the interior area.

He took his time to plant bricks of C-4 at various points, picking out containers that he thought would cause the most damage. He was not after a hit-or-miss fire-and-light show but wanted to create a volcanic bonfire that would be almost impossible to extinguish. Then, when the rocket-propelled grenades exploded, they would fly all over the place, igniting even more explosions. Cases of hand grenades would pulverize whatever was around. Fifty-caliber bullets would cook off hot and punch through other cases, and the entire thing would sizzle and boom for hours. Knowing the Pathfinders would be bringing in more ammunition of all kinds, Kyle decided to expend all of his C-4 but for a single brick to be kept back for an emergency. The det cord was strung, and the timers were all set for 0230.

It was almost midnight when he left the place as quietly as he had entered, moving faster once he got past the guard post. He wished he could have taken those guards out, but their bodies would have called attention to the fact that somebody had been in the area. Anyway, those two would have enough to worry about in a just little while.

At the edge of the final field, he stripped away the ghillie, broke down the rifle again, put it all in the drag bag, and, once again in his baggy Egyptian clothes, walked back to the waiting 4Runner. It was time to go pick up his people.

ABOARD THE USS *JOHN F. KENNEDY*
THE RED SEA

Tech Sergeant Bubba Talbot suppressed a smirk as he cocked the unique scarlet beret that identified him as an Air Force Combat Controller to just the right angle so the wind across the flight deck would not sweep it off his head; he was the man tonight. Four of the deadliest men on the planet walked with him to the Black Hawk helicopter that was sitting in the busy gloom aboard the giant aircraft: a two-man SEAL sniper team, a Marine Recon explosives expert, and some weird-looking dead-eyes dude with a big gun from the Christians in Action, better known as the CIA. All were sneak-and-peek gunslingers, and their job was to protect Talbot, the Combat Controller. The five experts had been chopped without explanation for temporary duty with something called Task Force Trident, assembled at Fort Bragg on the double, then flown across the Atlantic, and finally boarded the COD for the final leg to the carrier.

Talbot, the burly Air Force Combat Controller, had spent more than a year going through rigorous training on everything from advanced communications to parachuting out of airplanes to swimming underwater before being allowed near a battle zone. Four years later, he was one of the best in the business, a combat veteran, a dead shot with rifle and pistol, physically superior, fearless, and a respected brother within the tight special operations community. He had been at home watching television when he got the call to drop everything and get his ass over to Bragg.

For Bubba did something special, something none of the others could do, which was the purpose of tonight's mission. In exactly one hour, at 0300, the Black Hawk would deliver them to a designated spot on a beach in Egypt, they would slide down thick ropes while the loadmaster simultaneously lowered extra gear, and the helo would turn and return to the carrier. Waiting on the ground as their guide would be a Marine who had been caught behind the lines when the Iranian attack had hit. Must have been on a diving vacation, Talbot thought. Wrong place at the right time.

Once proper security was established, the show belonged to Bubba, the man who could talk to the sky and make amazing things happen. With his specialized comm gear, he would organize and bring in the main assault when it happened—everything from guiding helicopters toting giant fuel bladders for building a temporary forward airstrip to calling bomber strikes on targets and targeting the thundering offshore naval gunfire. *The Iranoids have no idea how much shit I can bring,* thought Talbot. He had no pity for his future enemies.

The Black Hawk noisily spooled up its engines, the loadmasters finished strapping everything down, and the five men of the Pathfinder team settled in for what was going to be a long ride over a lot of water because the fleet was so far away from the target area. They were patient men who were used to such intervals, knowing that by daybreak the insertion would be complete.

Bubba ran through his mental checklists and stared at his radios that had been lashed down nearby. He would not put on that heavy pack until they were only a few minutes out from the target. Only then would he replace his beret with a helmet. *OK, here comes Bubba and his boys.* Finally, he settled back, closed his eyes, and jacked up the volume on his iPod to let Johnny Cash wail the "Folsom Prison Blues."

The Black Hawk lifted away from the lighted deck, banked to starboard to reach clear space, and was soon swallowed by the darkness.

HOTEL ROW

It took thirty minutes of lying prone on the bathroom floor, a time during which Major Shakuri dared not summon his aide or call for help out of fear of starting a rumor that he was a coward. He would rather be dead than disgraced. Eventually, the nerves settled and the heartbeat slowed. Convinced that he was still alive, he struggled to his feet and took a long, soapy shower to wash away the imaginary blood that seemed to cling to him like a coating of accusation. The major smeared on cologne and brushed his teeth and put on a fresh uniform. Back to work.

His spirits rose sharply about midnight, when his intelligence officer arrived with good news that helped push away the memories. One of the objects of the manhunt that had been ordered by Colonel Naqdi, the mysterious archaeologist from Great Britain, Dr. Tianha Bialy, was back on the scene, not in hiding after all but checking into the elegant Four Seasons Hotel, and under her own name. Shakuri would go see her first thing tomorrow, and that would certainly please the colonel.

So, progress was being made, despite the bloody business in the park, and he was able to enjoy a late-night salad and fish dinner that was sent up from the hotel kitchen. He finished his paperwork at two o'clock in the morning, by which time his feelings of guilt were solidly back under control, so the major retired to his suite and took another quick shower before crawling, exhausted, between the clean sheets. He immediately fell asleep.

At two thirty, detonator timers simultaneously registered 00:00 and triggered the chain of explosions throughout the Iranian ammunition dump at the airport. Brilliant and silent flashes rent the darkness as fast as an eye-blink, followed immediately thereafter by earth-jarring *thumps* that seemed like the old gods of Egypt were angrily stomping the planet, and a heartbeat later came the first thundering crashes that stopped time. A false sun began to coagulate above the Sharm airport.

Kyle Swanson heard it begin from miles away, as he waited for the Pathfinders beside the shoreline in the north. The sky colored with pulses of gold and yellow and red as the ammo cooked off with wild abandon, each exploding crate feeding the ignition of its neighboring containers. Rockets began to zip out of the inferno only to fall back and explode elsewhere and start other fires.

The big hangar adjacent to the stockpile of ammo was crushed by the pressure; the roof fell in, and the big Boeing transport airplane inside was blown to pieces, along with the mechanics working on it. Deadly shrapnel scythed through the air, and the wild fire churned into a concentrated inferno within the first minute, oozing a giant mushroom cloud into the night. By the time the alert sirens started screaming, they were useless. No one needed to be told that something huge was happening.

Major Mansoor Shakuri was thrown off of his bed by the harsh detonations that shook the hotel like an earthquake. An instant later, one of the big windows in his bedroom crashed inward, and a shower of glass splinters lanced across the mattress where he had been resting a moment before. His head was woozy and his ears were battered, a staccato of major explosions as he scuttled into the dark bathroom and curled up in the tub, knees to his forehead and hands over his head.

A similar experience rocked Tianha Bialy awake at the Four Seasons Hotel, but her reaction was far different. She rolled onto the floor beside the bed, reached up to the night table, and grabbed her cell phone as it chirped. Omar was calling from the rooftop plaza and reported that the ammo dump was blowing sky high.

"There's no danger to us here at the hotel, but all hell's going on at the airport. Come on up and watch the show," he said. "Nobody's getting any more sleep tonight."

A peculiar-looking airplane known as an E-2C Hawkeye had been carving a long oval high in the sky far in front of the USS *Kennedy* for three hours, with its advanced electronics suite sweeping the sky and ocean alike, simultaneously monitoring a multitude of tasks. The Hawkeye's crew and computers were out there to detect any long-range threats to the carrier, which was a vital mission since Iran possessed both ground-to-ship missiles and submarines. Among its other duties was to monitor the flight of the stealth Black Hawk helicopter of the Pathfinders and act as a communications relay point for the ship.

Technicians had detected a new heat bloom at the Sharm airport, which also had shown up on satellites and was being tagged for further investigation. That did not skew the total attention of a crewman tracking the inbound Black Hawk, which carried a transponder that automatically registered its position on a radar screen. Suddenly, he blinked, then fidgeted forward in his seat as much as the seat belt would allow. The blip was gone! He did an automatic reset, and the screen did an instant reactivation, but there was nothing there.

"Charlie Brown, Charlie Brown," he spoke into his headset, calling the aircraft carrier's Combat Information Center, keeping his voice neutral. "This is Snoopy Two."

"Copy, Snoopy Two. Send your traffic."

"We have lost track of Red Box. Repeat, we have lost all signal from Red Box."

"Hold one." The tech in the carrier CIC checked his own screen, which confirmed what the tech in the plane was seeing. "Same on my screen, Snoopy Two. No signal from Red Box. Alter course for a closer look."

"Roger that."

The Pathfinder helicopter had disappeared. The CIC launched helicopters to the last known location and to vector any allied warships into the area. A covert insertion had changed in an instant into a massive search-and-rescue effort.

Going through the checklist, a Navy lieutenant dialed a number that activated the portable satellite telephone that was on the ground beside Kyle Swanson at the rendezvous site. After some buzzing interference while the connection was made and the proper code words given, the lieutenant said, "Bounty Hunter, be advised that the mission is off."

"Say again your last, Charlie Brown." Swanson looked up into the night out over the sea. No sign of any Black Hawk. The voice from the carrier confirmed the notification that the mission was now inoperative. Kyle thought the choice of words was interesting; the guy had not said it was "aborted" or "ordered terminated," just that it was "off," which left Swanson with no idea of what had happened to the Pathfinders and their helicopter.

That did not matter. He immediately moved out, stacking his gear in the 4Runner and hitting the road, back toward where the sky was absolutely glowing with deathly colors and thunder rumbled. Whatever happened with the chopper was no longer his business, because he knew all too well that unexplained shit happens in war. Plans can fail in a moment, and a new plan has to be implemented.

Meanwhile, the ammo dump was back there exploding like the biggest Fourth of July celebration he had ever seen, and that was just too damned good a diversion to pass up. He could still make something happen.

CAIRO

Colonel Yahya Ali Naqdi of the Army of the Guardians was sitting on the side of his bed in Cairo, taking deep breaths to control the emotions churning within him. It had been a rather pleasant night at the end of a work-filled day, and he had left work behind at five o'clock so as to have a very private dinner with a beautiful yellow-haired young Swedish woman who was hired because of her skills at pleasing rich men. It went on for hours. Their lovemaking had reached a fever pitch, and afterward she departed quietly with a full purse and left behind another satisfied customer. Naqdi had immediately fallen asleep.

The private military telephone beside his bed blinked a red light and purred softly, just enough to alert the occupant that he was being summoned. It took a few moments for Naqdi to unsnarl himself from the tangled sheets and deep sleep before he answered, and the operator, an enlisted man, politely said, "Colonel. You have an urgent call from General Khasrodad in Sharm el-Sheikh. He insisted that I connect him without delay."

Khasrodad? Why is Khasrodad calling me directly? General Khasrodad normally was the commander of Iran's airborne division and had been temporarily assigned to lead the commando forces down in the peninsula. Naqdi considered him competent and loyal. The general, however, answered up the military chain of command, and he was under orders that Naqdi was in overall command of the Egyptian invastion and that Major Shakuri was on site down there and should be handling whatever this was. The colonel took a drink of water from a bedside bottle. "Put him on. Don't listen in."

"Yes, of course, sir." The operator made the connection with a clicking sound.

"Has Shakuri called you?" The gritty voice of Khasrodad jarred the colonel. He was clearly furious about something.

"No. Why?" He looked at the small clock on the dresser. Four o'clock.

"Let me report, then." The voice was almost a venomous hiss. "I'm sure you're aware of his reprisals against the civilian population last night, but listen to this . . ."

Reprisals? He had heard nothing about any reprisals. The colonel was now wide awake, then stood up as the sound of explosions came through the receiver. "I have been out of contact this evening. What is happening, General?"

"Our main ammunition dump at the airport has been attacked by unknown forces and is in flames. It is so wild right now that we cannot get near it, much less contain the damage, which is going to be substantial. The cause is unknown, so I can't say whether it is sabotage or a military assault. I've taken steps to draw in our perimeter around the airport for better protection."

"Isn't Shakuri out there? Let me speak to him."

"That's the reason I'm talking to you directly, Naqdi. Your man Shakuri is not answering his telephone. I've dispatched an officer over to his headquarters to find him."

There was a pause. "Thank you for alerting me, General. I will come down to Sharm in person as soon as I can." Now for the delicate part. "Have you notified your superiors in Tehran?"

The general's tone eased. "Not yet, both as a favor to you, my old friend, and because I do not have enough specifics. I do not think your man Shakuri is up to this job."

"You have my gratitude, Medhi." It was a huge favor from an old friend, and a costly debt that would have to be repaid at some later date. "Now, let me ask you plainly. What is the overall situation in the area? Is this serious?"

"The ammo dump will be a hard blow to us, but it is not fatal. We can make do until we get some resupply and the Brotherhood reaches us, although we will have to be even more cautious. I hope those Brotherhood people get here fast. The reprisals in the city are a problem. In my opinion, those have put Sharm on the brink of switching sides, and the ammo dump blowing up shows weakness on our part. Serious mistake, Colonel. Very serious."

Naqdi sat back down, telephone to his ear, elbows on his knees, eyes closed. "For some reason, the major has neglected to inform me of any reprisals. Tell me what happened. From the start, old friend."

CHAPTER 23

For Kyle Swanson, it was now open season on Iranian soldiers anywhere he found them. So far, the big guns of the military forces of the United States and its powerful allies remained muzzled, and the diplomats were slogging along doing whatever it was that diplomats did. His MI6 partner was off doggedly pursuing her own agenda and of little help to him, and unfortunately she had taken along Omar, who would not leave her. Ah, fuck it. He drove on rapidly, watching the fire in the distance. The massive round of initial explosions had quieted, but there were new ones cooking off sporadically, still jarring and strong, and flames rolled across the airport, which meant firefighting was at a minimum. He believed that all the Iranians could do was form a tighter perimeter, try to extinguish the smaller fires, and let the big one cook unchecked until the things stopped popping.

A new plan was forming in his mind as he drove, pushing away the absence of the Pathfinders, for there was nothing he could do about that anyway. For the present, momentum and darkness and surprise were still on his side, and he wanted to strike again, to lay on even more pressure to knock the Iranians further off stride.

He pulled to the side of the road, shut down the Toyota, and used his small flashlight to study the crude map that Omar and Tianha had made for him showing Iranian strongpoints, tracing a finger across the northeastern edge of the city to a place they had labeled MOTOR POOL. An old saying, Napoleon or Frederick the Great or somebody, proclaimed that an army marches on its stomach, but modern armies didn't march much at all. Wheels, Kyle thought, remembering the hodgepodge convoy that had transported the first wave of invaders from the beach to the airport. He suspected that the Iranians did not bring any trucks with them on the airliners; it would have been a waste of space. A few small armored vehicles probably came in, but not plain vanilla trucks. Omar said they had officers all over town yesterday buying a small fleet of large-capacity vehicles from the locals. Those were all driven to a large garage that was being outfitted as a maintenance and fueling center for the military force.

His mind made up, he folded the map, cranked the SUV, and headed south along Al-Sheikh Zayed, splitting between the tranquil big hotels on his left and the burning airport ammo dump on his right.

A mile later, buildings became more numerous in a

light industrial area, and Swanson was able to use less-traveled roads, dodging into lanes and nooks when he saw oncoming headlights. Steadily, he wound toward the big garage that hulked on one of the wider streets. An apron of light in the big parking area of sand and gravel was almost as good as a WELCOME sign. A number of buses and trucks were parked in the yard, side by side with military precision, while the noise of power tools and voices came from the open bay doors. Mechanics were at work inside. A single soldier lazily walked the yard with his rifle across his chest, guarding the wide front gate in a weather-scarred chain-link fence and watching the ammo dump go up at the airport. Several workers were taking a break in the yard, with their attention also glued to the dazzling show on the horizon, and one man in a stained mechanic's overalls was in the wide bay door, wiping his hands on a rag. Kyle drove around back, into the shadows.

No one was there, as if any threat were expected to politely walk up and announce itself to the guy with the gun in the lighted front. There was absolutely no sense of panic, despite the rolling thunder from the airport still occasionally vibrating the ground and the buildings. The surprise of the initial blasts and shocks was over, and people with work to do were losing interest. He maneuvered the 4Runner until the mirror on the passenger door brushed the fence, and he left the motor running, got out and climbed atop of the SUV, then spider-dropped over the barrier. Moving in a crouch, he reached the first of three sets of fuel pumps and planted his last brick of C-4, with the timer set for thirty minutes. Since fences surrounding businesses are designed to keep people out, not in, Swanson found a wooden loading pallet leaning against the wire, stepped on it, grabbed the top rail, and pulled up, over, and out. He checked his watch and drove away. Total elapsed time inside, less than three minutes.

The 4Runner had been tricked out by Omar to provide tourists with comfort, but nothing had been given away that would make it any less reliable off-road, for some intrepid prima-donna adventure seekers would insist on heading out where no man or woman had ever been before, as if every square inch of Egypt had not been explored over the past few thousand years. Swanson engaged the rugged four-wheel drive and peeled away from the paved road and into the dirt, lights off and steering by the cold January moon. Mercury and Mars nearby hung like bright ornaments.

Ten minutes later, a halo glowed at a new checkpoint that had been established on the main highway, maybe a mile away. Slowing, he closed the gap to what he guessed was a half mile, beyond the reach of the light bubble, then stopped and switched off the engine so the exhaust vapors would not curl up like a smoke signal. Swanson dug out and assembled the rifle and put the laser range finder on the target. Just under half a mile: 2,640 feet or 880 yards. He could make that shot but wanted to be absolutely certain, which meant closer observation, so he walked forward carefully, letting his toe feel the way before planting his heel and shifting the weight. When he was almost on the edge of the lights, he went to his stomach and crawled until he found a small depression at the base of a sad old palm tree that would provide cover and concealment.

He settled in against the rock-strewn sand, brought up the stock of the rifle, and allowed the Leupold 10-power scope to carry him right inside the Iranian outpost. The laser range finder snapped the number right at six hundred yards. Just like at the motor pool, these guys still didn't get it, even with the ammo dump still thudding like a jackhammer; they did not understand the danger zone they were in, because they were elite fighters and everyone was supposed to be afraid of them. One rifleman was on the road to wave down oncoming traffic, a second was ten yards behind him, and a third, apparently the noncom in charge, was standing beside a Jeep to make sure the others did what they were told. A .50 caliber machine gun was mounted on the Jeep, but it was unmanned, apparently there to show passing motorists the soldiers meant business. These guys were asking to die, standing there with their dicks in the wind staring stupidly down a corridor of dark road, talking loudly, even laughing, and pointing out particularly impressive fireworks over the airport. According to his watch, there were two minutes left before the motor pool provided still another light show.

Swanson's fingers ran a final check of his weapon, a familiar task that was built into his brain. Then he slowed his breathing and ticked off the seconds in his head as he waited for the C-4 to blow. It did, and he went to work. His first shot took out the sergeant by the Jeep to keep him from getting the big gun going. By the time the middle man turned toward the motor pool explosion, Kyle's semiautomatic rifle had cycled in a new round, and he moved the scope just a hair, then pulled the trigger again. The man's arms flew wide, his AK-47 spun away in slow motion, and his knees buckled. The bullet tore through his chest.

The third soldier, the guy out front in the road, had reacted to the close gunshots but was running back toward the Jeep instead of into the darkness, or at least falling flat or charging toward the shooter. Kyle slid the rifle back to the original aiming point, and the guy ran right into the scope and caught a bullet through the spinal cord. Three shots, three dead targets, less than three seconds.

Swanson was up instantly, jogging back to the waiting 4Runner, breathing steadily and not looking back. The work at the outpost was done, and he still had more mail to deliver.

He went out into the desert, where there were fewer roads, and angled away from the main highway before looping around wide to the east to avoid the communities that were out that far. He parked again and used his cell phone to contact Bialy, who answered on the second buzz. "Are you and Omar in the Blue Neptune now?" he asked.

"Yes. We're good. Where are you?"

"Out shopping. Anything happening that I should know about?"

She almost laughed. "I should be asking that question, Swanson. We keep hearing these explosions, and the Iranians are running all around. Did you hear about the firing squad?"

"No." His blood chilled. They were executing civilians because of his actions. "Anyone significant among the victims?"

"The mayor of Sharm," she replied, reading the list of names. "Mohammed El-Din. The people aren't going to accept that one very easily."

"Who was he? Anything might help."

"The head of a prosperous local family. Omar says he has been mayor for many years and was well liked. Owned a good-sized business called the Gold Sun Water Equipment marina, which served the big hotels. The other victims seemed to be just a cross-section of citizens. El-Din was the example the Iranians wanted."

Kyle paused and thought for a moment. Most of civilization clung to the water, and the people of Sharm were no different, for water brought trade and money and success. He realized that he might have found the next step in his night's work. The Gold Sun should have what he needed, and it most likely would be closed because the grieving family of the mayor, who ran it, would be huddled together at their home. "OK. You guys stay safe."

"Kyle?" Tianha said, but he was gone.

Heading south again, he checked his position on the Toyota's global positioning system and found a small track that led to the back road to the Gold Sun Water Equipment marina. The tourism trade of Sharm depended on watercraft, for this was a world-famous diving spot, but even divers needed a break from the reefs and caves and coral, and they rented everything from sailboats to windsurfer boards and played around the beaches when not lying around the hotel pools. All of that had collapsed, and now the storehouses of the fun toys stood empty and locked. Just outside the city, he entered a wide rectangular area in which a central road was flanked by storehouses. Upturned kayaks lay stacked alongside like pancakes. A few palm trees loitered around the buildings, beyond the reach of the sprinkler systems of the hotel grounds.

He parked one street over and made a careful circuit of the area on foot, checking the rear of the buildings, the rooftops, the windows, the yards, other parked vehicles, anywhere that danger might hide. He saw no inside lights, although a few bulbs glowed feebly above some front doors. The place was deserted. He went back to the 4Runner and took it almost to the water's edge, parking behind a battered white pickup that bore the words GOLD SUN WATER EQUIPMENT in English.

The building extended out over the water, and a blunt pier outside extended inside, too, so watercraft could be sailed directly into the building. A metal roll-down gate sealed the opening. Kyle went to the glassed-in front, where the rental office could be seen. Colorful posters of underwater scenes hung behind a single desk and over a four-drawer filing cabinet. Two straight chairs were in front of the desk, with one cushy executive model behind it. Beside the front door, another passage led out to the waterside working area where all of the gear was stored. He kicked around at the decorative stone border until he found a heavy rock. In the middle of a night that was already filled with explosions and fires, nobody would even notice the shatter of the small glass window in the door. He threw it and was in.

The inner door opened into a wide space in which two concrete piers were separated by an open finger of water. Swanson switched on his flashlight and went directly to a rank of five jet skis that were cradled on lifts, and two more—a Yamaha and a Honda, both blue—were tied at the pier, ready to be taken out in the morning. He unscrewed the fuel caps and found that both had full gas tanks.

He went over to a broad piece of plywood that was used as a bench and table where wet suits were rented. Once again he was happy to be of average size, for he immediately found a full-length diver's suit, a face mask and snorkel, and a pair of swimming flippers.

He had constantly been alert for noises but had heard nothing except the lapping of the water, and he peeled off the sagging Egyptian clothes. As he began putting on the wet suit, there was a movement in the shadows, and a young man stepped out, pointing a pistol at him. Kyle stopped, with one foot in the suit, one out, then slowly raised his hands. "Don't shoot," he said in English. "I am a friend."

Merchants and businessmen throughout Egypt usually speak several languages, and he was betting this guy was one of those multilingual types who dealt with tourists from all over the world. Anyway, Kyle's knowledge of the Egyptian language sucked.

The young man stepped forward, but not too close. He was in his early twenties, wore an oil-stained T-shirt over baggy cargo shorts, and had a stubble of beard above penetrating eyes rimmed in red, as if he had been crying. The pistol remained steady. "You are an American?"

"Yes."

"The Americans are coming here?"

"Maybe. Who are you?"

The man walked to the left, not even looking down as he stepped through and around the gear, indicating that he knew where everything was. "Who are you?"

"I'm a tourist who was caught here by the attacks, and I am just trying to get out."

"So you were going to steal my jet ski?"

"Yes." A grain of truth helps the total lie. "Try to make my way to an American ship."

"You would never make it out alive through all the boats out there. You really are not an Iranian?"

In answer, hands still raised, Kyle spat into the water. To his surprise, the young man did the same and slowly lowered his weapon. "Those bastards executed my brother last night. Had you been Iranian, I would have killed you on the spot. You can lower your hands."

Whoa, thought Kyle. *This might be better than I expected.* "Your brother was Mayor Mohammad El-Din?"

"Yes." He said it with a grim face. "My name is Abdel El-Din. Now who are you, and why are you here?"

"First, I'm sorry about your brother, Abdel. I would have stopped it if I could."

Abdel pushed himself up to sit on the counter. A wall clock behind him showed the time to be just a minute or two after five o'clock in the morning. "Really? Just you?"

"My name is Kyle Swanson, and I am a United States Marine." Kyle nodded his head toward the outside, where explosions were still being heard. "I've been doing what I can."

"My brother was a good man, Mr. Swanson. We do not know why he was put among those people the Iranians decided to murder, for they were just picked up at random. He went to his death with his head held high, scornful of the executioners. My family made me hide out here to avoid also being picked up in some future sweep. I was asleep until I heard you break the glass out front."

"So I will tell you the truth, Abdel. I'm not really trying to escape. I've been fighting them on my own, but even my own government doesn't know I am here and what I'm doing. I really was here on a business trip, had a room at the Blue Neptune and everything. Now I just cannot let the Iranians take Sharm without a fight."

"I want to fight back, too." El-Din's face twisted with emotion. "Nobody asked those soldiers to come to our city."

"Fighting is dangerous work," Kyle said. "I'm trained to do this kind of thing. You aren't."

"Those Iranian pigs have come to our home and took my brother and shot him in cold blood. They are not wanted in the city. A lot of people feel just as I do. We were stunned by the suddenness of it all, but now we are getting angry."

"Do you think there will be an uprising?" Kyle believed he was witnessing the first spark on a sputtering fuse of rebellion.

El-Din gave that rueful smile again. "Maybe. Only Allah knows the future. I only know that I must do something to avenge my brother." He paused, took a breath. "So let me help you. You want a jet ski, I'll let you have it. And I know these waters well and can be of help out in the channels."

While he thought, Kyle finished wiggling into the wet suit. Another local asset in addition to Omar would be a definite advantage, and this job would be a good test to determine if the kid had any guts or if it was just bravado coming from grief doing the talking. Zipped up, Swanson said, "OK. You're on, Abdel. Here's what we're going to do."

CHAPTER 24

Abdel El-Din listened wide-eyed to the audacious idea, then immediately proved his merit by turning on all of the lights in the boathouse. Should anyone stop by to question why, he could say he was simply getting ready for tomorrow's business. In minutes, he was suited up like Swanson.

"We have to tow these things around frequently, so hooking them together is no problem," he explained. Tie-off rings were installed fore and aft, and Abdel pulled down a twelve-pound coil of steel links sheathed in tough plastic, with snaps welded to the ends. It took only a moment to hook the Honda so it would trail behind the Yamaha.

A small roll of duct tape was on a worktable, and he pocketed it, then walked to the big roll-up door and hit the red button to open it. The clanking of chains retracting on the pulleys sounded like a warning siren as the door was ratcheted back, and before it was fully open, Abdel already had mounted the lead jet ski and was puttering to the fuel station at the end of the pier. The second machine slid along behind, with Kyle in the saddle, thinking how having Abdel as an ally had already saved him a lot of work.

They tied off at the gas pump. El-Din opened the lock with his keys, and the two of them filled a group of red plastic five-gallon containers and lashed them all with loops of duct tape along the sides, front, and low back of the trailing jet ski. When the cans were secure, the men released the moorings and both skis drifted free. The Yamaha started with the first twist of the key, but Swanson made no attempt to start the Honda, for he was sitting in a giant improvised explosive device, and any spark could be spectacularly fatal. The lead ski hummed slowly to take up the slack in the chain, and Abdel sidled them out into the calm waters of Naama Bay, burbling along at a minimum speed, about three hundred yards from the beach.

Around the harbor, red and green navigation lights pierced the darkness. Swanson wryly noted the absence of the usual huge sleek yachts; the monied people who could leave had already left. Farther inland, the sky was still being chewed by the bonfire at the motor pool and the unrelenting flames at the ammo dump. That reflected brightness, plus the running lights of the big ships, made it easy for Abdel to thread a familiar path out to deeper water, and he put on a little more speed.

Kyle was glad to get a bit of breeze across his face, for the cloud of gasoline fumes made breathing difficult.

The skis drove farther out into the harbor at a minimum pace, sliding over small swells, with Abdel ready to rack up the pace if they were discovered or challenged. About three miles from the beach sat the target, the brightest ship in the harbor, the Iranian freighter that had brought in the original waves of troops and had since been off-loading supplies onto a barge anchored alongside. Hired laborers and soldiers moved the material into smaller boats that hauled them to shore. The ship was alight from stem to stern, but only colored warning bulbs were at the corners of the transfer platform. About a half-dozen boats were tied to it, for work had been shut down for the night.

Abdel looked back to check on Kyle, and Swanson motioned with a hand to head out even deeper, then circle back and come in from the blind side. The young Egyptian understood. They motored on unseen.

Major Shakuri answered the telephone in his office at the disgusting hour of five o'clock in the morning with an impatient response but immediately settled into a respectful tone when he heard that it was Colonel Naqdi. He sighed to himself. This had been expected.

"I have received a rather interesting call from General Khasrodad at the airport," the colonel said. He was still on his bed in Cairo, pushing away frustration and anger. "The ammunition dump has been blown? Why didn't you alert me immediately?" The voice betrayed only curiosity, not anger.

"The general had the responsibility of guarding those

vital supplies, sir. He failed." Shakuri was at his desk and looking at his notes. It was depressing. "It seems that about twenty are dead out there as of right now. Maybe . . . probably . . . more. Another one of the big planes was destroyed."

"You did not think that I needed to be informed?"

Careful, Shakuri said to himself. *Unstable ground here.* "Of course not, sir. I did not call for several reasons. There was nothing you could do, and you need your sleep. Allah, praise be unto him, knows how much I need sleep, too, and you work harder and longer than I do. I was planning to call you after daybreak, when we will have more facts, and possibly even have captured the saboteurs."

"I know, Major. General Khasrodad is given to panic when under stress. As you say, he had several thousand top soldiers at his disposal and should have prevented that attack. Is it still going on?"

"Yes, sir. It's quite a show." The grumble of explosions could still be heard downtown.

Naqdi steered the subject away from the airport. "Then you are actively hunting saboteurs?"

"Correct, sir. I have been forced to implement stern measures and requisition some soldiers from the general, who is resisting giving me any. He wants to pull his protection perimeter in tighter, while I want active patrols in the streets."

"What was this firing squad the general told me about? Something else of which I had been unaware." The voice had switched back to cold. "It seems you are very busy with things of which I know nothing. Are you keeping things from me, Major Shakuri? Am I going to have to come down there?"

"If you wish to come, of course, Colonel, but there is really no need. After the initial problems—again, the general's soldiers—I had six examples, including the mayor, shot in the public square to discourage any public uprising. We must be firm with this population. As the Americans said, 'When you have them by the balls, their hearts and minds will follow.'"

The colonel stopped himself before laughing. Shakuri was really getting a grip on leadership. "I agree, but please be careful with reprisals, Major, for killing somebody's husband or cousin might breed enemies."

"Absolutely, sir. Already, obviously, the one-for-one idea will no longer work. With more than twenty of our soldiers already dead tonight, we would have to execute twenty more residents of Sharm. Will the unarmed people of Sharm be willing to make such an exchange?"

"You know the path around that." It was a declaration straight out of the occupation rules established in Tehran before the invasion. Mercy went only to a certain point; then the iron glove was needed.

"Yes, sir. We must ruthlessly kill more, enough to instill fear and suppress their opposition. After the twenty, I will increase the ratio to two of them for every one of us. Women and children will be included."

"Very well." There was a momentary stiff pause. "I'll probably be down later today to see how things are going after all, but you seem to be doing the job as well as possible."

The major felt the pleasure of the compliment override the lash of reprimand. *He was doing a good job.* "Thank you, sir. Your visit might be the best way to settle the nerves of our general out at the airport. Now let me give you some good news. I was saving it for the morning report, along with the other material, but you will like this. That British woman you wanted, Bialy, has been located. Should we wait until you arrive to pick her up?"

"A good point, Major. Go ahead and arrest her, so when I come down, she will be waiting for me. I will let you know my travel plan. Anything on the American, Kyle Swanson?"

"Not yet, sir, but we will get him. Can I ask what your interest is in them?"

"They are spies, major. CIA and MI6. I want to personally interrogate them both."

Shakuri decided to push a step further. "Our intelligence people report she has been asking about someone with the code name of Pharaoh. Can you tell me what that is about, sir?"

A deep pause while the colonel thought it over. Shakuri had done well so far, but he did not need to know this. The Pharaoh was a one-man show, the colonel's mask as a valuable counterintelligence source and his ticket to freedom. "That sounds like another enemy for us to track down, Major. Find Swanson, and if you uncover the Pharaoh, arrest him, too."

"Absolutely, sir."

"Good. So why don't we both get a few hours of sleep? Good night, Major."

"I can't sleep, sir. The night isn't over yet." The major

hung up, still chuckling, feeling that the razor had been removed from his throat. But Colonel Naqdi did not understand that his blade had two edges these days, for Shakuri knew all about the colonel's backdoor ruse as being the Pharaoh, and his contacts in London and within the Egyptian military. In his time as chief of staff, he had burrowed quietly into everything he could find in the colonel's private files and the office safe, and even had followed him to determine his contacts. He had enough to confirm, if the need ever arose, that the man was a traitor. The question was, who was using who? If Naqdi held a razor, Shakuri believed he held an ax.

He, aware of his growing independence and ability, had not told Naqdi about the attack on the motor pool, and now he had been handed this report that a Guards outpost was wiped out. This could not be the work of a few upset civilians, for the signature of upscale ferocity indicated military activity. He would call back in a few hours, hopefully interrupt the colonel's sleep again, and warn him that based upon the latest information, there was a strong possibility that NATO special operation teams had been inserted.

Five thirty in the morning, with the bleak winter dawn only an hour away. *Please, Allah, let the rest of the night remain quiet.*

The two jet skis were side by side, bobbing together some two hundred yards from the hulking mass of the Iranian freighter that separated them from the shoreline. Abdel was in the water, having unhooked the connecting chain and let it sink rather than chance having it make a sudden clatter if they tried to stow it in the compartment under the seat. He had other chains back at the shop.

Then his attention turned to Kyle's ski. Tourists had a bad habit of thinking they were extreme sports athletes when they got a jet ski between their legs, and going too fast and making sharp turns was dangerous in a crowded water sports environment. Head-on collisions were not uncommon. Therefore, marina operators usually rigged governors to the jet ski throttles to limit the speeds, and El-Din was putting one in place on the accelerator that Kyle would use. It was a plastic wedge screwed onto the handlebar to prevent the throttle from being squeezed all the way back in an overenthusiastic grip. When he tightened the bolt, he swam back to his Yamaha and climbed aboard.

"Are you ready?" he whispered.

"Have to crank it up sometime," Kyle responded. "Might as well be now." While Abdel had dealt with the chain and the throttle, Kyle had used duct tape to secure both ends of the handlebar to keep the ski pointed straight ahead. "You go ahead and drive out of danger range. If something goes wrong, get the hell out of here. If not, come and get me."

"Or whatever is left of you."

"I'll creep in to about thirty yards from the midsection, light the rags, then jack the throttle back all the way and tighten it in place with duct tape. I will roll into the water."

El-Din nodded in agreement. "I will be right behind you. Just grab on tight as I pass and hold on until we get clear of the target and the blast. After that, you climb aboard and we leave in a hurry. Right?"

"Right. Let's get this done."

Abdel cranked his jet ski with a minimum throttle and little noise and scooted into a wide circle without creating a disturbing wake. Swanson took a deep breath and turned the key on his Honda. The engine spun to life without igniting the extremely flammable cargo, allowing him to exhale. He pressed the throttle slowly and the little ski slid forward, as if being summoned by the big boat, which loomed larger in his sight by the second. A hundred yards away, he could see a few figures moving around on board, but no alarm had been sounded.

Seventy-five yards, and he forced himself to concentrate on delivering the package perfectly, not on getting off of the homemade bomb as quickly as he could. Sixty yards, and the ski remained perfectly positioned, its nose aimed directly at the metal hull looming in front of him. Kyle revved it up, pulled the throttle back to its maximum position, and held on tight as the ski almost stood on its tail. When the bow hit the water again, he looped a turn of duct tape around the accelerator to hold it in place.

Jump, you crazy fool, he thought as the ski lunged ahead like a Thoroughbred out of the gate. A cigarette lighter had been kept dry in the neck of his wet suit, and he thumbed it once with his left hand, then twice, and the little flame caught. He touched it to a gasoline-soaked cloth that snaked from the filled gas tank tied at the front, then to another rag that fed into the rear tank. Somewhat surprised that he was still alive, Kyle Swanson rolled easily off and smacked into the water, careful not to kick away hard, which might throw the jet ski off course.

In the old days of wooden ships, enemy fleets and blockades were often attacked by ships that had been sailed into them while burning fiercely, thus torching the sails, spars, and hull. Swanson popped to the surface just in time to see his own version of a fire ship crash into the Iranian freighter.

"Oh, my God. Not another one!" Dr. Tianha Bialy had been awakened for the third time in a single night by a monstrous explosion, this new one sounding like it was just outside her hotel window that opened out onto scenic Naama Bay. She had been dozing in her wrinkled clothes, and her hair felt wild, her eyes were blurry, and a foul taste was in her mouth.

She staggered to the window as sirens and alarms began sounding around the harbor, where a ship was in obvious great distress. It took her only a moment to realize that the new blaze was engulfing the Iranian ship that had been so placidly rocking at anchor all day long, unloading supplies. A wave of flame from the starboard side was marching hungrily along the deck, fingers of fire licking around the wheelhouse superstructure while boxes and crates on deck started to ignite. There was another crash as one container of mortar shells blew apart.

Grabbing her binoculars from the night table, she focused tightly on the ship. Crewmen were unreeling hoses, and spotlights came to life from other nearby ships to give the scene an awful glow. A tugboat was already approaching, looping a line of spray from a mid-deck water cannon. There was a pounding at the door behind her, and Omar came in with his own key to join her and watch the fiery disaster. Another explosion, more muffled, rumbled through the ship.

"That one was belowdecks," said Omar. "They have big trouble out there."

"So do you think there is a guerrilla force at work in Sharm? Maybe a special ops team from outside that we don't know about? I mean, all of these attacks tonight have been severe." A sudden sheet of flame spouted from an open deck hatch, and two men with fire chewing at their clothes dove overboard, screaming. Then there came another thud below the waterline, but no accompanying flame, just a ball of smoke.

"No. I think our dangerous friend Kyle has been working hard all night long. That last explosion may have put a hole in the hull."

Bialy sniffed. "Impossible. He's only one man, and these attacks have been all over the place. The airport *and* the ocean? What do you think I should report to London, Omar?"

As he watched, the topside fire crawled swiftly across the deck, obviously out of control. A harbor firefighting boat arrived and started arcing water uselessly into the inferno, but the men on board had withdrawn in the face of the heat and the implacable moving fire and the danger of being blown to pieces.

"Don't call them quite yet. Look. The ship is starting to list to starboard." As the right side of the hull edged lower, the left side rose, pulling with it the platform on which unloaded supplies were waiting, and those boxes started to topple. More men leaped overboard and were picked up by circling small boats.

The tilt continued as water rushed unchecked into the ripped hull and all of the volatile material burned hard and fast, heating enough to burn the paint throughout the interior. The crew had not had time to block all of the watertight compartments, and tons of rushing seawater flooded through the open ports. The ship was not only tilted but was also going down by the stern.

"It's going to sink right out there in the harbor, isn't it?" Tianha's voice was hushed.

"Yes, it is. The Iranians are not going to be happy. I think the time has come for us to leave, Tianha."

"I'll call London. Then we can go." The telephone on the polished bedside table rang.

CHAPTER 25

THE FOUR SEASONS

Hello?"

"Am I speaking with Dr. Tianha Bialy?" A man's voice, rather deep, his accented English crisp. She snapped her fingers to Omar, motioning for something to write on.

"Yes, it is. Who is this?"

"My name is Major Mansoor Shakuri, and I am commandant of the Iranian peacekeeping forces in Sharm el-Sheikh. A thousand pardons for telephoning at such a terrible hour."

Bialy turned and sat as Omar handed her a small tablet and a pen. "It is no problem at all, Major Shakuri. I doubt if many people in Sharm have gotten much sleep tonight. There has been so much going on." It was a little jab at having so much trouble with his command.

"It has been rather noisy," he admitted with a subdued chuckle, "which means I will be very busy today hunting terrorists to protect this beautiful city from further harm."

So you can execute more civilians, you bloody monster? Instead of asking that question, she said, "Why are you calling?"

"Perhaps we can help each other," he answered. "It has come to my attention that you are trying to contact an intelligence agent who goes by the name of the Pharaoh. I can help you with that."

"Do you know who it is?"

"In fact, Dr. Bialy, I do. And I'm willing to share that information with your British intelligence service. Everyone knows you are with MI6."

"And what do you want in return for this man's name? You said we could help each other."

"I want your friend Kyle Swanson, of the American CIA."

"Kyle Swanson is no friend of mine, Major. We had to work together on a financial project for a few days, but afterward, he immediately left for England."

The voice hardened. "He did not get on a plane before the airport was closed. Therefore, he is still around somewhere. I want to find him for a few questions."

"Then I'm sorry, Major. As I said, we were not friends, and I have not seen him since dinner before the hotel was attacked. He told me good-bye. I told him the same thing. I cannot tell you something I do not know."

"I am sorry, too. The Pharaoh will not be disclosed unless Swanson is available."

Tianha let the moment of silence extend. "Major, give me a bit of time. Let me talk to some locals and make a few discreet inquiries back in London."

He changed back to a command voice. "I will arrive at the Four Seasons Hotel at exactly ten o'clock this morning, Dr. Bialy. Whether our visit will be pleasant is entirely up to you. Don't think of trying to escape, because I have men watching for you. Is that clear?"

"Very clear, Major. Thank you for the courtesy of your call. I will see if we can work something out." She hung up, threw herself back onto the pillow, and rubbed her eyes with her palms. Her thoughts tumbled with images of explosions and treachery and an unknown future. One thing was clear: Her mission had always been to find the Pharaoh, and he was almost within her grasp. She explained the call to Omar, who lay beside her, keeping his pistol within reach on the table.

"He wants a straight swap," she said, explaining the call. "Exchange Swanson to the Iranians for the Pharaoh."

"Then the major believes he has you boxed in. If you don't give Kyle up, then you will be arrested and never find the Pharaoh. It could be your death warrant, so in his view, you have no choice," he said, nuzzling into her hair, and she reached out for him. They lay in silence for a while, thinking.

"Kyle's still at the safe house?" she asked.

"He should be, but who knows what the man is up to?"

"Then suppose I let the major take me prisoner and force me to cooperate? That would buy time for you to get over there and warn Swanson."

"That's much too dangerous for you, Tianha. Once he has you, Shakuri won't let you go. As an MI6 agent, you could be hauled off to Tehran for interrogation, then buried out in some Iranian desert. C would never approve, and I sure as hell don't want you committing suicide."

"I won't ask C," she said and gave him a soft kiss. "You, my dear, will let me do it because I want to and because I am ordering you to do so."

"No."

"Omar, the major is coming up here with armed security. You are a wonderful bodyguard, but the numbers and weaponry are on his side. I don't want to see you killed, either."

THE MARINA

Kyle Swanson clung to the waist of Abdel El-Din as the young Egyptian piloted the jet ski in a mad zigzag dash back for the safety of the Gold Sun Water Equipment warehouse, careering wildly around buoys and boats to eat up the distance, finally slowing near the marina, where they scooted inside just as the darkness was giving way to another winter morning's light. Kyle had kept looking back over his shoulder toward the ship, which had become a ferocious inferno within ten minutes. He had expected damage, but nothing like what was happening aboard that vessel; it had been filled with flammable material and was being gobbled by the fire.

Then they were back at the little pier, tied up, and

Abdel lowered the outer door. Both men sat on the waterside pier in silence for a few minutes, just catching their breath after the tension-filled past hour. The strain of the continuing action during the night had left Kyle drained of energy, and he thought about how far he had pushed his luck by breaking almost every rule in the book on clandestine warfare. With daylight coming, he could get back to the safe house, get some food, and take a break.

"I've got to go," he told his new accomplice. "You did great tonight, kid, and you sure as hell drive a mean jet ski. Your family will be proud that you exacted such a vengeance on those who murdered your brother."

"Do you have a place to stay? You can stay here, if you wish." El-Din had not moved from his place on the pier.

Kyle stripped off the dive suit and toweled down hard to restore some warmth to his skin before putting his dirty local clothes on again. "I'm good. I can't tell you where I'm staying. You understand?"

"Of course. What do you want me to do?"

"You go to the police in about an hour. Report that your dive shop was broken into last night by thieves and two jet skis were stolen." He thumbed back at the office, where the broken window attested to forced entry. "I left plenty of evidence to back up the claim. You found one ski drifting and abandoned about a hundred yards away, but no sign of the other one. You took a quick look around and went for the cops."

Abdel shook his head in amusement. "That is almost the truth. So are you going to leave me out of any further action? I don't want to be left out."

Kyle stared at the earnest youngster, then picked up a loose business card from a rack on the counter. "I need all of the friends and assets I can get, Abdel, so it is likely I will be asking for more of your help. Meanwhile, stay in the background, and don't tell anyone what really happened last night, not even your family. Just continue working here. I'll find you. This thing is not over."

El-Din watched the strange American leave, heard the SUV engine boom to life, and saw the 4Runner drive away. His thoughts turned to food, and for some reason, he wanted an enormous breakfast. After that, he would contact the police. He was just full of energy.

Major Shakuri believed his overall situation was good. While being the on-site commander in Sharm, he could blame the army general at the airport for the military mishaps, and now he saw a unique opportunity born of that rising confidence.

Instead of being the whipping boy of Colonel Yahya Ali Naqdi, the major sensed that there might be a chance here to topple his vile boss, take his place, and leap forward in rank and privilege, maybe even become a general. All he had to do was inform Tehran that their man was selling secrets, almost on the open market, and the colonel would be gone forever. He was weary, but this entire operation was playing out much better than he could have imagined.

Already, he had the colonel dangling, and Naqdi's normally confident voice was sounding strained. He had told his senior to get some sleep; then he had awakened the colonel a short time later with really bad news.

"The transport ship! The ship was sunk?"

"Yes, sir. At present, we do not know if it was a torpedo or a missile from the infidel fleet, but nothing is being ruled out. It certainly had the look of a decisive military attack, and resultant heavy loss of life. I have asked General Khasrodad for his explanation for still another military failure." *And what do you care, you old dog? You had one of our ships sunk with a missile strike without giving the crew any warning.*

The colonel had grown agitated. "I sent you down there to run this operation, Major Shakuri, and most of the reports I receive are of new disasters." The voice was rising, and Shakuri could detect a little fear from the colonel at the sudden loss of control. Someone else was pulling the strings in Sharm el-Sheikh while he was in Cairo trying to oversee the entire operation to put Egypt into Iran's military grasp.

"Even after the earlier attacks, our army commander failed to take adequate precautions, sir. Apparently no one on the ship even saw the attack coming. The captain and his first officer are among the dead, lucky for them, for I would otherwise have them shot for their negligence. I regretfully recommend that after his dismal performance of the past twenty-four hours, you consider relieving General Khasrodad of his post." *And replace him with me.*

It was if the colonel were no longer even listening. "I must spend some time this morning finding out why the Muslim Brotherhood has been unable to come to our rescue down there, as they had promised. And then I must talk with our leaders in Tehran about the situation, and what the diplomats are saying. That will not be pleasant. But I am definitely coming down today, Shakuri, and you had better have some adequate explanations by the time I arrive."

Shakuri let the uncomfortable silence hang in the air, knowing the colonel would be feeling pressure from Tehran. *Push him harder.* "Sir, I recommend that you consider placing Sharm under martial law. General Khasrodad simply must get his soldiers out of their holes and into the streets."

"I will be there this afternoon, Major. Carry on." The colonel abruptly hung up his phone. No new orders. No asking about the spies. The Pharaoh was falling apart.

Major Shakuri snorted in disgust and brushed aside the call from his superior officer, who was too far away to change anything at all for a few more hours. Shakuri called aloud for the intelligence officer seated at his own desk outside of the main office and told him to bring in the lists, then ordered an aide to bring in a hearty breakfast. His intel officer spread out the sheets of names of candidates for the new round of public executions.

Yesterday, they had simply rounded up victims at random and treated them with respect before shooting them. The uneasy truce that followed evaporated with the overnight actions, so Shakuri wanted twenty more examples to be picked for death, men and women of substance, whose names would be recognized by the people of the coastal city.

The chief of police was the first on the list. A couple of large merchants, and a woman television reporter who had become too outspoken, fomenting resistance. A professor, a dockworker, a mother of three. The twenty would get their final visit to the park at nine o'clock that night after a day of severe questioning.

Having done all that he could for the moment, he instructed the intel officer to carry out the arrests. The spy business intrigued him. What would the rewards be if he could capture both a CIA agent and the MI6 woman? Meanwhile, the major had time for a nap before going to the Four Seasons at ten.

Once he had pried himself from beneath the thumb of the colonel, Shakuri had enjoyed the freedom of thinking for himself, and this whole spy business had intrigued him. All in all, this might turn out to be a fine day.

LONDON

"Bad business, this." The normally placid face of Sir Gordon Fitzgerald, the chief of MI6, was wrinkled with lines of tension. The man had been protecting England from foreign threats since the bitter years of the Cold War, and his office was filled with glass cases containing rare weapons and souvenirs from his long career. Soft leather chairs, a big desk, and tall dark cases of books in several languages served to emphasize his old-school manner. He did not have, nor wish to have, a computer, for he had others to deal with details, and the material he wanted would never be on the Internet. Through the decades, he had learned to recognize both the unusual and the inevitable, and the quickening developments in Sharm el-Sheikh qualified on both counts. A small war was blazing within a bigger one. "How much do you trust your American?"

Sir Geoffrey Cornwell snorted. "He's not 'my American,' he's our son. And I've never met a better man. I have total trust in him, C. Total trust."

"Forgive me, Jeff. I refer only to your evaluation of his rather unusual skill set."

"There is no one better in these situations."

Fitzgerald lifted a quizzical eyebrow. "There is always someone better."

A deep voice joined in via speakerphone from across the Atlantic Ocean. General Brad Middleton, the commander of Task Force Trident, was on the horn from his Pentagon office. "Actually, with all due respect, sir, I agree with Sir Jeff. There isn't anyone better at this sort of action. From what we've been able to piece together on this end, Gunny Swanson is raising hell in Sharm, and he is still on the loose."

The MI6 man had come to the same conclusion, based on a different set of facts. C cleared his throat. "General, I must apologize for not letting you know directly that we have been using Swanson as an unsuspecting plant to draw the attention of a potentially valuable secret source of information. I had assumed wrongly that the CIA, which was involved all the way, was passing along the plan. It was a massive mistake on my part, but I thought that everybody was on the same page over there since 9/11. Sharing all information, you know?"

Sir Jeff gripped the arms of his wheelchair. "You dangled him on the hook without knowing he was bait. That was inexcusable, C."

"I have extended my apologies to you both. Now we must move on."

"Not until Kyle is alerted to the situation." Jeff was showing his stubborn streak. "Just in the past night, he has caused extraordinary damage to the Iranians. If they think he is a CIA agent, they are definitely coming after him."

"That is probably happening even as we speak, which is why we must depend on his ability to react quickly and correctly to totally unexpected situations. I told our agent, Dr. Bialy, to give him a full brief, but she said it may be too late. They are not in regular contact. She hasn't heard from him in hours." The MI6 chief put both palms flat on his desk and rubbed the old wood as if giving it a good polish. To those who knew him, it was a habit that expressed great alarm. "After last night's exploits, he must be holed up somewhere alone, thinking he is safe. He is most assuredly not."

Middleton joined in. "An operator like Swanson is only as good as his last fight, sir. If I was talking directly to him as his commanding officer, I would ask, 'Gunny, what have you done for me lately?' Swanson may be holed up for a few hours, out of ammo, with no fresh intelligence about what we are thinking, and tired beyond normal endurance, but he will be ready for whatever comes his way."

"Let us hope so, General. The plan was thrown together rapidly, it is complex, and the time is short. At this point, our governments are protesting to the United Nations and threatening military options if the Iranians do not withdraw from Egypt. Only his continued success in this one-man war is holding back the decision to send in special ops teams. We're willing to give it another twenty-four hours."

CHAPTER 26

SHARM EL-SHEIKH

Swanson made it back to the safe house, locked the door, went to the bedroom and fell backward onto the mattress, fully clothed. He fell asleep with his hand on the Colt .45 that rested on his stomach, and the nightmare snatched him so hard that his body shuddered in physical response. An endless ghostly line of dead men shuffled toward the small pier at the jet ski marina and were being packed into a narrow black boat that could only seat perhaps a maximum of ten, but somehow there was always room for one more. Leaning on the steering oar at the stern was the Boatman, who grinned with stumps of rotten teeth in oozing black gums.

"You are doing well. I knew you would. I told you this would be your largest harvest ever. I can always count on you, Gunny Swanson," said the spectral im-

age, spreading an arm to help another zombielike passenger lurch aboard.

"Go away," Kyle replied in his dream.

"I cannot. You are killing too many to ignore. Hundreds."

"They are not men. They are my enemies. If I don't kill them, they could kill my fellow Marines."

The Boatman hissed a cackle of amused laughter. "A dissembling response. They posed no threat to your fellow Marines, who were not even here, and you killed them anyway. Fellow humans are dead or dying by your hand. Men who happen to wear a different uniform, that's all."

"Each is my enemy, you evil bastard. You know that. Quit busting my balls."

Behind the fluttering sheer silhouette of the Boatman was an entire sea of licking, low fire. "I think this is enough for me to transport for one load now. You keep up your good work, and we will visit again later." There was the cackle of a bodiless laugh, and the long, low craft nosed away into the flames.

Swanson cried out at the departing figure. "I didn't want to kill any of them! They were my country's enemies. And I don't want to kill any more . . ."

The final answer echoed back from a hole in the fire. "But you will. You have to, for more are coming."

Swanson jerked awake to a full sitting position, the .45 locked in a two-handed firing grip, as he heard the scratch of a key in the lock of the safe house's front door. He swung his feet to the floor and slipped prone at the bedroom doorway, with a clear firing lane to the front.

A light triple-rap knock, and the door opened about two inches and stopped. "Swanson? It's me. Omar. I'm alone."

"Step in backward and slow, keep your hands where I can see them, and close the door." Swanson's pistol did not waver from its line, and his eyes were intense and on the target.

Omar did as instructed, keeping his hands high, which pulled up his shirt high enough in back for Kyle to see the butt of a pistol in the back of his belt. "Pull out the weapon with two fingers, left hand, drop it, and kick it beneath the sofa." Omar did as he was told.

"Keep moving back toward my voice." Kyle got up and took a few silent steps. "Turn around, slow."

Omar did so and found the big hole at the end of the .45's barrel pointing right between his eyes. "Hurry up with your search or inspection or whatever this is, Kyle. We don't have much time. They're coming."

Tianha Bialy was at a big mirror in the bedroom of her suite, carefully applying the final touches to her makeup, deciding to pass on the lip gloss. A girl had to be careful around Muslim men, she thought. They would appreciate beauty in a woman and then just as easily treat her like a dog. Love, she had found over the years, had little to do with such a relationship. Anyway, she was not here to please anyone, for she already had a fiancé back in London as well as a lover, Omar, in Egypt. Satisfied with her understated look, she gave her clothes a final adjustment, then took a chair in the living room and calmed herself to await the knock on the door. It was almost ten o'clock.

Major Shakuri had been extremely busy all morning, imposing his version of logic and order on the situation that seemed to change every few minutes. He studied the updated damage reports from the overnight attacks and had a brief, unpleasant telephone conversation with General Khasrodad out at the airport. The man had no fighting spirit and very reluctantly gave Shakuri the soldiers needed for the evening's executions.

The major had approved the final list of the latest examples, but the overnight casualties to the Iranians had been high, and Shakuri had to keep his retaliation formula in some sort of perspective. Even at one-for-one, it would mean several hundred executions, which was an impossible number. The lesson, not the executions, was the important thing. So he would do twenty today, then declare the lesson learned before it turned into a general massacre. With the extra soldiers, he would then use martial law to restore calm in the beachfront city. The bodies this time would be left to rot in the park for a few days before being taken away by grieving relatives. *Examples.*

With those arrangements in place, he sifted through the news reports. The Muslim Brotherhood had promised to spark a spontaneous uprising of the people across the land, but that had not yet happened. Since winning political power through elections, the Brotherhood had to deal with all of the problems of any government, both in its own country and abroad. They had wanted power, and found it an uncomfortable fit. There were problems in Gaza, where militants wanted to secede from Egypt and form an Islamic emirate on the Israeli border. The Bedouins would not cooperate because they never cooperated with anybody. The old players in Hamas would not bow to the wishes of the new government, and al Qaeda despised the elected officials for not being radical enough. There were dozens of serious fracture lines within the Brotherhood, and powerful rival political parties. So when it came to stitching together a unified front with a separate rebel army, everyone wanted a slice of the pie. The idea that the Brotherhood would launch demonstrations against itself defied logic. That left the Supreme Council of the Armed Forces still intact, and the last thing the generals would allow was a competing army on Egyptian soil. The major wondered why the colonel could possibly have believed any differently.

While Brotherhood spokesmen on the streets were still forecasting victory, they had not come close to marching south to relieve the Iranians in Sharm. At best, it might be viewed as stalemate; at worst, it was the quiet before a storm, for the Egyptian military had not yet truly intervened.

Shakuri enjoyed this new ability to overwatch the entire situation, the feeling of control. It had a sweet taste, and he was reluctant to return that magic bottle of power to his boss when Naqdi arrived this afternoon. Shakuri was now absolutely confident that he could replace the general at the airport, for sheer incompetence if nothing else. Then he could turn his full attention to ousting his superior officer. To think that only a week ago, he had trembled in fear of the influential, magical Naqdi. Things change quickly.

First, he had to deal with these spies among them. He slid a pistol into the polished leather holster on his belt and stepped into the chill and pure morning light. Two uniformed soldiers, each with an AK-47, stood at attention beside his car. Major Shakuri believed that at that moment he was the most important man in Sharm el-Sheikh, if not in all of Egypt.

The ride up Hotel Row from the Blue Neptune to the Four Seasons was short, and he and the two escorts marched inside as knots of people parted before them. Scars of the fighting from the first night were still plentiful but were rapidly disappearing beneath the reconstruction by work crews. The smell of fresh paint was strong, and drills, saws, and hammers were busy.

They went up on the elevator to one of the higher floors and found the room number. He knocked with short, impatient raps, then importantly went to a rigid parade rest position, chin up, hands behind his back, pistol on his hip.

Tianha Bialy opened the door and gave him a quick once-over, thinking he looked somewhat silly with the military posturing. She stepped aside as the men entered, with the guards walking through the suite in a brief search. Shakuri sat down, uninvited. *Showing who is boss, like a little dog peeing on a lamppost,* she thought.

"Thank you for seeing me, Dr. Bialy," he said as his

eyes roamed over her. The soldier who had searched the bedroom returned, nodded to the major, and joined his partner at the door.

"Since this is a business meeting, Major, let's get right to it. Are you the Pharaoh?"

"Yes, I am," he lied, turning up his palms in a gesture of innocence.

"Can you prove that?"

"Give me Kyle Swanson, and I will give you everything you want."

"This was to be a fair and mutual exchange, Major Shakuri. My orders are not to proceed without proof of identity. A substantial sum of money is to be delivered to the Pharaoh, and we must be sure of the person with whom we are dealing."

"I do not carry an identification card bearing that name. I am sure you can understand." His eyes gleamed with quiet excitement.

"Then answer a question for me," she said, pushing the conversation. "Why should I, or anyone in British intelligence, trust what you say?"

"Because it is very dangerous for you not to do so." In a lightning move, the major reached forward and backhanded Tianha across the face, knocking her from the chair. "I did not come here to bargain with a British spy. I came because you have something I want." He lunged across and wrapped her hair tight around his fist, then slapped her again, and blood spilled from her lower lip. "Do you know where Swanson is?"

She wiped away the blood with her fingers, feeling the sting of the cut. She did not scream and did not seem frightened, which puzzled him. Instead, she watched him with her dark eyes. She had known the ruse she was running was dangerous, but she would stick to the plan. "I want the real Pharaoh! It is obviously not you. You're just an errand boy."

It was Shakuri's turn to be shocked. His word was not to be insulted and challenged by a woman. "And I plan to deliver you to him later today. First, I ask again, do you know the location of this CIA spy?" He gave the hair a vicious jerk and was pleased to see her wince in pain. "Do you?"

Tianha coughed, then gave a sarcastic smile. "Better than that, Major. I can take you to him." *They should be ready by now.*

He pushed her away and bent over with his hands on knees, his face close to hers. "Then let's go. My car is waiting."

Swanson patiently waited in an apartment two doors down the hallway from the entrance to the safe house, his eye pressed against the peephole, again feeling the familiar warmth of his blood flowing through him before a fight, his heart thumping in a steady beat to make the machine that was his body ready for sudden, maximum performance.

A woman and her child lived in the place, but they had been paid well by Omar after a brief negotiation to leave for the rest of the afternoon to avoid some possible trouble. After the previous night of flames and fire, it did not take much persuasion for the handsome Omar to convince them to vacate for a few hours.

When it was clear, Kyle walked quickly down the hall from the safe house and into the apartment, where Omar was already clearing the area around the door of toys and furniture to allow more freedom of movement. Neither man spoke, for the time was past for talking. Omar hurried back to the safe house rooms but did not lock the door. Kyle also left his unlocked, with a small piece of duct tape over the latch to keep it from engaging. It would open with a simple pull. The big pistol carrying the sound suppressor was in his right hand. It shouldn't be long now. *Why had Bialy put herself in harm's way?* She had hatched this risky plan and was now firmly snared in the hunter's net.

The door to the safe house was at the top end of a T of bisecting hallways, and Kyle was two doors down on the right side of the T stem, with the elevator at the far end. To get to the safe house, anyone would have to pass his position, and the only variable would be the positioning of the Iranians and where Tianha was placed among them. It almost did not matter how many guards there were, for they would be bunched together, and he planned to kill them all.

The cell phone vibrated silently in his pocket, and Omar spoke quietly. "I just saw them pull in downstairs. One officer, plus two bodyguards with AKs. Tianha is in front. On the way up." Kyle snapped down the lid and put it back in his pocket, then let his body settle into the alert mode with every sense tingling. He rested his left hand on the doorknob and watched the hallway through the fish-eye peephole.

There was no warning bell on the elevator, but

Swanson heard movement at the far end of the hall, and a woman's voice echoing in the stillness. "This way. It's that door right down there at the end." Tianha was announcing obvious directions to make useless noise that served as a warning. Her comment was followed by the heavy fall of boots in the hallway. Swanson sucked in his breath and exhaled slowly.

One bodyguard led the way, and the major steered Tianha by the elbow to keep her in front of him. The second guard brought up the rear. They stopped at the entry to the safe house, and the guards took positions a few feet away from the door, one on each side, flat against the wall, and brought up their AK-47s.

Swanson gently opened his own door a half inch and saw that they were about fifteen feet away, with all of their attention on the safe house entrance.

Shakuri pushed Tianha forward. If any bullets came out of the apartment, she would be the first to be hit. "Call him," the major ordered in a whisper, pulling his own pistol and standing out of sight to the side.

She knocked. "Kyle? It's me, Tianha. Let me in."

There was a pause and a shuffle of feet behind the door, as if someone were looking cautiously through the spy hole. Then there was a rattle of a chain as if the door were being unlocked. The two guards stepped back into the hallway, rifles pointed at the door, and Shakuri held Tianha tightly as a shield.

Kyle Swanson had silently opened his own door and was already in the hall behind them. His pistol was extended, a part of him, and he went for the soldier on his right with the first shot, which sounded like a cannon in the tight quarters. Swanson felt the kick of the recoil and saw the bullet strike the man just behind the ear. Kyle was already turning to the next target. The pistol crossed over the major and Tianha and steadied on the second guard, whose head also exploded before he could turn around. Bright red blood and pink and gray brain matter showered the walls, and Kyle moved in hard and fast.

In three steps, he was at top speed and hurtled into the major, whose face was covered in gore and who still did not realize what was happening. Swanson hit with a body tackle that slammed the Iranian officer against the wall as the door opened and Omar reached out and snatched Tianha inside to safety. Kyle pistol-whipped the officer, back and forth across the face, three times, letting the front sight gouge and tear at the flesh, then banged down hard on the skull with the butt of his gun and knocked Shakuri cold. Two kill shots and a takedown in less than ten seconds. His marksmanship and mixed martial arts coaches would have been proud.

He shoved the weapon into his belt and helped Omar drag the three bodies inside and dump them in the living room. They had no time to wipe down the walls and mop the hall, but at least the corpses were out of sight.

Tianha emerged from the bathroom with a stack of wet and dry towels and gave Shakuri a quick cleanup, pouring water into his face. "Wake up," she said. "You're going on a trip." The major was hoisted into a chair and cuffed with plastic strips, then gagged with duct tape.

His eyes blinked madly when he started understanding what had happened, and he stared at the slim man standing before him with arms crossed. It had to be the American.

"So you are the famous Major Mansoor Shakuri, and I hear you have been looking for me," Swanson said. "Too bad you found me."

Kyle seized the man's right hand and with a hard pull and a sharp twist broke the little finger. Shakuri jerked away in pain and tried to kick out, but Swanson just slapped him. "That was for ordering the assassination of an American citizen on American soil—an accountant who had done no one any harm, but was a threat to your efforts in Egypt."

Shakuri shook his head in denial, only to get slapped again with an open-hand strike that made him see stars. The bleeding on his face had resumed, and Tianha stepped in to towel him clean again.

"We've got to go," she said.

"Almost there," said Kyle. He took the left hand, stared into the major's terrified eyes, and broke the pinkie finger on that one, too, watching as Shakuri recoiled with the new slash of pain. "And that is for sending a team out to kidnap Lady Patricia Cornwell in London." He gave Shakuri the look of a wolf checking out a rabbit. "This next one is going to hurt," he said and tore away the duct tape gag. "I want to hear you scream on this one."

"But . . ." the major sputtered, as Kyle flipped the pistol around, and the excuse turned into earsplitting screams when Swanson hammered Shakuri in the stomach, breaking a couple of ribs, then once more in the balls, and threw a final punch that broke two upper front teeth. The screams came with every breath for a few seconds, then lapsed into moans of despair and pain.

"Pat's my mother, you asshole," Swanson snarled.

Omar put a hand gently on Kyle's shoulder and was surprised to discover that Swanson's muscles were not even tense. "That's enough of the torture. Save something for the intelligence types."

Kyle stepped back. "That wasn't torture, Omar. It was just plain old ass-kicking payback. I'm done with this piece of shit."

CHAPTER 27

Let's do it quickly," Omar said, his voice flat and under control. "This safe house is burned. Even with the bodies out of sight, the blood trail out there will be a big flashing sign when someone comes looking for them." There was no time to waste with scrub brushes and buckets of water to wipe up the blood, the goo of brain matter, and the white bits of bone that stuck to the walls and spread on the floor.

Tianha had watched in shock as Kyle had attacked the major, for it had been so quick and continual, one violent act after another. "You must have steel bands around your heart," she said when it was over.

Kyle dropped the used magazine out of his pistol and slid home a new one, then lifted his backpack, which was already on the kitchen table. The anger that he had displayed only a few minutes earlier had evaporated like a blowing fog as he adjusted to the developing situation, preparing for whatever came next. He did not answer her observations. "I'm ready. Let's move out."

Omar hauled the major to his feet, and Tianha slid a pillowcase over the prisoner's head for a hood. The thin cotton immediately soaked up the ribbons of blood from the facial wounds, and Shakuri groaned against the stabbing pain of the broken ribs and fingers. He was wobbling on his feet when he heard the American hiss, close to his ear, "You call out for help, I'll rip your throat open. Now move." Kyle did not have a knife in his hand, but the major did not know that.

Tianha opened the door, and the four of them went into the hallway and down the emergency stairwell, with Omar and Swanson dragging the reeling major between them. Within ten minutes, they were in the garage, and the moaning Major Mansoor Shakuri had been bundled into the windowless cabin of a scarred van.

"Come with us," Tianha said to Kyle, looking him in the face and noticing the exhausted eyes and the cheeks sunken from weariness. "We rendezvous with a Saudi Air Force helicopter about twenty miles to the north and will be across the border in no time. Then we fly this package straight back to London. Let's go."

Kyle reached into the bag and found the computer flash drive that had been given to him. No bigger than a domino, it was packed with vital inside information about the government of Egypt, the armed forces, and the Muslim Brotherhood. He pressed it into her hand. "Here's the digitized material the Egyptians gave us during our meeting. It never made it out of the country, but our bosses can still use it."

"You're not coming, are you?" She dropped the flash drive into her pocket. "MI6 has set up the extraction with the Saudis, our agents will be aboard, and we have a quiet place waiting in the desert where the major will be interrogated. Everything will be safe. We can clear out of this place, Kyle. Our job is done."

"Can't do it," Swanson replied. It was a Marine thing: first in, last out. "I still have some unfinished business here." He did not consider telling her about the earlier disaster with the American special ops chopper. Keep things upbeat. "You and Omar go ahead. You have an intelligence coup with these documents and your own personal observations, plus my debrief with Omar this morning, and a prisoner who has been getting headlines as the man in charge of the Iranian operation. If that major isn't your so-called Pharaoh, then he knows who is, and he knows a hell of a lot of other things. You did a good job when crunch time came, Bialy, and organized a great snatch-and-grab operation. Now finish it off. Get to your bird and extract your high-value target out of here."

"What about you? How are you going to operate with no safe house and no backup?"

"I have it somewhere," he said, reaching out to shake Omar's hand. "Good luck to both of you. Go."

"Stay safe, Kyle," said Omar. "I'll buy you a beer in London."

"Right." He tossed his bag into the 4Runner and waited until the van pulled away. Then he drove out into the veil of bright sunshine.

* * *

Swanson had to admit that he was bone tired, edgy, and agitated. He was squeezing the steering wheel in a death grip. He had been carrying on this singular one-man crusade from the moment the first Iranian troops had set foot on the beach in front of the Blue Neptune two days earlier, never knowing from one moment to the next where it was all leading. He had caused the Tehran military machine to stumble, but the stress and nonstop action were wearing him down. He fumbled around in the seabag as he drove and found a packet of Dexedrine "go pills," then chewed two of the amphetamines for a temporary, emergency chemical lift. He could sleep when he was dead and resting in the Boatman's skiff. Until then, he had work to do, and a Marine gunnery sergeant was not in the business of cutting anyone slack, least of all himself. He had been trained to go beyond the limits of endurance, to take it to the absolute max.

He threaded the 4Runner through the heart of the city, then turned out into the smaller, flanking neighborhoods. The usually colorful Sharm el-Sheikh was without any joy this morning, and the few people on the traffic-starved streets were scurrying from one place to another. Many shops were closed, and the central market was almost empty instead of being jammed with customers. At the big park where the executions had taken place, the bodies had been removed, but a pair of Iranian armored personnel carriers were parked back-to-back with their ramps down and guns manned. Maybe they were showing the locals who still held the big stick, despite the crippling attacks of the previous night. Stinking smoke still rode on the breeze. Along Hotel Row, the big buildings seemed like derelicts waiting for someone to give them a dollar, although the construction crews were still at work. A few foreign tourists milled about, looking lost and worried.

He drove back into the coastal business park where the Gold Sun Water Equipment marina was located, parked beside a shed about fifty yards away from the shop, on the opposite side of the road, and shut down the engine. He slid down in the seat, tucking his pistol beneath his thigh. Just like downtown, the boatyards were yawningly vacant except for a few vehicles. No police cars nor any men in uniform were around. Abdel El-Din was outside, nailing a sheet of plywood over the window that Kyle had broken last night, and the *rap-rap* of his hammer sounded like little pistol shots. At least the kid wasn't under arrest, which indicated that he had successfully run his scam with the local cops, who apparently had a lot more to worry about this morning than a dive shop burglary. Their city was falling into an abyss, and their chief was under arrest by the soldiers.

Kyle eyeballed each door and window in the yard. The sun, almost directly overhead, applied a flare of golden light on the whitewashed buildings. A motorboat chugged down the waterway, but no one stirred at the businesses. Doors were locked, all lights were out, and signs announced that the places were closed. Swanson eased from his SUV and quietly worked his way around the sheds, avoiding the gravel road and exposed spaces. At the water's edge, the hodgepodge of stacked canoes, paddleboats, jet skis, and other apparatus provided ready-made concealment. After scaling a small wire fence, Kyle ducked through the big door that opened into the Gold Sun Water Equipment pier. He crouched behind an overturned boat just as the hammering out front stopped.

Abdel El-Din came inside, sweating and wiping his head with a cloth, and gave a loud sigh as he sat down at his desk with a bottle of water. A voice behind him said, "Hello, Abdel," making the young Egyptian jump in surprise, his eyes darting around. "Swanson! How did you get in? I was working right by the door."

Kyle smiled and took a seat. "Never mind that. How are you?"

El-Din shook his head. "Things are bad. I reported to the police, like you said, and they were uninterested. I am OK, but everything is falling apart. Some kids have spray-painted the word DEATH on buildings across the city."

Kyle paused to let the Egyptian collect his thoughts, and then he said, "I've been through the streets today, too, and the few people that I saw look afraid. I understand that up to a point because of the attacks yesterday, but there's more to it, isn't there? What's happened?"

El-Din scratched at the sweat on his chin. "More people have been culled out for another firing squad. Twenty of our leading citizens have been arrested and beaten in the streets and thrown in prison. No one is allowed to see them. The whole city is in shock. We don't know what to do, other than hide."

"You know what to do, Abdel. You didn't hide last night, you fought back."

"Which means that I am responsible for these new executions." Tears welled in his brown eyes, and he turned away so another man would not see him cry. "I haven't told anybody about what we did, but my heart burns with shame and guilt."

Kyle shook his head. "That's just normal after-action shock, and you're feeling sorry for yourself. You went out there with me to avenge your brother, who was murdered by those same people . . . *before* you took action. You had done nothing to cause his death, and you are not the reason for this new round of executions."

"Why are they doing this? I thought they were supposed to be our friends."

"The Iranians must stamp out any challenge to their authority in this city in order to turn it into a permanent military base, and they will get meaner as time goes on. Take my word, kid, Sharm will soon become a militarized city, all of the businesses will die, and the worst elements of Sharia law will be ruthlessly imposed so they can create a big naval base that controls the Suez Canal and the oil shipping routes."

"Sharia law? Why bring that up? Are you just another American who hates all Muslims?" Abdel El-Din shouted the accusation. "You don't know anything about our culture."

"Bullshit, Abdel. I've worked alongside Muslims in the Middle East and Africa for almost as many years as you have been on this earth. This is not a religious thing but a cold political move by Tehran and the extremist elements of the Muslim Brotherhood in Cairo. Those soldiers out there who are running around shooting your friends and relatives are your fellow Muslims, not American or British troops."

El-Din was on his feet. "They came as peacekeepers to protect us during the uprisings that are sweeping the country. Look at how they put down the attacks by those fanatics on Hotel Row!"

"The Iranians came as part of a conquering army, Abdel, and I think that assault on the hotels was just another part of their plan to establish themselves. Are they acting like friends, or are they your new masters?"

"They will go back home when things settle down," El-Din said, not believing his own words.

"This won't stop with Sharm. They will expand across to Hurghada and capture that big air base because it is better suited to handle their fighters and bombers. Once they have supporting air power, they will have control of all of southern Egypt, and then they will never leave. But the rest of the world is not going to sit by idly and let Iran control most of the oil traffic. There will be a big invasion and all of Sharm will be crushed like a bug."

The Egyptian had his hands on his hips and sucked in deep and nervous breaths, trying to put his thoughts in order.

Kyle continued. "Look, Abdel, I really did get caught up in this mess by accident. Eventually I will be able to leave. Sooner or later, this is going to be your fight, not mine, although I am willing to help." Kyle stared hard at El-Din. "The only question you have to answer is whether you want to live the rest of your life beneath Iranian boots. Do you? If so, I will leave right now and you will never see me again."

Abdel rose and wiped away the tears, which had mingled with the sweat. His eyes grew hard. "No. I do not, but I am only one man."

"You told me last night that other people were as outraged as you by that first round of executions, so I don't think that you are really alone. Egyptians have not survived so many centuries by acting like a bunch of frightened rabbits."

El-Din regarded the slight American; no doubt this was a dangerous man. "So do you have another idea, like the one we did last night?"

"Yes. With a little help from your friends, I believe we can stop tonight's executions."

"Really?"

"Why not?" Kyle sketched out the possibilities, like a salesman pumping an inevitably positive response into a client. The clock read just after noon, which gave them nine hours to pull something together.

The muted purr of the twin-prop Cessna 421 was almost hypnotic to the pilot as he skimmed the private plane along the eastern bank of the Suez Canal. Not a ship was moving down there. Colonel Yahya Ali Naqdi had held his private license for many years, was rated for multiengine aircraft, and had, in a rare moment of weakness, managed to purchase the Cessna for his own use three years ago with money laundered through the Palm Group cover company. He had sold his masters back in Tehran with the idea of using it for covert reconnaissance, when in reality he just loved flying and treasured the feeling of freedom that being in the air gave to him. On his own plane, he was master of his own fate.

Getting a flight plan filed and the necessary permissions to leave Cairo had been brutally frustrating today. Since no one was really in charge of the airports due to the riots and pitched battles around Cairo, no one wanted to make any decisions. The colonel had to bribe his way into the air, arguing through multiple levels of bureaucrats that his unarmed plane was no threat to anyone, and that he was on a legitimate and urgent business trip for the Palm Group, which had holdings down in Sharm. Yes, he had been given assurances that the Iranians would let him land safely. The lies and money finally won approval for him to go but had burned several hours. It was almost six o'clock in the afternoon, only an hour and a half before dusk, as he neared the end of his flight and saw the canal widen to empty into the Red Sea. He banked slightly and dipped to a lower altitude when Sharm el-Sheikh appeared off of his left wingtip after the trip of slightly more than 230 miles.

The view was startling. Naqdi could see out to where the broken oil tanker *Llewellyn* was being held awkwardly in place by anchors and tugboats, surrounded by the sheen of a huge oil slick. Containment rings were in place, but heavy oil had coated the nearby shoreline, and the cleaning process was still days away from even starting. Another large oil slick marked the death waters of the *Babr,* the first ship to die, and the bow of the destroyed supply ship in the harbor stuck out of the water like a macabre monument. The city seemed quiet, and few people were out along the line of big hotels that dominated the long sandy beaches.

This is a war zone, he thought. Things had gotten messy. Ripping his eyes from the long line of idled ships that stretched out as far as he could see, the colonel banked back toward the Sharm airport, using the gray columns of smoke that rose from the destroyed ammunition dump as guideposts. He was eager to get on the ground and receive a full tour and updated briefing from Major Shakuri. His usually reliable aide had not been in contact since early this morning.

The colonel slid his radio headset over his ears, tuned in the military frequency for the airport, and requested landing clearance, which was immediately granted. The little Cessna passed by the charred and skeletal wreckage of the crashed Boeing airliner, made a featherlike touchdown, and taxied up to the control tower. He cut the engines, then pushed open the fuselage hatch and stepped out onto the tarmac. Shakuri was not there. Only a curious sergeant carrying a clipboard filled with papers stepped out to meet him.

CHAPTER 28

They abandoned the marina because Kyle believed it might very well be under observation by the police, although they had feigned disinterest in Abdel's report of the theft of the jet skis. Perhaps, deep inside one of those nearby buildings, a couple of cops with binoculars and a radio were waiting and watching. So Abdel took some time to sweep up glass and debris, then locked up and put out a CLOSED sign, just like the other businesses. The activity kept any attention on him while Kyle crept back out the way he had come in, still unseen. They met at the home of one of Abdel's cousins, not far from the public park where the executions were held, and El-Din went around the city to collect other relatives.

By dusk, they had a pickup team—nine men, including Kyle. The size was determined by Abdel selecting only people whom he would trust with his life.

The men were all members of the El-Din clan or the extended family, with a collective attitude of retribution. Each had brought at least one weapon, a mix of AKs and SKS rifles and even one old M-14, all with multiple clips of ammunition.

They were surprised to see the American outsider, and suspicious until Abdel vouched for Swanson's friendship and explained how he was a tourist with military experience who had been caught in the same vise that clamped them all. His local-style clothing and dirty appearance were explained away as part of his just trying to stay away from the Iranians until he could leave.

Kyle was lavish in praise of their bravery for deciding to come today, and he freely acknowledged Abdel as the leader. He himself was there only to help and offer advice because he knew a lot about how counterinsurgency works, he said. Eventually, the group accepted him.

On the other hand, he was struck by the fact that these men were not hardened desert warriors or lethal mountain tribesmen like those he had faced on battlefields throughout the Middle East, the kind of fighter with deep scars and hatreds. These were merchants, workers, fishermen, and city dwellers who had earned their livings from free-spending tourists and lived far from the fighting that roiled Afghanistan, Iraq, and Pakistan. Despite the political revolution erupting elsewhere, their lives had been calm before fanatics had stormed the hotels, killing people, and the Iranian soldiers showed up, almost in the next breath. Since then, their normal lives had vanished. Their eyes and muscles were soft, and their fighting experience and discipline were limited or nonexistent. The youngest was sixteen, the oldest around sixty. None had military training. Would they fight? Some would, some would hesitate, or spray and pray, and some might run away. He would not know that until the shooting started.

It did not take long for the meeting to collapse into a useless council of war, during which every member of the team gave his opinions, some of which were very wordy and long and, in the end, useless. Kyle bit his lip to remain silent, depending on Abdel to run this show. The kid let them talk until the general opinion drifted inevitably toward pessimism, and he stopped it there.

"My friends," Abdel said softly, politely addressing the hardest arguers as everyone remained seated on the scattering of cushions, the carpet, a sofa, and chairs. Some were his elders, which meant he had to step carefully or risk insulting them. "We have now heard all opinions, and the time for talking is done. The choice is simple: We either fight or run away. If we run, the Iranians will remain in control of our city, perhaps forever, and execute our people whenever they want, as they did with Hamid, and as they will do again tonight with others. If we fight, as a group, we can answer the Iranian violence with violence of our own. There have already been some significant attacks that have hurt the invaders, and I admit to you, my trusted family, that I am part of this rebellion. I will continue to fight. They want to own us, and we must not allow it."

There was an outburst of enthusiastic support in the room, eagerness replacing concern, words tumbling over other words, and Abdel asked them to gather close and pay attention to the American's scheme for a surprise attack.

Using a black marker on a large piece of cardboard, Swanson mapped out the park and the situation, with Abdel translating. The group peppered him with questions, and several went out to recon the park, returning with new details. There were ten posts in front of the sandbags, but there were twenty people to be executed. "Then they are planning to do it in two groups of ten," Kyle said. "Twenty would be awkward for a ten-man firing squad. This way, it will be ten soldiers against ten unarmed victims tied securely to the posts. One-on-one easy targets."

He pointed to the circles that marked the straight line of the firing squad, marked with the numbers 1 through 10. Then he drew in two lines of X's, four each, angled to obliquely face the soldiers in a classic ambush pattern. "Abdel will assign your positions," he said. "This way, you will have a good crossfire. Everyone will be assigned an exact soldier to shoot with your first burst of fire, and an alternate. And do not expect them all to just fall over dead, for a battle never happens that way. Just keep your discipline and remember your targets, trusting the man beside you to do the same. One of you cannot shoot all of the soldiers, so don't even try. Once the firing squad is down, take out the few guards who will be standing around. The crowd will panic, and the guards will be slow to react in the confusion."

Abdel translated a question from a man who bent

close to the map and pointed to the two rectangles representing the armored personnel carriers at the edge of the park. "What about these big tanks with the machine guns? They will slaughter us."

Swanson said, "Those are my own targets. I have some stuff that will take them out, and I will hit them at the same time you are ready to open up on the soldiers. They won't get off a shot."

"And when do we shoot?"

"That is an important point. Do not get excited and pull the trigger too early, or the plan will fail. We all attack at the same time, when the officer in charge of the firing squad calls out, 'Ready.' That will leave them locked in position and focused away from you. Abdel takes the first shot, and we all go. Attend specifically to your target first. No shooting in the air or celebrating or any of that until the job is done."

Abdel chimed in to close the little session. "Then we free the prisoners, grab some weapons, and leave the area before Iranian reinforcements can arrive." Abdel had them in hand, for they were all of the same family. With Swanson's help, they spent some time disassembling and thoroughly cleaning each weapon, right down to the butt plates, including unloading the magazines, cleaning them, and even polishing each bullet. The American said their lives depended on the guns working flawlessly, and the men understood their weapons had become filthy through seldom being used; one weapon had rusted to the point of being useless.

They drifted apart to have some tea and food, talk among themselves, and have some sleep as the afternoon sun lost its power and fell toward the horizon. Kyle lay down and closed his eyes, wondering how many of these men would live through the coming fight. They knew nothing of war. *The Dirty Dozen, they ain't.*

THE AIRPORT

Colonel Naqdi had changed from the civilian clothes he wore in Cairo into his regulation military uniform in order to announce his presence in Sharm with the full force of his authority. Insulted that no one had shown up to meet his plane, he stormed into the makeshift office of General Khasrodad bellowing, "What is going on here?"

Khasrodad unfolded slowly from the chair at his desk but did not salute. He outranked Naqdi by a full grade, but that meant nothing because the man was head of Iranian foreign intelligence operations, and as such was answerable only to the ruling council in Tehran. To challenge him risked losing not only your job but your life. "Welcome to Sharm el-Sheikh, Colonel."

There was no handshake, and the men locked stares. They were physical opposites. The colonel stood about five-ten and was a bit thick around the middle, with hair that was beginning to show gray. The general was a hard six-two and 210 pounds, a veteran commando leader who often ran with his men during their harsh physical training. He had led numerous operations, had been wounded in action, and feared nothing.

"I had expected to be met at planeside upon my arrival, General."

"And I assumed that your aide, Major Shakuri, would be doing just that, Colonel. I've been busy." The general swept his arm toward a window that gave a wide view of the airport destruction. The fires at the ammo dump had not yet been totally quelled, wreckage seemed everywhere, and the air was still hazy with smoke. "So I can assume that Shakuri did not show up?"

The colonel threw his beret on a desk and walked to the window. "I saw this from the air, and the sunken ship in the harbor. Incredible. No, I haven't heard from the major since early this morning."

"Nor have I, Colonel. That, however, is not unusual. He worked out of his own office down in a beach hotel and seldom communicated with me. I will send someone to get him, or you can go down yourself, if you choose."

"I would be grateful if you sent a couple of men, General Khasrodad." The colonel found a chair and made himself comfortable, allowing the general to resume his own seat. "Let's get right to the point, Medhi. These attacks. Are they the work of local partisans or foreign special forces?"

"Frankly, we don't know." The general spun his chair around and looked out of the window at the damage beyond. "The work has been very professional, but we have no proof, no enemy bodies, and no equipment that would identify any of them. Judging by the kill shots at other locations, we think at least one of them is an experienced sniper."

"Could they be from the Egyptian army? They

would have the proper training and be able to hide among the population."

"Once again, there is nothing definite. If it was the army, the population would be gossiping and talking about it. My intelligence people say there has been none of that, plus the army is supposedly being kept busy in the north by the Brotherhood rebellion." He had turned back around to look at the colonel. "From what I hear, that fledgling civil war is not going well."

The colonel snapped at the mocking tone. "That is not your concern, General."

"Yes, it is. If this far-fetched plan to overthrow the government in Cairo fails, then my forces here will be trapped here with no way out. So it is my concern, Colonel Naqdi. Very much so."

"You will not report that pessimism up your chain of command! That is an order, General. I am in charge of this operation. The rebellion will succeed, and then your troops will be reinforced and break out of this bottleneck beachhead."

"I understand the plan, Colonel. I just hope it works, for the linkup was supposed to happen tomorrow, and it obviously will not. No Brotherhood convoys with food and ammo and big guns are going to be arriving anytime soon, are they?"

"I admit that there have been a few setbacks, General. Such things are to be expected in any operation of this size, but heavy fighting continues as the Brotherhood army is making steady advances. You will continue to keep Sharm under control until the cities revolt and join the rebellion."

"Yes, Colonel." He had a map of Egypt on the wall of his office, and it was kept up to date according to intelligence reports from a variety of sources. No breakthroughs were shown, no columns moving south, no true advancement. Things were stymied, and Naqdi had not pointed out exactly where the so-called victories had been achieved. "Yes." He changed the subject. "If something has befallen Major Shakuri, should we continue with these executions tonight? I personally think they accomplish nothing other than driving more people into the arms of the resistance. We didn't come here to kill the locals, did we? I don't like the idea of creating a guerrilla movement where none existed."

The colonel was adamant. "Of course we must continue the punishment for what they have done. Without enough soldiers to really establish martial law in the city, we must instead make them fear our wrath and thus ensure cooperation. Twenty have been chosen to be shot tonight, is that correct?"

"Yes. In the park at nine o'clock tonight. All is ready, and I have posted two armored personnel carriers there to support the operation. Should I choose another officer to command the firing squad in the absence of the major?"

The colonel paced a few steps, deep in thought, then turned and walked to the desk and leaned on it with his fingertips. "Better yet. Let us demonstrate how serious we are about controlling the situation here. You, the commanding general, will take personal charge of the firing squad."

The general crossed his muscular arms and rocked

back on his heels. "With all respect, Colonel, I do not think that is a good idea. Are you making that a direct order?"

"Yes. It is."

THE PENTAGON
WASHINGTON, D.C.

Marine Major General Brad Middleton, commander of Task Force Trident, broke into a smile as he listened on the scrambled telephone link that spanned the short distance across the Potomac River to the White House. He raised his beefy hand, curled it into a fist, and pumped it up and down.

His operations officer, Lieutenant Colonel Sybelle Summers, was watching with her hands folded in her lap. Navy Commander Benton Freedman, the communications chief, was in another chair, scrolling through a highly classified dump of material that had just been delivered on his laptop. Master Gunnery Sergeant O. O. Dawkins was pouring still another cup of coffee, his inner combat antennae twitching. He looked over at Sybelle, who shrugged her shoulders, her face blank. The general was rarely this happy, particularly during an ongoing operation.

"No, we haven't heard much from him at all," Middleton told the White House chief of staff. "His instructions were to call if he needed us, but he has chosen to go silent." He listened to a final response, said goodbye, and hung up the telephone with a flourish.

The general made a show of getting some coffee of his own, keeping his staff in suspense. After a first sip, he checked to make sure no drops had splashed his tie, then turned to them. "Kyle is raising hell in Egypt, and his MI6 partner has come out with a gold mine of intelligence. A fuckin' *gold mine*!"

Back at his desk, he unrolled a synopsis: a couple of big airplanes, an ammo dump that had closed the airport to anything larger than a biplane, an entire motor pool, a goddam *ship* in the harbor, dead Iranian soldiers all over the place, a high-value prisoner, and Gunny Swanson still healthy and on the loose as of a few hours ago. He had refused to leave when offered the chance. Dawkins gave a low whistle of Marine-to-Marine appreciation.

Middleton added the firsthand observations from the MI6 agent and her local contact, plus the delivery of an accumulation of computer data that contained thousands of pages of internal reports about the current government, military capabilities, and financial infrastructure, along with detailed intelligence on the operations and personnel of the Muslim Brotherhood and its leaders. The international banks and companies that were the main money funnels were identified, as were specific financiers who were laundering Iranian money transfers, including specific accounts that could be frozen, and some ranking political figures who were being bribed around the world. The Lizard started a rapid-fire read of the documents that had been downloaded to him from the White House and muttered, "Wow. This impacts a lot more than that little adventure in

Egypt. We're talking about their nuclear program and covert activities in Africa and the Middle East. The Egyptians are giving away the store."

"Iran pissed off the wrong people," Dawkins growled.

"The president and the British prime minister have both been briefed," Middleton said. "The Egyptian ambassador to the United Nations will openly condemn the invasion, deny that the elected government ever asked them to intervene, and demand that they leave."

"What about on the military side?" Dawkins asked.

"We are positioning naval strength forward, in the Red Sea and the Med, to isolate the battlefield. The Egyptian sources are urging restraint and insist that the roots of the Brotherhood uprising are weak. The army has been repositioning its forces, cleaning out the disloyal officers, and says that they are ready to commit their main battle forces and handle it on their own. They felt they could stymie the Brotherhood with minimum units, and by God they fought them to a standstill."

"So will there be any more attempts by us to insert special ops teams?" asked Summers.

"No. No American or British or NATO combat boots on the ground. Except for Gunny Swanson, and he's just a tourist."

"So even if the Egyptian military and the elected government are really stronger than they appear, do they have the support of the people?"

"Looks as though at this point the people have not

joined the Brotherhood's calls for still more revolution. The regular Egyptians probably are tired of the turmoil of the past few years and just want peace," Middleton mused. "Maybe they are just waiting for some kind of spark."

CHAPTER 29

A little more than an hour after the sun had set, cutting the daylight from another short winter's day, the men who would comprise the ambush team knelt together in lines on mats and rugs to offer their evening prayers at 6:27 PM. Kyle Swanson stood away from the group, positioned so he could watch the area outside while they were at worship, and hoped they were getting things straight with their faith. It was more than just ritual tonight. He expected that these would be the last prayers ever offered by some of them.

After the worship came a period of excitement and almost childlike exhilaration as the men hugged one another, made promises of brave acts, and shouted encouragement. They left the house at staggered intervals, one by one, with their weapons tucked into baggy clothing, carried in parcels over their shoulders, or rolled up in a prayer rug. Kyle still hung back; Abdel was the one sending them out the door.

"Did you do a count?"

"Yes. Just as you said, so I will know exactly how many we are. That seems strange. I know them all."

"Trust the count, Abdel. You know a lot of people, and things are going to get confusing. After the action you will know exactly how many are missing, if any. The last thing you want is some outsider infiltrating your team."

Abdel bit his lip in thought. "Will some of them die, Mr. Swanson?"

"I can't answer that, but it's likely. Look, my friend, there will be a lot of bullets flying out there tonight; in fact, it will be two minutes of hell. We are up against professionals, and we can't allow them to recover from the surprise of our attack. We have to keep up our fire until they are all down."

"What are you going to do about the tanks? They could massacre everybody."

Kyle dug into his bag and lifted out a pair of gray hand grenades with yellow markings. "These are Willie Petes—white phosphorus—and they are absolutely brutal. When you start the attack, I will pop them into the armored vehicles, and I can guarantee destruction. These babies destroy and burn everything flammable, and that armored skin will keep most of the power inside the vehicle. You'll see big white clouds, and an explosion that will rock the town." He put them down. "Plus, I plan to shoot whoever is inside, particularly the guys on the machine guns."

Abdel nodded and got up to leave. "I hope I can do this."

Kyle just gave him an easy smile. "You've got the guts and the smarts to do this, Abdel. Remember that you are the leader and the others will take their strength from what you do. Now let's go save those hostages and kill the bastards who took them captive."

Abdel's eyes grew hard, and he pulled his cloak around to cover the AK-47 that rode on his hip. "The Iranians should never have come here," he said and disappeared into the thickening darkness.

Swanson snapped off the light and sat alone in the house for another ten minutes, readying his head for what was to come, letting his tactical mind take over. He had done all he could to prepare the team, and now it was his turn. Although he had indicated to Abdel that taking out the armored personnel carriers would be no big deal, it actually was. On a battlefield against a comparable force, the AICs were insignificant relics, but sitting in an open park with no visible opposition, these variants of the old Russian BMPs would be lethal if given a chance. Kyle would not give them that chance.

He guessed that the troops who would become the firing squad and perimeter guards had been brought to the square in the Boraghs, the Iranian name for their modified version of the vehicles. So the soldiers would be dismounted and outside, their attention turned away from the tracked vehicles, and the sharp sloping sides of welded rolled steel armor would be no protection for them.

Still inside might be the drivers, on the left front position, and they also would be idle, watching the show; probably they would have been pressed into service outside with their mates. The commanders who sat right behind the drivers might stay with the vehicles, but as officers, they would more likely be outside, on the ground, to run the operation. That would leave the gunners in place behind the DShK 12.7 mm heavy machine gun in the rotatable turret. All of the armor and weaponry were just piles of metal if not properly employed. Men were needed to operate the Boraghs, and Kyle planned to kill both the machines and the men.

He checked his weapons and casually opened the door, settling into the act that he belonged there, that he was just another man on the street. He left his black special ops beanie in a pocket for the time being. Do nothing to raise suspicion, don't stare at anyone, be totally unremarkable and stick to the shadows. Be invisible. Hide, blend, and deceive. It was a unique talent that was a vital part of who he was, something a sniper did almost unconsciously, and he fell smoothly into the rhythm of walking through the streets in a tangled route that would lead to the park, where he would come out right behind the two parked Boraghs.

Kyle soon realized that he need not have worried about being spotted. The streets of Sharm el-Sheik, almost empty and silent during the day, had become busy pedestrian thoroughfares as small groups of people, and many individuals who looked just like he did, walked with solemnity toward the execution site. Everywhere he looked, there was movement, and he worked his way into the moving throng. The city was awake and fearful and stunned; twenty of its leading citizens were to be shot to death in public by the Iranians, and there was nothing to stop it.

Swanson believed that the Iranian officers in the park eventually would notice the growing size of the crowd of spectators and alert their central command at the airbase to prepare a quick reaction force should things get out of hand. If worse came to worst, the on-site commander could have his soldiers get inside the armored vehicles, button up, and wait for help. Meanwhile, they would be able to shoot out through firing ports in the sides while the machine gunners raked the attackers. Reinforcements, Kyle reasoned, were not anticipated, and if called they would not move out with a sense of urgency.

Ahead, just around the corner, there was an aurora of light, and the crowd spilled into the park.

At 8:30 PM., beneath a scatter of stars, the prisoners were marched up the street from Government House to the park, flanked by Iranian soldiers and led by a captain. Instead of the formal uniforms of the previous night, the soldiers were all helmeted and in combat gear. The prisoners were battered—black eyes, split lips, swollen faces, cuts and bruises on arms and legs, and blood splotched on their clothing. They had endured a rough ordeal in prison as the guards tried to get information about the partisan forces in the city, and now they lurched more than walked, some having to assist others. The crowd howled with cries of despair as familiar faces were seen. Even the old police chief had been taken prisoner, under the reasoning that his officers might have helped the unknown resistance force. All of the uniformed cops on crowd control duty, Kyle noticed, had been disarmed and were unsmiling. Step by step, the cowed prisoners were herded into the bright lights that glowed at the execution site.

Swanson slid to the rear of the crowd and took position in a doorway about ten feet behind the armored vehicles. These were parked at an angle, ass to ass, and the gunners had swiveled their big weapons toward the growing throng of onlookers. He spotted Abdel in the front rank of spectators on the right side of the wall of sandbags, and when the Egyptian saw him, they exchanged silent nods. The kid was doing OK, learning fast on the job, just like any new lieutenant getting lessons from a veteran gunny on determination, leadership, and discipline. Abdel seemed confident, which indicated his men were in place, and Swanson could only hope they would all hold their fire and not open up too early to revenge the obvious outrageous treatment of their people. Each man on the team had a specific target, and everything depended on that opening burst. Shooting too soon would be a disaster.

The Iranian captain leading the awful parade of prisoners was a strutting little martinet who had been second in command to Major Shakuri at the first executions. He was proud that General Khasrodad had put him in charge of this one. He would tolerate no mistakes by his troops, or any intervention by the civilians.

The invisible partisan fighters hiding in Sharm el-Sheikh had to watch now as innocent friends and neighbors paid a blood price for the attacks on Iranian forces. The captain had also lost friends to the ruthless and cowardly actions of the rebels during the past few days, and there was no pity in him as he straightened his crisp olive green uniform. These people needed to feel his whip.

You're mine, thought Kyle as he studied the commander of the execution group. Then he switched his attention back to the Boraghs. The pair of back doors on each of the big APCs hung open, and each of those thick hatch covers served double duty as an auxiliary fuel tank. Inside, he saw the padded bench on which eight soldiers would sit in each vehicle, two rows of four leaning against a common backrest that was also the main gas tank. At the front, below the gunner's hatch, was ammunition storage. The Boraghs were universally hated by the troops who had to ride in them, because battlefield experience had proven that a land mine, an armor-piercing incendiary bullet, or a rocket-propelled grenade through the rear would utterly destroy the beast. A soldier's best chance was riding outside, where he might risk being hit by bullets but would have a better chance by being thrown away from the blast rather than cooking trapped inside. Swanson hoped the captain had been efficient enough to top off with fuel and ammo before coming to the park.

Twenty people were too many to kill at one time. They had done only six the first night, and that had required a firing squad of ten men. That same number of soldiers with AK-47s set on full automatic should be sufficient this time, too, if each was responsible for the death of only one Egyptian prisoner who would be standing immobile, tied to a post. The captain had to be economical, for his overall force was obviously smaller than the crowd that was gathering in the spacious park, trampling the grass underfoot to see the dreadful execution ground.

Each of the armored personnel carriers had brought eight infantrymen, for a total of sixteen. Add the dismounted drivers, and the captain had a total of eighteen on the ground in the large park, plus himself and a lieutenant who was his own second in command this time. The difference makers were the two machine gunners who remained in their overwatch positions aboard the tracks. Still, looking over the uneasy crowd, he thought about calling for reinforcements. He decided against it. The general would think he was not up to the job. *Where was Shakuri, anyway?*

The sad line of those chosen to be killed shuffled to a halt beside the big fountain, which the captain noted had been turned off as a silent protest against what was happening around it. He briskly counted off the first ten from his left. "Move these traitors to the wall," he barked. "The rest will sit down here under guard to await their turn."

Four additional posts had been planted before the long wall of sandbags that had been extended and strengthened, and an Egyptian captive was soon tied to each of the ten positions, with black hoods yanked over their heads. Two women were among the initial victims.

After binding the prisoners, the soldiers retreated across the killing field, picked up their weapons, and formed into line to become the firing squad. Three Iranians guarded the next group of prisoners seated on the grass, and the remainder of the soldiers stood at intervals facing the crowd. The captain then noticed that the police who had helped in the initial executions had vanished. No matter, because he neither needed nor trusted them. Both sides of the wide field between the shooters and the citizens tied to the posts were packed with sullen spectators who were remaining ominously quiet. Where was the weeping and the cries for mercy? Even those about to die were not struggling or calling out.

The captain took his position to the left of the firing squad, with his lieutenant standing a few steps behind. A final look around showed him that the gunners in the Boragh APCs at the edge of the park were ready in case of trouble. The squad had readied their weapons and were squared away, so the captain decided to get on with it.

"Attention!" he yelled.

Kyle Swanson had quietly pulled on his special ops black beanie and rolled it down so that his face was hidden but for his eyes and mouth. When the captain roared his preliminary order, Swanson elbowed roughly through a few people in front of him, uncovering his M-16A3 as he went. He was only a few steps away from the open rear doors of the armored vehicles when he snapped the rifle butt into his shoulder and put two quick bullets into the head of the unsuspecting machine gunner facing away from him on the right, then cycled and did the same thing to the one on the left. Both targets jarred forward against their weapons and bounced back, dead. "*Now!*" he shouted as loudly as possible, grabbing a white phosphorus grenade from his left pocket. He pulled the pin and flipped it into the open door of the left-side Boragh as he dashed between the pair of APCs.

The first volley of shots that came from Abdel's group on the right side of the crowd was a long clatter of gunfire that indicated little discipline, but it was effective, and three members of the firing squad staggered and collapsed like discarded dolls. The volley from the second ambush team on the left took down another two Iranians, just before Kyle's grenade exploded inside the fuel-laden Boragh armored personnel carrier, which seemed to expand like a balloon before blowing up with overheated shrapnel, which instantly penetrated the adjacent APC and detonated the gas and ammunition inside. The heavy explosions thundered, and the rolling concussion smashed Kyle Swanson facedown into the grass. For a moment, he lost his breath and had to struggle to lift his eyes as the gust of searing wind broke over him and the swelling noise shook his body.

When he regained his senses, the crowd was scattering, and the gunfire had increased in volume. The ambushers were shooting, but so were the remaining Iranian soldiers, who were trained troops and altered their aim from the prisoners to the threat of the unexpected attackers. The captain and his lieutenant spread out to direct the fight, stunned that their backup units of armored vehicles with the heavy machine guns had been destroyed.

Kyle was up and running again when the renewed fire from the ambushers clipped two more Iranians, but one of those went spinning down with his AK-47 spraying on full automatic and ripped two of the prisoners still tied at the posts. One attacker dropped with red holes dotting his white tunic, but the initial surprise had worked to make the manpower score more even, and the silence of the terrifying machine guns emboldened Abdel's men. From the fleeing crowd came a couple of the policemen who had retrieved their weapons and joined the fight on the side of the rebels, and the two final Iranian guards who had been herding the seated prisoners both fell.

Swanson was only twenty yards behind the Iranian officers, and he went to a knee, steadied, and shot the lieutenant three times in the center of his back, then was up and moving again, understanding that the casualty rate had definitely swung to the plus side for his guys. Just as he thought they would win for certain, he saw Abdel take a round, blood blooming at the left shoulder as the youngster spun and hit the dirt. Nothing could take the steam out of this attack like the sudden loss of an inspirational leader, but the Egyptians had already tasted victory and kept crawling and running forward. Kyle heard the wounded Abdel calling encouragement. More men fell on both sides.

People returning from the crowd braved the crossfire to free the prisoners from the poles and rush them to safety. Others picked up fallen weapons and joined the battle.

The Iranian captain was screaming at his dwindling force and firing his sidearm at random targets when he felt the barrel of a gun press against the back of his head and heard a voice say in English, "Hey. It's over." Swanson double-tapped the officer, and the head blew apart like a melon. A few more extended bursts of gunfire, and the attack was finished. The park lay bathed in blood and wreathed in smoke.

Kyle jogged over to where Abdel was pushing himself upright, holding a hand to his left shoulder but smiling broadly. His people were rejoicing; the prisoners were free, and the Iranian firing squad lay dead. Onlookers stripped the soldiers of their guns and ammo. Swanson slung his own weapon and started to tend the wound, but he was pushed away by two women who seemed to know what they were doing, while others formed a protective circle around the young man who had come out of nowhere to defeat the invaders and save their friends and neighbors.

Abdel grabbed Kyle with his right hand and pulled the black-masked man toward him. "You knocked out the tanks, just as you said."

"Forget that. You led this attack, and just look what you did, pal," Kyle said, watching the confidence grow in Abdel's eyes. "You're the leader now. They want to join you."

It was a flesh wound, and the nurses had him bundled up, with his left arm in a sling. "What next? Just let everybody go home?"

"No. A column of reinforcements will be coming in from the airport. Stop them and you win the entire battle."

"Show me how." A broad and enthusiastic smile crossed his handsome face, and Abdel held his rifle high while people cheered and cell phones and cameras snapped pictures and made little movies that would soon flood the Internet. An unknown man wearing a black roll-down mask was right beside him.

CHAPTER 30

You disobeyed me!" Colonel Naqdi shouted as he stormed into the command post at the airport, and his furious eyes were like daggers. He did not care that other, lower-ranking men would hear what he had to say to their commanding general. The man was finished! "I told you to personally take charge of tonight's executions in the park, General Khasrodad. You ignored my direct order, and look what has happened."

"Keep your voice down, Colonel Naqdi," Khasrodad replied in an equally hard tone. "We're organizing a counterattack, and I have no time to waste arguing with you. Stay out of our way."

Radios crackled on different tactical frequencies, and aides hurried in and out with reports and orders. Naqdi felt the eyes of the staff members scalding him and moved to one side to watch. He could wait a little while longer to deal with the insubordination. Let them stew for the time being and wonder what he was going to do.

The general was committing the last Boragh armored personnel carrier that had been airlifted in with the troops, this one armed with a cannon as well as the big machine gun. A bus that had been confiscated would follow it, tailed by three pickup trucks, all four filled with troops. Forty elite Iranian commandos with automatic weapons were ready to roll and eager for a fight, tired of being forced to stand by as a defensive occupation force. The officer in charge of the relief convoy reported that it was ready, and the general gave permission to set it in motion.

As the string of headlights went through the front gate, the general turned to Naqdi with a snarl. "Now. What do you want?"

Colonel Naqdi would not accept being bullied. "I wanted you to do your job, Khasrodad. I demand an explanation of why you were not down there as ordered."

"Because my proper position is here at the headquarters, where I can see the big picture and command my entire force. You want a martyr with a sword on horseback. That's stupid thinking." He walked to a wall map of Sharm el-Sheikh and put his finger on the execution park. "We are going to reestablish control and get our men out of there."

"How bad is it?" The colonel had heard only fragmentary reports on the fighting.

The general let out a long breath. "We don't know. Local observers have told us that it was an ambush and heavy fighting, with both of our armored vehicles destroyed. I don't understand why the captain did not call for backup forces, or even withdraw, if he saw such a threat developing."

"It was your poor leadership. Do not try to fob it off on some captain." Naqdi made his decision on the spot. "General, you are relieved of your command. I shall take over here. I order you to leave immediately."

With every soldier in the room watching, Khasrodad turned slightly to his right and spoke to a monstrous man standing nearby. "Take this man out of the command post, Sergeant Major. The colonel is confined to his quarters, under guard."

"No! You have no authority over me, Khasrodad. I refuse to be arrested." The sergeant major grabbed Naqdi's bicep with a huge hand and squeezed hard. It felt like the arm was being torn off.

"Very well. Then take him outside and shoot him, Sergeant Major. The charge is cowardice in the face of the enemy."

"Yes, sir." The big NCO shoved Naqdi toward the door.

"Cowardice? That is absurd, and I shall tell our senior leaders in Tehran of your insubordination and ineptness."

"No. You will tell them nothing, for in about two minutes, you will be dead and out of my fucking hair, you interfering dog. This whole thing was your plan, and it has blown up in our faces."

The colonel slowly raised his hands in surrender.

"I'll go. But you know I will still report this insubordination to Tehran."

"So will I, Colonel. So will I. Now, leave."

The convoy of reinforcements encountered no opposition as it trundled out of the airport beneath a spangle of stars. The headlights were bright and the ride smooth along the paved highway. In the distance lay Sharm el-Sheikh, most of it wrapped in darkness but with a few of the big hotels still gaudily lit. Those bright lights drew the eyes of the soldiers, when they should have been studying the road ahead and the buildings around them. The traffic circle that was the first checkpoint was directly ahead, and the armored personnel carrier led the way into it, now entering the more populous section of Sharm, although the streets were empty.

The APC had to slow a bit to handle the curve of the traffic circle but arced around smoothly, followed by the other vehicles. The driver saw the main road's exit just ahead and steered for it, ready to accelerate. His commander was right behind him, mentally picturing the distance left to the park, and he ordered his radio operator to alert the base that they were through the first checkpoint and continuing on.

Simultaneous flashes popped through the darkness as three rocket-propelled grenades erupted from the ground floors of three different buildings at the exit, and the first one burst against the side, taking off a track. The second bored into the weak rear doors to explode inside, and the third skipped under the APC and went off like a land mine beneath it. In an instant, the powerful armored vehicle leapt upward in a fiery ball and crashed back to the roadway, everyone in it dead, its big cannon useless, and the burning hulk blocking the forward exit.

From rooftops and windows, men jumped up and let loose with a typhoon of gunfire at the troops in the bus and trucks, and a final RPG flashed out and drove like a burning lance into the last truck, which had just entered the traffic circle. It detonated, and the incinerated vehicle rolled to a halt to seal off the exit. The other vehicles were now trapped inside, and the soldiers bailed out of the trucks, harried by the gunmen firing down on them. The Iranians opened up with their own weapons, unable to see their targets, just raking the upper floors and roof edges around them. They knew that they were supposed to charge into the buildings and take the fight to the enemy, but most of their officers were dead, and every soldier there felt alone.

The whole column had been destroyed, at least a quarter of the force was dead or wounded, dancing flames surrounded them, and gunshots were blinking from every dark building, making more of them fall by the minute. The shouts of Egyptian rebels fell on their ears, and as soon as one Iranian soldier began to run, so did the others. Safety lay beyond this deadly traffic circle and out of this deadly ring of gunfire. The airport was the only place to go.

Swanson watched them go from the rooftop of a corner building, thinking, *Well, that's the end of that.* His M-16A3 rifle was slung across a shoulder, and he had rolled up the mask, feeling a sense of relief for the first time in days. His fight here was over, and he could leave.

Abdel El-Din, with the bloody shirt and youthful enthusiasm, was the hero. Kyle's guidance of the youngster in any future battle would be replaced by that of the police chief, a former army guy who knew what he was doing. As soon as he had been freed from his execution post, the old man had grabbed a gun and started shooting at Iranians. His men followed his example, and he threw open the police armories to get better weapons for the civilians who wanted to stand and fight the invaders. Kyle had advised on setting up the traffic circle ambush, but the chief didn't need much help, due to his twenty years of military experience. He positioned the RPGs and a pair of light machine guns, then lined men along the surrounding rooftops and the upper windows, but he let Abdel give the order to fire. The chief, too, understood that the charisma and bravery of the young man was a force unto itself, a focus around which the people would rally. About a hundred men from Sharm el-Sheikh were now already fanning out to collect more volunteers and establish roadblocks.

"How you doing, kid?" Swanson asked.

Now that the excitement was calming, Abdel was feeling the effect of his wound. He was pale and weak, leaning back against a wall as a doctor worked on him. "I am good, but it hurts."

"He must go to the hospital," the doctor said. "The wound is not serious, but the bullet is still inside. It needs to be cleaned out and properly repaired. He has lost a lot of blood."

The police chief stroked his beard and examined the young man who had made this all happen. "Then let's get him over there," he said. "We've got things under control for now. We have our guns again and can go back to being policemen and protecting our citizens."

"I don't want to leave," Abdel protested. A grimace of pain twisted his face, and the doctor prepared a needle and inserted it in the forearm. Abdel looked at Kyle; his eyelids fluttered and closed.

"He turned into quite a soldier," Kyle said to the chief, who nodded agreement. "Not bad for an untrained man who rents jet skis to tourists."

The chief laughed, then spoke in remarkably good English. "I understand that he reported a couple of jet skis were stolen from his business recently, the night the ship blew up in the harbor."

"That right?" Kyle scratched his ear.

"Ummh. I've been meaning to get around to investigating that soon." A wink. "Don't worry. I'll keep watch over him from now on. If I cannot persuade him to become a policeman, maybe he will be mayor or something." He extended his hand, and Kyle shook it. "From what Abdel told me before the fight, your hand was on this rebellion all the way, sir. And I saw the way you handled your rifle."

"A young man's imagination. I was just hanging around, and now I'm going to check into one of those big hotels. I'm just a tourist, and I think it is best if I go home now."

"Where is your home? Are you American, British?"

"Best of luck, Chief." Swanson turned away and

disappeared into the crowd that had come out at night, unafraid, to fill the city streets.

THE AIRPORT

Colonel Naqdi was in a room that had been set aside for his use, surfing the Web on his laptop. His unfinished business with General Khasrodad would have to wait, but he had not forgotten the arrogant senior officer, nor the big sergeant major who had actually laid hands on him. Eventually, he would deal with them both.

The high-definition resolution on his screen brought the rebellion of Sharm right into his room. Every news channel was broadcasting pictures of the uprising, and the social media sites were alive with individual reports. Naqdi did not have to crawl back over to the general and beg for a report about the convoy of reinforcements, for its fate was there for all to see; any child anywhere in the world with access to a computer could watch the shameful, crushing defeat of the Iranians both at the execution park and later at the traffic circle. Elite soldiers had turned and run like cowards.

The one outstanding figure in the narrative and the photographs and news reports was a young man who apparently was the leader of the rebellion, a rather heroic-looking fellow who was now getting worldwide attention for his bravery. He was shown fighting, cheering his men on, talking seriously to older men, including one wearing a mask, and finally refusing to be loaded into an ambulance because he was wounded. His name, the reporters said, was Abdel El-Din, and he normally worked at his family's seaside marina. The colonel studied the various scenes, clicked on several specific pictures, and downloaded them to a printer.

Naqdi finally turned from the computer, for the news was not going to change. Of more immediate concern now was his own survival. The general would do whatever he could to save the remainder of his command, but that was no longer the colonel's problem. In fact, he was under a peculiar kind of arrest, for while no guard stood outside the door, the entire airport had become his prison. He went outside for a walk. Dawn was just about to break in the east, and that gave him the idea. He quickened his pace over to a hangar into which his own plane had been taken. He could fly out of here anytime he wanted! Get back to Cairo and find some levers of control, out from under the thumb of this failed general, and into the welcoming arms of the Muslim Brotherhood.

Several mechanics in stained coveralls were in the large building, and, since he was still in his military uniform, he had no problem ordering them to fuel the plane, do a preflight check, and move it out of the hangar to the apron, prepared for an immediate takeoff. While they did that, he returned to his quarters to gather his computer and civilian clothes. Should he tell the general he was leaving? Why bother? He would find out soon enough.

Naqdi came back outside and saw that the mechanics had been quick. The light tan plane was sitting there, waiting for him in the first glow of the new day. He would have the props turning in five minutes and be gone in ten, abandoning the failures of Sharm to the general.

Four stubby MiG-21 fighters bearing the red, white, and black rondels of the Egyptian Air Force kicked away from the military base at Hurghada on afterburner and headed across the Red Sea toward Sharm el-Sheikh only a little more than fifty-one miles away. The old but agile planes steadied up at 1,300 miles per hour, rocketing across the water and the ship-packed channel that led into the Suez Canal. The pilot of each plane started checking down his weapons systems immediately after takeoff, because they would be in attack mode in a matter of moments. Each had a 30 mm internal cannon and a pair of 500 kg bombs hanging on wing pylons.

They flew due east, then broke into two pairs as they began a low circle back west so they would come out of the rising sun. Radars all around, including at the airport, would paint them brightly, but that was immaterial this morning. This fight would be over in the blink of an eye, and the pilots would be back at Hurghada in a few minutes for the debriefing and a big breakfast.

The four MiGs dropped out of the sky like an aerie of hawks and came streaking over the runway in line, popping eight large bombs right down the centerline, then zoomed up, flipped over, and came roaring in again, emptying their cannons on any targets the pilots chose. The series of explosions followed by the booming chatter of the cannon fire and the shriek of the jet engines on afterburner stunned the entire Sharm airport, not so much for the damage inflicted but as a signal that the Egyptian military had made up its mind and was coming after the Iranians.

No one was more shocked than Colonel Yahya Naqdi as he was running toward his plane, only to dive hard onto the tarmac when the bombs began to fall. He was battered by the bomb blast concussion waves and watched helplessly when a strafing MiG zoomed directly overhead and chewed his little plane to bits.

CHAPTER 31

THE BLUE NEPTUNE

Karam, the concierge, looked up from his desk in the refurbished lobby of the Blue Neptune and saw a man with a familiar face standing before him. "Mr. Kyle Swanson? Are you all right?" The visitor was dirty and unshaven, dressed in the clothes of an Egyptian workingman, and carrying a worn duffel bag.

"As you can see, I didn't make the plane out before the Iranians landed, so I would like my old room back for a few days, if I can get it."

"There is still fighting going on in the city, sir."

"Not much longer. It looks as if the Iranians are bottled up at the airport now, and the executing of citizens is finished once and for all."

This man was a big tipper and always seemed to be a harbinger of useful information, so Karam started running the profit possibilities. Peace would mean a return of commerce to normal levels, and his family could benefit from that by getting an early start, bringing in fresh supplies and repair material. They could rent trucks, buy food elsewhere cheap, hire African immigrants for labor . . .

"Karam? Hello? My room?"

"Oh, pardon me. Of course, Mr. Swanson. Fortunately it escaped damage during the awful attack."

"Believe it or not, I still have my key, since I did not have a chance to check out properly before the shooting started. I hope my suitcase is still in your left-luggage storage room, and I would like it sent up immediately. Also send up a medium steak, potatoes, and a salad, with a twenty-four-bottle carton of bottled water. A stack of fresh towels, too. Can you do that?"

"Yes. Of course. Welcome back, sir. May I ask your immediate plans?"

"Not very complicated, Karam. I'm going to shower until my skin falls off, eat a huge meal, and then sleep the rest of the day. I don't want to be bothered."

"Depend on it, sir. Have a good rest. Whatever you need, sir, just call me."

In the distance, toward the airport, they heard the running thumps of exploding bombs and the whine of attacking jet planes. "What was that?"

"Just someone carrying on the good work, Karam." Kyle rapped the desk with two knuckles and headed for the elevators. Those distant explosions meant the Egyptian military had finally gotten off its collective ass and decided to do something about the foreign interlopers.

The only question was, would it be a prolonged fight to the death, or would reason take hold and things finish peacefully? The Iranians could not win, but they had to decide how they would lose.

He went to the suite, unlocked it, and stepped into a cool, clean area that seemed to be on a different planet. The Blue Neptune had been badly damaged, but if his guess was right, that little mercenary concierge, Karam, had made a small fortune in organizing rebuilding and repair. Now, at least in his suite, nothing seemed out of place. Even the little soaps and shampoo bottles were in a wicker basket, and colorful fresh flowers stood in glass vases. The broad window in the bedroom opened onto the harbor, and fresh air blew in. He took a deep breath, looking up as a lone helicopter flew along the coast, heading north: a Sikorsky SH-3 in Egyptian colors.

THE AIRPORT

The Sea King chopper, adapted for executive transport, had cushioned seats and extra sound-absorbent padding around the cabin, easing the nerves of Brigadier General Mohammed Suliamin of the Egyptian general staff. The flight had departed Hurghada as soon as the MiG fighters returned and reported their total success. It was Suliamin's job to negotiate a settlement. As the big bird approached in a wide circle, the pilot radioed for landing permission and advised that General Suliamin would be on the ground within five minutes to confer with the base commander. Permission was given, and the Sea King settled down near the control tower. The hatch opened, stairs were lowered, and Suliamin, looking fresh and rested in a crisp uniform, stepped onto the tarmac.

Brigadier General Medhi Khasrodad of the Iranian Revolutionary Guard walked out to meet him while the helicopter blades were still revolving, and the two officers formally exchanged salutes, then retreated into the darkness of the operations center, where a pot of hot tea and plates of warm breads were waiting. All maps had been removed and the radios turned off, and the two men were alone.

"How did you get yourself into such a mess, Medhi?" The two generals were on a first-name basis from having bumped into each other frequently during their respective careers, usually at conferences in foreign capitals.

Khasrodad shrugged his big shoulders. "Politicians, Mohammed."

"As always," replied the Egyptian. "Did they really think this would work, dropping you into Sharm on the hope that the Muslim Brotherhood would ride to the rescue?"

"I don't know what was said in the halls of power. I guess they determined it was worth a try, to capitalize on Egypt's ongoing political unrest and seize control of the Suez and the Red Sea ports. The Brotherhood was supposed to destroy the moderates and take over your government, and the Egyptian military would become a puppet that we would operate, an unpredictable knife on your border with Israel."

"Preposterous. Our general staff doesn't care who the president is. The generals will never give up power in Egypt."

The Iranian agreed and poured some more tea. "So let's get to business. What offer do you bring?"

General Suliamin did not open his briefcase. "First, admit that your military situation is hopeless. You have no heavy weapons, no airpower, no offshore naval support, no armored columns rushing to save you, no more ammo, food, or supplies. The Muslim Brotherhood realized it was not an army and is pulling back on all fronts, cushioning its extreme demands in hopes of gaining broader support for their candidates in a new round of elections. As you said, politicians.

"Meanwhile, I have all of those things I name, and more, not counting thousands of local citizens who would like to destroy every one of you. How many men do you have left, Medhi? About a thousand?"

Khasrodad sidestepped the question about troop numbers. "My men are highly trained, Mohammed. They are not some riffraff off the streets. We could fight a long and hard battle to the last man before you overran us."

"I might point out it was riffraff from the streets of this little city that defeated your elite troopers. But why opt for a full battle when the result will be the same in the end? You are locked in place by the desert and the water, so we would just stand off and bomb the crap out of this place before ever having to move in ground troops. With a snap of my fingers, I can call in those pesky and deadly American drones to eradicate some final pockets of stiff resistance and simultaneously take pictures of your ignominious defeat. You might give us a bloody nose, General, but you have no hope of victory."

"Are you demanding an unconditional surrender?" The Iranian sucked in a deep breath. "You want us to stack arms and parade in shame through the streets so old women can throw rotten fruit at my men? I will not allow that."

"No, not at all. You have done some terrible things here, but we have no intention to make you and your country lose face in the international arena, brother, for we are of the same region. Our countries are bound through antiquity, and we will undoubtedly share common interests in the future. Right now, we just want you gone."

"So, how?"

"The same way you came in, by air. Egyptian aircraft will take you back to Tehran. Leave behind your guns."

"The runway is useless."

"I can have engineers and heavy equipment here to repair that within a day." General Suliamin paused. "The one final thing is that, regretfully, you must stay behind as my prisoner, the man who led the invasion. You will be treated honorably and eventually repatriated back to Iran."

Khasrodad nodded, and a bitter smile crossed his face. "I understand. That's fair enough. I will recommend that my senior commanders in Tehran accept these terms, particularly that idea of following the UN request. Now I have something extra, my friend, something that will make this your lucky day. Instead of fighting to the death, I'm going to present you a gift."

General Suliamin crossed his legs. "What kind of present?"

"I want you to take someone prisoner in addition to myself. The fool who planned the whole operation is a top intelligence officer by the name of Colonel Yahya Ali Naqdi, who has been organizing this for months, if not years. He operates out of Cairo but flew in yesterday to bother us. The public executions were his idea. You don't have to treat him with any honor whatsoever as far as I am concerned. In fact, I almost shot him myself yesterday. You can now do it for me."

"Where is he now?"

"I have him under arrest in the barracks." The general went to the door and told his sergeant major to go bring Naqdi, on the double. "When do we get started on this withdrawal?"

"Withdrawal? Once back in Iran, you can call it anything you want, maybe a strategic redeployment of troops at the request of the United Nations, which you claimed asked you here in the first place as peacekeepers; but on our side, it has to be a surrender because of the insult to our territorial integrity. We will let the diplomats sort out the final terminology." General Suliamin opened his briefcase and handed the Iranian a three-page legal document to make it official, including a schedule. "I will bring some troops over today to take over your perimeter outposts and keep the locals away. Do you have any of those transports left?"

"Only three that are still airworthy. We can use them for the airlift." He finished reading the document. "I have to obtain permission before signing."

"I know. I will go back to Hurghada now and send a couple of staff members back to work with your people and finish the details." He stood and shook hands with the defeated general.

The sergeant major threw open the door and barged into the room without knocking. "Sir! Colonel Naqdi is gone!"

THE BLUE NEPTUNE

The ringing telephone did not awaken Kyle Swanson, nor did the knock on the door of his rooms. The knock became a pounding, and still he didn't stir, for he was buried in clean sheets and soft pillows, snoring and relaxed for the first time in days. Finally, Karam, the concierge, unlocked the door with his master key and allowed the chief of police to go inside and shake Kyle awake. It was eight o'clock in the morning, and he had been asleep for only a little more than an hour. Swanson groaned as the burly Egyptian cop called his name loudly and shook him roughly by the shoulder.

His eyes opened, bleary and unfocused until the face of the chief swam into view. Kyle pulled a pillow over his head and said, muffled, "Why in the name of all that's holy are you here, Chief? What does a man have to do to get some rest in this place?"

"Get up, Mr. Swanson. Something urgent has happened."

Kyle lowered the pillow and read the bedside clock and groaned. "Urgent? I thought the fighting was over."

"That it is. In fact, a surrender is being arranged, but that's not why I am at your bedside. You must get up."

"This had better be good." He shucked off the sheet and sat up, wearing boxer shorts. A bottle of water was on the table, and he gulped at it.

"An Iranian officer, a colonel, drove up to one of our roadblocks and surrendered to my men, saying that he had important information." The chief of police found a chair and made himself comfortable. "And he asked for you by name."

Kyle closed his eyes for a minute. It could only be one person. "Let me guess; he calls himself the Pharaoh, right? Says he's some kind of spy."

The chief blinked. "Yes. How did you know? We have him downstairs."

"Oh, double shit," Swanson said, getting to his feet and yawning. "OK, Chief. Give me a few minutes to dress and make a few calls, then I'll come right down."

"We are holding him in an office area that had been confiscated by another Iranian officer, a Major Shakuri."

"I heard that guy was taken off the street a few days back by British intelligence agents. He also claimed to be some kind of big intelligence dog. Was it that long ago? Jesus, I can't remember. So much has been going on. Anyway, Major Shakuri is currently the property of MI6 and the Saudi Arabian government. I'm going to shower again to wake up and will meet you there in fifteen."

Colonel Naqdi had been in the intelligence service for many years and had learned that a good agent always has a back-door emergency plan for himself. His ambitious operation to plant Iranian troops in Egypt had failed due to that incompetent general and the spineless weasels of the Muslim Brotherhood, so it was time to save his own hide. The idea of getting out through Cairo had vanished when his airplane was destroyed, so he was into his secondary scheme of trading information for safety. It was time for the Pharaoh to step forward and start revealing actual state secrets, which meant he could never return to Iran. Too bad, but the world was a big place, he had a number of bank accounts abroad, and if he could get beneath the protective wing of the United States and the British, the colonel could look forward to a long, comfortable life.

This was the payoff moment from planting those seeds over the past months with MI6, which certainly shared the information with the CIA. They liked what he had given them so much that a pair of agents had been dispatched to work closely with him. He had always stayed just beyond their reach, always one step ahead, always tantalizing his would-be masters with what he might reveal about what was happening in Tehran and about the workings of the minds of the fanatic mullahs and that crazy president. He could even discuss the nuclear program with enough authenticity that his questioners would accept the information as being fresh, although it was not. In fact, a lot of the material he passed along was common knowledge in Iran's intelligence circles. With his rank and reputation, he could spin his cooperation to be dependent upon how well he was treated. He was thinking more in terms of Miami than Guantánamo, or Ireland instead of Romania.

That was his frame of mind when the office door swung open and the chief of police came in with a slim man wearing a dark business suit, shined custom-made shoes, and a silk tie over a light blue shirt. He was about five feet nine and weighed probably about 150 pounds, with sun-bleached brown hair and piercing gray-green eyes. The colonel could not stand up because he was handcuffed to his chair, but he went on the offensive immediately. "You are Kyle Swanson of the Central Intelligence Agency," he announced with authority in his voice.

"Wrong," the man replied, taking a chair.

The policeman stood behind him. The last time the chief had seen Swanson, he was dirty, sweaty, and in Egyptian clothes; now he was in the neat clothes of a successful, cold-as-ice business executive.

"I don't know where your information comes from, but I don't work for the CIA. You did get the name right."

"Then some other American intelligence agency. Rumors are often inaccurate on details. Which group you work for is unimportant."

The man slid a leather billfold from his inside jacket pocket and pushed a business card across the table separating them. "I'm a businessman who just happened to get caught in the middle of your stupid invasion of Egypt. That was some kind of fucked-up fight from the start, huh? It must have been planned by idiots."

The card identified Kyle as vice president of Excalibur Enterprises, based in London. The colonel read the card and twirled it on a corner while he thought. "It has been no secret that you and Dr. Tianha Bialy of the MI6 were sent to Egypt to find the Pharaoh. Well, here I am, ready to accommodate your questions on a matter of vital importance."

Kyle turned in his seat and looked up at the chief. "Is this guy for real?" The chief shrugged. "Bialy was looking for you, but she and I were together only for a few days, working on a project for my company because she is a recognized expert in Egyptian affairs. She had some local guys helping her out with the spy stuff, and they worked hard to keep me in the dark. That was how I preferred it."

The colonel remained unruffled. "You are a clever man, Mr. Swanson, but you forgot one thing."

"I forget a lot of things, but nothing important, like whether I'm a spy."

"You got too close to the spotlight of publicity, sir, when you were helping out the young hero street fighter in the rebellion. I saw your picture with him during the fighting."

Swanson smirked. He had been wearing the mask. "Bullshit. You're just fishing now."

Naqdi unfolded one of the pictures he had downloaded. It showed Abdel El-Din listening to a masked man with a gun over his shoulder. "The rifle, Mr.

Swanson. Everybody else out there had out-of-date and common weapons like the AK-47. This man is carrying a 5.56 mm Colt-made M-16A3 assault rifle, the latest generation preferred by American Special Forces. I suppose it could have just been there by accident, but I don't believe so. The masked fellow fits your physique. This is you, Kyle Swanson."

Swanson laughed aloud. "You are letting your imagination run away with you, Colonel. Somebody with a telephone camera snaps an out-of-focus picture and you come up with a story to match what you want it to be? You're wrong again, but let's wrap this up. What do you want?"

"Very well. Have it your way."

"Chief, could you excuse us for a few minutes? This won't take long."

"Should I know what is being said?" The chief was already moving toward the door. This man Swanson was a mystery: a warrior, then a businessman, now becoming something else right before his eyes.

"Probably best that you don't."

When the Egyptian had left them alone, Swanson sat down again. "Talk. Get to the point."

"You know my work as the Pharaoh, so you can assume that I possess an incredible amount of information that I am willing to pass to your government, with a few conditions, such as my safety."

"Information like what? Sell me."

Naqdi turned sly and condescending. "You have neither the rank nor the skills to interrogate me, Mr. Swanson. All I want from you is a safe-conduct escort to

Washington or London. Inform your superiors that I will give them the inner workings of the Iranian Army of the Guardians to start. From there, we can move on, all the way up to, and including, the nuclear program. Is that enough of a sales job?"

Kyle leaned back in the chair and laced his hands behind his head. God, his neck was in knots. "Well, let me break this to you gently. While you were waiting, I was on the phone with MI6 in London and my boss in Washington. The decision is simple: No deal."

Naqdi swallowed hard, and his face blanched white. "What are you saying? I insist, no, I *demand,* to speak with someone higher than you."

"Too little, too late. Everyone agrees that you are unreliable, untrustworthy, a liar, and that you are just trying to lay down some disinformation fog to save your ass. We doubt that you know anything at all that we don't already have on file in triplicate in some agency's file cabinet. As for the paper-shuffling side of things, like with the Palm Group in Cairo, your chum Major Shakuri beat you to it and made his own deal first. He's giving up everything, and he had been logging your private dealings and secret communications for months. Other sources have cracked your financial network. You've got nothing left that we want."

"You took Shakuri?"

"Yep. Chalk that one up for Dr. Bialy. So we're done here, you and me. By the way, I really don't work for the CIA. You know that the United States operates a big-league intelligence and counterterrorism network, Colonel, but it also has a few guys like me—I can go anywhere in the world and do anything I want, no questions asked. So count yourself lucky this morning that I haven't broken your fat neck right here at this desk, or pitched you off the top of this nice hotel, you arrogant son of a bitch." Swanson unfolded from the chair and opened the door for the chief to return.

"Take me to the British, then. Let me talk to them!" Naqdi's voice grew shrill, and he tried to stand, jerking on the handcuffs until the steel cut into his wrist.

"This guy is all yours, Chief. I think he has a lot to answer for to the Egyptian police and military, or you can just mail him back home. The mullahs in Iran would love to talk to him, knowing that he has turned traitor and is peddling all of their secrets."

The cop unlocked the handcuffs and pulled Naqdi to his feet, saying, "Or perhaps there should be one more firing squad in Sharm el-Sheikh. He should feel how it is to be tied to a post with a bag over his head, like I was."

"Your choice, sir. It's not my affair," Kyle said. "I'm going back to bed."

CHAPTER 32

Egyptian troops flooded into the Sharm airport, disarmed the Iranians, and kept them under loose guard. They were easy prisoners, for they had nowhere to go even if they escaped, and they willingly helped fill the holes in the runway and mixed hot asphalt that would patch it up temporarily. The Egyptians could get around to laying rigid concrete later, but this would be enough to handle the commercial jets that would be used for the exodus back to Iran. Their commander, Brigadier General Medhi Khasrodad, signed the surrender papers in a private meeting and was allowed to stay with his men until they were safely evacuated. The Egyptian and Iranian troops arranged soccer matches for exercise. Khasrodad knew that his military career was over, and he did not really want to return to Tehran, but his family was there. He would not abandon them, although he was certain to be imprisoned and probably executed when he returned. Maybe something could be worked out. He didn't know.

Abdel El-Din remained in the hospital for a few more days, then went back to work on the beachfront, which was already returning to normal. The still-mending arm wound prevented him from doing a lot of heavy work, but there was still plenty to do because business was phenomenal as tourists and residents flocked to the Gold Sun to see and cheer the hero of the rebellion. After a week, he accepted the invitation of the chief of police to go on a fishing trip for a few days, out on the water and visiting little shoreline villages where no reporters could find them. By the time the trip was over, Abdel had agreed to become a cop.

A short time thereafter, the decayed body of Iranian Colonel Yahya Naqdi was found in a desolate stretch of desert to the north. The corpse sagged against the ropes that lashed it to a tall pole; a hood was over the head, the body was riddled with bullets, and scavenging animals had been feasting. An official notification of his death was sent to Tehran.

Kyle Swanson missed all of that. The day after his private talk with the colonel, and a full ten hours of sleep, he made arrangements through the hotel concierge to go home. A private helicopter was chartered and was waiting for him on the beach in the morning. No more suits, no more local clothes, no more weapons. Today it was back to jeans and sweatshirt and running shoes, and he climbed into the chopper easily, buckling in beside the pilot.

The Red Sea appeared glassy smooth as Kyle looked

down from the helicopter at the long thicket of tankers and other vessels that were starting to unsnarl the knot of shipping that had gathered at the mouth of the Suez Canal.

"Oil prices will go down today," the pilot said over the headphones.

"Take me for a quick tour so I can get a good look," Kyle replied.

"It's an hourly rate," said the pilot, and Swanson replied he didn't care. His plane would wait. For the next forty-five minutes, they cruised the unchallenged sky in lazy circles, hovering for a few minutes to watch the cleanup crews that had finally contained the oil slick from the sunken tanker.

The Hurghada airport was still operating its commercial side, and he could see that the military area was still armed to the teeth, ready for a fight if the deal with Iran fell through. The chartered bird sat down easily on the concrete apron within walking distance of a gleaming white executive jet bearing the insignia of Excalibur Enterprises, which had been dispatched by Sir Jeff. Once he was welcomed aboard and made comfortable by the hostess, Kyle heard the big Lear's twin engines whining to life, and it was climbing into the cloudless sky five minutes later.

THE PENTAGON

"Hey," said Lieutenant Colonel Sybelle Summers when Kyle walked into the inner sanctum offices of Task orce Trident. She didn't look up from the screen on er computer.

"Hey? That's all?"

Commander Benton Freedman leaned back in his hair in his adjoining office and looked at him with isinterest. "You back? Want to go over your expense eport?"

"Yes, I'm back. Glad you noticed. No, on the ex- enses."

Master Gunnery Sergeant O. O. Dawkins walked in rom the hallway and punched Kyle hard enough on the rm to knock him sideways, then kept on walking to a ig door and announced, "Gunny Swanson, sir."

"Is he in proper uniform?" asked the gruff voice of Major General Bradley Middleton.

"Yes, sir. He's in his service alphas."

"Then haul his ass in here."

Swanson blew out his cheeks. Not a decent *Hello, ood job, let's get a beer* in the bunch. He walked into Middleton's office, came to attention, and reported in.

"You know the commandant?"

For the first time, Kyle was aware of another man, vho was rising from the couch by the window, a tall nan with neat gray hair and a penetrating set of green yes that matched his uniform tunic, on which were six ows of honor ribbons, the gold jump wings of a master arachutist, and four silver stars on each shoulder. Gen- ral Oden Harrison smiled warmly. "Welcome home, Gunny Swanson."

Kyle was able to stammer, "Thank you, sir. Good to e back and to meet you."

"Well, thank you, and I thank General Middleton for allowing me to come into his secret bat cave and hang out with the team for a few minutes." Sybelle, the Lizard, and Double-Oh had filtered into the room and stood alongside the general's desk. Middleton stood, which surprised the hell out of Swanson.

General Harrison came closer, and in his hands was a small oblong black case, which he used both hands to open. Inside on a bed of purple lay a ribbon of dark blue with a white stripe down the middle and a gold medal beneath it. "I'm proud to represent the president of the United States today in awarding you the Navy Cross for your actions against an enemy of the United States."

Kyle could feel the blood rushing to his face in a blush, but he controlled himself. He accepted the medal and shook the commandant's hand.

"You saved an untold number of lives and helped prevent a possible war," said Harrison. "It was an outstanding performance, son. Just outstanding." The general paternally slapped him on the shoulder. "Medal of Honor and now two Navy Crosses, two Silvers, and one Bronze with a V. You're going to have more medals than Chesty Puller before you're done."

The Trident team let out a round of cheers and applause, and the general made his good-bye and left.

"Dawkins, open that bottle of champagne," ordered Middleton, moving to his wall safe. "And you, Swanson, give me that damned medal. You can't wear it for a year or two until this heat blows over. The citation goes in your classified file, and even that is redacted so that it doesn't show much more than your name."

Kyle reluctantly handed it over. "I just got it and you're taking it back? How's that work?"

"Awww. Come and cry on Mommy's shoulder," said Sybelle as she wrapped him in a hug.

A cork popped, Dawkins poured glasses for each, and they toasted Kyle's return. "Good stuff," said General Middleton, wiping his mouth. "Now everybody take a seat and let's get going on a preliminary debrief, all the way back to the sniper attack on the Maryland shore. Just the overview first, Kyle, then I can go brief the White House, where the Man is waiting for word. After that, we can get to the details. You know the drill."

"Yes, sir."

"Since you can't wear the Navy Cross for a while, is there anything that we can give you? The president will probably let you have South Carolina or Idaho if you want it."

Kyle unbuttoned his green jacket, knowing this was going to be a long session. "I'll settle for two weeks of vacation."

"Back to the beach and your cheerleader girlfriend Maddy?" teased Sybelle.

"You're dating a cheerleader?" Dawkins curled his lips in distaste.

"My last vacation was interrupted," Kyle said.

"Good enough. Two weeks' leave. Permission granted," said the general.

"After the expense report," added the Lizard.

Read on for an excerpt from the next Sniper Novel
by Gunnery Sgt. Jack Coughlin, USMC (Ret.),
and Donald A. Davis

ON SCOPE

Coming soon in hardcover from St. Martin's Press

PROLOGUE

FALLUJAH, IRAQ

The afternoon sun was motionless in the scalding sky
and Staff Sergeant Kyle Swanson, wedged between the
floorboards of a decapitated two-story house, cautiously
wiped sweat from his eyes with a dirty handkerchief. A
hundred and ten degrees out there, with more to come;
heat merciless enough to bake a plate of cookies or sear
a man's soul. He drank some warm water, then returned
his aching eye to the telescopic sight of his 7.62x51mm
M-40 sniper rifle. Far away was gunfire. He had been in
the hide since before daybreak, part of a deadly anvil on
which a huge hammer was about to slam down as part
of Operation Phantom Fury. If everything went right,
the insurgent forces that controlled this dusty city beside the Euphrates River were about to receive a crippling body blow.

More than two hundred armored vehicles of the United States Marine Corps had just crossed the start line to the east, accompanied by some two thousand Marines and soldiers of other coalition countries. Judging by the increasing volume of gunfire, the insurgents had been ready for them, but the bad guys in Fallujah were always ready for a fight. They were determined not to lose their ruthless grip on the people in Al Anbar Province.

"Blue Dog One. They're coming our way." The quiet voice in his earpiece was Blue Dog Two, Staff Sergeant Mike Dodge, whose own six-man team was entrenched a half-block behind Swanson's. Each position supported the other.

"Ready here," he said, running through a mental checklist still again: squad automatic weapons, M-203 grenade launchers, M-16s, even two sniper rifles, plus Dodge's radio gear to call in roof-scraping Cobra helicopters and fast-moving fighter-bombers. They were the anvil. When the tanks and APCs and infantry struck hard from the front, the insurgents would roll back into the perceived safety of the city, smack into the waiting Marine force planted in the two buildings that dominated a broad street that was empty of traffic.

There was no doubt the enemy would put up a good scrap, for they owned the home field advantage in this stronghold forty miles west of Baghdad. Their deposed dictator, Saddam Hussein, was believed to be hiding somewhere in the stubborn region known as the Sunni Triangle, where he was protected by fanatic loyalists. The Iraqi force was comprised of members of Hussein's ruling Ba'ath Party political apparatus and government, elements of the Republican Guard, some remnants of the Iraqi Army, and a growing number of Sunni Muslim guerillas and foreign fighters. They owed their allegiance, their very existence, to Saddam. If they lost, none of them had a bright future in a new Iraq that would be ruled by their religious rivals, the Shiites. The burps and thumps of automatic weapons fire rose in volume and came closer. Explosions popped on the horizon, and the usual thick haze of dust and dirt churned.

The Swanson and Dodge teams had inserted during the darkest hours and, after linking up, had made their way into the eerie stillness of the city before the sun came up. Mike had set up in a house beside a junk-littered field, while Kyle arranged his guys across the street and a half-block up, but within sight of the other team.

Straight down the avenue was the broad entry plaza and main doorway of the Haj Musheen Abdul Aziz Az-Kubaysi mosque complex, a domed citadel that had surrendered its protected status as a religious site when it was turned into a base for the insurgency. Trashed by looters and air strikes, the remaining mountain of jagged rubble had become a fortress. That was the prime target today. Whoever controlled that palace and its underground bunkers had the city. From his strong position, Kyle Swanson believed he held the keys to the front door. He watched gunmen pour out of the structure and up over the walls and head for the fighting. He reported the movement. The sniper teams were the eyes and ears of the assault force, gathering intelligence and picking targets, and only later would they exercise their trigger fingers. Let the big assault force do the heavy

lifting and roll a couple of Abrams tanks up the main
street in front of the old mosque, supported by a battal-
ion of Marines. The bad guys would be concentrating so
hard on the armor, and not even know the snipers were
at their backs until it was too late. When the hammer
closed the trap, the guns of the anvil would erupt to take
out specific targets, such as officers and radio operators.

The forces were almost fully engaged now. Kyle
checked his team, all of whom were veterans that sup-
pressed their eagerness with professionalism, and then
he let his fingers wander over his big sniper rifle, wiping
away dirt. *Ready.* He was happy that Mike Dodge was
at his six. The Marine Corps was a large organization,
but a rather small family, and over years of service any
one of them met many others. He and Dodge had been
friends since their miserable days of basic training at
Parris Island and later during Scout/Sniper School.
They had gone off on their own careers, but stayed in
touch. Both had served in the first Iraq war, and afterward, Kyle had been an usher at Mike's wedding two
years ago. The bride's name was Becky.

Now it was November 2004, and they were back in
the Sandbox with the Third Battalion/Fifth Marines for
another round, this one called Operation Phantom Fury,
with the goal of taming the wild city of Fallujah.

"Blue Dog One. Hear that?"

"Copy. Fire decreasing on the outskirts. What's going on, Two?" Dodge had the big radios. There was no
answer. "Blue Dog Two?"

"Yea. I was just over on the main freq. The attack
has stopped. Repeat, the attack has stopped."

Kyle kept his eye on the scope. Insurgent fighters were flooding back into the city. "Blue Dog One to Blue Dog Two. They're coming our way. I don't see any of our guys chasing them."

Dodge's voice was calm but urgent. "Dog One, we are ordered to exfiltrate immediately. Something has fucked up and the attack stopped at Phase Line Butler."

"They want us to leave a place that is filling up with enemy fighters in broad daylight? Let's just stay here and keep quiet until it gets dark." He wanted to know what had gone wrong, but shit happened in war and he would think about that later. Staying alive was now the higher priority.

"Negative. Those bad guys are being flushed right toward us and they will be in every building. We don't have until dark."

Kyle could see it unfolding. The attacking armored force had drawn up in a line outside the city and was laying down a massive barrage that was driving the insurgents back and making them hunt cover. The Marine infantry, however, was not in pursuit, although the enemy was scattering like a gaggle of scared cats. *Coming this way, fast.* "You're right, Blue Dog Two. This is untenable."

As if to make the point, a fighter seeking safety from the barrage threw open the booby-trapped door of their building, and the explosion shook the entire structure and drew the unwanted attention of other enemy elements in the area. They swung away from the stalled attack and opened fire on the sniper positions. Kyle's team answered with a hail of automatic weapons.

Swanson squeezed off one shot that took down a dumb gunman standing in the middle of the street and spraying bullets from an AK-47 held hip-high. *You watched too many movies*, Kyle thought. Then he popped a second man on the plaza, who looked like he was giving orders.

"Blue Dog Two. You guys stay out of this. You haven't been compromised."

"Negative, One. We'll engage from here to take some of the pressure off and you guys bound back to us. I've called air cover and the choppers for the extraction from the field next to our building. You control the fight, and I'll control the air."

Swanson clicked his microphone to let Dodge know the message was received, then let the fight talk to him. Bullets were crashing into the mud and clay building where they hid, and the Marines were answering with outgoing fire that was disciplined and deadly. "Corporal Burke! We're leaving. You and Ridgeway fall back to the Two position when they start firing." The two Marines slid from their hides, gathered by the rear door, and when Mike Dodge and his crew opened up, the pair broke cover and pounded across the street and into the safety of the Blue Dog Two position.

The element of surprise was gone, and the gunmen would be ready for more Marines to make the dash. Swanson and his spotter, Corporal Boyd Scott, came down the broken stairs of the house with Kyle calling out, "Reynolds and Thomas! You're next. Stay low and move your asses when you see the smoke." Swanson, kneeling at a window, tracked an insurgent who was closing in and put a bullet in him. Scott fired smoke grenades with his M-203 launcher and a soup of thick gray smoke bloomed in the street. Reynolds and Thomas took off running and made it to the house half a block away.

The firefight was getting serious as more insurgents joined in and the acrid smoke started to swirl away. "Now us, Scott. Shoot and scoot." Kyle slung his long sniper rifle over his back and brought up his own M-16A3, then followed Boyd out. The bad guys were firing blind, but with everything they had. Bullets whined off buildings, skidded along walls, and kicked the pavement. He could see Mike Dodge not far ahead, standing in the window, firing carefully over their heads and into the mob behind the smoke. *Movemovemove!*

Halfway across, Boyd Scott was hit. He spun left and crashed onto the ground. The corporal had been struck in both the neck and the head and was bleeding like a fountain. His helmet had been torn off and rolled away like a hubcap off a Plymouth. There was no time for emotion or emergency treatment, so Kyle dropped his weapon and grabbed the shoulders of the wounded man's armored vest and began staggering backward, pulling the bleeding man with him as more bullets sang around them. The possibility of being shot himself by slowing down to help a buddy did not enter his thoughts; Marines don't leave other Marines behind.

Then someone else was at his side, also grabbing the downed corporal and yelling something incomprehensible in the roar of the battle. Mike Dodge had left the safety of his building and leaped into harm's way to help, and the two of them stumbled into the shelter together while the other Marines laid a hurricane of fire up the road toward the palace. A corpsman leaped over to take charge of Scott.

"You were a fucking moron for coming out there, Staff Sergeant Dodge."

"Saved your slow ass, didn't I?"

"Shit you say. We were almost in the door before you even moved."

"Screw you, Staff Sergeant Swanson."

Kyle got busy placing the remaining Marines in tactical positions, and Mike went back to the radio. The incoming fire was growing, and two more Marines were wounded within the next three minutes. "Watch your rate of fire," Swanson called as he jumped from team to team. "Help's on the way. Don't let ammo become a problem."

The first Cobra helicopter gunship wheeled in and made a gun run straight down the boulevard, and another scoured the rooftops on the left side, where enemy shooters had gathered to get a better vantage point over their target. As the first team of snakes pulled out, another set of helicopters came down to continue the counterattack, and above the roar of the hellacious firefight, Kyle heard the deep-throated thudding of an approaching CH-53 helicopter, their big taxi out of there. Corporal Scott died before it landed.

On the way back to base camp, Swanson wiped his face and drank some water and thought about what had happened. No way was that a successful mission, not with one Marine KIA and two WIA. It wasn't an unsuccessful mission, either, because the insurgents had been battered pretty well. He might never know why the original plan had been changed. What was it they said about battle plans not surviving the first shot? This was Iraq. It was just another mission in a long and dirty war. He listened to the *thunking* rhythm of the helicopter blades and figured that he owed Mike Dodge a beer.

CHAPTER 1

BARCELONA, SPAIN

Their careers pushed Swanson and Dodge in different directions after that. Mike Dodge, with a wife, chose a more conventional path, while the single Kyle Swanson was swept up in special operations. Two years later, when Marine Corps Brigadier General Bradley Middleton was kidnapped by mercenaries and terrorists in Syria after the first Iraq war, Swanson went in and got him back, but was mortally wounded in the fight, buried in Arlington, and posthumously awarded the Congressional Medal of Honor. It was huge news throughout the nation and the Corps, and Mike and Becky mourned the loss of their friend.

But things are not always as they seem, and three years later, Mike was shocked one evening to answer the front door of his two-bedroom home in Oceanside, and find Kyle standing there, alive and well, beer in hand, ready to regale Becky with wild stories. It had all really been a major league Pentagon paperwork mistake, he said, and they couldn't very well take back the medal, nor unbury him. Instead, they had bounced him around on special assignments until someone could figure out an appropriate job for a dead guy.

The surprise reunion became a party that continued at a seafood restaurant on the coast highway just south of Del Mar. Back home about midnight, Kyle got down to the business part of his resurrection and the surprise visit. First, he swore them both to secrecy, making them put their hands on the family Bible.

"Everything I told you earlier was bullshit," he admitted. "I'm sorry, but I had to see how you were both doing before I divulged the actual story. Tell no one what you are about to here, not tomorrow or ever."

Swanson then confessed to Mike and Becky how he had been officially washed from the records to help create a totally black spec op organization that was known as Task Force Trident. It was a handful of specialists who answered only to the President, and was turning the War on Terror on its head by taking the fight right to the enemy's doorstep. Some really bad people had been learning there was no safe place to hide if they attacked America and its allies, and that there would be no martyrdom awaiting them, nothing but a bloody end. Trident could access any and all assets of the U.S. government to accomplish its missions—drones and SEALs and Delta Force and B-52s and computer geeks and federal agents and local cops and forensic psychologists could be called as needed for support. There were no paper trails to back-track, and no punishment for carrying out the strikes, which were cleared personally by the President of the United States.

Kyle said that Trident had reached a stage where he really needed a partner he could trust out there in the boonies, and who was better at this game than Mike Dodge? Mike looked ready to sign up on the spot. Becky pulled back.

Think about it and talk it over, Swanson urged. Let him know tomorrow. Bumps could be expected in both pay grade and expenses. Big bumps, Kyle said. The Dodges talked all night before turning down the offer. It was the right move for them, Swanson admitted, but he at least had to try.

Instead of running and gunning in dangerous special operations, at the end of another five years, in 2014, Gunnery Sergeant Mike Dodge found himself in command of the Marine security detachment at the U.S. consulate in the peaceful diplomatic backwater of Barcelona, Spain. He wore a coat and tie to work, com-muting from the two-bedroom apartment where he lived with Becky and their one-year-old son, Timmy. The place was all the way to the Reina Elsinda station, last stop on the Metro's L-6 line, and it was a quiet life, a good life for a man with both a sense of duty and a family.

On a bright Monday morning, when Dodge stepped from the train station, he immediately had a prickly feeling along his arms and neck that sent him into a state of alert. He saw nothing out of the ordinary, but the gunny had often felt that special tingling just before trouble broke out back during his combat tours in Iraq and Afghanistan.

At least on the surface, everything seemed fine. A line of Spanish locals and citizens of other nations wanting to obtain visas and process business permits had been forming for the past hour at the main gate to the consulate. All were orderly, standing there for a specific purpose, reading newspapers and drinking coffee.

Four Spanish cops were in front at the barrier that controlled vehicle entry. Dodge walked over to exchange greetings, and they confirmed that there was just the usual morning traffic and pedestrians.

Dodge walked into the consulate through the heavy main door, crossed the polished stone lobby floor, and was greeted by the day-shift guy, Corporal J.V. Harris, in uniform at Post One behind the bulletproof glass wall. Dodge eyeballed him to be sure he was squared away. J.V. stood six-two, with a square chin and broad shoulders, and was an imposing figure although he was only twenty years old. Buttons on the short-sleeve khaki shirt and the buckle of the white web belt were in exact alignment. A holstered pistol rode on the hip of his dress blue trousers, and the white cover was perched firmly on a high-and-tight haircut. "Top of the morning, Gunny," Harris called out, buzzing him through the reinforced transparent entrance to the business area. "Another excellent damned day in our beloved Marine Corps. Sergeant Martinez is in the back." Rico Martinez had been the night man and would be changing into his civvies to go home.

"What's the threat assessment?" Dodge asked.

"Low. Martinez reports things were quiet all night. Nothing since I came aboard."

Dodge's eyes studied the young Marine. "Are you sober?"

"Of course, Gunny."

"And the guys at the House?"

"Absolutely. It was sort of a rough night in Barcelona, but if you want them, they can be on deck quick enough."

Dodge shook his head. That meant they were probably as hungover as sheets flapping on a clothesline. He couldn't shake the itchy, warning feeling. "Matter of fact, I do want them. Call over there and get them up. And you stay sharp."

The big door hissed closed and locked. Harris added, "The RSO and the consul-general are already back there." The RSO was the Regional Security Officer for the Department of State's Diplomatic Protective Service and technically in charge of overall consulate security.

Dodge walked down the hallway, his eyes flicking to every door. Several consulate workers were at their computers at the front counter, getting ready to deal with the morning line. *I'll keep Martinez around for another hour,* he decided.

It was less than a minute before eight o'clock when J.V. Harris picked up a secure telephone and dialed the House, and the telephone rang once, twice, three times, but no one answered. He hung up, planning to wait a few minutes and give them one more try before reporting to the gunny, who would rip them all a new one if they didn't answer. Corporal Harris hung up and buzzed the security lock again, to allow a consulate worker with a big ring of keys to exit through the barrier so he could open the heavy, bullet-proof main door. The business day was about to begin.